FORGET ME NOT

Cover Design by A. Thomson

Developmental Editing: Kelli Mazanec

Line Editing: Charlotte House

Beta Reader: Marlee Talbot

Contents

BOOK PLAYLIST

POWERFUL - MAJOR LAZER, ELLIE GOLDING
I'M WITH YOU - VANCE JOY
DRIFTING - ON AN ON
HARD PLACE - H.E.R.
OCEAN EYES - BILLIE EILISH
WAKE UP ALONE - AMY WINEHOUSE
COSMIC LOVE - FLORENCE + THE MACHINE
WHITE BLANK PAGE - MUMFORD & SONS
HOME - EDWARD SHARPE & THE MAGNETIC ZEROES
DO I WANNA KNOW - ARCTIC MONKEYS
MIDDLE OF THE NIGHT - ELLEY DUHE
ROLL ME AWAY - JACK SYMES, NAT LEFKOFF
PUT IT ON ME - MATT MAESON
FIRE AND THE FLOOD - VANCE JOY
ASTROVAN - MT.JOY
SEASIDE - SEB
IDK YOU YET - ALEXANDER 23
WAVES - MIGUEL, KACEY MUSGRAVES

AUTHOR'S NOTE

Hello readers! I'm happy you're here. Before you get lost in my little world, I do want to warn immediately that this book contains extremely explicit sexual content. And not just a sprinkle of it, a generous helping. Please take that into consideration before you flip the page. I'd also like to warn for specific triggers such as drug use, gambling, gaslighting by a romantic partner, emotional infidelity, and graphic violence. If all this floats your transport—enjoy!

To Joe. The other half of my shooting star.

PROLOGUE

"*They'll kill me first, you know. Before I've had the chance to taste you.*"

"*I won't let them.*"

"*Dream girl, I applaud your altruism. But unless the sky suddenly becomes starless and there's a tear in the cosmic thread, I may never be graced with keeping you from my darkness.*"

"*It's not your fault. What happened to him.*"

"*Then why did every day on this moon feel like a sentencing? If the atmosphere didn't bring me to my knees, the predators still kept me afraid of my own shadow. My only solace is sleep.*"

"*You've kept your promises. You're here repaying that debt like an honorable man. All the while this life has made you a shell. Those people don't care about you, they care about what you can do for them. You've figured it out before, many times.*"

"*I've lost every friend, but you.*"

"*I'm not your friend, Silas.*"

"*No, you are my reason.*"

"*And you're the one who survived, for a reason. The universe doesn't operate on chance. Don't allow the last seven cycles to let you forget that.*"

"*When I leave here tomorrow, I intend to never come back.*"

"*I'll follow you wherever you go.*"

1
FORTUITY

I t would take at least a cycle and a half for the transport ship to make its way entirely back to the Otera. Back to the dense, bustling, mainland planet I fucked off of several moons ago with Logan.

Let's go rogue for a little while, he had said. *Stick our feet in the sand.*

So we did just that. Traveling as young lovers do, still yet to stake a permanent claim in a safe and explored stratosphere, and with not much more than a couple duffle bags between the two of us. It was divergent from our normalcy, refreshing. We hopped on a connection pod with whatever currency we had jingling in our pockets, found a twinkling constellation orbiting a habitable planet on the map, then threw the dart.

The Glades were perfect. A beautiful oceanic moon, thriving culture, black sand beaches. The climate kept our skin glistening happily during the day, bodies warm to the touch—and at night the breeze danced through the billowing curtains of our cozy bungalow and wiped the sweat off our bodies tangled between the sheets.

We spent every day wrapped in barely enough clothing to cover ourselves. Drinking in the sun as we laid across the sand, dining with the locals on fresh aquatic dishes, shopping through markets of the indigenous villages. We learned new languages, practiced new traditions, engulfed ourselves in the freedom of a holistic culture that was worlds away from the life we lived on the Otera.

I became consumed by the salt-fleshed nature all around me. Food and drink, efflorescence, incense, oils, natural medicines, the fruits of the land that were recycled into every edge of society.

And the sex was invigorating. When we felt that good all the time, were that *tipsy* all the time, we couldn't help but screw each other senseless.

Logan and I were welcomed outsiders getting fat on the feeling of a life that didn't exist on the Otera. We thought several times about ways that we could stay on the island forever, different odd jobs we could do in that foreign society to keep us submerged in it. We even sold our own personal belongings to the locals for a while to spread ourselves thinner—things they could only find on the mainland. But, eventually the money had to run out.

If we leave now, we'll have just enough tally to catch the return back to the Ote, Logan had said. *If not, we're stranded here, Eliza. The next freighter doesn't pass for another three cycles.*

So that was that.

We spent a final night in paradise listening to the waves as they rocked us to sleep, and like every single night before that one, like clockwork, I still dreamt about *him*.

The man with the ocean flecked gaze and sideways smile who came to me so often in my sleep I just learned to expect it.

I didn't know his name, or how many years he'd had before him—where he was from, or how he was in my head, *constantly*. But, he had been a perpetual stronghold in my life since I was young. An imaginary friend, a *lover*, the reason I couldn't wait to drift to sleep and visit my dreams.

When I opened my eyes it was with a content sigh, rolling sidelong to face the man who laid in bed with me.

"Hi." I smiled.

His tousled, ash brown locks fell rebelliously in front of his eyes, one a calm sapphire sea, the other emerald, deep and unmistakable like moss in the night. The glint in his stare was mischievous as he smirked back at me.

"You've been having fun," he said. "I have a rightful concern you may forget about me."

"I've tried."

I reached out, tracing the silver half-moon scar that hung from his brow with my thumb.

The man feigned insult, grabbing my hand to place it over his heart as if it were breaking. "I'm wounded by your brashness, Birdie. You would miss me."

He was right about that. I twisted my fingers into his own, nodding at the longing look in his eyes before I answered, "Like the rain in a dusking drought."

There was a comfortable silence then, one where we both basked in the unsaid. He and I spoke to one another like this often, drawn out quietude, mirrored expressions. Our own secret conversations, even under the curtain of my closed fantasy.

He swept a stray blonde strand of hair away from my forehead, tucking the coarse, tangled wave behind my ear. "Are you ever going to tell him about me?"

"About the imaginary man who haunts my dreams?"

My fingertips had found their way to the plush skin of his bottom lip. He was so beautiful to look at like this, bare and vulnerable, as affected by my touch as I was by just his mere presence.

"Is that all I am now?" His voice was honey thick, tied up in a low seductive drawl that hung off his tongue as one eyebrow shot up in question.

"Yeah." I sighed and kissed the knuckles on the back of his hand. "That's all you are."

After that I couldn't sleep. I sat up in bed, watching Logan snore beside me, pulling out my worn leather journal to write about the man in my dreams for what seemed like the thousandth time.

I was a vassal to my own imagination. There had never been a time in my life that I felt completely in control of my own desires. Even when I thought I had found the same happiness I craved in those fleeting hours asleep, I still caught myself wishing to float into unconsciousness on occasion.

I sat in the darkness so long I resorted to a tincture of natural oils to aid in the rest process, and it wasn't long before exhaustion overtook me again.

Along with the tranquil sound of the waves, sleep swept me away like the tide.

The next day, our link pod touched down on the transport right around the same time a man named Silas was boarding his own connection vessel on the Pulp. His ship's cargo was heavy with a precious trove he'd spent seven cycles searching and scraping out of the moon's murky, yellow flesh with a fine toothed comb.

He planned to catch a ride on the freighter ship back to the Otera and trade his way to riches—sticking around just long enough to make his peace with the mainland, and then become a ghost. Gone in the starstruck dust.

Silas kicked his little ship into orbit without a second look back, scattered belongings that he was in too much of a rush to stow away floating in zero gravity around his head. Books, dog-eared and browning around the edges from wear, several samples of dried flowers picked during his planetary travels weaseling their way out of the folded pages. Stray oxygen packs, a dirty compression shirt he'd stripped himself of minutes before, long forgotten empty wrappers from stale protein supplements.

It had been seven long cycles out in that toxic, viscid forestry alone. It took him twice as long to extract without a second set of hands, and he swore under his breath on more than one occasion that as long as he lived, he'd never play the Mako again without a partner. He'd never maraude a moon for its sustenance lest he knew beyond a shadow of a doubt he would make it out unscathed.

That was of course behind him now.

Silas hadn't been entirely alone though, by his own standards. He had his novels, and a shoddy radio with adhesive tape holding the metal antennae at just the right angle for a station to sift through. He had a handful of weathered photographs found on a job once upon a time, and sometimes he'd look at them and imagine the scenarios come to life—giving the people names and stories.

He had even befriended a blue bird for a while. They both ended up at the lone watering gully at the same time a few mornings when Silas slipped in to bathe. He would whistle at it, tell the warbler about his day, speak to it like an old, mute friend. Eventually though, the bird stopped coming around.

And then he had me. The girl that didn't exist.

For as long as Silas could remember, I took up a stable residency in his dreams. As a friend, a partner—a paramour.

The latter were his favorite nights out in the unforgiving Pulp. Falling asleep, and then finding me there in bed with him, always stark nude as the day I was born.

"You're tired, Silas."

My voice was angelic to him, like a calming whisper.

"The strength of these old bones does deceive me, Birdie," he agreed, pulling me on top of his body and parting my legs over his hips. "But you'd sooner call me manic than tired if I ever wished you away for sleep."

I dipped down to catch his lips with mine, our tongues sliding together in a quick movement before pulling away.

Silas held my waist while I stretched up on wobbling knees, just high enough to reach between our two bodies and stroke him. The groan he let out was low and deep as I dragged the tip of his cock through the wet valley at my core.

"You're doing so good out here on your own, Sy. You deserve a break."

I always slid down onto him perfectly, and he filled me tight, watching as I took a beat to savor the blissful feeling of being so full, body slick and wanting, before lifting my hips and riding him back down again.

"Maker and all his men—fuck," he breathed. "I have never felt a euphoria near comparable to the likes of you." His tangled hand in my hair pulled me down against his mouth again as I rocked my hips against his faster, biting at his bottom lip as he kissed me.

Silas was careful with his hands, kneading me as I rode him. He pushed and pulled, guiding me at his pace, licking the supple moans out of my mouth as they left my throat.

"Can you take me harder, little bird?" The question sounded more like begging than an inquiry. The unabashed groan that slipped from his lips had me whimpering against his ear. "That sound." He half sighed, half chuckled, delirious on how close I was getting him. "You make me depraved, dream girl, you make me—oh, fuck."

With feet planted firmly underneath him, he wrapped his arms around my body and hammered upwards, matching the wave of my hips with his thrusts until the tightening feeling in his shaft became devastating.

"Don't you dare stop on me," he warned shakily. "Don't—don't you dare."

"Come for me, Silas."

He pressed his face into the slope of my chest, muffling his pleasure into damp skin as his body shook. Before he could even pull out entirely, Silas felt the warm drip of his own release trickling down to matte the wiry hair at the base of his stomach.

Just like that night, he would often wake up in briefs sticky with his own seed, cursing himself alone in his bed and wondering who and why I was. A fever dream, his own personal form of glorious torture.

NOW

"Quit fucking stealing off my plate." I jab a half eaten wafer at Logan across the table. "You'd think you hadn't eaten for days."

Even as I say them, the words feel silly. My partner is more than obviously not starving. He's tall and effortlessly lean, square shoulders, strong arms, a rough line to his jaw. He has daggers for eyes, sterling gray, and thick strawberry blonde hair that he habitually tucks behind his ears while he speaks.

"Oh, come on, babe." He stabs at the plate again, grinning as I spar with his utensil. "You know you won't finish that."

I give in and let him pick a stray piece of meat off the tray.

"The food on this ship won't be the same as it was in the Glades," I say, tipping my body back against the cushion of the booth. "It's back to reality."

"Well, not completely." Logan's fork is abandoned as he takes a swig of his drink. "I mean *yes*, when we get home—but we still have a long ride on this transport before we hit the Otera."

I look around the communal dining area. The place is like a shopping center food court, several ticky-tacky shacks with different cuisines lined up next to one another. Every-which gender and species scattered about at their own little tables. Maybe families that are traveling to visit more of their own, maybe friends headed to a vacation spot. Possibly a lone straggler starting a new life on whatever system the ship happens to pass.

There's a giant screen hitched on one of the walls showing arrivals and departures, next destinations, systems we're passing through currently and what's on the literal horizon. The red, blinking alarm light attached to the screen indicates there's a pod on-load docking currently in the garage bay.

This system of intergalactic travel has opened the gates to millions of new unimaginable discoveries, allowing ventures well beyond the mind's capability of what exists in a space that never ceases to unfold.

And yet, "I just wish there was more to do on this thing," I complain.

Focusing again on the meal in front of me, I notice that quite a bit more has gone missing off the plate. I point an accusatory fork in Logan's direction, but before I can berate my boyfriend over the obvious lack of food, he cuts me off.

"Ah look, new travelers just pulled in." He gestures in the direction of the steel elevator doors across the room as they open, and a drove of people make their way into the common area. Bags in hand and confused looks on their faces as they try to find their way through the busy quarter.

"This is a great place for people watching," he adds. "Getting to judge everybody immediately, you know? It's kind of fun."

I ignore him for the most part, only giving the arriving group short glances as they move their way into the space.

There's a family with young children that amble distractedly behind their caretakers. A couple, probably ten years older than Logan and I, mid-to-late-thirties, holding hands and heading toward the health food concession. A group of girls follow, giggling and whispering to one another, preoccupied with a communication tablet they're all looking at.

Then a man. Just—one man.

My neck tilts to follow him, curiosity and *shock*, blurring the edges of my vision.

Shaggy brown hair curls over his forehead, and even half-hiding his eyes, the stark blue and green irises still puncture the veil. He wears dark cargo pants tucked into half tied boots, and a waffle-weaved, black long sleeve shirt that's wrinkled enough I can still notice it despite the color. His olive skin gives way to scratchy looking, unkempt stubble; it starts halfway up his neck and peppers his cheeks and chin in patches. A faded half moon scar hooks around the brow on his left temple.

There's a sudden tightening in the cavity of my chest like my heart is in a vice grip, and I'm left mouth agape as I take the stranger in.

One ratty duffle bag slung over his shoulder, a thick, soft-covered book stuffed into his back pocket that I can see when he turns to the side. His disparate eyes that dart around adapting to the area are familiar in a way that pulls me like a current.

I know you.

It's like I can't breathe. I pinch my own skin in an attempt to wake myself from the daydream I must be in—but I can't, because it's not. All of a sudden my mouth is wet, too wet, and I try to swallow down the nauseous feeling climbing its way up my throat, but it's a meager fight. I feel my skin flush, hot and feverish.

Logan catches my attention for a second, reaching over the table to grab my hand. "You okay, Lize? You don't look so good."

Fighting off my queasiness, I take a deep breath as I dart my eyes back in the direction of the man; then lose it all over again when I see his gaze locked in on me as well.

We still, making absolutely no attempt to hide the fact that we're both staring at a stranger in a crowded room.

The sloven doppelganger has a look on his face like he's wounded, shifting his eyes slightly to take in the way Logan has my hand wrapped in his own before finding my stare again.

Noticing my line of sight, Logan turns to look at the man too, giving him a once over and a quizzical eyebrow raise before turning back to me. "Get that guy a razor, am I right?" He jabs a thumb over his shoulder.

My stomach flips once more, and this time I realize that I can't contain the sick feeling making it's way up my windpipe. I bolt from the table, making my way through the maze of people and nearly reach the restrooms before I'm forced to swallow the first heave; choosing then to abandon my plan all together and double over a metallic trash can to yack instead.

It can't be him, I talk myself down, head still half in a receptacle. He's not real. *He's not real.*

I consider wiping the remnants of spit across the back of my sleeve, but just as I stand up a hand reaches out to offer me a stack of napkins.

"Thanks," I say before getting a good look at the person in front of me.

I freeze again as I do.

The man of my every dream is standing there, as dumbfounded as I am, taking in each inch of my face as he's done a thousand times before, but somehow, this feels like the very first time.

And then he speaks.

"If it makes you feel any better, Birdie, your affliction is one I can sympathize with all too well right now."

2
AMBIVALENCE

There's something to be said about slow motion. It's like—life improvising. Like, the universe is asking for a moment to figure itself the fuck out.

That's what it feels like with him in front of me.

As if every moment leading up to now was somehow completely insignificant, and fate had carved a road for me, but left it unpaved.

We're suspended in a truncated reality, and I'm pretty sure that life just whispered in my ear to *wing it*, because not even the all knowing universe was prepared for this plot twist.

I take the much-too-thick pile of napkins from his hand and notice the weathered, dimpled scar that's burned into the meat between his thumb and forefinger; one that I've come to know well in my sleep.

I immediately think of every time I've kissed it. Every time I've traced it with my own fingertips, or bit down into it when it's covered my mouth to stifle a pleading moan.

"I didn't mean to startle you," he says, scratching the stubble on his cheek like he's looking for something to do with his hands. "I'd love to claim it as my own sheer acuity, but unfortunately you do know how to part a room."

Looking around him I notice the sea of prying eyes, the people trying to get a glimpse of the girl who just emptied her guts into the trash can. When they notice me, everyone resumes, save for the vague whispers and occasional nosy glance. I think the teenagers in the corner might have started recording my humiliation, just in case.

"I'm sorry," I finally say, forcing myself to laugh along with the words. "Very attractive of me."

It's Silas's turn to gawk now, and somehow I'm even more beautiful to him in the flesh. He can't help himself from looking directly into my eyes, mapping them from the deep blue pigment of my irises to the flutter of long eyelashes batting against my cheeks. He takes in the freckled complexion of dewy skin, draws his sight down the soft span of my jaw, and then his mouth turns up in a subtle smile as his gaze lands on the trembling pink of my bottom lip.

With all the time he's spent inside his head with me, committing my face and body to memory, this feels more like a pleasant nostalgia than an introduction.

"What's wrong?" I ask, blotting the napkin against the corner of my mouth where I notice him looking. "Is there something on my face?"

He smiles wider, shaking his head in response, and if it were anyone else I might think they were pitying me, but not him. He has this awestruck sparkle in his eye like he's discovered a new constellation, and it makes me smile back at him like I'm seeing the modish formation of stars as well.

"No—no it's just," he pauses to collect his thoughts, "I feel like I know you from somewhere."

He knows how he knows me, of course. The most stable relationship his life has ever had, coming in the form of a reoccurring dream woman—but he's not about to say that.

A scraggly nomad, still in the same clothes he's been donning for two days, hair unruly, beard unkempt, just off a toxic moon after six too many cycles and telling a strange, beautiful woman that he sees her naked when he goes to sleep at night.

Yeah, that won't go over well.

And I know how I know him, obviously. His admission isn't half of the extent to which I know him, but it feels right in the uncertainty of the moment.

"Yes," I agree. "You look very familiar to me, too."

He nods, watching me throw out the excess of the paper napkins, and then sticks an open palm out as if it could cut through the thick sheen of ice neither of us are doing a particularly great job at breaking.

"Forgive me, I'm normally much better with introductions, I'm—"

Before he can get the last word in, my partner is at my side, slithering his arm around my waist and pulling me against him.

"Babe, you good?" Logan interrupts. "Must have been that mystery meat or something." He notices Silas's outstretched hand and takes it, shaking it quickly. "What's up, man?" *Head nod.* "I'm Logan."

Silas gives him a sarcastic head nod back, then wipes his hand against the pocket of his pants and puts it inside.

"Silas," he answers plainly, shifting his eyes from Logan back to me.

"Ah, Book Guy."

Logan points to me, as if we'd had some sort of long conversation about the man in front of us and the book in his pocket in the infinitesimal amount of time he's been on the ship.

Silas just slaps his back pocket and points back at Logan like he's in on the joke.

"Yup that's me, 'Book Guy'." He takes the worn paperback out of his pants and makes a minor show of the title. "It's a good one."

I study the cover. It could have been a deep green at one point but the color has faded significantly, and I can see the dips and creases of pages that have been used over time.

"The Master and Margarita," I recite. "I've never read it."

Logan runs his hand up my back and Silas notices in his peripheral, but he pretends he doesn't.

"One of my favorites," Logan lies. I can see Silas's ears perk up. "Can't say I ever carried it around though."

He laughs a bit too loud for the situation so I chuckle along with him to guise it.

"I didn't know you'd read Bulgakov," I say to Logan, looking up a few inches to meet his eyes.

"Long time ago." He waves his hand exaggeratedly away from the group of us.

"A book such as this one stays with you long after you've put it down," Silas interjects, thumbing the brown pages. "Humor me, Logan, I'm always interested to know a fellow readers' favorite part."

He knows what he's doing, and if it weren't for the suave way he twists his vernacular, it would be even more evident.

Silas's work has taught him to weed out the good and bad. The trustworthy from the shifty. He supposes that if he weren't so interested in me, that he'd have left the conversation as it stood and wished Logan and I both safe travels to the Otera. Now if he found a way to keep me in his presence longer, he would take it.

The surly look on Logan's face dies quickly, and he lifts the hand that's on my back to run it through his hair.

"That's a tough one, man." He blows a raspberry through his lips, like he's having trouble sifting through all the scenes of the book in his brain. "I couldn't just pick one. You know what I'm saying, right? It's a disservice to Bulkov."

"*Bulga*-kov," Silas enunciates, nodding at Logan like he understands where he's coming from.

I hide my embarrassment by dipping my head to stare at my feet, but when I look up again, Silas is looking back at me. Taking me in once more. After a few seconds he clears his throat and offers his hand for the second time.

"Well, it's been my pleasure to meet you..." He stops where he's stuck on my name.

"Eliza."

"Eliza," he repeats back slower, stuck on the syllables, letting them dance on his tongue.

It felt like a word he just couldn't remember. It was there, tauntingly familiar, but he could never get it out, and here I finally was to fill in the blank.

I take his hand in mine and shake it softly. And as if it weren't before this moment, everything becomes real. Not a dream, I'm not asleep. He's real, and he's standing in front of me, and he doesn't disappear into dust when I touch him.

"Keep this," Silas says when we finally let go of one another. He hands me his copy of *The Master and Margarita* and I'm slow to take it from him. "I implore you, those pages have seen enough of me for twelve lifetimes."

"Are you sure?"

He smiles, nodding his approval.

"Certain, Birdie. It's a long ride to the mainland—you're gonna need something to keep you occupied." He shifts to face Logan, giving him a half-assed salute. "Logan."

"Yeah, see you around, man."

Logan waves back and we both watch Silas make his way to the exit doors. He looks over his shoulder at me once, as if it might be the last time he'd get a chance to, before breaching the opening and disappearing through it.

"Interesting guy," Logan decides once he turns back to face me.

"Yup," I agree as I waft through the pages of the book in my hands. I notice unintelligible scribbling of ink marking the insides of the novel, and realize it's Silas's own little notes written in the margins.

"C'mon, let's go sit back down." Logan starts to pull me toward our abandoned table but I stop him.

"You know what, I'm still not feeling that great, mind if I head back to the pod to lay down for a little bit?"

He cups my cheek with a large hand and I lean into it thoughtfully. "No, of course not. I'll come get you for dinner."

I should have just started reading the book front to back like any sane person would do. Glance at the dedication, skim the prologue, and then get down to the gritty.

But, if I'm being honest with myself, the promise of Silas's own thoughts penned across the pages was more enticing than any story I could have read.

I fan through the book again while I sit cross-legged on Logan and I's shared bed. I notice the color of Silas's ink switches from black to blue and back again, sometimes within the same chapters. Sometimes it's pencil instead of ink. I imagine him writing in the worn paperback, putting his pen down to continue reading and losing track of it, or opening the book back up another day and realizing he doesn't have a pen at all, scouring his surroundings for anything to write with.

I stop on a page where he's underlined a paragraph.

I read it a few times, in different tones and cadences, and out loud to myself.

"You spoke your words as though you denied the very existence of the shadows or of evil. Think, now: where would your good be if there were no evil and what would the world look like without shadow?"

"You'll need to explain that one to me, Silas." I fan the pages again.

"Even at night, in moonlight, I have no rest... Why
did they trouble me? Oh, gods, gods..."

I follow the words into the margin where Silas left a note: *Can't
rest while I'm sleeping. She doesn't let me sleep when I'm dreaming.
She.*
My body responds to this in a weird way. Somehow feeling
like I'm eavesdropping where I shouldn't be, like I'm reading
something not meant for me. I close the book quietly and tap the
cover with my fingers, thinking maybe I should find him and give
it back.
But then again, he knew what was written in this book when
he gave it to me. He knew I would see it.
I continue through the pages, stopping when I see a paragraph
circled several times in black ink.

"Love leaped out in front of us like a murderer in an
alley leaping out of nowhere, and struck us both at
once. As lightning strikes, as a Finnish knife strikes!
She, by the way, insisted afterwards that it wasn't
so, that we had, of course, loved each other for a
long, long time, without knowing each other, never
having seen each other..."

The last lines, *'without knowing each other, never having seen each
other'* are underlined, and etched into the margin in strong capital
letters Silas had written one word.
YOU.
I bring the book down onto my lap and stare ahead awhile,
marinating in the quote, stroking a finger over the word inked
into the page in his handwriting.

I get this strange notion that he knows the things that resonated with him in this book will either be a deterrent, or like a light bulb switched on for me. A shared epiphany perhaps. Maybe just a twisted way of making me feel closer to a stranger.

There is no denying the shocking resemblance he shares to the man in my dreams. From the dichromatic eyes, to the befitting scar across his temple. The burn mark, the rough Shakespearean drawl of his voice when he speaks.

I pick the book back up and sift through again, stopping on a dog-eared page and another underlined group of words.

"But what can be done, the one who loves must
share the fate of the one he loves."

Then Silas's addition in the empty space on the page: *In fate I will find you.*

The notes go on and on like this for dozens more pages, circled and underlined, fragmented pieces of literature strung together like a puzzle. Some of Silas' notes are more decipherable than others, some paragraphs have no explanation, others are littered with asterisks and stars, like his own personal key.

I spend an hour reading through it, another hour laying flat on my back staring at the ceiling in contemplation. Before I even have a chance to close my eyes and rest, I hear the door of the pod slide open with a clang as Logan makes his way inside.

"How's my girl feeling?"

He scoots up next to me on the bed and I groan a bit, burying my head in his chest.

"I've been better," I admit, sighing heavily as Logan scratches his fingers through my scalp.

"I made dinner reservations."

"Dinner reservations?" I lift my head. "There's a restaurant on this thing?"

"There is exactly *one* restaurant on this thing," he answers, adjusting a bit to be face level with me. He leans in and captures my lips in a quick kiss. "We have an hour, though." He kisses me again.

"Hmm, a whole hour," I ponder. "What ever shall we do?"

Logan winks and slides down my stomach, lifting the fabric and planting a few kisses to the skin there. I laugh as he tickles my sides and slides my pants down my legs, taking my panties with them.

"I'll be down here if you need me," he teases. I bite my lip to stifle a smile.

As soon as he parts me with his tongue my hands are tangled in his hair, guiding his mouth until he finds that perfect spot.

Logan loses himself in it, sucking and licking sporadically, reacting to my body, letting me take the reins. He licks a heavy stripe through my core and plays with the little bundle of nerves there, which has me arching into his mouth, holding him against me while he works.

It feels amazing, but it isn't enough. My body demands the friction of him inside of me, so I pull him up by his chin and guide him on top.

"I need you to fuck me."

He kisses me roughly, pulling the zipper down on his pants and I wrestle them off his legs until he's hard at attention and grinding himself against the wet center of my body.

"Like this?" he asks, pressing the tip of himself inside of me and pulling back out again. "Tell me how you want it."

"Hard," is my only answer. I pull him against me again, until his cock catches and is sheathed completely.

Logan's hands find my pebbled nipples beneath my shirt while he rides me out. I have both my arms wrapped around his neck, and as he buries his face in my throat, kissing a trail to the bottom of my ear, I close my eyes.

Like a switch, all of a sudden my mind is elsewhere, hanging in the balance between fiction and reality.

When he lifts his head again he's Silas, sweat stricken and exultant, filling my body with heavy strokes as I thrash underneath him. He picks up his pace, driving me wildly into the mattress and I reach a hand up to feel if he's real. My thumb runs against the hair of his full mustache and slides down to catch on the flesh of his bottom lip. He flicks his tongue out, licking my finger into his mouth and sucking on it.

"Fuck." I drop my hand down between our two bodies to touch myself. "Keep going."

Silas stays steady while I play with my clit, the friction of him inside me pairing heavenly with the stimulation, and I know I'm close. I pull him down and he meets me halfway, closing his mouth over mine as I spar with my orgasm.

"You're gonna come for me, Birdie?" I nod back at him. "Let me feel it."

The rush overcomes me even quicker than I expected, blinding me for a second as my climax hits its peak. When I come to, and the room has finally stopped spinning—It's Logan pinning me to the bed with his dense, satiated body. I feel my thighs painted slick with him and run a hand up his spine as the guilt washes over.

Every time before this I'd dreamt myself naked and underneath Silas, it wasn't anything more than that. A dream. An impossible scenario with a non-existent man.

Now it feels different.

Not just because he *is* real, but because I *want* him to be. I *know* him to be.

And I'm not dreaming.

.✦

After Silas left Logan and I in the common area, he circled the ship twice on foot just to calm his own racing pulse. Get his mind right.

There I was, an angel in front of his very eyes. The deity of his every waking dream come to life.

His most sacred companion was latched onto the arm of another man, and there wasn't a Maker damned sane thing he could do about it.

Yeah, he gave that book to me on purpose. He had Logan to thank for that, and if all it got him was the empty win of proving the man a liar, he would still take it. Commit to the gamble with no other cards to play.

If I read it and figured I knew Silas in the same way he knew me, that was the best clue he could offer without leaving himself completely vulnerable.

When he finally returned to his pod, the exhaustion of the previous days' travels caught up with him. Finally unhindered by the constant work and paranoia of looking over his own shoulder, he was able to relax for the first time on the ride back to the Otera.

Silas slipped into the beginning stages of sleep easily, at peace with the ambient background noise of space helping him along. It took almost no time for the vision of me to show up there with him, sitting at the edge of his unmade bed.

"So I'm real, huh?" I tsked.

"Don't ridicule me, sweetheart. You're with another man, I think I'll leave the detriment of explanation to you."

"I don't want him, Silas." I slithered to his side, tracing my fingertips up his torso. "It's always been you."

"Well, now you're just being malicious."

He let me climb on top of him and straddle his middle, granting me a chaste kiss before pushing me away softly.

"If I cannot have you out there, I won't allow myself the tactless pleasure here either."

Silas forced himself awake and sighed, running a tan hand down the expanse of his face and cursing under his breath.

He needed to get me out of his head. Spare himself the endless disappointment seemingly following him from point A to Z.

I didn't wait for him. I *didn't* want him. To no one's fault, and that was the hard truth of it. One thing he did know, was he wouldn't survive this cycle and a half trip to the Otera if he couldn't find another way to occupy his time.

The restaurant is absolutely bustling, which makes sense. The only semi-social thing to do while traveling through space comes in the form of eating and getting inebriated until your heart's content.

The waiters are dressed in button down shirts and intricately knotted ties, and it feels fake fancy, but I'll take what I can get.

Logan pulls me along with him by my hand into the venue and a hostess seats us at a sparkling booth. The lighting is decent, yellow hues to keep it homely.

This could be a proper date.

I finagle with my menu for a minute, flipping it over, back and front, and cajole with Logan over the cocktails. When our waiter approaches the table I look up with a smile that dies on my lips immediately.

Just past their head in my line of vision is Silas, sitting up at the restaurant bar with a tumbler of amber liquid in one hand, the other slung over the backside of a woman in the bar stool beside him. He talks close to her face, leaning in to whisper something in her ear and they both laugh.

I feel that familiar tightening in my chest again and snap back to look at the waiter when Logan's voice interrupts my zoning.

"They asked what you wanted to drink, Lize."

"Right, sorry—not feeling myself today." I scan the menu with my finger and point at a drink. "This one sounds good. Thank you."

I find Silas again when the waiter walks away. He's playing with the tiny straw in his drink and scanning the restaurant while his date takes a swig of her own. He sees me across the room already looking at him and lights up a little, lifting his drink toward me with a nod. As he takes a sip from his glass and sets it back down I shoot him a friendly smile in return.

Then, with a devious wink as the woman turns back to face him, he doesn't waste any time at all leaning down and putting his mouth on hers.

3
COVETOUS

LAST NIGHT

S ilas initially wanted to fuck her like he would have fucked me.

Long lingering strokes and the heavy weight of his dick stretching her so full her eyes would roll back in her head. He thought, ineptly, that if he fucked her that good, that thoroughly, word of it might crisscross the transport's gossip grapevine a few times and fall on my ears.

It was self-complacent, he knew that. Unfair to the lovely woman attached to his arm and grabbing at the buckle of his pants before they even reached her pod. Silas realized quickly after he got her undressed that he couldn't fuck her like he wanted to fuck me, simply because, well—she *wasn't* me. He couldn't pour that type of endearment into someone else, even if it was just pretend.

He was attracted to her, which wasn't abnormal, Silas was attracted to a lot of people, had slept with a lot of people, but a relationship? Never. I was that empty hole for him, one that someone else's presence couldn't fill no matter how many ways they tried to squeeze into it. So Silas wasn't going to fuck her like he'd fuck me.

No.

He was going to fuck her like he needed to *forget* about me.

Nipping at her dark skin as she moans, lacing his hand through the hair at the nape of her neck as he takes her hard from behind. With lips finding purchase in the crook of her neck, Silas licks the salt from her skin—using his other hand to play with her as she rocks her hips down against him. "You like that?"

She smiles over her shoulder from where she's knelt on all fours, flawless umber complexion knotted in pleasure while Silas splits her wet center open over his cock.

If not for the circumstance, he may have found himself completely enamored by the woman. She demanded attention without asking for it, reeling Silas toward her across a crowded room of people at first glance.

"I know you do," he answers himself.

With every thrust, Silas can feel a jolt in her spine as he caresses it, even more violently when he circles the thick flesh of her ass, then brings a harsh palm down against the skin there with a sickening crack.

She whimpers into the open air of the pod, fists clenching the thin white sheet of the bed as a rush of slick escapes her.

Silas clings to that feeling. It's been so long since he's felt the grip of another person around him, the desperation in a pussy when it reaches its limit. Seven cycles in the wild of the Pulp was a sentencing, one he took without choice, but the company of a callused hand is naught compared to the welcoming choke of a primed body.

Curling himself over her back, he lets his damp forehead settle between the blades of her shoulders and unleashes harder, her warm walls only beckoning him tighter and tighter the deeper he pushes himself.

Then he closes his eyes for a beat, and the mix of alcohol and lust sends his head spinning through the starless space behind his eyes as he drifts into a daydream where he feels... *me*. Where he can imagine he's taking *me*, instead.

"You are so gorgeous."

He slides his fingers around the woman's ribs and massages the plush, full mounds of her chest as a familiar heat ignites in his groin, sending a sweat to his lower back and a buzz up his spine. He can't think of me like this without losing composure. Not when I'm so near, not when I'd looked at him with those vexed, indigo eyes across the bar and taken his heart further in my tiny palm.

Silas wants that look again, underneath him, begging for him, dripping in satisfaction.

He nuzzles the skin on her back, lathing his lips in sloppy open-mouthed kisses as his thrusts become erratic.

"Spank me again," she asks.

Silas lifts his head with a snap, the fantasy he'd conjured of me fading promptly into the stark contrast of actuality.

"Please." She bites her lip. "Do it again."

He obeys, bringing his palm down on her tingling flesh once more and reveling in the sting of his own skin as well. Silas kisses her neck, then slots his nose against the sharp outline of her jaw.

"I can tell you're gonna come."

She replies in terse nods as her eyes slip closed in pleasure. "Yes—*fuck*, yes."

As if the sound of his voice alone brought her to that high, Silas cords his palm over her mouth to quiet her, pumping in quick, deep strokes until he feels her legs start to shake under him.

"That's it, go ahead."

With a groan and one final long stroke, she brays into the skin of his hand and spills around him. "Divine." He hums. "Fucking beautiful."

The woman's body goes limp underneath Silas as he pulls out, stroking himself and falling back against the frame behind the bed exhausted. He jerks his still hard cock slowly—*agonizingly*, compared to what he'd just done to her.

Discontent to leave him in wait, she shifts and props up on her knees, leaning down to take the head of his dick in her mouth without bothering for protest.

Silas groans deeply, keeping his eyes closed and head tipped back against the wall as her tongue swirls around him.

It's easier to imagine me this way though, as a fucked up little fantasy of my naked body knelt next to him and sucking him off. His conscience twists with knowing nonetheless, but he's far past the point of worrying about his morality.

Silas isn't a good man, he has never claimed to be, and with his eyes closed I don't belong to another, I'm *his*. My backside sways gently beside him, my mouth takes him all the way down to the base.

He laces his fingers in the woman's hair, pressing a little firmer on her scalp and she lets him, leaving the pace up to Silas as he lifts his hips to match the way he's bringing her throat down around him.

"Fuck that's good," he breathes as he cords his other hand through her hair then too, holding her head with two palms to fuck her mouth.

He isn't being tender, there's too much gnawing at him to feel guilt over using her as an outlet. Taking it out on the woman bent over his lap is a broken way to heal, but he welcomes the possibility of a missed stitch as she grips hard enough into his thighs to leave a mark.

"So good for me, Birdie." He pants. "Make me—making me come." His eyes are screwed shut, his forehead beading with sweat as he feels his shaft start to pulse before he comes undone in the warmth of her mouth, down her throat.

When Silas reluctantly opens his eyes again, she's wiping her chin with the back of her wrist. He leans down to capture her lips in a quick kiss before slinking all the way into the thin mattress.

"That was amazing," she fawns, which has the corner of his mouth lifting into a smirk as he skates his fingers absentmindedly down her spine.

If one thing is true of Silas, it's that he's a thorough lover, and a giving partner in whatever sexual endeavor he finds himself.

Still his ache remains unsatisfied.

He thought he could level the playing field by sleeping with someone else. Not that he ever physically slept with me, but it felt like he had. A hundred times, a thousand times. And yes, he'd had sex with other people of course, in his travels, on the job, but never knowing I was real, or tangible—never while I was sitting in a fucking pod down the corridor with another man.

"Why'd you call me that?" The woman's soft voice fills the silence of the room again.

"Hm?" Silas mumbles, neither here nor there anymore, his mind in a static limbo.

"Birdie." She runs a long finger up the span of his stomach, drawing little lines with her nail through the hair on his chest. "You called me Birdie."

Silas grinds his teeth and presses himself further into the pillow, counting the lights on the ceiling twice over before meeting her eye. He doesn't like that she latches onto that, because it isn't *for* her. He slipped and fell too far into the reverie in a moment of weakness, and that name doesn't belong to anyone else.

"Force of habit."

"I could get used to it," she flirts.

As if the house lights have flipped on and the act is complete, Silas shifts his weight into his palms and pushes himself to sit up. He quickly finds his briefs on the floor next to the bed and snags them from the tile. There will be no getting used to it or repeating of the past. The entire situation all of a sudden feels depraved. He wants to be elsewhere.

The sex was supposed to make him forget about me, not *crave* me.

Silas knows innately that there will never be another woman to replace who I am to him. That there isn't meant to be. And maybe I know that too, but he'll have to fight for it.

If the universe put him on this ship with me it's for a reason, a final test. He arrived alone on the transport with nothing but a bag of foreign gems, but he isn't leaving without me. He won't be damned to live only in his dreams.

"I enjoyed this," he says, pulling his briefs up his legs and tucking himself into them. He stands from the sheets and twists rather awkwardly to find where his shirt had been tossed in the heat of things.

The woman watches him get dressed and reticently finds her own dress splayed across the floor, shrugging it over her head with a faint frown. "You can stay."

"I'm partial to my own sleeping arrangement," Silas lies, finding a subtle way to end the evening as he bends over and picks her panties up off the floor. She makes her way around the bed to where he stands in front of the door and takes them from him. It's apparent she isn't yet ready for the night to end, but doesn't press the issue.

"We'll have to go to yours next time, then."

She lifts to her tiptoes to kiss Silas one last time, which he returns with a sad smile and an empty nod before stepping outside the pod.

4
VEXATION

NOW

I had watched the entire booze-induced philandering go down between Silas and the mystery woman from across the restaurant.

From the *very* distasteful tonguing, in my opinion—to the lingering way his hand played with the seam of her little gold dress where it fell on her thigh—all the way to the moment he signed the tab mere minutes later, guiding her away from the bar with a playful pinch to the meat of her ass.

It wasn't fair for it to hurt me, I knew that. Especially not with Logan sitting an arms length away, spoon feeding me several different tapas from the platter he'd ordered. Somehow it all gave me a sort of *introverted* feeling. Like someone who was watching a person take credit for what was theirs, but was too shy to speak up.

Only, Silas *wasn't* mine. He wasn't the man in my dreams that was devoted to me, he was free to do whatever—*whoever*—he wanted.

Yet, I still wouldn't let myself fall asleep last night because I was angry with him. I didn't want to see him when I closed my eyes.

"You need a fucking coffee," Logan observes.

He's trailing me down the hallway toward the concession area, my annoyance with the events of the night before bleeding into the morning, the exhaustion obviously not helping my mood either. I roll my eyes and push the doors open into the common area. "I barely slept."

Logan catches my wrist in his hand, twisting me around. "Still not feeling good?" He cups my jaw and rubs two soft thumbs down the span of my cheeks.

I wish I could tell him the truth: that I feel perfectly fine despite the aching pit of anomalous jealousy over Silas fucking another woman. I don't even know if he fucked her, I'm just jumping to conclusions, and how dare I anyway?

"Yeah," I decide to agree with a soft smile. "It's probably just travel sickness." I kiss the inside of one of Logan's wrists before he drops it away, and then make my way to the self-serve coffee area.

I regret it almost immediately.

Silas has his back turned facing the machines, hair still bedraggled like he couldn't bother to comb it before the caffeine hit his system. I think for a second to detour and skip the coffee for something stronger all together, but it's too late when he turns around and sees me standing there first.

The smile he offers is shy, one that feels like it should be followed by an apology, but the buzzing tension between the two of us tells him otherwise.

"'Mornin'," he says, voice no higher than a whisper, prompting him to clear his throat.

"This fucking guy." Logan claps a hand down on Silas's back like they're old friends. "I'm surprised you made it out of bed after the night you must have had."

My partner has always been forthright in his social advances, never shying away from intimate and sometimes even inappropriate conversation. A 'people person', he would say in defense. Over-sharer, I would argue.

Silas shifts awkwardly, scratching the back of his neck with his free hand and focusing on me. He tries to gauge my reaction to the conversation, but I must look just as horrified as he does.

"Seriously man, I'll be honest when you first got off the docks I would have never guessed you had that type of pull."

Logan steps around Silas to grab two cups off the countertop as he speaks. Silas and I remain locked in on one another while my partner pours our coffees, silence speaking every unsaid word.

I'm sorry, I see written in his eyes. *Me too,* I say back.

"You gonna see her again?" Logan asks, pulling both our attentions back to him as he hands me my barely-hot-enough cup of liquid.

"Never even got her name," Silas finally answers, taking a sip from his drink.

He thinks somehow that this admission may save him some sort of face, subtly letting me know that he didn't even care enough about the woman to ask her name. All hopefulness dies on his tongue when I scoff into my own cup.

Logan swings an arm around my shoulder and crowds me into his side. "Don't mind this one," he says to Silas. "She's been in a mood since dinner last night."

"That is *not* true." I shake my head dramatically, like I've just been accused of murder, and I see Silas's eyebrow shoot up like he's just *solved* said murder.

I need nothing less than this man believing he has some sort of affect on the state of my being.

"Oh bullshit," Logan presses. "You said it yourself, you couldn't even sleep last night"

"Enough, Logan." My cheeks flush, and if the situation could get any worse I'm sure it would. "Silas doesn't want to hear about it, he seems like a pretty busy guy."

"It may surprise you just how interested I am," he retorts, crossing his arms over his chest and fitting me with a sly smile.

"Fine, fine." Logan raises his one hand in mock surrender and turns his attention to Silas again. "What's the *busy guy* got going on today?"

I wince at the way he words that, and Silas keeps his eyes on me for a few more seconds before entertaining it.

"I hate to be so formulaic," he says, chuckling to himself, "but I was actually headed to find the library on this thing."

I shrug out of Logan's grasp and cross my own arms, feeling a sort of lingering embarrassment, like caging myself inside my own body might hide me from it.

"Book Guy." Logan repeats the previous days' sentiment to Silas again, snickering along with him. "Well, hey man, let us show you where it is. We've got nothing going on today—or any spin until we hit the Ote."

"We don't have—" I begin.

"I'd be elated for the company," Silas interjects, heading toward the doors to the long hallway. "It's been quite some time since I've had any."

Logan and I follow him, and I hang back a bit and let my boyfriend walk beside Silas. I watch them both converse languidly, measuring them next to each other.

Logan has a few inches of height on Silas, but Silas makes up for it in width. His broad shoulders fill the back of his relaxed long sleeve nicely, and I can see the way his shoulder blades dip and curve against the lines of muscle down the planes of his back.

As if he senses my eyes, Silas glances over his shoulder and checks on me, ignoring whatever it is that Logan is chatting his ear off about for a few seconds until I smile at him, and then returns to listening.

"So what do you do, man?" Logan asks.

"I'm a *Mako*. You're lucky enough to catch me on the come back from a moon we call the Pulp."

I walk a little faster to hear him better, interested in everything that is Silas. The man himself and how he came to be walking in front of me. Maybe it would explain some things. Why I see him every night in my dreams, why I'm cursedly in love with him despite just learning his name a day prior.

"So you're like a miner. Very cool," Logan says.

"No, not really," I correct him. "The miners uncover artifacts. Planetary cargo and such to help them better understand the historical significance of moons and their dwellers. Most of the things they find end up being brought back to the Ote and placed in museums for tourist attraction. It's really somewhat of a pity that they don't erect similar places on the mother moons themselves—the people there are robbed of their own significant histories for our brief entertainment."

Silas slows down a bit to fall into step with me, listening to my explanation as Logan continues ahead.

I turn my attention to him as I say, "You dig for the same things, but not for the same reasons."

"That is right, Birdie," he confirms, giving me an impressed nod. "I'm afraid my line of labor deserves no more praise than those you speak of though."

"Look at you Lize, you know your shit." Logan turns a bit to bump my thigh with his knuckles. "Book Guy, meet Book Girl." He jokes pointedly at Silas and Silas takes the bait to brush me with his knuckles as well.

"I've met you a thousand times then, Book Girl," he says. "In a thousand stories."

His gaze shifts to mine, saying something with his eyes again that I can't quite decipher over the rapidly beating sound of my heart.

"She does read a lot," Logan interrupts, completely oblivious. "Eliza studied—" He frowns. "What was it again? A long name for a lost appreciation."

"Intercultural-specific text," I remind him. "I had a draw toward the Earth-aged classic."

"My little collector, she's got a lot of books burning a hole in our shelf space back home."

"I'm somewhat of a collector myself," Silas admits. "I find a certain depravity that I can cling to among early human literature. I relate to the longing."

We all round a corner of the ship's hallway, stopping in front of an elevator. Logan hits the 'up' button and I watch as blinking lights start descending from the floors above us, catching Silas's eye over Logan's shoulder.

"I do read a lot," I manage. "But I like to keep my books unlittered with love letters—in case someone reads them after me."

Silas smirks, watching the elevator spring open as Logan walks inside first. Then he holds his hand out to keep the door from closing and steps to the side so I can go ahead of him.

"It's impressive," Silas comments as I pass, a grin still rampant across his face. "I wouldn't have expected someone who was too ill to sleep to have spent their night reading my annotations." He follows me into the elevator, studying my face as the doors shut behind him.

"So what do you do out there digging all by yourself?" Logan asks. "How long are you gone for?"

Silas clicks his tongue. "This time around I was out there for seven cycles—not a hell I'd banish anyone to by the way, before you think me formidable."

"Fucking *Maker*." Logan draws out the words like he's in pain, bending at the waist a bit. "How do you manage being alone all that time? I'd go insane."

"I wouldn't say I'm entirely by myself." The elevator halts at a new floor and the doors screech open. "I read," Silas starts, waiting for Logan and I to walk through the opening first before following close behind. "I study the foliage. Sometimes I meet a bird or two." We all see the glass entrance of the library in the distance, and Logan makes a silent gesture toward it. "And I'm never alone in my dreams."

All three of us stop in front of the double doors and my eyes flicker to Silas's. If there's a moment of realization, it should be this one. A subtle way he's trying to tell me something that I don't know if I want to be true.

He searches me for a reaction, a flicker of divulgence, and I think maybe I could just—tell him.

Tell him I'm never alone in my dreams either, tell him what he already knows.

"That's poetic man," Logan says and Silas and I both break our gaze to look at him. "Here it is, *ye olde* library." Silas holds his hand out to shake Logan's in thanks. "Hey listen, why don't me and you go grab some drinks later? I want to hear about the Mako thing some more, yeah?"

"I very much appreciate the invitation," Silas says, looking for a way out of it, "but—"

"Oh, come on, what do you have going on? We're all stuck on this thing for more than a cycle—please? On me." Logan urges. "This one is sick of me, she could use some peace and quiet." He darts a thumb in my direction.

Silas looks back and forth between Logan and I, finding my eyes, and I shrug at him like I don't know the right answer. He struggles with the obligation and quickly realizes there's no viable way out of it.

"I'll see you there, then."

Logan is already more than half in the bag and canoodling with the less than optimistic bartender by the time Silas meets him at the bar. He counts a shot glass and two empty bottles in front of

Logan, and a third half empty clutched in his palm before he even sits down.

"I started without you man," Logan says, slapping a heavy hand down on Silas's shoulder when he takes the seat next to him.

"I can see that."

An already unappetizing evening has suddenly become even less so. Silas can't remember the last time he found himself in a crowded lounge, leisurely sipping cocktails, without the weight of the world crushing his neck. Even last night, with the woman from the bar, he couldn't wait to shed the background for something smaller and less consuming.

It wasn't always like this. When Silas was young he spent many dark nights beneath the glow of neon lights, rubbing shoulders in throngs of people, forgetting his own name. But that hadn't been his way for a long, long time now.

Apart from being out of place here, he feels unsettlingly self-conscious beside my partner. Sizing himself, still in the same clothes he'd been wearing earlier, against Logan's cleaner, crisper pair of slacks. He can't help but compare their likeness, their gaits. Lucidly pondering what I might find attractive or exceptional about the man sitting next to him. The things Logan has that he hasn't.

My boyfriend's hair is long but well-trimmed, styled into an impressive mop that nearly touches his shoulders. Short, golden stubble with hints of red weaving through the fuzz on his jaw. Silas knows when a man is attractive, he's given into that inclination many times, and he can't help now but notice his and Logan's very opposite features. The only time Silas has ever felt groomed was during his seldom stops between digs. When he could find a straight razor and clean the hair from his cheeks and neck, take a blunt scissor to the furling hair over his ears. After seven cycles on the Pulp, he's become brazenly unkempt in contrast.

Around the two men soft music plays, and the late dinner crowd of travelers have either found their way back to their pods, or sunken deeper into the black leather booths under dim light. The room means to give off a night-clubby feel, no doubt coaxing the lonely, bored patrons on the freighter into a more welcoming setting to mingle.

Silas gives the bartender a nod toward Logan's empty bottles as she approaches, to let her know he'll take one.

"She's nice." Logan points at the slender woman working behind the counter when she walks away. "She'd probably fuck you."

Silas shakes his head and looks around, hoping that there's no one within earshot of the pair of them that might mistake them for friends. "I'd hardly say a woman being nice to you means she would sleep with you, Logan."

"Nah man, you know what I mean," his words are slurring as he takes a sip of his beer and points the neck of the bottle at Silas. "Like, if you're looking for someone to sleep with again—you know, she looks nice. She looks like a woman a man would want to sleep with."

Apart from the deranged way in which Logan chose to describe it, she *is* attractive. Short black hair chopped just below her ears, purple eyes and thick makeup lining them. There are silver earrings dangling like chandeliers from her ears that sparkle along the curve of her jaw, and she wears a black button up top that's tight across her chest. She has a mysterious demeanor that eats Logan alive and intrigues Silas for the second she's turned around pouring his drink.

She returns and shuffles Silas's beer over to him, pushing another in Logan's direction, too. When Silas gives her an anxious look, she shrugs.

"I told her to keep'em coming," Logan explains. "And a couple shots!" He shouts as she walks away again.

Silas sips his beer and watches the bartender grab a shiny bottle off the top shelf, pouring two shot glasses, despite his less than enthusiastic expression.

"So tell me about that chick from last night," Logan smiles wildly.

"And to think you dragged me down here to talk about my job."

Logan gives him a fake pout. "Anything to get the girlfriend to cut me loose for a night."

As if he wasn't irked enough already, this *really* doesn't sit well with Silas. Thinking then of all the time he wishes he had with me, all the time in his life he's spent imagining what he would do with me, if given the chance. If I were really his.

And here Logan sits, happy to spend time without me. Happy to leave me alone in our pod for the night so he can get drunk at a shitty transport bar and make passes at the fucking wait staff.

It's hard enough for Silas to pretend to endure the man sitting next to him. Pretending to condone his blatant disrespect of me is a quickly crumbling disposition.

The bartender returns, placing the shots on shiny coasters.

"It hardly seems like you're in shackles," Silas answers plainly, downing the contents of the liquor.

As if given permission to divulge, Logan laughs to himself. "Eliza is wild, man. To be completely honest I don't know what to do with her half the time. You ever have a woman like that? Looks like an angel, but she's a fucking firecracker in bed." He does his shot too, crinkling his nose at the aftertaste as it slides down his throat. "She likes it *rough*, like..." He shakes his head as if his mind is racing with the picture of me. "And the body on this girl." Logan releases a whistle and closes his eyes, his body sways unsteadily in the chair.

Silas taps his fingers idly on the bar and stares in the direction of the door, anywhere but at Logan, afraid his face will give more away than he's willing to admit—not that Logan would remember it anyway. Inebriated son of a bitch.

Silas has a sudden inclination to punch him, to crack the bones in his nose for talking about me like that, for talking about *his* girl like that—and half a mind to leave him at the bar and go to me right then, finding me alone.

Logan didn't know Silas, or the twisted, hardened past that followed him like a shadow. He couldn't have been sure that the man he'd invited for a drink wouldn't take advantage of his situation and endanger the lonely girl he knew was lingering nearby in their pod.

Yet he sits here, a fountain of unprompted, unsavory information about *Silas's* dream woman.

"Do you get off on it or something Logan?" Silas asks, trying to understand the betrayal. He crouches in closer to Logan's face. "Another man imagining your partner naked? Imagining how she'd take it?"

Logan sips his beer, laughing lazily, like he can't even comprehend what Silas is saying. "Woah, man." He laughs again. "Fine, you know what? Just tell me about being a pirate—jeez."

Silas leans back against his chair and sighs, downing the contents of his glass and waving a hand at the bartender to end the night.

Logan is too drunk for this conversation, and Silas is too nettled to treat him with an inkling of more respect.

On any moon, had someone referred to Silas as a pirate, he'd have leveled the man instantly. That was an insult that you didn't throw around to a Mako, the insinuation of pillaging and taking advantage of a land's people was one that didn't go unaddressed. The disarrayed state of Logan was all that gave him pause.

"You wouldn't understand if I did."

As Silas settles their tab, Logan sways off his stool and nearly collapses against the bar. Silas reluctantly picks him up, shrugging Logan's dead arm over his own shoulder so he can support his weight, then drags my partner toward the door.

"Stay with me, Logan," Silas says, kicking them into the corridor hallway. "Which way is your pod?"

For whatever reason, the thought of Silas and Logan sharing a few drinks is keeping me on some catastrophic edge of anxiety.

What are they talking about? I know better than Logan actually giving a fuck about makoing. He thought Silas was a miner, for Maker's sake.

I sit down on the unmade bed and fling my head backwards into the pillows, sucking my teeth as I try to imagine what their conversation might sound like. I quickly abandon that line of thought when the image of Silas and Logan at the bar reminds me of the way Silas looked sitting there with that woman last night.

"Fuck," I curse myself and slam a lazy fist against the mattress. I thought I couldn't escape him when he only infiltrated my dreams, but this was another level.

My eyes slip closed and I begin to think about him again, about the way he *kissed* her. I imagine the brush of his mustache against her upper lip and lift my hand to ghost over my mouth in the same place.

Against every fiber in my body screaming at me not to, I think about how it probably felt skating down the inside of her thigh, tickling the warm skin there.

Instinctually I bring my hand down to touch between my legs, squeezing my eyes tighter and seeing Silas' shoulders spreading me apart, feeling his lips kiss a line up to my center.

I sigh and push a hand beneath the band of my panties, sliding my own finger up the wet seam of my slit. With a press down, I let it dip inside of me, imagining it's Silas again—but the fantasy is immediately shot to hell when I hear the loud bang of a fist against the outside of the pod door.

"Fuck!" I yelp in surprise, collecting myself as quickly as I can when the door starts to slide open. I see Silas first, ducking his head and stepping through.

"Where's—what are you—" I ramble, smoothing down the wrinkled mess of my sleep shorts.

He shuffles past me, dragging a half conscious Logan behind him. I shake my head in embarrassment, pinching the bridge of my nose as Silas makes his way to the bed I'd seconds prior tried to pleasure myself on. He shrugs my boyfriend off his shoulder and let's him drop face down onto the rumpled sheets.

"All yours, Birdie," Silas jokes, straightening his shirt from where it shifted off his shoulder.

"I—" I stutter.

Silas tries to make his way to the door again so as not to impose on my space uninvited. He has one leg out the small opening, and I can't explain what possesses me at the moment—a need to know him, to be close to him perhaps, but I stop him either way.

"Stay." I tell him, rather than ask.

He studies my face for a second, knowing there's no way he'd ever deny me, regardless of time, space and circumstance. He doesn't say anything but he doesn't leave either.

"I might need your help," I justify, unsure if the excuse is even necessary. "If—if he wakes up."

Silas swallows a thick lump of uncertainty. He's not the man to take advantage of a situation, but how I'm looking at him, pleading in a way that makes it hard for him to breathe, there's little left between selfishness and self-righteousness for him.

He doesn't say a word but he nods, putting his hand out for me to grab and motioning his head toward the empty hallway. I follow him, closing the latch to the pod behind me when I do.

5
EPIPHANY

When Silas and I step out into the hallway it's quiet. It's quiet, and empty, and when I look around my eyes burn slightly as the lights are just a little too bright. The trilling sound of space that's normally placid is deafening, because the implications of Silas and I being alone can only end in one of two ways: platonically cordial, or like it usually does in my dreams. Naked, all consuming, never close enough to one another.

My slinky outfit leaves little to visualize, not that he couldn't already, and I think I probably should have grabbed a sweatshirt before leaving the pod, but when I turn to go back in, Silas is already standing in front of me.

It takes a second before either of us even realize we're still connected at the hand, and another second passes before I let go, because it just feels so *natural*. Like muscle memory.

I'm *supposed* to be holding Silas's hand, he's used to it. He already knows the smallness of my palm trapped in his own and the dainty tips of my fingers against his knuckles.

Silas isn't sure where to go from here, standing alone with me in a hallway. He knows where he wants to be, of course—pressing me against the cold metal wall of this fluorescent lit corridor, tasting me for the first time, the *real* first time.

He wonders, what if he just does it? Just leaps across the narrow space separating us and takes me like he wants to. Slow, hungry kisses, desperate breaths as both of us struggle for air.

I'm looking back and forth between his eyes like my train of thought and his are one and the same.

His gaze flickers to my lips as he darts his tongue out and licks his own.

I *am* thinking about it, the seemingly implausible what ifs.

But as quickly as the feeling comes it goes. In a trice, like the weight of the moment is too heavy on my chest. I can't explain the pressure, but somewhere in the invisible movement of the universe something snaps its fingers and reminds me of the reality of the situation.

I think I know the man in front of me, but I don't.

I think I might be dreaming, but I'm not.

I think I must be in love with Silas—but my partner is passed out on our bed just beyond the door behind him.

I clear my throat and find a line in the floor tiles to trace with the tip of my sock. "So, was it really that bad?"

Silas looks down too, letting his teeth worry his bottom lip.

He thinks for a second to tell me just how bad it really was. That he'd mistaken Logan for a common idiot, when he's truly just an ungrateful mythomaniac. Silas could get past him lying about the book, it worked to his advantage anyway. A little white lie that did no more harm than good. But then the pattern resumed when Logan lied about the reason he wanted to meet him at the bar, not to mention the borderline inebriation before Silas even got there.

He could tell me about the way Logan talked about me, my body, my bedroom habits. To a man he met the day before, nonetheless.

It made his skin crawl thinking about what Logan might have said if he were talking to a friend.

But no, that's not the type of man Silas is.

He wouldn't capitalize on another man's misfortune, if he could even call it that. To use Logan's faults against him would be a dirty game, one he didn't want to play.

When Silas does finally have me, in his arms, his bed, he wants it to be on my own accord—because I chose him, not because I resent Logan.

"No." Silas eventually shakes his head. "No, we've all been there time and again, Birdie." He keeps his eyes on the ground as he speaks and I wonder if it's because he's lying. "Liquor is fickle in its loyalties."

I'm almost positive he's keeping something from me, but I decide it's probably better left unsaid. I walk a few more steps down the hallway away from the door so as not to make too much noise with our conversation, though I'm sure the ship could enter a black hole at this point and Logan wouldn't so much as snore.

"So, you never got to tell him about makoing then, I assume?"

I watch Silas take a couple long steps in my direction to close the gap again, and he hardly attempts to stifle a laugh. "Regrettably, I wasn't awarded the pleasure."

I laugh with him, sliding down the wall to sit on the floor. I cross my arms over my chest and shrug. "Well, I'd still like to hear about it."

Silas mimics my movements, hesitantly joining me against the wall, elbows bumping from the closeness. He stretches his legs out across the tile and runs his hands down the dark fabric of his pants from hip to knee. He has a soft smile on his face when he turns his head to look at me.

"Where shall I begin?"

The way Silas talks about his work, about anything, is like he's speaking in poetry. Twisting metaphor and anomaly like a matured vine through his language, it's as if I'm simply listening to my favorite story.

If I closed my eyes I would see it, the endless Pulp he describes. Trees as tall as mountains, thick grasses and brush, an atmosphere heavy with yellowish hues from the endless pollen—a mother planet that wades on the horizon day and night regardless of the climate.

Everything has to be controlled, he tells me. It's an integral part of the dig, readying the site and preserving your safety in several steps before extraction.

"Not every place in these surrounding galaxies is deemed safe for travel, some will never be. The Pulp is toxic, you can survive there for small bouts of time, but long term it's completely unlivable."

I nod and he gives me a wink before continuing.

He says the earth is gifting the harvest, and you must treat it as such. Take care of the land, respect it, and it will respect you.

I watch him closely as he describes the process of extracting crystal from the silt, one of the most highly requested jobs of a Mako. He practices the movements with his hands so I can see, like a pantomime and a picture show.

Mostly, Silas digs for natural resources and left-behind rarity's from civilizations on planets unexplored; metals, oil, gems, jewels. On occasion a client will be looking for something more specific and be willing to pay an outlandish tally to possess it.

The galaxy is ever-giving and largely undiscovered. His job takes him places people have never gone before, and to places people would never *want* to go.

Centuries ago, when humans began migrating from the Ghost Earth in the solar system to the newly discovered Alzaec system to inhabit the Otera—everyone got greedy. It was a quest to spread and conquer, to put down roots on planets and moons that hadn't been claimed or well protected. Many important discoveries came from this of course, but it's the nature of any creature or animal to be possessive over what they believe is theirs.

That's where the Mako's were born.

When people of power were too prim to get their own hands muddied, but wanted a cut of the extraterritorial anyway, they started contracting diggers to go boots down on unexplored planets and do the bidding for them.

There are other men like Silas, often contracted in the same ways he is, to provide for a client or do the dirty and often dangerous part of new-celestial exploration. Meeting someone else in the wild of a foreign planet could be either your greatest salvation or your greatest threat.

He opens his palms in front of him like he's cupping something in his hands, another silent gesture, and smiles when he looks up to see me enamored. I'm staring into the empty space there, as if I can see the nonexistent mineral he's just described to me with my own eyes.

"What does your client do with it?" I ask. "Was this past dig a special task?"

Silas seems to bristle at my acquisition. The tension that he's obviously trying not to convey creases a wrinkle between his brows before he irons it back out. Still, I'm left wondering if there's more attached to the Pulp moon than he's disclosing.

"Lavish jewelry probably." He scoffs a bit. "The gem itself is glorious, it can be used for many things. The pigment for ink, the shell for plastic, but most incredibly it harnesses a sound energy that's inconceivable to our ears but harmonic to animals. This could be unbelievably advantageous to agriculturists. It's a rare, valuable substance. I hate to confess that it's been depreciated into no more than something to show wealth."

"Unfortunately beauty does tend to bring out the ugly in people." I lament over the centuries old juxtaposition. "It sounds truly stunning, Silas."

"The most beautiful thing I've ever seen," he says. I nod as if I agree, imagining the sparkling blue geode inside its fluorescent bubble. Like seeing the night sky captured in clear quartz.

When I look up, Silas is still watching me, basking in his own staggeringly obvious innuendo. My cheeks run hot when I realize.

It's easy for him to treat me in such a way, because he already does every night when he sleeps. And sure, he's talked to *dream* me about makoing, or maybe dream me already knew the ins and outs of it because I'm subconsciously connected to him. But having this conversation here in a shared reality, captivating me with his work, is better than any dream.

"It's refreshing," Silas says, his mouth yet to present anything less than a beholden smile. "Speaking with someone that shows genuine fascination in how I make my living."

I grin back at him and shrug, pulling my knees into my chest and wrapping my arms around them. "So you sell everything for tally?" I ask. "You've never even kept one thing?"

"I've learned very well to deflect the burden of temptation," he says. The dusting insinuation is there again, but he brushes it off. "When we arrive at the Otera everything will be sold or traded. Debts will be settled, arrangements made—and then I'm gone again."

I furrow my eyebrows, a stinging sense of worry pings in my stomach at his words.

Gone.

I don't want him to be gone. The thought of this freighter docking at the Otera in a cycle or so and having to say goodbye to Silas already feels wrong. It already hurts.

I've just found you.

"Gone? Gone where?" I ask without hiding the hint of frenzy. I twist my body to face him better, knee bumping and settling just against his thigh. His one eyebrow raises quizzically at my blatant unease.

"Undetermined," he says, starting to feel homesick as well, if home were a person. "This dig was auspicious to say the least, and I now have the somewhat taxing fortune to settle wherever I please."

I think about what that must be like, having complete freewill to pack your life up and just, *go*. Go wherever you want, have a sense of security, start anew.

I wanted to stay in the Glades forever just a few days ago; I would have done anything to make time stand still. Now as I'm sitting next to Silas, in a beaming hallway, on one of the thousands of transports floating through the endless black of space, it's evident there's several forces at work that brought the two of us together.

"I suppose I'd enjoy the menial labor of opening a bookstore," Silas continues. "Perhaps, teach literature somewhere."

I smile, even through the ripples of jealousy I can feel threatening to make waves. I can picture it so clearly, Silas standing behind a small counter, shelves of paperbacks and hardcovers alike littering the walls around him. A perfect disarray that only makes any sense to him, and if you ask for a book he already knows exactly where it is—right where he left it. No promises on the state of the secondhand or if the pages are penned and keyed in his little language.

I selfishly picture myself there too, lounging on a chaise across the room with a pen tucked behind my ear, flipping through Silas's copy of *The Master and Margarita*, making my own annotations next to his.

"I can see it," is all I reply.

Silas knows it's unbecoming to stare, but he can't help himself the way I look sitting next to him at the moment. Blonde hair tousled around my scalp, eyes silken with exhaustion because of the impious hour of the night I was all but kicked out of my own bed.

I look so *soft* to him. Like a comfortable type of soft, where he wants to lay into me. He wants to envelop me. *Feel* me. It's brazen and obvious, but he lets his eyes fall down my neck, slink to my chest, and remain.

I know he's looking and I do nothing to shirk the moment—almost enthralled at the thought of him drinking me in.

Silas sighs low in his throat, swiping his tongue out to wet his lips at the sight of my nipples, puckered through the thin fabric of my shirt.

He knows my naked body. He's seen it, made love to it, traced the curve of my spine with his fingers and his lips. He can map my beauty marks from memory like a constellation. *One right there*, he thinks, letting his gaze travel down my body further. *One there—and there.* I know I should stop him or cover myself, but it's so unbearably sexual despite the lack of physicality that I can feel myself getting aroused.

Silas has to snap himself out of it, remind himself where he is, why he's on the floor of the hallway with me in the first place.

Logan's passed out in the bed he shares with me, and Silas won't do that. He won't be a beacon for infidelity, and he suspects correctly that I wouldn't be that person either. He closes his eyes for a beat and then opens them to look back at my face.

I'm still not completely disposed of the moment, and I want so badly to tell him that I see him in my sleep. That I can't stop thinking about him. If there's a reason the two of us are both here, a reason I'm watching the man from my dreams come to life right in front of me, it's celestial. And Silas has hinted at it enough that he feels it too.

"Why do you stare at me like that?" I ask.

Silas perks up at my question, not expecting it, but also not opposed to my blatancy. He struggles for a second, deciding the right angle to take before he answers. "Just trying to remember where I've seen you before."

"You haven't figured it out yet?"

He senses a speck of discern in my voice, like the answer is obvious and I'm just waiting for him to see it too.

"Have you?" he deals back.

It's a peculiar thing, how we've managed to tangle ourselves in this game. Like we're playing cards and haven't yet deciphered that we picked the same suits—that the other will always have what we need to win.

"It's starting to come back to me," I say.

To this, he closes his eyes again and lets his head fall back against the metal wall with a dull thud. Silas decides that if I leave this hallway thinking he's a lunatic, he'll take that chance. The circumstances of this entire exchange, this entire coincidental meeting in space, may never be so opportunistic again. He's bending his own rules to take advantage of Logan's current state, but if he misses the window and never gets to have this conversation, then rules be damned.

He goes about it in his own very Silas-esque way, the way he imagines a remarkable love story should. Unfolding itself in hyperbole and indelible prose that sticks with you long after it's over.

Even if I don't choose him after all of this, he wants me to imagine the story as what it could have been. Wherever I end up tucked away in the universe, forever thinking about the type of love I could have had with him.

"You know what, I *do* remember now," he confesses, opening his eyes again to find me.

I sit up straighter and my eyebrows wiggle in what I imagine looks like a muddle of excitement and confusion.

"You were laying in a field of green, on a big old blanket." He watches my expression change completely to confusion. "Yeah—in a little yellow sundress and hat made from straw. The sun was beating down on you, and you were reading a book."

My confusion crosses the line into disappointment as he speaks, thinking he *must* be mistaking me for someone else. A pretty memory with another person.

I shake my head and laugh, cutting him off. "That couldn't have been me."

He nods his head, like he's never been so sure of something. "Oh it was you, Birdie." He smiles, thinking about it again. "A reminiscence I visit frequently."

I smile back, closing my eyes to imagine it for myself.

"I'd never forget your face," he says. "And you knew my name. You said to me, '*Silas, what took you so long? I've been waiting,*' and then I joined you for a while."

Something clicks in my brain that tells me he isn't mistaking his recollection—he's just the only one of us who would remember it. Much like every contented interaction I've ever had with him before he landed on this transport.

If he's reciting a dream to me, there's a thousand I can declaim to him too.

"I—I think I know where I've seen you too, actually," I say, voice so low it might as well be a whisper.

Silas feels a ball of nervous energy knot in his chest, several emotions like strings flipping over one another until they're a fraying mess he knows won't easily untangle.

"I was hiking one afternoon," I start, and Silas knows immediately. He knows it's a rendering of a well loved dream I'd had of him.

"You were sitting on a rock at the head of the trail, right where it opened up to the river delta, and you were writing in a little journal."

It's his turn to picture it now, this scene of himself that's carved into my mind. To live my memory as if it's his own.

"I could hardly hear you over the waterfall," I continue, "but you called me Birdie, and yelled something about how the water was so exquisite, that I needed to jump in."

Silas drops his head back against the wall again, still holding my gaze. He wants so badly to reach out and touch me, or hold me, because this is more emotion than a body alone can endure. A feeling of fate barreling in like some insane, extraterrestrial being that was impressively late for the party.

I have no idea how long he's waited for this, he thinks.

How long he's waited for me.

While Silas is almost positive now that I share the same connection through my dreams, he needs to hear me say it.

"My evocation may be a bit divergent from yours," he tests me. "You see, after our rendezvous—I woke up. It proved to be just a dream."

I don't mean to be so conspicuous, but his admission makes me gasp like I'm struggling for air. I'm heavy with the realization that I'm not crazy. I'm not alone.

After all this time in my life, feeling that I was experiencing a one-sided pleasure with a man that didn't exist and never would, he does. I grip his hand where it's resting on his knee and squeeze it.

"I knew it," I whisper. "You see me, too."

Silas squeezes my hand back and nods in haste. "Every single night when I go to sleep, Eliza."

It's less the disbelief than it is the shock that leaves us speechless. Trying in both our own little bubbles to wrap our heads around it.

What it means—*why*.

For Silas he's always afforded himself the shred of faith I was out there, never taking any more than an arbitrary lover. This moment for him is elation, prophesied ambiguity.

"Maker, fuck," I lament, scratching at my forehead while I think. "I didn't want to say it when we met, you know how insane I would've sounded."

"I can agree I shared that sentiment," he says, thinking back on when he first saw me in the ship's concession area.

"What the fuck are we?"

I'm past exasperation, my mind zig-zags to make some type of connection. Regardless of this shared epiphany, I still don't want to admit to certain aspects of my dreams. I still don't *know* Silas, I decide. And just because *my* dreams pin him and I as lovers, doesn't mean that his do the same.

"We're bonded," Silas answers, and that feels undoubtedly true.

He likewise is sharing my feelings about not admitting to a more intimate relationship—at least not yet. At least not with Logan in the picture, without giving me time to sit with what he already knows to be fact, that he and I are fated.

I stand from the floor abruptly and Silas jumps up on my heels to shadow me, worried I'm freaked out about the situation.

"Stay here," I say, stopping him from following me. "This is gonna sound crazy, but I keep a journal of my dreams. When I wake up or if I can't sleep, I write them down."

Silas stops in his tracks and watches me make my way back to my pod in a state of utter wonderment.

A whole *journal*, filled with memories of us. Penned into pages, recorded forever. He scolds himself for never keeping something similar, not having something to offer to me in return.

I slide the heavy door of the pod open as quietly as I can and take in the limp body of Logan spread across the entirety of the bed. The mattress is pushed into the corner to open up more space in the room, which makes it impossible to reach my journal tucked between the sheets and the wall without crawling over him. I sigh and shake my head, whispering a flustered *fuck* to myself.

I decide to take the chance and crawl over him anyway, easy so as not to rattle the bed too much, already preparing for the inevitable squeak of the springs. Logan doesn't stir when I lean my body over his, reaching as far as my arm will allow to snag the journal from its hiding spot. I sigh in relief and begin to retreat, but before I get fully off the bed Logan groans and flips over, roused by the creaking metal. He pulls me against his body and wedges his face into my hair.

"C'mere baby," he mumbles. "I love you." He kisses the crown of my head and then attempts to kiss my face.

"Go back to sleep," I hush him softly. "You're drunk Logan, stop."

He lets me wiggle out of his grasp, but before I can get off the bed I look up and see Silas standing in the doorway watching me. His hands are in his pockets and he's leaning against the small hatch of the pod.

He can't help but feel hurt. Not because of me, never me—but because he spent the last, however many minutes of his life, completely engulfed in a far fetched fantasy.

Silas let himself get too enthusiastic. The stark realism of the situation hit him like a bullet charge when he saw me just now with Logan, wrapped in his arms. Regardless of my intention to return to the hallway.

I wave the journal in the air and stand from the mattress. "Got it."

Silas gives me a regretful smile and nods in the direction of Logan already snoring again behind me. "Another time."

I drop the hand that's holding the journal down as he pulls the door halfway and pauses to look at me a final time.

"Sweet dreams, Birdie," Silas says, then clicks the slide shut, leaving me standing alone in the center of the pod.

6
VOLITION

S ilas closes the door and stays there for a while—he isn't sure why. Maybe with some shred of hope that I'll follow him outside anyway despite his very cut and dry goodnight.

He holds his breath for a minute and leans his forehead against the metal slide, listening for the sound of me moving around inside, shuffling my belongings, sifting through the journal by myself.

Selfishly, he imagines me hesitant to lie with Logan and get some sleep, though he knows I've barely gotten a wink in two days.

It actually stings him a bit to think it's been that long since I've dreamt about him.

When Silas doesn't hear anything, he peels himself off the metal and backs away, deciding to drop the self pity and let me sleep, to go and get some sleep himself while the clock still says its night on this hovering transport.

I hear him leave from the other side of the door, pressing my ear against it with a palm over my mouth to hush my erratic breathing.

I knew he was still standing there, probably just as aghast as I was. Trying to understand this intense attraction that leaves us both airless and clueless. I battled with myself as I waited, half ready to go to him in the hallway with my journal anyway, to show him some of my dreams, and find out about his, too.

The sound of his feet traipsing down the corridor snaps me out of it.

For the better, I think, looking back at Logan. I tiptoe toward the bed and squeeze in next to him.

The clock on the wall reminds me that my talk with Silas bled into the early hours of the new spin, and I squeeze my eyes shut to force myself to drift into some semblance of sleep.

When Silas gets to his pod it's just how he always leaves it.

An organized mess.

The dim overhead light he keeps on flickers as he slides his door open and plods inside.

There's so many things unsaid, and he's angry at himself the more he sits on it. Why didn't he just stay? I *wanted* him to stay. He could tell in my face when he closed the door that the night wasn't over for me. I wanted to show him the journal.

Silas throws himself onto the shoddily made bed, kicks his boots across the floor, runs a tired hand down his face and stares at the ceiling.

He couldn't handle it.

That buzzing feeling of getting too close to the flame when he knew he was inches away from being burned.

He hardly fights it when his eyes start to feel heavy, still in his clothes from the day, not even bothering to take them off. It's immediate, the way I show up when he succumbs to his sleep.

"I wanted you to stay," I say. Silas is facing me in his pilot's chair, I'm perched on the edge of his bed.

"You know I couldn't."

"I know you're afraid," I challenge, smoothing the sheets with my fingers.

Silas sucks his teeth and shakes his head back and forth like he doesn't know what else to say. He knows his mind is taunting him with the image of me, telling him all the things he won't allow himself to believe in his waking hours.

"You're afraid I won't want you back, that you'll scare me away, that you won't be what I imagined you would be—afraid you won't satisfy me."

"All this supposition, Birdie," he bites, now staring daggers through me. *"None of the answers."*

I stand from the bed and saunter toward him, my clothes wishing themselves away as they would in any of his dreams. As I squeeze myself between his open legs, he holds my hips, staring up at my body, past my breasts to see me looking down at him. My choppy hair frames the outline of my jaw as it hangs around my face.

"Is that what it is, Sy? Hm?" I caress his cheeks in both palms. *"You don't know if you'll satisfy me?"*

He turns his head and nuzzles the soft hair above his lip against my wrist, not breaking eye contact with me as he does.

"You haven't made love to me in days, maybe you can't..."

He cuts me off. *"Birdie, don't delude yourself. You know I'm not one to feign naivety—the satisfaction isn't lacking if you're here begging for it."*

Against his promises he lets me straddle his lap, pressing myself firmly into the junction of his hips. I feel the way he hardens instantly. Silas runs his thumbs back and forth against my smooth skin and leans forward to press a chaste kiss to the valley between my breasts.

I smirk at him when he meets my eyes again, rolling my hips lightly over his. *"So make me beg then."*

Without another word he licks a thick stripe up the middle of my chest to the dip of my collarbones, kissing the skin there before nudging *his sharp nose against my neck and trailing it up to my ear. He laves at my pulse with his tongue, then bites down into it as I sigh.*

My hips are rocking into him while he works, searching for the friction that makes my eyes close and my head dip back. And I find it for a second, but Silas steals it from me just as fast—shifting his body away from my grinding core and pinching a puckered nipple between his fingers to snap me out of it.

"Beg," he says. I bite my bottom lip, giggling at him, but not giving in.

He continues, cupping that same breast in his hand and leaning down to lap my peak into his mouth. He stares at me as he sucks on the tender flesh, bringing a whimper to my lips when he scrapes his teeth over the bud.

The untended nipple receives the same attention from him then—keeping the first caught between his fingers as he licks at the other.

I wrap my arms around Silas's head and thread my fingers through his hair, holding him close to my chest. There's a spark of delight in my center when he sucks the peak hard enough to tug it away from my body.

I start carving my hips against his again, and I pull his head up to to catch his lips between my own. My tongue slides through the narrow opening as I lick into his mouth.

Silas breaks away when I get too greedy, bunching the hair at the nape of my neck into a fist to draw me off of his lips.

"Beg," he demands.

I try to hide the whine that escapes my throat, but I can't. Silas is the one who chuckles now, running both his hands up and down the junctures of my ribs. He slides them down to cup my ass, kneading the flesh and pulling it apart so that the cold air of the pod hits my core.

When I don't give in he stands, helping me off his lap and walking me backwards until I hit the mattress. I fold into it without protest, and Silas kneels on the ground in front of me, catching the backs of both

*my knees in his palms and pushing my legs apart until I'm completely
exposed.*

He smiles at how wet I already am, glistening and ready for him.

*He can feel my muscles tense as he trails his nose from the inside of
my knee down my inner thigh and my hips buck toward the sensation.*

*I wait with bated breath for him to lick into me, and when he doesn't
I whine again, pressing up onto my elbows so I can see his face.*

*Silas awaits my eye contact before spitting down onto the throbbing
bundle of nerves at my peak. My spine arches when he does it.*

*"Gods..." I groan, feeling the ghost of his lips over the place I want
him the most. I lift my hips to try to force it, but he holds me down with
a forearm.*

"Beg."

"Please, Silas," I sigh. "Please."

I'm still awake before Logan is, but that gives me time to meander
to the communal showers and take my time under the pressured
faucet. We have a small stall in our pod that only kicks out enough
lukewarm water to soap my body once over before it turns ice
cold, so if the opportunity arises to have a long, hot shower—I
take it.

I hum to myself as the water splashes my back, melting the
tension from my shoulder blades and warming my spine and
tailbone as it flows downstream.

I take my time, close my eyes, and think about this whole
fucked up trip. How I felt so irrevocably in love with my boyfriend
mere spins ago and now my mind is entirely occupied by Silas. It's
more than a clouding of him. He's a thick fog in my brain that's
stubborn to lift, leaving me blind as to what will come next.

The sound of a robotic voice rumbles through the ship-wide
intercom speakers hitched to the wall. The bustle of conversation

and faint music within the communal space comes to a halt while everyone in the room listens.

Floating today over the Continental for scheduled refueling, pods may disembark but must return before the end of the spin.

The comm clicks then and recites the announcement in several different languages as I turn the water off in my shower.

I wrap a towel hastily around my chest, tucking it tightly to my body as I pull the curtain back to step out of the stall. I'm forced to stop short as soon as I do, because Silas is standing just across the way.

He can't see me, his body turned away and facing a wall mounted mirror in the main congregation area. There's a thin white towel draped around his hips as he takes a razor to his cheeks, his hand moving across the soapy flesh languidly and precisely. His muscles flex and release, I can see the way that beads of water still drip down the olive skin of his back where he couldn't reach to dry it.

He's exactly as I imagine him—taut, glowing, scar-slashed skin. Damp, dark hair curling at the ends and threatening to fold over his ears.

He turns a bit more and I step back into my stall, pulling the curtain slightly to hide myself.

When I'm satisfied he hasn't caught me, I take in the peaks of his chest as they give way to his tapered waist, then my eyes fall to the firm slat of his stomach and the spattering of wet hair that gathers at his lower belly and starts to trail beneath the towel.

As if he can sense eyes on him, Silas stands still for a moment and then turns in my direction—but before he has a chance to see me, I pull the rest of the curtain closed and press my back hard against the cold tile of the wall.

"Shit," I mutter.

I give it a few minutes just to make sure, and when I build the confidence to peek outside the curtain again, he's gone.

Back in our pod Logan is awake, still lying in bed and scrolling a communication tablet with a pair of sunglasses on his face.

"Weather looks great on the Ote," he says.

I put all my toiletries back in their place and throw my laundry into the shared hamper.

"What about on the Continental?"

"Good..." The word has a tail on it like it's a question.

"So we should go down there," I say to answer his silent inquisition before it actually becomes one.

Logan groans into his pillow and pulls the blankets up his body, abandoning the comm tablet to play into his ailment. "Lize, I'm way too hungover." He moans again. "Do we really have to go?"

I pout and shake my head at him, both sympathetic to his position because I've been there myself, and annoyed that it's keeping me from exploring the Continental for the day.

Off the ship—fresh air, clear mind.

I've never been there before, and I'm not sure when the opportunity will present itself again, if it ever does.

Eventually I sigh and give in, joining him on the bed as he pulls me into his side. "It's a good day to just veg out. You can take care of me," he offers with a smirk and a wink. "You know, whatever that means to you."

I snort, shoving his shoulder and standing back up. Logan gives my ass a playful swat as I walk away. "Give me the booty, I need it to survive."

"Best I can do right now is breakfast and some hydration," I tease, grabbing a key and wallet before making my way to the door. "I'll be right back."

There's not *that* many places you can go on this thing, I tell myself as I make my way into the dining area and notice Silas almost immediately—again.

It's closer quarters than I realized. And maybe it's just the agony of the dream-lover-stranger situation, but when I look around at all the other people moving about, I don't recognize anyone, regardless of them traveling alongside me just as long as Silas. Possibly longer.

He's tucked into a small table, nose deep in another book, and I can see the steam piping off the top of his coffee in front of him.

He doesn't move a muscle as I wait in line for my food—the only motion I detect is his mismatched eyes, flitting back and forth across the pages.

I decide instead of pretending I don't see him, to just face the situation head on and walk over. It's only polite, I tell myself. He still doesn't notice me despite the close proximity, and I almost feel bad pulling him out of his literary trance.

"Gone with the Wind," I say. Silas looks up from his book immediately upon hearing my voice and smiles. "Haven't read that one either."

I take in his now closely shaven face. The grooming accentuates the sharpness of his jawline and highlights the small patches of his beard that have begun to gray. His hair is still slightly damp, and I'm close enough I can smell the woodsy scent of soap permeating off his skin.

"I'm afraid I can't offer you this one as a gift," he says, pulling a placeholder from his pocket and fitting it into the page before closing the book.

I frown a bit, fumbling with the foil wrapping on the sandwiches I'm holding.

"Because it's from the library," Silas adds, motioning for me to sit across from him instead of stand.

"Makes sense why it's not dog-eared and written in then," I tease as I sit down.

I drop the two sandwiches on the table and feel like maybe I should offer the second to Silas as I dig into my own.

He chuckles, reaching over to pick up his coffee and tenderly blowing at the brown liquid before taking a sip.

"So what is it about?" I take a bite of my food.

Silas furrows his brow in thought for a minute before he says, "It's about a lot of things. Love, survival, growth." He flips the book in his hand and looks at the back cover. "It's about a young girl who believes she's in love with someone, and she spends all her time and happiness on convincing herself of it, when the man she's truly meant to be with is there all along."

I stop chewing and hold Silas's blue-green eyes while he speaks.

"By the time she realizes she's not really in love with the man she's spent her whole life chasing, she's much older and the one she's always loved has moved on."

Silas sips his coffee again and thinks about his very one dimensional review of *Gone with the Wind*, knowing selfishly that there are several important parts of it he's omitted to appeal to mine and his situation.

"So it's sad," I quip, unable to say anything else while my mind ping pongs between Logan and Silas.

"Yes," he answers. "I suppose it's sad."

I take another bite of my sandwich and think as long as my mouth is full that any silence surmounting between the two of us isn't my problem to fix. Unfortunately for me, Silas thrives in silence and makes it very apparent that he enjoys just sitting here with me, watching me eat, trying to read my mind.

All of a sudden he's reminded of his own dream last night, the way I looked underneath him, the coo of my voice as I came.

I bring my thumb across my bottom lip to clean a drip of straying sauce and Silas watches that too.

I know it's wrong, but I make a minor show of popping the finger into my mouth and sucking it clean, feeling a weird exhilaration from the way he hasn't even attempted to look away. A staticky voice blares over the intercom and we break to stare up at it.

We are currently floating, it is now safe for all pods to disembark to the Continental.

Silas takes a last sip of his coffee and then fastens the lid back onto the travel mug. "That's me."

I feel an immediate rush of jealousy wash over me.

Silas is going down to the Continental, and I'm stuck in the recycled air of the transport for the remainder of the spin. I could be exploring, eating fresh food, visiting real places.

"Lucky," I say as I stand with Silas from the table. "Surprisingly Logan doesn't feel too great today, he'd rather just 'veg out' in the pod." The line comes out with all the sarcasm I can muster, and Silas registers the disappointment like it's seeping from my body.

He doesn't let himself think about it for more than two seconds before offering, "I'd be glad to take you, Eliza."

My eyes light up, and my stomach hurdles over something grand at the sound of my name dripping from his lips again.

"Everyone should see the Continental."

I truly didn't expect his proposal, but something in my body tells me I'd be damned if I don't take it. I'm having more and more trouble denying that I want to spend time with Silas, especially after last night—finding out we both dream about each other, that we share a bond that I'm implicit to explore further.

And this way, Logan can recover on the transport and I can still enjoy the moon below it. It's beneficial for everyone.

"I don't want to impose," I voice, not to seem so eager.

"No such thing," Silas answers, smiling at the genuine look of excitement on my face.

I look behind me at the double doors leading back out into the hallway and then down at the now cold sandwich in my hands.

"Umm, yeah," I pause. "Yeah okay—I'd love that, actually." I smile and a small giggle escapes with it. "I just—I have to run back to my pod quickly and grab some things, is that okay?"

"Meet me at mine," Silas says. "I'm docked at X43"

"I'll be quick," I promise him, then take off through the doors.

The walk back to my pod is more of a jog. I can't help the nervous excitement that flows through me like a stab of adrenaline.

I try to practice what I'm going to say to Logan, but instead of saying anything when I return, I just start packing miscellaneous items into a bag and wait for him to ask for himself.

"Whatcha doin'?" he does ask, sitting up from the bed for the first time all morning.

"I'm... packing some things, for the Continental," I murmur as I continue sifting through a crate, as if what I said was completely normal.

"But we're not *going* to the Continental," Logan asserts, pointing across at the tinfoil covered sandwich I abandoned on the table. I pick it up and toss it to him.

"I ran into Silas in the food hall actually," I say very nonchalantly, zipping my backpack closed and slinging it onto my back before I turn back to Logan. "He offered to give me a ride down."

Logan's a bit taken aback, I can tell, and his eyebrows furrow into a surprised confusion.

"I didn't realize you were so comfortable with him."

"It's just a ride," I point out. "This way you have the whole spin to relax, get better." I walk over and put my palms on both his knees, then lean down and kiss him.

"Do we even know if we can trust this guy?" Logan asks as he rubs the tip of his nose with mine.

"He could have left you passed out at the bar last night, and he didn't," I remind him. "He carried your heavy ass all the way back here."

"I guess."

"I'll bring you something back," I say, followed by another chaste kiss.

Logan watches as I make my way back through the door of the pod to leave. "You better!" he shouts before I slide it closed behind me.

"X40," I whisper to myself as I walk the bright hallway to Silas's pod. "41, 42..." The door to the next pod is ajar and I stop when I read the number plaque bolted to the wall. "X43."

"Come on in, Birdie," I hear from behind the slide as if Silas has been listening for me.

I push the door open and drop down the small step into the pod, seeing him messing with some yellow buttons and levers on the pilot's console to my right. I look around the space and take it in as best I can without seeming nosy.

He has little collections of flowers and stones scattered about on a desk, right next to stacks of tattered books and pages as expected. Hung up on one wall there's a canvas printed with a map of the galaxy, it's spattered with bright red X's and pictures pinned to the material here and there.

There's some clothes thrown in a somewhat organized pile at the edge of his bed, and the blanket is half tucked into the space between the spring and the mattress.

I can tell it's all very obviously the work of a man trying to make the room suitable for me in a short amount of time.

I grin, imagining Silas returning from the dining area and tidying his pod for my approval.

When I glance back over, Silas is sitting in his pilot's chair watching me over his shoulder. "Ready to go, Birdie?"

I nod and walk towards him, plopping down in the copilot seat and buckling myself in. I rummage for something in my bag for a second, finally pulling my journal out and smiling when I show him.

"Look what I brought."

7
DESIDERATUM

I t takes more concentration than you'd think to disembark and land a pod. The middle part is what's easy, the copacetic autopilot from point A to B.

While Silas calls in our departure to the main transport and navigates his way off the loading dock into the free fall of space, I let my eyes wander again. Seemingly busying myself with the mechanical soundness of the vessel, but in actuality trying to catch another glimpse at the place he calls home.

I look over my shoulder, straining my neck a bit, but Silas doesn't notice. He's too occupied with the push and pull of levers as he swerves through the jetty of pod traffic en route to the Continental.

His bed looks comfortable. Outfitted in a dark gray woven quilt and white sheets, two pillows of which I can tell one is definitely the favored.

I picture him laying there asleep, the blanket rumpled just above his waist, every hard dip of his torso and chest bare. In my vision he has one arm slung up over his head, the other with an open palm draped across his stomach. His dark eyelashes fan down against his cheeks like wings, and I can see the soft rise and fall of his rib cage as he's breathing.

It's an incongruous feeling, imagining him alone in his bed, knowing that's the place he sleeps—and where he dreams about me when he does.

This he's confessed as much.

I fight a spark up my spine as I consider how, in a way, I'm in that bed with him every night. His memories between those sheets start and end with me, as my own dreams do with him.

I begin to think about how I finally let myself sleep last night, and how Silas was in my head in an instant, inescapable.

"You can't avoid me forever, Birdie."

I was back in the hall with him again like he'd never even left me standing alone.

"I realize that."

"Do you?" He stepped across the narrow passage to meet me, lifting my chin between his thumb and forefinger so I was forced to look at him. "I don't mean dream me, I mean real me."

"Me?" I voiced accusingly. "That's rich coming from the man that just walked away. You had me, and I was willing." I swatted his hand from my face lazily and tried to step away, but his arm jutted out against the wall to cage me in.

"You know why I had to," he said. "There's no use playing second fiddle to another man."

"Like I didn't end up in this position by just living my fucking life. You didn't exist to me, Silas. Does that somehow make me the bad guy?"

"You tell me." He drew my attention back to his hypnotizing stare, and I fought the helpless feeling I had to kiss him as he crowded me against the cold metal. "It's your dream, Birdie." We shared a few seconds of pregnant silence, watching each other's lips part. He weaved his hand through my hair, and when I didn't move away he took it in stride—pressing his mouth to mine until he felt me melt into it. Without pulling away he asked, "Does this make you the bad guy?"

"Silas," I mumbled as I averted my eyes, but the syllables came out breathless. He waited for me to finish the thought, and when met with

silence he continued on, slipping his tongue through my lips to tangle with mine.

"You have to tell Logan," he whispered against my mouth, kissing down the column of my throat as his knee pressed into the space between my legs.

I let out a quiet laugh that towed the line between condescension and desperation.

"Tell him what? Hm?"

Silas trailed his hand down my spine until it caught on the waist of my pants, sinking beneath the material and gripping my ass.

"That it's always been me," he growled into my shoulder. "That it will always be me."

"She daydreams too." Silas's voice catches me off guard. I shake my head, dramatically ridding myself of the intense space out.

He's been watching me for far longer than he'll ever admit.

"Admiring your pod," I fib in an attempt to save any kind of face in the situation.

Silas hides his smirk when I struggle to ignore the crook in my neck and turn back to face the exterior windshield. The other pods I can see through the dirty portal look like shiny metal shrapnel suspended in the air.

"You'd never guess what I had to do to get her," he goads.

"Hmm." I tap a finger against my lips a few times. "Did you have to *kill* somebody?" I guess teasingly, hardly containing the laugh that bubbles from my throat.

In another situation perhaps the silence that follows the joke would be less discomforting, but Silas just nods his head a bit and lets the insinuation speak for itself. For a guy that thrives on verbiage the lack thereof makes me squirm in my seat.

"For real?"

I burn a hole in the side of his head with my glare, waiting for any type of placation to my understanding that I'm on a foreign pod, headed toward a foreign moon with a complete stranger—who may very well happen to be a murderer.

Silas clears his throat and gives me his best menacing pout, then holds his hands up in mock surrender as he stifles his own laughter. "You made it too easy."

I lean over and smack his shoulder playfully, letting out a long, exaggerated sigh and huffing at the harmless joke that nearly caused me a voluntary ejection from the shuttle into the dark unknown.

"Bastard."

Silas flips a few switches to pull the ride into a cruise control, then folds one leg over his lap and focuses his energy on me.

"All jokes aside Eliza, I'm no stranger to the hazards of my trade." I copy his laze and pull both my legs up to crisscross on my own chair. "I've given more than half my life to the harvest, and have found with every passing cycle a more pressing need for the winsome of retirement."

It's both interesting and sad the way Silas weaves his love of makoing with his detest for it. I know from just a few conversations that he's indebted to his own lifestyle, and also indebted to himself for carrying it on so long.

"I don't mean to cause any chagrin, believe me that's the last thing on my mind with you—but for the sake of utter transparency, I'll let you know that when it comes to violence, my hands aren't clean."

Silas watches my cool expression closely, seeing the flicker of apprehension go out like a lighter without a flame. For some twisted reason his admission puts pressure on something deep within me, tripping a spring in my abdomen that says to hell with fight or flight all together.

"You don't scare me," I say to him.

Silas keeps his eyes on me long after my declaration, even as I turn away to ogle at the rapidly oncoming moon as we descend.

Outside the windshield the Continental horizon makes its first appearance as the pod begins to drop into the moon's gravitational field. The surface is cerulean, deep greens thrown over it in patches like a blanket, swirling sands throughout. Silas finally shifts to face the circuit board once more and mutters, like an afterthought, "Well, you certainly scare me."

I've read about the Continental moon before, its sprawling mountain ranges that give way to greener pastures, valley's and winding rivers in-land, and an abundance of farmable animals throughout. On the outskirts of the port city there's an ocean as far as the eye can see.

The land is a puzzled mixture of suburban country and small city life. It's not unlike Earth once was, which is why many have migrated here over time from the Otera.

"There's much to do here," Silas says as he helps me step out of the hatch and into the fresh air. "We couldn't possibly cover everything with only one spin."

I'm happy to be grounded, to feel the hardness of dirt and earth under my boots. I sling my backpack over my shoulder as Silas locks up behind me, then look ahead at the bustling city outside the docking port.

The weather is warm, the kind of climate that lets the heat prickle your skin and the wind wipe it away before you start to sweat. I'm more than comfortable in cargo slacks and a tee, a light flannel wrapped around my swaying hips. Silas is more accustomed to humidity after his long stay on the Pulp, so the temperature here is refreshing.

"Well let's get going then." I smile when he stands at my side.

The walk is short before the journal starts to burn a hole in my bag. I decide to rip off the proverbial bandage, pulling the overused notebook from the satchel as Silas watches me in earnest with a sidelong glance.

Of course I already know the extent of these pages. Adored memories I visit often, writing about them every chance I get. The journal itself is an index of sorts for me, one I can flip through and analyze, try to find themes or recurring incidents.

Before he was Silas, the man in my dreams was just *mine*. The companion to my life's woes, my confidante, my friend, my lover. For the sake of this trip and my relationship with Logan I know I can't let him in on that last intimate detail—but all the ways in which Silas makes love to me are inked into the yellowing pages of the leather bound journal as well.

"Where should I start?" I ask him as I fan the pages under my thumb.

"At the beginning, of course," he says like it's the obvious answer.

Silas's feet drum up some loose gravel on the sidewalk and he gives a short greeting to another pedestrian walking past.

"I can't start at the beginning, do you see this thing?" I wave the thick journal at him. "You said it yourself, we only have a spin."

He expression remains unconvinced.

"I'll flip through, you tell me when to stop," I offer, then let the pages slide through my fingers in quick flashes.

"Stop."

I read the first line to myself and smile. Looking up, I notice Silas trying to peek over my shoulder at the scribbled writing.

"This is a good one," I assure him, then start reading.

"He taught me how to cook last night. Well, he tried. I just kept eating all the raw ingredients and getting a slap on the wrist."

I pause to gauge his reaction as he walks beside me, his face is softened into a pleased grin.

"We managed a dessert—I was only helpful in setting the timer, but I did learn the correct way to whisk an egg. I was more interested

in watching him do everything. Maybe the lesson will stick, maybe it won't.

He's much better than me at a lot of things, I've noticed. I like to think it's my subconscious showing me what I'm capable of through someone else's eyes."

I skim the rest of the entry quickly, noticing a long and detailed bit about licking batter from Silas's fingers which inevitably leads to something else entirely.

"So how did it turn out?" he asks, watching me read through the remaining paragraphs in my head instead of out loud. I look up from the journal with a flushed confusion at his question. "The dessert," he clarifies. "Did it taste good in the end?"

I clear my throat and skip to the very end of the page. "I guess I couldn't get the timer right."

"Unfortunately for us, we never got a proper taste, the pastries burnt to a crisp while we weren't looking."

Silas chuckles and I drop my embarrassed disposition to laugh along with him, humored by the reality that even in dreams there's imperfection.

Although you're the storied author of your own thoughts when you're asleep, you can't control every outcome.

"I've read a cookbook or two," he remarks.

"Of course you have."

Silas fits me with a playful eye roll, and then explains that he took a contract job for a dig on a moon called the Shade when he was young. He couldn't understand why it was such good pay for such a small job, or why older, more experienced Mako's had been happy to pass the opportunity on to him.

"The place was cold and dark, cycle after cycle." He cringes, thinking back on the near frostbite and chapped skin every day of the job. "There were only two other dwellers in the sector, they lived and managed a general store, mostly expired rations and discarded items left behind by other tradesmen they were attempting to resell. The only literature available were cookbooks."

"And you bought them?"

"I can make a fantastic stew." He winks in my direction. "It'd be my pleasure to *actually* indulge you—no burning the dessert though."

I nod happily, but it quickly falls flat when I remember that that can never happen between Silas and I. That there's no viable timeline or setting back on the transport where a domestic encounter between the two of us exists.

All of a sudden I wonder what Logan's doing, if he's resting or sick, if he's thinking about me as well.

Silas understands his overstep and recoils. He doesn't know if I'm upset because I'm uncomfortable with the insinuation, or upset because I want the same things he does, and can't justify it.

He points across the intersection to a cafe on the corner, bright red awnings drape over the sidewalk and there's several people sitting at tables, enjoying a meal.

"Hungry?" he asks.

I brighten up again at his suggestion. "Starving."

The food is a welcomed distraction.

I know I must look like a wild animal the way I'm shoveling the contents of my plate into my mouth, but I couldn't care less. It's a ways away from the slop I've been tolerating on the transport.

I close my eyes and tip back against my chair while I chew, groaning contentedly as the sun beats down on my face.

"Good?" Silas asks, although he knows what the answer must be. He's entranced by the way I'm glowing under the light, the way that the little frizzing hairs around my head are dancing in the dim breeze, how I tuck the strands behind my ears and they still manage to fall loose every time I laugh a little too hard, or move a little too fast. The way my freckles seem to multiply in the sunshine.

"Oh, you *so* have to try this," I say, opening my dark blue eyes again and lunging a fork back at the plate.

Silas reaches over with his utensil, but I bat it out of the way and lift my own speared with a decadent pasta toward his mouth. He meets my eye, like he's sure I'm about to correct my mistake, but I just press the food further in his direction.

Silas takes the bite, chewing slowly as I watch him in eager anticipation, and when he slumps back into his chair with a satisfied lick of his lips, I beam. "Absolutely delectable, Birdie."

"Right?"

Without asking, I take a forkful off his plate, scooping the meat into my mouth and groaning again. Silas laughs through a smile at my ravenous appetite, the way the food loosens my mood, the expressive nature of my relaxed state. He's staring at me again and I let him.

"You've seen me a million times, I haven't changed," I tease. He purses his lips in a tight smirk at being caught.

Rummaging through my bag, I pull the journal out again and begin to fan the pages.

"Stop," Silas says, and I flip it open.

"We were down at the ocean this time, I don't know how my mind managed to conjure such a perfect sunset but it did.

I've always been a fan of wading in the shallow waves and letting myself float over the breaking currents, but he warned me I'd end up washed away from shore or eaten by a sandling.

He wasn't technically right, but the sting of a plasma fish thankfully hurts much less in my dreams than it probably does in real life."

"Ouch," Silas reacts. "Well, I did try to warn you."

I shrug, loading my fork and finishing the last of my meal. "Wasn't the first time, won't be the last."

"No, I bet not." He chuckles at my newfound directness with him.

Silas basks in the fluidity of our conversation, at how easy it is to talk with me and be around me. He tries and fails to reel himself in a bit, to remind himself that this isn't what he thinks it is. It's not the spoils of a hard fought competition, it's simply just the beginning.

"Do your dreams about me follow your settings?" I ask.

"How do you mean?" He takes a sip of his drink and furrows his brows curiously.

"When I had that dream of us, I was at University By the Sea on the Ote. That's where I studied," I say. "It's like you were there with me."

He nods his head in understanding. The dreams the two of us have aren't ever random happenstance, they're rewritten scenes in our developed memories.

"You do indeed follow me wherever I go, Birdie," he answers, thinking fondly of all the places I've accompanied him, and all the ways I've always been a constant in his life.

"This might sound weird, but I'm less *scared* to do new things sometimes," I confess, "because I know you're there."

"I don't find it weird at all." He smiles. "I feel the same way."

When our empty plates are cleared, Silas leaves more than enough tally on the table and motions for me to tuck the journal away again. "Come on." He offers me his hand. "There's something I'm elated to show you."

"What the fuck is that thing?" I gawk across the open field from where Silas and I are perched on a wired fence.

It's a massive mammal, from what I can tell. Thin legs, taller than me alone, and a hulking frame for a body covered in coarse brown fur. It looks oblong and awkward, one stiff and angry antler sticks out of its skull and gives me a headache just thinking about it. The animal truly can't be bothered by Silas and I standing there making googly eyes at it.

"It's called a magdor," he says, clicking his tongue to get its attention. He doesn't.

"A mag-dor," I accentuate, forcing my lips into a pucker. "Yeah that fits, that thing is a beast."

Silas pulls me along down the fenced area of the trail where there's posted signs that warn of the wildlife beyond the wire and advise you not to feed the animals in the sanctuary.

It's a breathtaking property, somewhat of a protected park on the moon where the vegetation grows wildly and naturally. There's mountains as far as I can see, tall, pointed, and capped with ice and snow. It's hard to believe in the temperate weather where we're standing that a cold like that exists on the Continental.

I point a bit further down the field as we walk under a shade of trees. "Look! Look, another one!" A second smaller magdor is nearby, making its way in the direction of the first.

Silas is thriving on my excitement alone, happy just to be able to give me a new experience, a memory with him that will transcend the pages of my journal. He stops us under the shadow of a tree that's thick with yellow blooming flowers.

"How did you know they were here?" I ask him, plopping down on the soft grass and waiting for him to join me.

"I didn't," he admits as he drops to lean against the trunk of the tree. "But it's mating season, so..." He stifles a laugh at my agape look. "I hoped."

"Dinner and a show," I joke. "Such a gentleman." I start to rifle through my bag again and swallow the poor taste of my wording.

This couldn't be considered anything more than two strangers getting to know each other. Two strangers becoming friends.

"Aha!" I exclaim, pulling first the journal from my bag, followed by a small bottle of liquor I smuggled from the pod. "A drink?" I offer, and Silas takes the neck from my grip, not lost on my prior inference.

"Trying to get me drunk and take advantage of me, Eliza?" He spars. He knows it's a dangerous game, but one without a referee. The day has felt unsurprisingly natural, and where there's room to flirt on either end it's been all *but* unintentional.

Silas tries to tell himself that I only needed him for a ride to the Continental, but he's smart enough to know that if there wasn't the slightest bit of attraction, I would have declined his offer.

I would have stayed on the transport with Logan.

"In your dreams," I parry, and that *is* unintentional. It makes my skin hot the second it leaves my mouth, and I steal the bottle back from Silas to rid the cap and take a heavy swig.

He watches me swallow, following the liquor as it makes its way down my throat. When I look at him again he shrugs and takes the bottle fresh off my lips, brings it to his, and drinks.

The sun is angled in a way that tells us it's clear past midday, but not late enough to break into the pink of dusk. If I have a chance at surviving the palpable tension that vibrates between myself and Silas, I'll need to be a lot more drunk than this.

"Read me another one," he says, handing the bottle back to me. This time he reaches for the journal and flips a page open, but I snag the leather before he has a chance to get a look at it.

His eyebrow raises inquisitively, but I just take another generous sip from the bottle before looking down at the page. The alcohol tries to creep back up my esophagus as soon as I do.

On paper, Silas and I are in bed together, his face buried between the hot skin of my thighs, fingers prodding my heat open as he pleasures me with his tongue.

I choke on the bitter liquid when I try to swallow it again, then cough into the crook of my arm attempting to catch my breath.

"Judging by that conspicuous reaction, this one ought to be good?" he quips. All of a sudden I feel my skin break into a thin sweat.

"It's boring actually," I lie to his face, unable to imagine the riposte if I were to truly read my own words off the page. "Bird watching or something—we can just pick a different one."

"Nonsense," he assures me with a confident shake of his head. "I happen to love bird watching."

I sigh, knowing there's no clean way out of this. But as the desperation threatens to take over I'm reminded of something that helps disorient the conversation.

"You know, I never asked you why you call me Birdie," I say. The subject change isn't lost on Silas, but he likes this new line of questioning enough to ignore it. "Is that just—your thing? Or is it *me,* specifically?"

He smirks and lolls his head to the side to meet my eyes, part of me collapsing under the heated gaze. I can't tell if it's the early workings of the alcohol warming my body from the inside out, or the intense proximity between the two of us alone.

Or maybe, it's the voice in the back of my head reminding me of the journal excerpt I just gracelessly cast aside.

"It's just you," he avows. "The little bird that follows me around and sings me to sleep at night."

"Sounds like I can get pretty annoying," I jest, taking another sip from the bottle.

Silas shakes his head as soon as the sentiment leaves my mouth. "Undeniably my favorite part of every day."

He's not trying to be subtle anymore, and it's not a deterrent like it should be, but rather a provocation. I worry my bottom lip between my teeth and let the bottle drop to my lap as we're left just looking at each other.

I'm not sure if it's him or I that leans first, but our shoulders press up against one another, and he's so close that I can count the seldom gray hairs that pepper his jaw.

In any other circumstance, any other *universe*, if we both were dreaming, the more than apparent next step would be to just—kiss. The attraction is so heavy it muddles my thoughts.

Silas doesn't want to make any first move because he knows what that makes him—a *snake*. Intentionally pursuing me despite knowing I'm attached to someone else.

While he doesn't like Logan with even a fiber of his being, he can't say that the man has ever wronged him. It would make it so much easier if he had. To have a reason to close the gap between the two of us right now—lay me down on the grass and show me the feeling we're both so desperately craving.

I feel myself start to give into it, leaning in further to his darkening eyes and thinking: *to hell with what's to come.*

There's a reason I'm right here, right now.

But the universe is a volatile bastard, drumming me up and then beating me down in the same breath. A long grunting croak from across the field distracts Silas and I from one another, and I look up to the ever fascinating scene ahead.

"They're actually fucking," I say with open-mouthed astonishment.

Silas looks on, just as awestruck at the two magdor in the field coming together.

"Maker be damned, it *is* a show."

The remainder of the day is a mix of things. Silas tows me around from spot to spot trying to fit the best experiences of the Continental into the quickly moving spin. I read to him as we go, a dream about watching the rain outside the window as we drank coffee, another describing the buzz of a small tattoo inked into my skin that I would never have gotten without his insistence.

There's one about my university graduation once upon a time, but I skirt around the bits where the celebratory cake became a sexual prop—though I'm sure his ears were buzzing to hear it.

Silas stops at a few places along the way to buy little things: a book, an extra bar of soap, some questionably sourced native candy.

"Really?" I laugh as he unravels the colorful tinfoil and pops the contents into his mouth. He unravels a second and hands it off to me.

"Don't knock it 'til you try it."

When the sun finally does dip below the skyline, painting the remaining clouds in purple and orange twilight, I fight the sadness creeping up on me as we make our way back to the pod.

This was a near perfect day, the only hang up was that it had to end.

While Silas messes with the operating system on the vessel, I collapse into the creaking copilot chair and yawn. These last three days have knocked me clear on my ass with exhaustion, and it's not bound to get any better when we return to the transport.

My sleep, while normally pleasant and uninterrupted, has been stunted by the man to my left and the man waiting for me back on the floating ship as well. My body is all but begging for the relief of slumber.

Silas notices, he sees the heaviness of my eyelids, and the limpness taking over my limbs as they uncomfortably fold over themselves on the little chair. He takes his own seat next to me as the pod ascends from the Continental, the trip back up will be longer than the first as the transport drifts into movement, but quite a bit less turbulent.

"Go rest, Birdie" he says, motioning backwards, over his shoulder. "Exhaustion never did anyone any good."

I look back as well at the welcoming bed he's referring to, pinching my eyes closed at how amazing I know it would feel to just *lay down*. But I know it's not a good idea to fall asleep with him so close to me; Maker forbid I find out I talk in my sleep. I yawn again and Silas gives me a pressing look.

"Go on." He reaches over and unbuckles my intrusive seat belt. His fingers accidentally graze my lap and it makes my spine tense. "You need a few more dreams to write down." He winks like it's a joke, but it's the farthest possible thing from it.

It's an innocent gesture, offering me a place to take a nap, but in the back of his mind the vision of me asleep in his bed makes Silas's chest ache.

He thinks of every time he's woken up and wished I were still there, tried to reach over and feel my skin under his palm but was met with cold sheets.

Having me this close to him, the thing he's hungered for all his life but can't yet devour, must be a punishment for every sin he's ever committed.

I'm hesitant to stand from my chair, both because I don't want to seem intensely eager, and because I know it's wrong. I shouldn't be sleeping in another man's bed regardless of how guiltless it seems. I have to talk myself down.

It's not a big deal, nothing has happened, he's just being nice, you could use the sleep.

Silas senses my apprehension and nudges me again. "Do you need an extra blanket? Or do you need me to carry you?"

"No, no." I say, finally working up the courage to stand and walk toward the bed. I feel the soft ruffle of the linen when I sit down on it and run my fingertips over the woven quilt. "Wake me up when we land?" I task him.

Silas smiles and nods from his vantage point, watching me lift the blanket and slide my body between the weathered sheets.

It takes several long minutes, more than half the ascent, before he's confident enough in the soft hum and slow evenness of my breathing to turn back around to face the window into space.

Silas loved to float like this, watching the stars go in and out of focus. It's the only place he's ever felt could be a home to him, the black limbo of space between terra and transport, the ever expanding night surrounding him like a heavy blanket, a safe quilt.

In those short distances from his jobs back onto the freighter he felt weightless, almost as much so as when he was asleep.

This day on the Continental was everything for Silas. A delighted cameo of what his life is meant to be, *could* be, with me. So many times on this trip he felt like he was simply living out a very vivid dream.

He knows me, intrinsically. The care free breeziness I exude in every experience, my witty retaliations that make his ribs tickle in adoration. He's known me like this all his life, he feels. The way his dreams and now reality seamlessly flow, as if just a natural change of hands, is an homage to that.

Silas sneaks a peek over his shoulder again at my relaxed face tucked into his sheets—his blankets, his pillows—and wonders if he'll be able to smell me there tonight after I've left him. He has to shake the pain of me returning to Logan as it stabs at him.

After all of this, after every dream I've recited, every branded page of my journal telling stories of the two of us, he can't be the lone half feeling like there's more than just chaste connection to be had here.

He looks over at my bag draped around the copilot's chair, imagining all the tales of us that went glossed over today on the Continental. The missing pieces he might never know if we're not given the chance to be alone again on our journey to the Otera.

What he does know, is that I've fallen into the heavy stages of sleep at this point, and that if he wanted to read more, he has time to do so between now and the pod on-load that he's dreading so sincerely.

Against his conscience, he leans over and digs into the satchel, feeling around past the nearly empty bottle of liquor and a few smaller items he can't quite identify by hand, before he grabs a hold of the leather bound journal.

Glancing back at me once more before he does, Silas flips the binding open to a new page and allows himself to divulge.

It was my birthday yesterday. Nothing special, just another number and another lifetime it seems that I've been playing pretend. I suppose I have nothing to complain about when it comes to being thankful. The friends and family I surround myself with love me endlessly, but still I'm always searching for the next best thing. Next best place, next new adventure, next answer to this dream man in this dream puzzle.

He knew it was my birthday of course, like he knows everything about me. My thoughts, my fears, my secrets. He told me he'd been waiting for me all day, and truth be told I felt the same. Nothing compares to him. The way he carries himself, the way he talks to me, the way he loves me.

The way he makes love to me.

Silas feels his breath catch in his throat, goosebumps rising from his neck down his arms like pins and needles on his skin. He affords himself another panicked look back in my direction to find me still deep in sleep, then turns back around and continues on.

My birthday was like a holiday for him as well. He left me breathlessly satisfied, fucking me over and over again until I couldn't think, couldn't walk. I've never felt something like this, something so intensely real and raw like when he's inside of me, stretching me, claiming me.

I crave it when I'm asleep and it follows me into the day, distracts me from reality to think about the ways I need him so wholly. Need this man who doesn't exist to me.

He wished me a happy birthday with his lips, his tongue, that perfect stubble gentle against the sensitive skin between my legs even after he made me come. Drawing more and more warm release from my body until we were spent and the insatiable need for each other was quelled.

Waking up just now was no surprise, my panties slick and ruined, sticking to my thighs. A nightly occurrence I wouldn't dare resent.

"Fuck." Silas sighs deeply, the word comes out coarse with dryness from the way his jaw has been entirely agape.

He doesn't need to look down to know he strains mercilessly against the seam of his pants, throbbing and swollen by my words.

I'd been hiding these intimate interactions from him all day, circling the excerpts carefully to give him enough to paint a picture, but not nearly what was necessary to fulfill the masterpiece.

He fidgets aggressively, searching for relief without providing it for himself.

We both have been keeping the true essence of our dreams to ourselves for different reasons, but now that Silas knows this about me, he wants to confess for himself.

He wants me to know there's a dangerous satisfaction to explore, that he wants me in all the ways this journal says I want him.

The pod beeps in warning as it begins to make its final climb. We're within a short distance of the transport, but Silas reads on, flipping the pages again and finding more to leave him staggering against the headrest, closing his eyes to imagine exactly what I describe.

I love the sounds he makes when I ride him. Choked grunts into the skin of my chest, breathless panting when I slow my hips to take him as deep as I can.

His usual loquaciousness all but undetectable, because the way I fuck him leaves him speechless.

He loves to taste every inch of me, lick the sweat off my skin, wrap a tender hand around my throat...

The shrill sound of the freighter's comm system filters through again and sidetracks Silas as a a female voice says he's safe to re-dock in X43 and to make his approach.

He lays the journal open-faced in his lap and gears the pod toward the open bay, distracting himself for at least a few minutes with the precision needed for a safe landing. There's a jetty of pods queued outside the massive freighter, awaiting space traffic command and humming slowly along until reaching the open mouth of their correct docking portal. Silas clicks out of autopilot, maneuvering the levers and buttons on the dashboard, his own vessel beeps and groans like warping metal as its jets turn.

The clattering in the cab stirs me as well, and I'm pleasantly surprised to find myself in Silas' space still, in his bed. I can see the top of his head bobbing over the seat and it makes me intensely happy that I was able to wake from a much needed rest and he's still here with me.

Not a figment, not a pipe dream, just in the flesh, Silas. My Silas.

I lean back into his sheets again, inhaling the scent of his skin on the cotton. He's all around me, warming me, comforting me.

To be honest this was the most satisfying nap I've had in longer than I can remember.

I kick the blankets back from my body and stretch my limbs, ruminating on how instead of something new, my dream of him this time was a romanticized retelling of the day we had just spent together. Walking the streets hand in hand, tied up in one anothers embrace. A re-imagined fantasy of giving into my desire to kiss him under the shade of that yellow flowered tree.

I feel so comfortable here in his pod, like I belong. And I know now that moving forward and lying to myself about the feelings I harbor for Silas will only teeter the line of impossibility. They already are. I'm disappointed in myself for letting it get as far as it did.

If I've learned anything from this day, it's that I need to tell Logan about my bond with Silas, and there's external forces at work that tether the two of us together in a way that breaches platonic.

I can show him the journal, I can beg for forgiveness, but I know in my heart that keeping this from Logan any longer will be a deep gash through our relationship that may never heal.

I stand from the bed and tiptoe over to Silas, careful not to break his concentration as he brings us to a safe landing back in its lane way. When I find myself close enough to catch a glimpse over his chair, the sight of my open journal splayed across his lap grips at my chest so tightly it steals the air from my lungs.

"What are you doing?" I chastise him, reaching over his shoulder and snatching the notebook from his thighs.

My blood boils in a mix of anger and embarrassment, more so the latter. A short look down at the page is all I need to see what he was reading, and I can't bring myself to stay in his presence as I feel a welling bout of tears sting threateningly in my eyes.

"Wait." He jumps from his chair to follow my rampant exit, trying to stall me as I pull my bag from the back of the copilot's seat and stuff the journal into it recklessly. "Eliza, listen to me."

"Just, stop." I frown, holding my fingers to the bridge of my nose in a pinch. "You weren't supposed to read that." I tremble a bit as I speak. "You weren't—"

He grabs my bicep and holds me still, scared I'll take off if he doesn't, scared I'll change my mind about him if he can't explain himself.

"These things that you write about me..." He moves his head with mine as I try to avoid his eyesight. "They're kindred sentiments. I know them all too well in my own mind's eye."

I let myself look at him, and know he's telling the truth.

He's careful with his acquiescence, drumming his thumb against my skin comfortingly as I wipe a small tear off my lashes before it has a chance to drop.

The emotion in itself is overwhelming and terrifying.

I can't entertain the conversation with a clear mind. Not after the day I've spent with him, not after I promised myself I'd talk to Logan first.

Admittedly finding Silas sifting through my journal behind my back hurt me in and of itself, and there's no clear or logical conclusion to come to when both of our judgments are clouded in heightened emotion.

"I can't do this right now," I say to him, adjusting my bag onto my shoulder again as I break free from his grasp. "I—I just can't, Silas."

When I turn and leave he follows me into the hallway, not trying to stop me, but silently making it known he's still there. Still going to be there, whenever, if ever, I'm ready.

8
FALLACY

I decide to give myself thirty seconds to let the tears flow. Just thirty fucking seconds because *wow*, this day went to complete and utter shit so fast.

One minute I'm tossing in Silas's bed sheets, committing the smell of him to memory, and the next I'm storming out of the pod with my shoes hanging from one hand, and my dignity swinging like a knotted yo-yo from the other.

Like a walk of shame but the only thing that got fucked was my ego.

So, thirty seconds. And not because I'm sad or even embarrassed at this point, I got over that the second I stepped out of his pod, but because I'm *angry*.

Angry at Silas, angry at myself for having feelings for Silas, angry that I wrote them in that Maker forsaken journal and that he *read them*—and I deserve the release.

I'm not even sad, damn it. I'm just fucking emotional.

After about ten seconds I end up mocking my own stifled sobs for how pathetic they sound, and wiping my tears away before they even have a chance to hit my cheeks. *Stop fucking crying.*

Maybe I should be thankful Silas took it upon himself to read the journal, because it saves me the endless beating around the bush about it.

Now he knows.

He knows that I dream about him in ways that leave me thrashing and gapingly empty between my sheets when I come to. Releasing choked breaths into the palm of my hand, grinding against a ball of bundled sheets between my thighs until I feel the sweat break on my back and warmth spill onto my fingers.

Fuck, this is so embarrassing.

I swing my bag around on my back and clip the parcel of it under my elbow, digging through with one good hand until I feel the cool glass of the liquor bottle on my fingertips.

There's no way I can just, *go back,* to Logan like this.

Not in this state.

I can feel the skin under my eyes puffing and swollen. My hair is probably disheveled from my fucking beauty nap. Not to mention my overall mental incapacitation over the fact that I spent the entire day with another man and I *wanted* him. I convinced myself so wholeheartedly that I wanted Silas in that bed, and that I was going to tell my long-term partner *all about it.*

I laugh at myself, a self deprecating, *how-stupid-are-you,* kind of laugh, and decide I need to give myself time away from either of them to figure it out.

The alcohol slips down my throat like a sunburn at first, the second gulp piggy-backing off that one, and by the third shot I'm feeling a little better about the situation.

In reality I'm walking around the ship like a drunk chicken with its head cut-off. Smiling and tipping the neck of the bottle at whispering passersby, listening to chatter behind closed pod doors, sitting on an empty bench to read my own depraved words off the page Silas had bookmarked when I caught him.

At some point I end up staring out the observatory windows into the black hole of space, wondering: *If I jumped out this window, how long would I fall for? Is there a bottom?*

"I'm already at the bottom," I mumble, pressing my forehead to the glass where it leaves a mark. I try to smudge it away with my fingers, but it only makes it worse.

I'm barefoot, and one look at the transport clock hanging from the wall tells me it's long past when Logan would have been expecting me home. The liquor ran out a few breakdowns back, and it's staggering how quickly the reality of the situation douses me in water and sobers me up.

"Fuck." I groan outwardly, realizing it's time to make a decision.

Even if I decided that I didn't want Silas, and that he wasn't who I thought he was, it still wouldn't erase the fact that the journal *exists*.

I've innocently kept it from Logan because there was nothing to say. It was just dreams up until a few spins ago, and Silas was just a handsome, nameless figure of my vivid imagination.

Well, he's not that anymore. He knows it, and I know it, and the words that left his mouth before I stormed out of his pod are still ringing in my ears.

These things you write about me, they're kindred sentiments.

Despite his voluble redundancy, the only thing that statement could possibly translate to, is that Silas feels the same way about me.

His dreams have crossed the line from wholesome to sinful as often as mine do, and the sheer thought of it makes me hot.

I wonder if he sometimes goes there with me just because he *wants* to. If he's ever forced himself asleep in the middle of the day just to feel me.

Now my mind is elsewhere again, notwithstanding the fact that I'm in a crowded ship's terminal. I find myself dozing off thinking about his skin against mine, his mouth on my throat, his palm around his—

Yeah. I have to tell Logan.

It was a nice thought, and while I expected it might be made easier by my late arrival and Logan jumping to his own conclusions, that's so far from actuality that it gives me whiplash.

"What is all *this?*"

Logan smiles proudly at me in the doorway as he sucks the sticky remnants of butter and honey from one of his fingers.

Behind him, spread out on a counter that doubles as a work desk is not the most aesthetically pleasing buffet, but still a dozen or so open platters of food waiting to be eaten.

"You're back!" He greets me cheerfully, leaning over to plant a kiss that finds purchase half on my cheek, half on my lips. He's overly excited to turn around and take in his own handiwork from my vantage point. "I know it's kind of late now," he muses, "but—breakfast for dinner, your favorite."

Logan motions to the containers of food like a ringmaster would at a circus, and that feels so fucking ironic I can't help but smile at it.

He really did pull out all the stops.

I meander to the table and look at the different plates—baked goods, pancakes, eggs paired with savory meats, some blended juices and parfaits. A bottle of bubbly alcohol that makes me wince at the empty one I'm trying not to rattle around in my bag at the moment.

I'm rightly speechless, because I imagined this would be an excruciating ordeal if anything.

Logan, still half-hungover, lazing in our bed, feeling sorry for himself and interrogating where I'd been for the last several hours since the pods docked back from the Continental.

Truthfully I don't even think he noticed the time of spin while he was spending it getting this all ready for me.

"Logan I—"

"I'm sorry," he says, dragging my bag delicately from my shoulder and tossing it somewhere toward the bed. "I wanted to say I'm sorry for last night, and today, because I was a shitty fucking boyfriend."

I start shaking my head to disagree and he stops me with a warm hand on my cheek. "I should have taken you down to the Continental today," he insists. "I should have just sucked it up and taken you, because you wanted to go and it's been killing me all day thinking about it."

Fuck fuck fuck fuck. This is not good.

I think about how amazing my day with Silas was. I wouldn't have changed it for the world, minus that hiccup just there at the end that's figuratively kicking my ass right now.

"And Silas seems nice enough for some drifter who never learned how to use a comb, but there's a reason he's a loner."

Because of me. The voice in my head screams. *Because he's not alone.*

"He's probably got a couple screws loose up there," Logan lands on. "It was negligent of me and it'll never happen again. I promise."

I want him so badly to stop talking and making this harder for me. Logan's assessment of Silas based on their very brief encounters is biased at best, and doesn't even scratch the surface of the type of man I know he really is—but I have to remind myself that Logan doesn't know Silas the way I do.

And Silas isn't trying particularly hard to leave Logan a lasting impression.

"Okay." The corners of my mouth struggle into an appreciative smile.

He has the right intentions, and if it were any other person, any other strange man traveling planet to planet that offered me a day on the Continental, I would have laughed in his face.

But it wasn't any other man, and how was Logan to know that?

"I know you haven't slept, and you haven't been feeling good." Logan smooths some fraying blonde hair away from my forehead. "I wanted to do something nice for you."

I feel myself soften for my clueless, well-intentioned partner.

I had just spent three cycles on the Glades completely lost in Logan, exploring untraveled culture, cultivating our relationship, planning a future and unapologetically in love.

It only took three days for Silas to completely unravel that, and it just isn't *fair*. Three days isn't enough time for me to truly figure this out, regardless of how strongly I believe I feel about him.

I *will* tell Logan. But not right now, not yet.

Not until I can clear my head and rehearse a premeditated script of all the things I first need to say to Silas. There are too many things to discuss before I make any type of rash decision.

"Come on, before everything gets cold." Logan ushers me over to the bench seat with him and hands me a fork.

We take turns trying all the food, Logan fills our glasses and makes a toast to *getting the fuck off this transport,* while I do my best to sip the liquid. I feel the stabbing pain in my chest again at the prospect of time dwindling on our trip back to the Otera, because it means my buffer for discretion is nearing obsolete too.

"You're being quiet," Logan notices as he organizes the leftover scraps of our meal into more compact containers.

I crawl to the head of the mattress, folding into the pillows with a tired sigh. Truthfully there's not much for me to say without making everything worse for myself.

"Tired," I grumble, letting a hand rest over the peak of my stomach. "Full."

"Long day?" Logan follows me onto the bed and sits by my outstretched feet. I nod wordlessly. "Get anything good while you were down there?"

My tired eyes fling open, and I put a frustrated palm to my head as I sit up straighter. "Shit, Logan." I can hear the disappointment in my own voice. "I didn't bring something back for you."

He reaches out and cuffs my ankle with his palm, rubbing faint circles into the bone. I was so caught up in everything Silas all day that I literally *forgot* about Logan.

I forgot the one thing I promised him before I'd left the transport.

"I'm so sorry," I say, but he doesn't seem to mind whatsoever, continuing to run the same palm up my calf to my knee.

"Don't be sorry." He brushes a light kiss over my shin. "You were exploring, you were having fun. I know you, head in the clouds half the time. Sometimes I don't know if you're here or there." He chuckles at his own revelation, but I just wince a bit.

If only he fucking knew.

"I'm still sorry anyway," I say, feeling a faint tingling in my core as Logan skims his fingertips up the inside of my thigh.

I'm stuck here, between faithful partner and wandering soul. My conscience is half inside my body, half knocking on the door of a different life.

"Well, make it up to me then."

He pulls my knee across his chest so he can fit between my parted hips and kisses the inside of my knee, working his way down to bite into the meat of my thigh.

I drop my head into the pillows. "This is hardly *me*, making anything up to you."

I can feel Logan's smile against my skin as he hooks his fingers into the waistline of my pants and pulls the material down.

"Oh, but it is." He groans as he gets a look at my pussy, toying with the damp slit to wet his fingers before curling them inside of me.

I can't help but arch into the sensation.

I *needed this*. I needed to let off some steam, let myself be gratified—have a fucking orgasm by someone else's hand for the first time in days. I'm exhausted, and the dip of his fingers inside of me feels so good because I've been wound up like a broken toy with no release.

Logan leans down and pairs the thrust of his hand with kitten licks to my clit, moaning his own approval, and the vibration is glorious. His laps at my pulsating nerves while his fingers rub a perfect place inside of me.

I can feel myself getting close to where I need to be. The tension siphoning itself from my body is like a warm bath, coaxing me loose, clearing my aura. I shudder and groan with relief, threading a hand through his hair, and when I look down to watch Logan pleasuring me, our eyes meet. It's something I didn't expect, and it shifts my perception.

My partner is watching me thrash and moan over days of pent up tension that have nothing to do with him, and *everything* to do with Silas.

The intense attraction drawing me to him that I can't yet decipher between that of a forbidden fruit or genuine longing.

I know how Silas feels in my dreams, the way he plays my body like an instrument to which only he knows the strings. It's driving me wild to know that type of pleasure could be laying in a pod on the other end of this transport.

The flames in my lower belly are extinguished immediately. Logan still works at me frantically, kissing my cunt up and down, fingering me with merciless abandon, but the mood is completely lost. I squeeze my eyes closed to try to bring it back, but all I see is Silas and that douses it even more.

Even so, I can't hurt Logan's feelings with this.

He's doing everything right, it's just my fucking mind playing games with me, to no fault of his own.

So, I bear down on his head once more, grinding my hips into his mouth and moaning like he's rocking every inch of my world. "Getting close, baby?" He pauses to catch his breath. "Gonna come for me?"

I lie and nod my head, biting my lip as he dives back between my thighs. This is as good a time as ever, I think. I can't prolong this complete failure of a sexual endeavor any longer.

"Just like that." I moan, canting my hips into his face again. "I'm—I'm gonna come, I'm coming."

I arch my back dramatically, pulling a little too hard on his hair and making a show of myself as I fake what looks like a mind shattering orgasm from Logan's point of view.

He moans along with me, doubling his vigor, no doubt unable to breathe with the way I've got my thighs clenched around his head. When I finally let go, my chest is faux heaving and I've slung a wrist over my eyes to hide the reality.

"Fuck." Logan pants, pulling his fingers from inside of me. He lifts them to his mouth to lick clean and I hope like fucking hell he can't tell the difference in viscosity.

I pull my pants back up my legs in shame as he collapses next to me against the pillows, but sincerely I'm glad the ruse is over.

I can't decide what's worse: having an orgasm and picturing another man, or faking an orgasm because I can't live with the guilt of it.

"You'll sleep well now," Logan says, kissing my cheek and my jaw before he nestles his head into the crook of my neck. "Love you."

He starts to snore within minutes, but I'm still lying awake, staring at the ceiling like every other night on this prison of a transport.

I'm so inconceivably fucked if I don't figure this out, and figure it out fast.

Eventually I do fall asleep, losing the staring contest between myself and the dim overhead lights in the pod. It's not long—it's never long before Silas joins me, perched on his elbow with his chin in his palm.

"Just shut up," I say before he has a chance to speak. Silas's pompous grin speaks everything he wants to without even opening his mouth.

I loll my head towards him just as his smirk turns into a full blown self-approving smile.

"I said shut up." I groan again.

"Shall I pick up where he so complacently left you off?"

I lean over and pinch his lips together with two fingers, as if that'll keep him quiet, trying not to giggle at the pout he gives me.

Instead, he pulls me over his hips with little effort, and I squeak at the abrupt change of positioning.

"I can think of a divine way for you to shut me up, Birdie," Silas teases, squeezing my ass until I shuffle up his body and am seated more so on his chest. "But you know I love talking."

I shuffle even closer, hovering over his face with my knees on either side of his head. Silas looks up through long eyelashes like this is a punishment he's more than willing to take, jutting his tongue out to lick his lips as he savors the view.

"No more talk-"

His tongue is on me before I can even get the last word out.

Silas doesn't need to sleep tonight to go there with me. He lays on his back with his face turned into the soft give of his pillows and his cock in his hand.

Just as he suspected they would, his bed sheets do smell like me, even in the brief amount of time I spent laying between them.

The faint scent of my hair taunts him into finding release with his eyes pinched closed and his dick hard and wanting between his legs.

He grinds into his palm, picturing the filthy things I admitted to dreaming about him in my journal.

He imagines me just the way I described it: taking him slow, all the way to the hilt, bouncing against his hips until we come together, mouths all over one another.

The smell of me lingering pulls at him desperately until he lets go into his own hand, grunting against the sweat slicken sheets as he calms down.

Silas thinks about it all night, unable to sleep, because in his own depraved way he doesn't need to, he already has me.

IN THE MORNING

I'm doing this blatant ignorance thing, where if I don't leave the pod, there's no way I'll run into Silas. No way I'll be forced to have a conversation I haven't convinced myself I'm fully ready to have yet.

Logan is milling about, squeezing himself into our crawl space of a shower, because apparently he'd rather do literally anything than leave me alone after yesterspin. I realize I'm a bitch for thinking that.

He's worried about my well being, and he wants to be there for me if I need it, but the only thing I need today is a little bit of space and some peace and quiet to sort my erratically disorganized brain.

While Logan's cleaning himself up mostly out of my sight, I start to rehearse what I'll say to Silas—how I'll exude the confidence needed to breach the undesirable topic.

"So you have sex dreams about me too," I whisper to myself like I'm speaking to Silas and then wrinkle my nose in disgust. "No." I scoff.

"Do you want *me,* or do you want my *body?*" I try again, a little more aggressively as if I'm interrogating him.

"I can't throw my whole life away for this! I don't even know you!"

The shower head stops and Logan peaks out from behind the small curtain. "Are you talking to yourself?"

"Fuck." I jump. "No I'm not, I'm—reading out loud."

Logan scans my surroundings for the book I'm reading but his search comes up short. "Right," he drawls, stepping out of the shower in a towel and busying himself getting dressed.

I just need the time to *think.*

Uninterrupted, no bullshit, me on me time. Logan hawking over my every move as he basically promised he would last night isn't doing me any favors.

"I'm hungry," I insist. "Would you go grab me some food?"

"There's all those leftovers from last night," he says, pointing to the cooler. He pulls his shirt over his head and then musses his dark blonde hair between his fingers.

"Yeah I'm not in the mood for that, I want something more salty, something fried."

Logan thinks to sigh but reels it in, still noticeably a little irked by my solicitation nonetheless. He realizes after a brief standoff I'm not taking no for an answer.

"Any more requests from the princess?" he asks, filling his pockets with carry around items before heading toward the door.

I shake my head, and he bows to me like a servant before leaving me alone in the ambient quiet.

Unlike me, Silas wants to do absolutely anything *but* sit in his pod all day.

He wants to see me as soon as physically possible, talk to me, tell me everything his mind has been playing on repeat since I left him last night. Be it a muddled string of incoherent prose or not, he couldn't care less.

There's a beautiful authenticity to a random outcry of love in Silas's mind. A shout it from the rooftops type of clarity to be felt by just letting his words speak for his heart.

He perches himself in the dining lounge for a long stay, knowing that I have to come in here at some point—but he still wants the exchange to seem organic.

Propping a book he's read a thousand times open to a random page, he peeks over the binding at the door inconspicuously, waiting for the first sight of me.

It feels like hours have gone by when Logan finally comes trotting in with a less than pleased look on his face.

Silas abandons his book like a used tissue, springing up with the hope that I'll no doubt be tailing my partner into the room as I always do.

But I'm nowhere to be found, and to his dismay, Logan sees Silas sitting all alone and makes a beeline toward him like a man with something clearly on his mind.

Golden brows furrowed, chest accentuated more than usual.

A typical show of masculinity to make up for having been tossed over Silas's shoulder and handled like an oversized rag doll two nights prior.

Silas is a bit caught off guard by the infringement, all of a sudden concerned that the reason I'm not with Logan in the dining area is because I told my partner about *him*. That it was possible I left Silas last night and returned to Logan to spill the intimate details of our mind-bending relationship and day spent flirting on the Continental.

Now Logan is barreling toward a befuddled Silas with an annoyed but nonviolent expression, and all he can do is stand and face the threat head on.

"Logan," Silas says, giving the man an inquisitive eyebrow raise when he finally stops in front of him.

Logan puts his hands on his hips and sighs. "You know I can't even be mad at you man, I'm just mad at myself."

Silas braces a bit, because *fuck*, this is exactly what he thought it was, and he doesn't know if he should be elated or ready to put up a fight.

Logan seems a bit blasé to have just learned that his partner has feelings for another man. Regardless, Silas takes that with a grain of salt. It would be a mistake to assume nothing could surprise him anymore.

"I wanted to thank you," Logan continues, "for offering to take Eliza to the Continental yesterday. I fucked up, I should have just done it myself."

Silas's guard drops again. He's confused at the direction of the conversation—maybe it's *not* what he thought after all?

Logan waits a second for a reply, and when he doesn't get one he offers Silas a handshake in gratitude instead. "Seriously, I owe you," Logan adds on. "For the other night at the bar, and for yesterday. Lize enjoyed the Continental, so at least I can rest now knowing she was in good hands."

Silas returns the shake, still eyeing Logan with an apprehensive confusion although he's confident now the man is just horrific at making an introduction.

"Of course. How is she today, by the way?" Silas tries and fails to brush his eagerness off like a comb with all its teeth missing.

"Good, man. I think she just needed the rest—hasn't been sleeping a fucking wink since a few spins ago, it's all this travel, you know?"

Silas smirks, knowing the real reason why I haven't been sleeping. I've been torturing myself to steer clear of him in my head because it's a conflict of interest in my real life now.

"Oh, I know." Silas gives Logan a pat on the shoulder. He looks down at the hand like it's hot coal. "I know it well."

Glancing toward the concessions, Logan finally remembers he's there to find me something to eat. "I'll let you get back to it then," he says, pointing at the discarded decoy of a book on the table behind Silas.

Silas looks back, because he forgot what it was he was supposed to be 'getting back to', and then turns and nods. "Tell the little bird I said hello."

"Right," Logan replies, squinting at the nickname and then spinning on his heel to walk away.

Well at least I know I won't find her here, Silas thinks as he swipes his book from the table and leaves the crowded area behind.

Much like my impromptu cry last night, it takes little to no time to get bored of my own voice practicing lines to Silas in the pod.

I settle on something like: *we need to talk about the depths of our dreams*, and, *I can't commit to a one handed desire, it's not enough for only the physical to be reciprocated.*

So fucking wordy, but he'll probably appreciate that anyway.

The back and forth is rehearsed in my mind, but it's one of those things where if Silas doesn't follow the script I've so graciously planned out, it'll throw the whole thing into cahoots and *that* I am not prepared for.

I tap my foot against the floor impatiently, waiting for Logan to return with the food that I don't even want. The silence is deafening the longer I spend sitting, and I can already feel myself starting to rethink the entire thing.

No. No way.

"Fuck this," I mutter, bounding to my feet. I'm going to find Silas and get this over with.

There's only so many places he can be besides his pod. I'll look for him in public first, Maker forbid this conversation has to take place behind the closed doors of his space. I'm already expending enough strength to stay away from his bed again.

I know I can't try the dining area immediately, Logan is probably still there. And if I can think of anything worse than finding Silas in his pod, it's finding Silas and Logan in the same place. It would force me back to square one when I'm already on this mission and ready to take the leap.

The observatory and the library are the only other two places he would be unless he's injured or showering.

I shake the latter thought free from my brain as quickly as it comes and force myself to focus on the task at hand. The observatory is much closer, so I trek in that direction until I'm face to face with the glass doors.

The dome skylight is black as night above the spacious seating area, and long metal benches stretch from one side of the room to the other like an auditorium. There's ten—maybe fifteen bodies moving on the other side.

I scan quickly, hoping that I don't find Silas after all, because I can hear my own deafening pulse in my ears the harder I look.

"Shit." I turn and press my back against the entry. I must have hoped too hard. Through the transparent barrier I can see him there, idling with another worn book just under his nose. "Fuck."

All of a sudden I'm rethinking it again, pinching my eyes closed like that'll just make him *disappear*. "Don't pussy out now," I scold myself.

I inhale until my ribs expand and bite my lip in the same place I've grown accustomed to doing so, feeling the dim sting of raw skin tethering me to reality.

Silas is *lucky* that someone like me is dreaming about him. I'm a hell of a fucking catch, and *he* should be the nervous one right now, not me. I've done nothing but attempt to get to know the man better, even going so far as to omit the extent of my disposition to retain modesty.

He's the one that crossed a line.

The pep talk puts me on a pedestal for long enough to breach the doors and without a second to adjust, Silas's eyes are off the book and on me like he's been expecting me all day.

His hooded gaze hits me like bricks, but I march forward despite it. Silas can sense that I'm here for him specifically when I don't seem surprised in the least to find him loitering in the communal space.

I was looking for him.

What a commodious coincidence.

I trek on, squaring my shoulders and he stands and takes a stride toward me as well, but with only steps between us, another body fills the gap, whipping into the frame in front of Silas like a gust of wind that leaves him stumbling backwards and off kilter.

"Hi again," the imposing woman says to him.

I stop in my tracks right behind her, and feel the blood in my veins go cold.

Silas is dumbfounded, looking back and forth between the two of us.

I know it well enough that the confusion she thinks she sees is actually mortification etched across his face. He opens and closes his mouth a few times but nothing comes out.

"Mori," she says. "From the other night."

Silas nods and focuses again on me, he knows that I know exactly who she is.

The ploy he used to get my attention, the one night stand he wishes never happened.

Maybe Mori really thinks Silas doesn't recognize her, because she makes a flirty gesture with her fingertips framing the underside of her chin when she says, "Maybe *Birdie* jogs your memory?"

When the words leave her mouth Silas squeezes his eyes closed like he's been shot.

I physically feel my chest drop into my stomach.

Hot and cold waves prickle my skin like my body isn't sure what to make of the situation. My mind knows there's an ailment, and it's going through all the factory settings it has to fix it, but the wound isn't physical. My brain can't quite process that.

When Silas opens his eyes to own up to the situation he can see the pain stricken across my face so clearly it fucking burns him. My mouth agape, eyes glossy *again*, on account of him.

"Maker, I'm so fucking stupid." I scoff, spinning on my heels to try to escape.

I'll be damned before I become the girl on the ship known for throwing up or crying in all the public spaces.

Silas lurches past Mori to grab a hold of my arm and twist me back around.

"Stop," he pleads with me. "Stop running from it."

"Let go of me, Silas." I rip my arm away from him and lift my chin, the tips of our shoes touching.

My tears sting but the initial shock stage is dissipating and hellbent anger is taking its place. I manage a bitter, malevolent laugh like I can't believe what's happening.

"You're like some cosmic magician, just hypnotizing all the dumb fucking women on this transport into sleeping with you."

"That's not what this is, Eliza, and you know it." Silas is wounded by my mockery, but willing to take the hits because he knows they're deserved.

I swing away again, flipping him off over my shoulder as my steps take me further away. "She probably sings you to sleep every night too."

"Is this what we're doing to each other?" He shouts at my back. "Is this our thing? Leaving everything unanswered? Don't walk away from me."

I ignore his insistence, seconds away from making a break through the door, but he's not yet done grasping at straws.

"Logan says you're not sleeping at night—it's because of me, no use denying it!" He raises his voice and I pause in stride to hear him out. "It's because ever since you saw me you've been riddled with the guilt that you feel something you shouldn't."

I'm facing away, but Silas can still make out the way I shake my head in protest.

I feel the weight of his words heavy on my shoulders and my chest, trying to crush me, and the truth of it punctures my skin, but I won't let him see me bleed.

"Where'd you read that one, asshole? The Great Gatsby?" I yell back in spite, then kick my way through the doors without looking back.

When I go, Silas nearly pulls his own hair out of his head, crushing his palms over his eyes and growling in frustration.

As much as he wants to, he knows following me will do more harm than good. He's spent his entire life in situations far more precarious, but not until now has he ever doubted his ability to overcome.

9
COGITATION

He still waits for me to come back for some asinine reason. Hoping that if somehow the woman from his dreams came to life, then he might also have the power to turn back physical time.

Silas would put a stop to this entire dramatic miscommunication before it started, see the woman from the bar coming from a mile away, and find me himself instead of waiting around.

But, that's not how our story would read, he muses. All the pages are already written, fated, we just have yet to reach the resolution. What's any novel without gripping conflict? What's any chapter without a purpose?

His hands are on his hips, one knee bent *just so,* that his weight is slightly shifted, and he runs a long thumb through the crease of his eyebrows to iron the discomfiture from his face.

There's a dozen or so passengers pretending they aren't watching Silas's every move, and while he realizes that we weren't the least bit discreet, these prying eyes are anticipatory—waiting for the other shoe to drop.

When he finally turns around, the wrinkle between his eyes returns in full force.

"Mori—"

"I guess it's difficult to be more memorable than that." She crosses her arms combatively over her chest but her voice isn't malicious, it's soft. Sad, even.

Silas didn't intend on an attachment from Mori, but he should have known better. Been more honest with her, told her he was working through his own affairs instead of stringing her along like bait.

I showed up in his life with a beating heart and flesh to my skin and all couth shot out the door for him, because he would have done anything in those moments to bandage the wound.

"I sincerely apologize if I lead you astray," he says to her in a subdued tone, hand over heart. "If I'd known when I took you to bed that half my soul would walk out those doors a moment ago on account of it—"

A sharp crack across his jaw stops Silas mid-sentence, and if he wasn't already sure of the eavesdropping bystanders watching with bated breath, the choir of gasping gives it away.

He rubs gingerly at the red flush of his cheek and gulps down any self pity. Her reaction was more than deserved, she had every right to be hurt and feel used.

"That was for her," Mori says, and Silas's eyes flit up to meet her own doey brown gaze in surprise.

Had the timing been right, he may have enjoyed her company in ways beyond a single shared encounter. But as it turns out there are always several pieces at play on the game board that is the cosmos.

Silas tilts his head in confusion, thinking maybe the slap has stunned him into an alternate storyline, but Mori's subtle smile tells otherwise.

"Go after her then," she says a bit louder, somewhat accusatory and with a harsh push that he desperately needs. "Before she's written you off like I would."

Silas lifts Mori's assaulting hand and kisses her knuckles in gratitude, barring the stupefaction to nod his apology and thanks all in one. It's a fleeting interaction as she nudges him in the direction of the exit with her chin.

Maybe watching me leave was the incentive Silas hopelessly needed. While I was every ounce the woman in his dreams—heart, mind and body—I was also never so catastrophically out of his control.

When he closed his eyes at night he never had to *fight.* We never argued, we never disagreed.

Silas doesn't know what it's like to displease me, or disappoint me. But even after this, he wants to. More than anything he wants those parts of me too. The wild, angry, sarcastic, passionate edge of the woman he's never even dreamed into existence.

He wants to know where my mind goes when I can't seek him for solace.

"Thank you," he murmurs gratefully, holding Mori's gaze for a moment before striding after me out the door.

Silas nearly jogs through the bright hallways toward my pod, the magnetizing pang of adrenaline piercing his heels as he goes.

It's not enough this time to give me bits and pieces of himself in order to keep me close. If these last four spins have taught him anything, it's that concealment is a detriment, not a safeguard.

The longer we hide from one another the thicker the fog of regret will be when it all comes to an inevitable climax.

He knows it won't be easy, he knows my stubborn head and sharp tongue will battle him like they've shown to do, an unfamiliar song and dance we've yet to choreograph together.

But if I truly feel the way about him that I've written I do, that I've dreamt that I do, there's nothing in Silas's mind that will truly keep us apart.

He rolls his sleeves up to his elbows as he walks along, scratching the shadow of stubble on his jaw in a nervous tick as he rounds closer to my docking port. There's a small bend to the wall before the recognizable metallic door to my pod inches into sight.

"Shit." Silas grunts under his breath as he stops short. The rush that was just kicking through his veins now vibrates with no place to go.

Logan is idling in front, one brown paper bag slung under his armpit, the other clamped between his teeth. He has two go-cups for drinks in either hand as he wrestles the door open with the heel of his shoe. He gets it, finally, shimmying inside the hole of an opening before the slide slams closed behind him.

Silas presses his back against the cold, metal wall and looks at the ceiling in complete frustration.

All that build up for nothing. All that mental preparation shot to hell because he wasn't quick enough. And if he's being honest, he'd entirely forgotten about the moving part that is Logan until he saw him standing there just now, juggling food from every limb that was undoubtedly for *me*, sitting on the other side of that door seething at him. I was probably happy to see my air-headed partner now that I had a solid reason to write my dream lover off.

But if anything, this gives him a chance to think things over, mull through his options. Silas curses again under his breath as he reluctantly pushes off the wall and starts back in the direction he came. Scorned at the loss of momentum, and the circumstances he finds himself in as a whole.

Maybe this wouldn't have been the right time to come to me. The events of the observatory are still raw and festering.

He knows his intentions are clear, but they come from a place of desperation, and there's no telling how I might react to that.

If he tries to force something so important into fruition now he could come off as unhinged, forlorn—disingenuous.

Above all, Silas is a strict believer that everything in the universe happens for a reason. So there's nothing good that could have come from this, he decides. Not yet.

I'm not even in the pod, anyway. Fuck no.

I'm washed up at the transport bar because the only constant in my life at the moment is liquor. This entire situation is so ass-backwards it's laughable. Silas is a cunning fucker, I'll give him that.

Dream bond.

I scoff into the overflowing martini in front of me, leaning over to slurp the clear liquid off the top without touching the stem. A solo olive is speared through the middle, bobbing in the drink, and I imagine that olive is Silas; pulling the green veggie out of the glass and biting it off its stake in one breath.

Mori showed up at the perfect time, my angel from above, warning the sheep before the wolf in plain clothes sunk his teeth in. I was so blinded by the thought of Silas finally being real to me, that I never stopped to think about how fucking *insane* that was.

So what, if he's a carbon copy of the man in my dreams? That doesn't mean I *know* him.

He's not the same man, and I gave him the benefit of the doubt because I'm a *good person,* when I really should have just treated him like the dirty Mako he is.

A snake, just looking for his cut of change and a quick fuck.

If it weren't for the ruggedly handsome exterior, and the devastating intensity of his eyes—I wouldn't have even looked twice. Him and I are nothing alike.

Loquacious, pretentious *bastard*.

He uses all these big words to get you to lean in real close while he speaks, but it's nothing but a spell. The fact that he reads a lot of long, tired, literature doesn't make him intelligent. It doesn't make him *legit*.

I take another generous sip of my drink that leaves the glass half empty, feeling the initial swimming of a head-high do a backstroke behind my eyes.

A dark hand holding a liquor bottle fills the glass back up, and I straighten my spine. I hadn't even noticed my body had entirely slumped over sideways against the wooden bar.

"You look like you've been through the ringer, honey," the man says, topping the martini glass off and plopping another fat olive into the fray. His voice is sweet and comforting, with a sugary pitch not unlike my own.

I look up through thick eyelashes and give the bartender in front of me a tired smile.

He's striking. Velvet smooth brown skin and hair as light as honey, shimmery gold. It's a staggering contrast to his pigment but entirely befitting. One eye is as dark as the deep space outside, black and mysterious, the other as tawny as the hair on his head. Heterochromia, just like Silas. I could probably spend all day simply looking at him.

"Is it that obvious," I reply, chuckling beneath the words.

He gives me a loaded smirk, gesturing toward the empty seats on either side of me.

"I know a midday crisis when I see one."

I appreciate the bluntness, lifting my glass toward him in beholden cheers. He reaches just below the counter and pulls a little shot glass from the shelf, pouring himself a drink to match mine.

"To shitty fucking men," I toast confidently, reaching out to clink the clear rim of my glass with that of his own. We both drink.

"Maker approves," he says when he brings the bottom of his empty shot back down onto the counter.

"Yes!" I exclaim. "That is exactly what I needed to hear."

The bartender gives me a doubting eyebrow raise, watching me fiddle with the stem of the glass to keep my nervous hands busy.

"So a man's got you drunk mid spin."

"Not *a* man," I correct him. "*Two* men."

A humored sound leaves his lips, and his head tilts dramatically. "Oh so you've been *busy*," he jokes.

I let myself laugh too, it's a breath of fresh air. "I wish," I settle on, giving myself a second to sip the martini again. "It's a lot more complicated than that."

"Well I like complicated things," he says, gesturing again at the quiet room. "And I'm stuck here anyway."

I like the idea of it, getting all of this off my chest to a complete stranger—an outsider with no ties to any of the people involved. I could use the clarity, the opinion of a person taking all sides into account and giving it to me straight.

Up until now, if I ever needed someone to talk to I just went to sleep. Silas was my confidante, my voice of reason.

Now he's my fucking problem.

"I'm gonna need another one of these first," I say, downing the drink and wrinkling my nose at the burn. The olive sits idly at the bottom and I pop it into my mouth as a dull chaser.

He nods amusedly and uncorks the bottle again.

"Do you believe in *bonds*?" I ask him.

"And fur cuffs, and pretty leather whips too."

We both find this humorous.

No I mean like, *soul* bonds." I flail my hands around a bit to mock my own words.

"I don't believe in anything I've never seen," he says, matter-of-factly. "I'm a realist, baby."

My expression is disappointed, but understanding. I have to be practical.

"But love," he continues, "that's its own kind of magic."

A blithe smile curls my lips and I take a swig of the new drink in front of me. "What if everything in the universe is already decided, you know? What if it doesn't matter what I do anyway, because I'm just along for the ride?"

"Well then you're living your life in the passenger's seat. Which one of these men are you letting pilot?"

I feel a familiar, twinkling cloudiness in the corners of my eyes when I try to look around. Like it's hard to focus on anything not directly in front of me. Alcohol is a pleasant, punctual, bitch.

"Hm," I hum, sitting back against the cool bars of the chair, contemplating. "Well my boyfriend—"

"Your *boyfriend*!" he hoots. "Maker forsaken, she's attached."

He's talking to himself, or his God, or someone a little above his head and to the left when he speaks. I laugh at the dramatization, realizing that what I'm saying *is* ridiculous, and that's why I'm saying it. Speaking it out loud so it's not just stuck on a loop in my own brain.

"Listen, listen." I calm him, hearing a faint slur to my own voice. "I have a partner, *yes*, okay, I know. I thought you said you liked complicated things?"

The bartender makes a gesture like he's zipping his lips shut and locking them. I hold my hand open in front of him and he places the invisible key in my palm with a playful roll of his eyes.

"But this other guy," I say, shaking my head back and forth, struggling to find the best way to describe Silas. "He—he lives in my mind. I can't escape him if I try."

I twist the olive around on its skewer in the glass between my two fingers, watching the thick liquor disperse around it. The bartender tilts his head, listening to me.

"I've only *actually* known him for less than a cycle." I sigh at my own insanity. "But it feels like a lifetime." The olive gets a fresh new stab from me as I lament.

He reaches across the bar top and steals the invisible key back from my open palm, unzipping his lips.

"So you don't want to ruffle any feathers."

I nod and sip from my glass again.

"Because you're not sure of the new guy's intentions."

"Well I'm fucking sure now." I scoff, pointing to the martini in front of me as an indicator. "He slept with someone else."

"You don't fuck your boyfriend?"

I stick my tongue in my cheek because he's right, but that's not the whole story. That's not the reason Silas is the glaring number one on my shit list right now.

"I was ready to give him a chance," I confess, bitterly. "But I wasn't special, I was just another woman on this transport."

"And you know that?"

"Basically, yes." I scowl. "I didn't let him explain, anyway."

The bartender watches me pinch my nose and down all of the clear liquid, chewing on the olive again. He takes the lull in conversation to straighten from where he'd leaned over against the bar.

I feel a head rush, the tranquil buzz setting in nicely.

"If you're looking for my input, I'll be up front and say miscommunication is half of your problem. But the lover in me also wants to tell you that I think it's all about who you want to wake up next to in the morning." He relaxes against the counter behind him, crossing his arms lazily over his chest.

I think about Logan and Silas, two completely different sides of the spectrum where I'm concerned. My soft, doting current lover is a stark contrast to the gruff, yet affectionate man from my dreams.

"But how will I *know*?" I ask him as if he holds all the answers.

The doors to the bar creak open and I can hear a shuffle of feet inside, the bartender gives me a last deliberate glance before the steps file closer. "I think you already do."

"What are you doing here, Eliza?"

I hear Logan's distressed voice behind me and grimace, because I'm drunk and alone at the bar in the middle of the day and I left him with no explanation or idea of where I went.

I swirl around in the chair, realizing immediately that the abrupt change of station was a bad idea as the liquor swirls in my stomach.

"I'm sorry," I try, knowing there's no good reason as to why I'm here, or why I sent him to get me food and then fucked off for a couple hours unbothered.

"Sorry?" he repeats. "For—what? For sending me on a food run to come back to an empty pod? For disappearing for hours without a note or a link message? For finding you drunk at the bar in the middle of the day?"

"Yeah." I sigh and pinch my eyes closed. "All that."

Wading on the stool, I wait for Logan to continue the deserved beration. When he doesn't, I lean forward and put both hands on his shoulders, focusing on his stern gray eyes.

"I'm sorry," I say again.

He can tell I'm not completely within myself, and it's frustrating beyond belief because it's been *days* like this. There's something taking a toll on me that for some reason I'm too afraid to share with him and that's just, not like me.

"What is going on with you?" Logan pries, fixing his stare from my eyes to that of the bartender's standing behind the counter top listening.

"It's complicated," he says to Logan with a shrug.

There's a lot of pacing in Silas's pod. A lot of grunting as he does, a lot of mumbled monologue and whispered cursing—head hanging. He's probably opened and closed his flexed fist a thousand times, stared at the wall, stared at the ceiling, chewed his own bottom lip raw.

There's no easily found solution in his reflection.

The only way he can fix this is through communication, he needs to *talk* to me, see me, get me one on one with him like we were on the Continental.

Silas needs to show me, somehow, that he is who I think he is to kill this distorted version I see. For now he takes the next best thing.

"Talk some sense into yourself," Silas says, rolling over in bed to find me staring at him.

"You screwed up," I tease as I tap the end of his nose. My finger trails down to his mustache, over his top lip and he bites at the wandering digit.

"I'm the casualty of fantastic misunderstanding." He huffs.

"More like the curator of your own fate."

"Now we both know that isn't true." He rolls his eyes. "I'm stuck with you."

"You love me," I say close to his lips, nudging his nose with my own and then backing away so he chases me.

"I love you," he agrees. "You're a thorn in my side, nonetheless."

My hands trail beneath the blankets and Silas pulls in a ragged breath. He's used to my touch, but he'll never tire of the way it steals the air from his lungs even in dreams.

"How do I make this right," he mumbles, eyes fluttering when my palm wraps around him under the sheets. Soft strokes break his concentration as I pull his cock until he's stiff and pulsing between my fingers.

His hands wander too, between my legs, coaxing a whimper from my throat when they dip inside me and circle my clit so lightly that I shiver.

We're breathing jaggedly into each other's mouths as we touch, the only thing Silas knows besides the broken sounds of my pleasure and the slide of his finger inside of me, is the stack of books sitting in his vision just over my shoulder.

And then my voice when I whisper, "I think you already know."

10
AMALGAMATION

T he mixture of exhaustion and alcohol was proving lethal for my mental state. Logan was on to me, Silas was still gnawing at every exposed and dangling wire in my head—and everything the bartender had said was like salt in an open wound the more sober I became.

I succumbed to it all early in the morning against my will, hypnotized by the dim blue buttons on the pod's control panel and unable to fight my body's dying need for a power down any longer.

I feel Silas before I see him or hear him. His warm, strong tongue setting fire between my thighs.

He parts my center with his nose, burying himself deep inside me, purposefully, and then catching the over sensitive nerves at my peak between his lips.

With a gasp I buck into his mouth, skating my fingertips down the length of my torso, tracing my hardening nipples as I go.

When I cord my fingers through the short waves of his dark hair he looks up, kissing my mound as he does.

"I'll never tire of the taste of you, Birdie," he says, dipping his tongue again into my pussy, watching me through dark, enticing eyes.

I hum at the sensation, squeezing my thighs tighter and crossing my ankles behind his neck.

When Silas speaks, the whispering puff of his breath against my core is already overstimulation enough to know he's been pleasuring me for a while now, torturing me for release.

"Can you spill for me again?" he asks, unanswered. "I think you can give me one more—just one more time on my tongue, yes?"

My eyes flutter shut and I bite my bottom lip to suppress a ragged, pathetic whimper. Maker, I could come from just his voice alone.

He groans something soft and weighted into my cunt as I scratch at his scalp, tugging the soft hair in tandem with the way he laps my clit.

It's a delighted pain I feel, so sensitive that with every touch of his tongue there's a buzz that runs deep into the bones of my hips and simmers like a warm blanket over my skin, making me wetter, needier.

Silas pulls my thighs tighter around his head, digging his fingertips into the thick flesh to ground himself as he works me harder—he's heavy and begging between his own legs, leaving a splotch of precome painted into the sheets below him.

He has me wound so tightly, hurtling towards the edge, but suddenly I hear my name being called, my real name—I open my eyes to it.

The voice is as foreign to Silas as it is to me. Intruding, interrupting, not at all coming from his mouth, and we both stir when we hear it again. My name, muffled like the horn of a far away train getting closer.

But Silas's expression isn't confused like mine, it's vexed. He crawls up my body and kisses me once, chastely. I try to follow him with my lips.

"Until tonight," he says.

The distant voice gets nearer and louder, until it forces me from my sleep into reality.

Logan is sitting next to me, shaking my body lightly, chanting my name next to sprinkled, *good morning*'s, and *wake up*'s.

"Hey," he finally says when my eyes focus. "Wake up."

"What time is it?" I grumble, shielding my eyes from the main fluorescent directly above my head.

"It's after mid spin." Logan reaches down and brushes a platinum hair from my forehead.

I curse myself silently before opening my eyes again. Pissed I fell asleep, pissed I let Silas seep into my dreams—pissed I enjoyed it and was too unconscious to snap out of it.

I drag my hands down my cheeks and sit up. My skin is clammy, I can feel it.

Maybe I'm not as sober as I thought.

I can vaguely remember the night before. Logan taking me home from the bar, helping my flimsy body into bed, trying to talk some sense out of me, but giving up after the thousandth 'I'm sorry'.

"My head hurts," I say to him, pouting.

Logan reaches over me to the night table, plucking two little circles and a glass of water off of it and handing them to me.

"I figured it would."

I sigh and fumble the pills in my hand, swallowing them both in one sip.

"Look, I'm—"

"Sorry." He cuts me off. "You're sorry, I know. Trust me."

"Right." I chuckle nervously.

"Are you ready now to tell me what's been going on?"

No, definitely not. There's no explanation for the mess of my life over the last four spins that won't ruin my relationship with Logan. Maybe if he asked me a day ago, I'd have spilled my heart about Silas and come clean to him about my dreams, but there's no point anymore.

Regardless, I still owe him *something*. A reason, a *good* reason, for my mental lapse of judgment. My disappearing, my drinking. I can't brush it off and say it's nothing, when it's more than obviously something.

"I just—I don't want to go home yet," I mumble. "I don't want to be back at the Ote, because then that means it's over. It's back to reality."

I struggle not to picture Silas.

I'm not lying to Logan when I say I don't want the trip to end. But it's more so that I don't want to be forced into a life where Silas is a stranger again, no matter how much I convince myself I hate him now.

There's only five spins left on the transport, and those days will either feel like the longest or shortest of my life.

"Come here," Logan says sympathetically, pulling me against his chest. "I know you loved the Glades, I know you wanted to stay." I nod into his shirt. "You'll be back there one day, I promise."

"I'm just having a hard time coming to terms with life not always being like I dreamt it would be." My voice is muffled as Logan leans down to kiss the crown of my head.

"Nothing is permanent," he assures me. "Nothing is forever."

I sigh and collapse backwards into the pillows again.

I know that isn't true. I know there's one thing that's forever for me whether I like it or not—and the truth of it is still sticky between my legs, like a shameful reminder.

"I need a shower," I groan, rolling my eyes playfully when Logan nods his head in agreement.

"You definitely do," he says on his way to the door. "Meet me at the concession, I'll get you some lunch."

I'm still slow to rise when he leaves, turning over to press my face into the blankets for a few minutes before I decide to move.

When I look up from the mattress I catch the evanescent green of Silas's copy of *The Master and Margarita* staring back at me from the nightstand.

"Get out of my head," I murmur, swatting at the book and sending it crashing to the floor of the pod somewhere out of sight.

⊹

The shower is longer than I intended it to be. I spend a prolonged amount of time just standing under the water and playing with the puddle forming around the drain with my toes.

I know I let the liquor get the best of me yesterday afternoon, and maybe I overreacted with Silas, but the sting is still there, the needle still stuck in my skin and swollen.

He didn't owe me anything, but he didn't have to *lie* to me either. About the nickname he gave to me, pretending it was something special or sacred between the two of us, like I felt so deeply that it was.

Before I even knew Silas to be real he had given me that name, in my mind I was Birdie to him, and maybe that's why it hurt so much. It was an invisible string connecting the Silas in my dreams to the Silas in reality.

I soap myself down distractedly while I think, washing my face with my shampoo accidentally because I'm too busy monologuing in my head.

If he knew I was the woman in his dreams when he first saw me, like he says he did, then why did he sleep with someone else? It was different for me, I was already attached to Logan, already in a long term, invested relationship. I couldn't just drop everything and go to him—the random doppelgänger that showed up coincidentally on a transport headed to the Otera.

If Silas was really serious about exploring that connection with me, he wouldn't have done that. He wouldn't have fucked Mori.

I rinse quickly, ready to get out of my own head and escape the shower stall that's become a locker of contemplation.

I don't want to keep Logan waiting any longer than I already have, so I hurry to get dressed, giving my tired complexion a once over in the mirrors before I leave to find him in the dining hall.

Silas's collection of books is more grandiose than the freighter library's. He skims the aisles, plucks a title or two off the shelf every once in a while to read the fine print on the back, then replaces them. He's the only one there, save for a self checkout bot of some sort pedaling around behind the counter.

He had hoped to find some untapped inspiration hidden between the pages of a story he may not have read before. An omen of sorts staring at him as he walked along—perhaps a golden spine glowing promisingly between bookends.

Yet all there is are encyclopedias, twelve different volumes of galactic atlases, and a thin selection of the classics which he scoffs at, because he has them all already in their original covers.

Silas spent the morning dawdling around the ship again, looking for me by inserting himself in all the nooks and crannies of the transport. Desperation didn't look good on him, he knew that, but if I was planning on avoiding him by sticking myself to the wall in my pod, at this point he would be loitering outside with a scraper.

If I would just *give him the chance* to explain this all, he would tell me anything I needed to hear.

How he couldn't stand the thought of me with Logan that first night, so he slept with someone else to placate the pain. How he still imagined me when he fucked her, eyes closed, picturing my face and my naked body writhing just so he could come.

How he *used* her.

He used somebody against everything in his nature because the mere thought of the woman he's searched the stars for being with someone else gutted him down to his bones—and he just wanted to feel *wanted* again.

Silas was never one to practice healthy coping methods.

He leaves the library empty handed, trudging through the luminescent halls, down the rarely used stairwell to avoid the elevator. Figuring that he'll start over again, get a coffee, meander in the dining area and look for glimpses of my golden hair or graceful frame in the background of people.

If he comes up short again he'll move on, hit the observatory, the docking floors, the fucking library another time if he needs to. He doesn't get what he wants but he gets *something*: Logan. My partner is in the cafeteria, tucked away at a booth by himself with two trays. Silas's stomach does a flip when he looks around, but I'm nowhere in sight.

That second tray *has* to be for me, he knows it is and if he wasn't at his edge—if he wasn't despairing, the last possible thing Silas would be doing is engaging in a conversation with Logan, but what other option does he have? It's below the belt, cornering me in a place I can't escape, but if it forces me to look at him, *really* look him in the eyes, that may be all he needs.

So he approaches anyway.

"Flying solo again?" Silas goads, cursing himself internally for playing clueless. If there's anything significant he has on Logan, its intelligence.

Logan's mouth is half full of something, but he still chuckles at Silas and reaches a clean hand out to shake a wordless hello. Silas looks around and adjusts the collar of his shirt awkwardly, regretting his decision to walk over more and more as the seconds pass waiting for Logan to swallow his food.

"She'll be in soon," Logan eventually says, gesturing to the other side of the booth. "Sit man, sit."

Silas stalls for a second. This is exactly what he was hoping would happen but still it feels dirty.

Him and I are getting good at playing games, but now he's pulling a wild card by using my significant other to his advantage, and he hasn't done that before. He hasn't needed to.

"If it's not an intrusion," he says, shrugging as he slides to the middle of the hard metal.

"At least if you're sitting there I don't look like a fucking loser eating alone." Logan laughs.

There's a few seconds of silence again, and Silas raps his knuckles against the table while Logan takes another bite off his fork.

He realizes he didn't really have a plan when he walked over here, no dialogue thought up in his mind to hold a conversation, he doesn't even have anything to say to Logan if not pertaining to me.

"So, what uh—what model is your pod?" He hiccups. Is this the kind of thing two men would make small talk over?

Silas isn't used to much company besides a revolving-door dig partner, or an enemy on a moon he has to smooth talk his way around. His usual loquaciousness is generally off putting to most—as if he speaks in tongues—and that's an easy way for him to decide who's worth a conversation or not. When he's not forced to dumb himself down to appease an acquaintance.

I always understand him though. I speak the same language.

"Treszka-004," Logan says proudly, but Silas already isn't listening. "Gift actually, from my father."

His eyes flicker over Logan's shoulder like an instinct, just in time to see me breach the doors and trot into the area. My hair is still damp from the shower, and I've since thrown on loose fitting joggers and a plain gray t-shirt. I seem lost for a second, and Silas braces for my reaction as he watches me look around, scanning the lines of people and the sea of tables before I see him.

He focuses back on Logan who hasn't stopped droning on about the pod, nodding his head along to make it seem like he's paying attention. Silas is truly just waiting for my feet to unstick from the floor and the furrow of anger to iron itself out of my brow.

I can't fucking believe him. I know damn well my boyfriend is clueless, but I know just the same that Silas wouldn't have been caught dead at that table with Logan without a motive. He's desperate and conniving, trying to pin me in a place I can't move.

Well if he wants so badly to force my hand I'll let him—and I'll make sure he regrets every second of it.

When I slide into the booth I huddle into Logan's side immediately, stretching my neck to kiss the underside of his jaw and then his cheek. He wraps a cozy arm around my shoulders and tilts his head down to look at me.

"Hi." I smile, inching up to catch his lips with mine.

Silas stares uncomfortably, clicking his tongue silently against the inside of his bottom teeth, but he doesn't look away.

He knows I'm instigating him. I'm trying to hurt him, and if that's what I want to do, he'll take the lashes.

Logan has to break the kiss himself, and he chuckles uneasily out of it, glancing at Silas across from us and his deadpan expression. "I should let her sleep this late every day," he jokes.

Silas smirks at me, only. "Have any good dreams?"

Without thinking about it I kick my leg out under the table and snag his shin. "Shit—sorry."

Silas licks his bottom lip and sticks his tongue in his cheek. "No need for an apology," he says. "It's likely just my karma evening itself out in the universe."

I give him a judgemental eyebrow raise and start unfurling the wrapping of the sandwich Logan has sitting on the table for me.

"Maker." I sigh when I lift the bread. "This is wrong."

"I'll go fix it," Logan says, grabbing the sandwich from in front of me and standing.

"No—no it's fine, it's fine." The words leave my mouth so fast it's hard to decipher the language. "I'll survive."

"Seriously Lize, not a big deal."

"I'll go." I scramble to get up and my partner presses me back into my seat with a heavy palm.

"Sit. It'll take two minutes." He winks.

I can feel Silas's eyes on me as Logan walks away. I close my own and sigh at the miscalculated self sabotage. This is the last place I wanted to be, vulnerable to his voice, his face.

"Don't say a word." I warn him with a pointed finger, matching his glare so he knows I'm not backing down.

"It's hardly fair of you not to afford me at least an explanation," he says anyway, leaning forward with his forearms on the table so his voice only carries between the two of us.

Silas isn't going to let me run the show like he's been doing. Waiting for me to come to him, cowering in his corner so as not to rock the boat.

"I think Mori pretty much explained it," I snap back at him, leaning in as well.

"I meant everything I said to you two days ago," Silas says bluntly, looking around to find Logan at a counter. He's gauging the amount of time he might have for this. "I want you in all the same ways you want me."

"I *don't* want you," I bite, despite how his words set my lower half aflame as soon as they leave his mouth. Silas sits back against the booth again, feeling a twinge in his gut. "Maybe I was fucking blinded, and I thought you were a different person, but I can see clearly now that you're not."

He knows I'm out to hurt him, to divvy the pain he would no doubt be feeling if the situation were reversed, breaking his heart in ways he didn't know it could. Yet, he tries to keep it cordial, chipping away at this wall I've built in front of him without disturbing the foundation.

"You can't control your own emotions, I get it Birdie. You're confused, I'm confused as well. Neither of us could have ever seen this coming, not in the way it's panned out at least. I *know* you."

I try to chalk up my oncoming attitude as Silas's inability to take my word for what it is, but it's truly just his calm, sensible demeanor and every fiber of my being telling me he's right.

Because how dare he try to tell *me* how I should feel?

"Fuck off, you don't know me." I scoff. "You don't know anything about me, and I don't know anything about you."

Silas sees Logan turning back toward the table with a new sandwich folded in paper for me, and realizes this isn't going to go how he wanted it to. There's nothing romantic or poetic he can say, and there's not enough time to chip away anymore either, the wall has to come crumbling down.

"No, but you know what I do know, Eliza?" he grits out, leaning in closer again. "I know that when you're riding him, you're thinking about me. Me inside you, me tasting you, me whispering in your ear while you come on my cock." He takes in my parted lips and the short way my breath catches when he pauses. "If you can live with that guilt, live with yourself—then be my guest."

Silas keeps his eyes on me as Logan returns to the table. Giving me a chance to say anything at all before knocking his knuckles on the countertop and standing up. My gaze remains ahead, on the empty space he left there.

"Enjoy your lunch," he finally says, nodding at Logan before he brushes past him and leaves the room.

Logan slides back in across from me to take Silas's place, but I look through him. I'm still holding my breath, trying to catch up, to hit reboot on the blank space of my mind. It's just a broken record in there with Silas's voice on repeat.

"Fixed it," Logan says, pushing my sandwich back to me.

I offer one look down at the new tray and shake my head.

"I'm not hungry anymore."

The rest of the day wastes away like a rainy spin.

I tuck myself into the pod with Logan and do menial things, trying to keep my mind off Silas by staying busy.

I sort my laundry into separate bins from where I've been neglecting it on the floor, tidy the junk, reorganize Logan's piloting manuals he's left open across the circuit board, and then get around to downloading my camera's memory onto a server and link it to my tablet.

After, I sit cross-legged on the bed with Logan and swipe through the pictures from the Glades.

There's one of us climbing the jagged rocks of Monsoo Metor on a hike overlooking the island, then another of the setting sun when we finally reached the top. I flip fondly through portraits I took of local artisans from the street market one afternoon, attempting to immortalize the people and place itself so as to never forget.

I stop for a while looking at one photo of a gray-haired older woman. Her skin glowing an ageless golden brown, the corners of her lips lifted and the pockets of her apron stuffed full of coins. The table she stands behind is covered in gemstones and crystals, homemade candles and incense, essential oils, teas, tinctures and holistic powdered medicines.

I continue on and see a few photos of myself sprawled across the black sand on the beach, shielding my eyes from the blinding reflection of the water and laughing through the embarrassment of my partner acting as a personal photographer.

"That's my favorite one," Logan says, pointing at one of me in a red swimsuit, looking over my shoulder at him.

I card through some more. Pictures of the food we ate and people we met that I was lucky to snap photos with, because we'd likely never see them again.

I get to a few of Logan and I, the camera is extended out his arms length away, my head on his shoulder—another in the same spot where I'm on my toes pressing my lips to his.

I feel myself becoming emotional, not because I miss these memories, but because attached to every one of them is Silas.

In my dreams at night, on these same sands, in these same places. Whether subconscious or not, there aren't any experiences in my life detached from him, and I'm thankful for it, but it guts me.

Logan doesn't deserve the pain I almost caused him over this. When we get to the Otera, Silas is going to move on with his life just like he always has, a nomad, a straggler, a permanently home-bound vagabond searching for *something* to keep him moving.

My life is more cut out of stone than that. It's planned, organized, routined. This trip with Logan was the most spontaneity I've ever known.

When the photos are through I switch on a film, Logan roams through the titles as I join him under the covers of the bed and fold into him.

I hardly focus when it plays, rewinding my day over and over again from the salacious dream I was awoken from, to the stand-off with Silas in the lounge. The way his words pierced me and stole the air from my lungs.

Silas wasn't one to show anger, this is the closest I've ever seen it, pointed at me nevertheless. Maybe it wasn't anger, but frustration. A cold-blooded last resort to drop the wistful prose and tell me exactly what we both knew to be true.

I look over at Logan when the film hits its halfway point and see his eyes are closed, chest rising and falling rhythmically, a low snore hums from the gape in his mouth that I hadn't noticed over the movie's projection.

I inch off the bed silently, intending to walk to the small toilet stall in the pod, but trip over something on my way, nearly twisting my ankle. I glance up from the floor at Logan who remains unbothered and reach out to the object of my demise.

It's Silas's book, half tucked under the bed where I must have glossed over it earlier.

I laugh at the irony of it, that he's everywhere all the time now when all I want is for him to go away. In my head, on this transport, tripping me up in my own pod. I sit the book on my lap and trace the faded black cat staring back at me on the cover.

I need to give this back to him. Omit any ties or reminders that will hold me back when I get to the mainland.

If I keep this book it'll forever be a palpable token of the cycle and a half where Silas was real to me, and how cruel the universe was to do that. Showing me everything I've ever wanted and why I can never have it.

There's just too many outlying variables.

I pull a sweater over my shoulders and slip on shoes, tucking the book under the fabric of the shawl to hold it tight against my body. I look back at Logan with loving intention before stepping out of the pod and into the brisk, bright hallway.

The door slides closed behind me with a soft click, and I wait there for a moment to listen for him stirring. When he doesn't, I take off the way to Silas's pod, for what I expect will be the last time.

He's still awake.

Truthfully, he's waiting for me.

Silas is trying to keep his eyes open as long as he can, flipping through the pages of the books on his desk with his feet propped up on the edge of it until I come.

The way he knows me is intrinsic. I can fight and say that he's not the same person in my dreams, but he is. The same way I'm the same person in his.

He's grown with me, learned and loved and experimented with me. He's cried, he's felt my pain and my happiness and my nervousness—sometimes one at a time, sometimes all at once. He knows I'll come to him.

Still, when Silas hears the soft knock outside of the pod it stops his breathing.

He was waiting for me, but it feels surreal when he looks up from his book at the sound of shoes shuffling beyond the door. He takes his feet off the desk, waiting in the chair until he hears another louder knock again.

"Silas?" I mumble against the slide and press my ear to the cold metal.

I hear him moving about behind it, the sound of a chair scratching against the floor, then a few seconds later the hitch of a lock being pulled back.

I retreat a step when he slides the door open, his brown hair is tousled like he's been raking his fingers through it, a white short sleeved tee clings to his arms and chest, he's dressed down in cotton shorts. I've never seen him so soft like this.

He takes me in for a moment too, no doubt thinking the same string of things before looking down the hallway on either side. He silently gestures with his head for me to come inside and I follow him, standing just within the open doorway while he takes a seat at the edge of his bed facing me.

"Where's Logan?"

"Asleep."

"And here you are, in another man's pod. Why?"

"I just wanted to give this back to you," I say, pulling *The Master and Margarita* out from under my cardigan and tossing it toward him. He catches it clumsily, like it wasn't what he was expecting.

"That's not why." He shakes his head, tapping the book against his knee.

"It is."

My temperament is far from where it was this afternoon with him, and he knows it's because he hit a nerve. I've been sitting on what he said for hours and whether I believe it to be the reason or not, it brought me here to him at this very moment.

If I didn't want him, I would have steered clear of him, not shown up on his pod step while my lover slept alone down the hall. I was sick with a need to be close to him.

"No, Eliza, I think I know why you're here." He turns the pages of the book in his lap purposefully, as if he knows the index like the back of his own hand. "I think you know why you're here too."

I shrug at him, crossing my arms over my chest and chewing on the skin of my thumb.

He looks down and reads off the page he stopped on.

"Who told you that there is no true, faithful, eternal love in this world." He looks up at me and recites the last words of the line from memory. *"May the liars' vile tongue be cut out."*

I shake my head and shrug again. "Silas, I don't understand—"

"I remember the first time I ever read that," he says. "Young blooded, still trying to figure out this celestial *empress* in my brain every night. Why she chose *me*, why she loved *me*—and no one believed me." He shakes his head at the memory. "I always knew though, that somewhere I'd find you, and I'd be naive in my deliberation that it would be easy."

Silas closes the book and reaches for another. He flips through the pages and stops on one that's all marked up, even I can see it from my vantage point across the pod as he clears his throat.

"'Every heart sings a song, incomplete, until another heart whispers back. Those who wish to sing always find a song. At the touch of a lover, everyone becomes a poet.' I wrote right here in the margin." He points to the open book at the scribbled ink. "It says, *'She and I love in ways that can't be explained, bottled, written, or imitated. Our love is for the stars.'"*

It feels like hands are tightened around my throat. I know if I open my mouth no words will come out, so I just lick my lips and swipe a welling teardrop from the corner of my eye.

"You're here because we can't stay away from each other," he says. "It goes against all the powers of the universe."

I'm stunned into silence, resorting to folding my sweater over my chest as tightly as I can, like it might protect me from the inevitable.

A last thin sheet between myself and Silas to be torn away.

"I'm sorry that I hurt you, and I will spend my life atoning for those missteps, but I'm not the one lying anymore. If you want to walk away from *this* because of it..." He trembles a bit, motioning between the two of us. "Well, then that's on you, Birdie. I'm laying it out here, I'm ready to do that. Are you?"

I'm taciturn, worrying my lip raw as he speaks. There's something in his ocean eyes dragging me into the unknown that finally pulls me under.

I see Silas like I do in my dreams suddenly, feeling the fusing of the two men that I've fought so hard to keep separate into one, because they are one.

All this time Silas has been grounded in the reality of this cosmic intertwine—that dream me, and real me are one in the same, but I've been stubborn to allow myself the satisfaction.

I can't fight it anymore.

I nod my head to finally give him some semblance of an answer, still stuck on the floor tiles afraid to move.

"Close the door," he says.

I hesitate, swallowing what feels like the last tie to the life I've lived thus far, because I know beyond this decision there is no going back—and then I do.

11
RHAPSODY

P atching a tear in anything will only work so many times before the blemish grows too large, too scathing. The adhesive just gets weaker and weaker the more you replace it, the problem grows too large to surmount. Eventually, you have to decide to either rid it, or restore it—or find a new thing all together.

That's what the last five spins on this transport have felt like. Only, it's a hole in me the shape of Silas, and the bandage is every fucked up way I've tried to convince myself to stay away from him.

Every reason I've conjured to forget about him.

Well, there isn't a bandage in space that will explain why I snuck out in the middle of the night and ended up behind the closed doors of Silas's pod. There's no rehabbing that.

"We may both find it beneficial for you to find your voice right now, Birdie," Silas murmurs.

His own cadence is caught in his throat over my sudden agreement. It's as if a world doesn't exist beyond the spherical walls of this airless pod. It's just me and him, some weathered paperbacks, and the muffled sheets of his bed that prickle both our skins in lascivious implication.

"Why did you fuck her?"

Silas squints a bit, licking a subtle line into his bottom lip. His jaw clenches then softens.

"That's easy," he says. "Because I couldn't fuck you."

I bite my tongue. Nothing about this is easy, but for some reason I feel it doesn't need more explanation than that. The raw truth tickles my insides and feels like it opens a tiny door to a cage in my stomach—all at once a thousand wings flutter through the cavity searching for escape.

"I was blistering from the burn of it. Of finally *finding* you—and you were with another man." He shakes his head free of the memory. "She was a balm."

I want to tell Silas that he doesn't have to continue, but he takes my hesitation as a running cue, stumbling heedlessly into the prose I love so—keeping me planted with his words.

"If it's the nickname you're looking to extrapolate..." He sighs. "Then you must already know I couldn't touch her without thinking of you." He let's that settle on my ears, giving me just enough to understand while still sparing the explicit detail. "Does that make me depraved?"

Maker. Why do his words sear my skin?

"No," I manage, imagining Silas using this other woman as a placeholder for me, as a means to an end. Calling out for me buried inside someone else. "I get it."

"I suppose then that we've both mastered the art of playing pretend," he says.

There's hardly room to pretend with him. I can hold my breath for as long as I want, but eventually my heart will beg me to keep beating. I pick nervously at the raw cuticles of my fingertips. "Did you really know it was *me*, all this time?"

Silas shifts on the bed, making room beside himself for me to sit. "I want to show you something," he offers, thumbing into the pages of the book again, anticipating my reply.

I approach him in a slow stride, shuffling my feet across the gap until I'm standing directly in front of him. His eyes level with the thin fabric over my torso.

He wants to reach out and touch me, pull me between his legs, nestle his head into the soft give between my rib cage while I climb into his lap like he's so used to.

In a dream, Silas would have me pressed against him, whispering adoration in my ear and down my neck. But here, all he can give is a tilt of his head and a hand to guide me onto the bed next to him, yet he still does it with hesitation.

It's an unparalleled restraint to have me so close yet so far away.

"I've been searching for a way to show you how I dream about you," Silas murmurs. He reaches to the side, swiping several books from the desk's ledge onto his lap and onto mine. When he's done there are dozens of them scattered around the two of us.

"Can I read to you, Eliza?"

Just as I had for him with my journal that day on the Continental, Silas lets the worn, brittle pages of book after book slip through the weathered callous of his fingertips.

"Stop," I tell him. The cover of the novel reads *David Copperfield*, Charles Dickens.

"She was more than human to me. She was a Fairy, a Sylph, I don't know what she was - anything that no one ever saw, and everything that everybody ever wanted. I was swallowed up in an abyss of love in an instant."

He looks up at me nervously as I watch him recite the words he'd underlined and circled.

"There was no pausing on the brink; no looking down, or looking back; I was gone, headlong, before I had sense to say a word to her."
Silas doesn't search me for a reaction right away. Perhaps hoping that somewhere down this line that's been drawn in the sand, I'll decide to take the leap and join him on the other side without pressure.

He closes the book and pulls another from where it's laid between the two of us. I read the cover quickly before it's tossed open. *Anna Karenina.*

He fans the pages again while I look over his shoulder, waiting to see one painted with annotation, long dried with ink.

"Stop," I whisper.

Silas fumbles past the page and has to wet his thumb against the corner to find it again, my lips twitch into a faint smile at that.

"He stepped down, trying not to look long at her, as if she were the sun, yet he saw her, like the sun, even without looking."

Although he doesn't have a journal of dreams like I do, this feels, in its own chaotic sense, all the more romantic—more special. Analyzing the way Silas searches for me in all his favorite stories, past the premise of the books, at times pushing aside whole themes and overtones to carve my shape into them. All his life, the time he spent awake, away from me, was still marked and scribbled and doused in me.

I realize he *did* know that very first spin, handing me *The Master and Margarita*, that he didn't have to find me in those pages anymore, because I was standing right in front of him. That, maybe I would need them to find *him*. Be it metaphorically or literally—tripping over the thick binding when I'd given up hope.

Silas opens another book, *Siddhartha*, and notices I've begun to lean against him. My shoulder pressed into the meat of his bicep, my cheek frosting against the cleft of his tee. He's watching me through the hood of his thick eyelashes while I'm preoccupied with the flip of the pages.

He doesn't hear me tell him to stop the first time, I have to say it again, louder.

"Sorry." He clears his throat as I crane my neck to look at him, then lands on a passage and scans it quickly. "A favorite of mine."

"So she thoroughly taught him that one cannot take pleasure without giving pleasure, and that every gesture, every caress, every touch, every glance, every last bit of the body has its secret, which brings happiness to the person who knows how to wake it. She taught him that after a celebration of love the lovers should not part without admiring each other, without being conquered or having conquered, so that neither is bleak or gutted or has the bad feeling of being used or misused."

Silas looks back down at me again when he's through, and I'm already watching him.

I understand why he talks the way he does: languid poetic sentences, meaningful words wound in rhythm like a song, argot that devastates me to speechlessness. Silas simply speaks like he's always in love.

"I like it too." I smile, running a finger into the margin over a cluster of his handwriting. "What did you write?"

He almost hesitates, but decides against it, chuckling under his breath as a faint blush rises to his cheeks above the facial hair.

"It says, *'My pleasure comes in pleasuring her, so we conquer each other. I think more often than anything about what she might taste like coming apart on my tongue.'*"

I feel a prickling heat rush to my cheeks now as well. Not just my cheeks, it leaks down my neck, warms my chest and settles low, simmering on hot coals in the pit of my stomach.

"I wasn't supposed to read that," I blanch, mimicking what I'd said after he read my journal.

He shrugs. "Fair is fair, Birdie."

Silas reads to me like this for a long time, we take turns picking the novels up off the bed and flipping through them. Some are more worn than others, tagged and ripped, but my presence is in every one. Permanently etched into the banks of everything he's ever read and carried with him in his travels.

At some point I inch myself back to lean against the wall, legs stretched out, feet dangling off the edge. Silas leans back too, propped up on his side by an elbow so I can still follow along with him.

"There is a heat of love, the pulsing rush of longing, the lover's whisper, irresistible - magic to make the sanest man go mad."

I open my eyes where they had been closed, my head propped against the cool metal wall, lost in the gravelly baritone of his voice.

"Which is that?" I ask, leaning in closer to the open pages.

"The Iliad."

"That's a good one," I mumble back, returning to my perch against the wall. Silas hardly stifles a smirk.

Somewhere in the passage of time I feel myself soften away from the scared uncertainty of who the man beside me really is.

Untinted by outside forces, letting myself breathe into what he's telling me, admitting in thousands of words—trying to make me see the only way he knows how.

Silas doesn't love me like all the characters love their counterparts in these books—because it's more than that. He loves me *through* them, in pieces, like patchwork on a quilt, a stitch here, a pattern there, never completely sewn together. Like he hasn't yet read his favorite story, but he's constantly trying.

"Do this one," I say, handing him a book. It's thin and faded a grayish blue now.

"Wuthering Heights," Silas notes, sitting up and sliding back to join me against the wall. He grunts a bit as he does, rolling his shoulders a few times, rubbing out his tired limbs. "You must have read this one before?"

"I have," I chime, impatiently nudging him with my elbow.

The tanned paper cards softly through his fingertips as he waits for my nod.

"Stop." I place my own fingers over his to halt the movement. Silas stiffens at my touch, but I remain there. My shaking palm pulls his hand away to reveal the open page of the book where one little line is underlined.

"He's more myself than I am. Whatever souls are made of, his and mine are the same."

I lean my cheek into his shoulder and close my eyes, squeezing them so tightly I see colors dancing against the back of my eyelids. Silas flexes his fingers to remind me we're still connected, but instead of pulling away, I thread my knuckles between his, and he folds his thumb over mine in return.

"Will you ever forgive me?" I whisper.

My lips press against the fabric of his shirt as I speak, and he can feel the warm hum of my breath on his skin through it. Silas shakes his head side to side, as if he doesn't know what I'm talking about, then studies the way my little fingers clamp over his own like he's seeing it for the first time.

"Forgive you for what, Birdie?"

I lift my chin up to rest atop his shoulder. The way I'm facing him, I can see up close the fine lines where his eyes crinkle, and the spots where the sun has permanently kissed his skin.

"For not waiting for you," I mumble again.

Against everything, because he shouldn't, he knows he *really* shouldn't, Silas reaches up with his free hand and cups my chin, caressing my cheek as I look at him. His thumb glides like a cloud against the bone there.

"Don't ever apologize for living the fullest life you could find. If not for that, you wouldn't be here with me right now."

I nod, closing my eyes again and leaning hard into the palm of his hand while he touches me.

I feel it like a beating pulse. There is no more dream Silas, or dream me, we both just simply *are*. Come into our final form, existing on the same plane. He's been so patient where I haven't, so fair, disciplined. I feel I owe him so much more than an empty apology.

"When I saw you that day everything changed," I admit. "I tried so hard to fight it, but even when I wasn't sleeping—you were still my every waking thought."

Maker, I'll test his resolve as far as it can stretch and he knows it. He wants to *engulf* me, sweep me underneath him against the soft give of this bed and show me how badly he's wanted me. To kiss my lips until they're bruised, and then more to lull the pain.

"You've been trying not to sleep at night to avoid me," he whispers. "Meanwhile, Eliza, all I want to do is sleep, because that's the only place I can have you."

I know come the morning all my actions between these closed walls will have consequences. They'll garner explanation and penance, and Logan will never forgive me and he doesn't have a reason to. As I see it, laid out for me now, the damage is already done. I'm in love with someone else, and I always have been. That emotional truth will hurt far more than ever the physical.

"You can have me now, Sy."

He tips his forehead down to meet mine. I can feel the soft brush of his hair against my skin, the quiet, skittering of breath fanning in and out between his lips.

I put my hand over his on my cheek, just to keep him from letting go. "You were right about what you said. I want you. Even with Logan, I've wanted it to be you."

It feels so fucking shameful to say that out loud, but it makes Silas's skin bristle like a sudden gust of wind on a warm day. He could have everything right now, if he wanted to. He could taste me, make love to me. It twists in his stomach and punches a hole through his chest because I'm finally telling him, *yes, yes, yes.*

It's more than he needs, but still somehow not enough.

"I—can't, Eliza," he stammers, lifting my chin to draw my eyes away from his lips. My eyebrows thread in confusion. "Not until you're irrevocably, unreservedly mine."

I know he's right, he deserves that much, I *owe him* that much. To know that I won't sleep with him here and now, and tomorrow find a reason in Logan to stay away again. He doesn't know if his heart could take that, giving half of his soul to me and being left empty. Having me once in a moment of weakness, and then never again.

"It's so hard to crave a person that I cannot touch," he utters.

I unwind my fingers from his, bring my palms up to his face and look right into him. "I'll make this right," I promise. "Let me go and make this right."

Silas doesn't want me to go, he doesn't want to see me walk back through the door of his pod, because it's another waiting game. Another blank slate of uncertainty.

The things he knows about my relationship with Logan are surface level, but it's not enough to say that there isn't love there, and it terrifies him. Even after all of this, after we've both laid our hearts out on the table, across the sheets of this bed in book after book—he won't be ignorant to the universe. If it's been this hard for this long to finally have me, what's to stop it now?

"Come back to me," Silas says as I stand from the bed. "I'll be right here waiting."

12
DELIVERANCE

B y the time I close the latch behind me in my pod it's the early hours of the morning.

I hadn't realized how much time I'd spent laying across Silas's bed, carding through his books, listening to the low hum of his voice as he read to me.

For him and I, time stood still within the tin walls of that space, because it was a mere blip in the eternal loop we'd already spent together. But on the transport, the cabin lights within the hallways whirred to faux dawn as I skated through.

I turn around from the door and Logan is laying on his back in bed, two hands folded behind his head. It's too early for him to be awake, but he is—none too happy when he turned over in his sleep an hour earlier to a cold and empty slot next to him where he should have felt me.

"Where've you been?" he asks. The words are so full of annoyance it would sound rhetorical if not for his lack of knowledge.

I brace myself against the door and hang my head a bit, wincing at his tone. I knew this wasn't going to go well down any path it took, but the rocky start has already set me paces further back than anticipated.

Truthfully, on my way here I didn't think much on my toes. I expected Logan to be asleep for at least another hour. I thought I'd have enough time to gather my thoughts and string together something coherent and *pliable* to feed to my boyfriend that might soften the blow of it.

Five spins is all it took to twist me from my happy, hopeful relationship into a tailspin of cosmic romance.

All the edges are blurred now around Silas. He's that North Star shining luminescent in the foreground that my life has always been traveling toward, everything else is just filler.

"Just trying to figure some things out." I sigh, chewing on that raw spot in my bottom lip again like it's an anchor.

"In the middle of the night?"

I let a humored puff of breath leave my nose—he's right, it sounds fucking insane. What could I possibly be figuring out along the barren walls of the freighter that I couldn't dissect in my own pod? A brisk walk to clear my head? Some staring out the windows of the observatory, maybe? But all of those options are rooted in dishonesty.

I left the pod when Logan fell asleep and I knew exactly where I was going.

"Okay, yeah," I agree, letting my shoulders drop from where they'd cranked up to my ears. "I've been lying to you."

Logan pushes himself up by his palms to a sitting position on the bed and the sheets fall to his waist. He looks so bare and vulnerable—so easy to hurt from where he sits. The usual flirty, quirkiness of my partner is gone and replaced with worry, laced in anger and betrayal. I can see it in his eyes that he's already reluctant to ask for elaboration, so I relent.

"I think this trip made me realize I'm not going to be happy with life the way it is anymore," I say. "That's what's really been going on with me."

This won't be a short conversation, nor sweet, or confounding or liberating. Not in the sense that I want it to be. Yes, it will mean

Silas and I can be together, but I'm losing a *friend*, and someone I had grown to love whether it be only a sliver of the word or not.

I'm stuck to the door, waiting for Logan to move or say something. To sigh, to cry, to pound his fist against the wall, to laugh at me, to scream at me, to tell me he already knows I'm in love with someone else.

But he doesn't—he's confused, but not torn.

"Did I do something?" he finally asks, opening both his palms in a shrug. "What's making you think that?"

You didn't do anything at all and that's the problem, I think. I wish you would have done something to make this easier.

"No," I shake my head. "Life on the Ote just isn't what I want anymore, and I've been having these—*dreams*." The word comes out like I'm trying it for the first time on my tongue.

"What do you mean, dreams?" His eyebrows cord together and touch between two wrinkles. "Your entire existence is on the Otera, Lize, your family, your jobs—*me*."

I let my eyes wander around the room as I listen, folding my arms over my chest. Here I am, surrounded by my own belongings, in my own pod. My clothes are tucked away neatly in drawers, my books on the shelves, shoes scattered about on the floor, camera and comm tablet on the nightstand. All my toiletries pepper the tiny bathroom walls. This pod is *lived in*. What am I to do about that? How am I going to eradicate something so fully and abruptly? Shift my life from one moving unit to another?

"We had our fun on the moons," Logan continues. "We've been gone way longer than we should have, and it's fucking with you—it's giving you some false sense of *'life'*." He exaggerates the final word in air quotes. "You know we don't live the same life as those people on the Glades, right? You miss your parents, you're exhausted, you're *hallucinating*, apparently, having weird dreams now."

I plod toward him, crawling over his outstretched shins and digging into the crevice between the wall and the mattress. My fingers find the familiar binding of my journal where it always is. "Don't laugh at me, please," I mumble, holding the notebook up. "I know it sounds crazy, and maybe you still won't find a reason in all of this to believe me, but—I've been having these dreams since as early as I can remember. And I've always kept track of them here."

I hold the thick leather close to my chest and sit back on my heels, wondering how to go about this explanation, where to begin, how to fit Silas into it at the centerfold.

"I have *vivid* dreams about someone else, another man," I confess, pausing to let that linger. "I've always had them, every night, and I've never told you." I flip into the journal and turn it around to show him. "Please, just look," I say as I push the pages at his chest.

Logan takes the book from me and sets it on his lap, then flips the cover over and skims a page. A minute later he does it again on another page, then again after that. Silently working through my entries.

My eyes are trained on his face the whole time looking for a reaction. For hurt, or realization—a sudden awareness that the person I dream about is punched like a staple through all things Logan and I. That I was sleeping with him, and then drifting into unconsciousness and making love to someone else.

Eventually he closes the journal, seeing all he needed to see, or maybe just bored with it, and tosses it in the space between the two of us on the bed.

"I should have told you," I acknowledge, unable to deal with the silence eating my insides like a parasite any longer.

"It's just dreams, Eliza," Logan objects, folding his fingers into each other over his stomach. "You can't control them."

"It's not, though." I sigh. "It's never been just dreams, it's more than that. Didn't you read what I wrote?"

"So—what? What does that mean? All of a sudden you're gonna rip the rug out from under me over a shadow in your head at night?"

"I told you, it's so much more than that."

Before I even knew Silas existed, the prospect of life back on the mainland was unappetizing. If I had it my way, Logan and I would have stayed in the Glades indefinitely—found a life beneath those speckled system constellations. But as the universe would have it, we were destined to this transport. I realize now that even the extra cycles we were able to milk out of the Glade moon acted as an orchestrated circumstance. Had we left a cycle before or after, I would have missed Silas on the travel-back all together.

"What about your family?" Logan asks. "I think you're jumping to conclusions because you've had too much time to think, Eliza. We've only got four spins left on here, barely. You need some land under your feet, some grounding."

Maybe he's right about some things. What am I going to tell my parents? I left home on my partner's arm to explore the outer systems, and am going to return a straggler, bound to a man they've never seen or heard of. A *Mako*, nonetheless. I can hear the disdain in my mother's voice already.

"You're reading too many books." Logan chuckles, running a few fingers through his overgrown hair. *"This..."* He reaches out and grabs my hand, shaking it a bit to make a point. "This is real."

I frown, looking down at his grasp as he tries desperately to pull me over the fictional threshold he thinks I'm stuck behind. It does read like a fantasy—my soulmate bound to my dreams until all of a sudden he's not. The denial, the conflict, the fall out, the grand realization that we can't stay away from each other any longer, and then what?

"I'm sorry," I tell him, inching my hand out of his.

Logan shrinks against the wall behind the bed, recoiling from my apology. I try to open my mouth again to speak and he cuts me off.

"Don't."

He closes his eyes and lets his head fall back, thinking about how this got so fucked up so fast, what the change was, where things started to go wrong.

"How do you know I'm not that guy for you?" he snaps. "What is there in your head that isn't right here? Call me fucking crazy, but I'm really not understanding this."

If there is a time or place to finally tell him about Silas, it's now. I can get this guilt-riddled burden off my shoulders and trade it for transparency. It probably still won't make any sense though.

Logan is hurt, visibly. He's angry, and confused, and he can't palpably grasp the notion of a man in my dreams meaning more to me than he does. Especially not after all this time together, in what we both perceived as love and commitment—and I can't expect him to.

Now I'm going to tell him that the other man has been here all along, doing shots with him at the transport bar? It's *a fucking lot*—and it's sudden, and we're in the middle of the sky, floating four spins from the Otera still, with nowhere to escape to after I drop this massive weight on him.

What happens when I tell Logan it's Silas? He just concedes? He leaves me to run off into the sunset with another man like it's a shift change? Maybe he'll even help me move my things from his pod to Silas's, shake his hand, thank him.

No.

The only thing that can come from this admission is malice. Logan has a soft exterior, but he's territorial. He won't let this go easily. There's no real *reason* to drag Silas into it when Logan could retaliate against him if I do. Nothing permanent can be done until we get back to the Otera, and that's the shitty truth of it. I'm protecting both of them by leaving Silas out of the fray.

What this comes down to, is *me*.

I know in my heart that my relationship with Logan is over, and *that* is the only explanation I need for ending things with him now.

Even if Silas and I don't make it off this transport together, the sheer fact that I'm enamored enough with another man to risk everything, means that Logan and I wouldn't have made it much longer anyway. I would just spend the rest of my life looking to fit Silas into all those missing pieces.

"I just know that you're not," I finally say.

Logan is sodden, his right leg under the sheets bounces impatiently, nervously. "How do I change your mind?"

I shrug and hold a palm to the clammy heat at the back of my neck. "You can't."

He chuffs satirically, pulling the blankets back and standing up in front of me. "So that's it, you're done with me? Over some dreams and post vacation blues?" His height is intimidating, softening in a way. "I think you're making a mistake. Give it until we get back to the Ote, and if you really feel this way then—fine. Then I'll have to live with that."

"No," I push back. "I know I sound crazy, but I care about you, Logan. And I can't string this along when I know I'm just going to be looking for someone else in you. It's not fair to you. You know it's not."

He puts two big hands on my shoulders, centering me to look up at him.

"Eliza," he pleads. "What about all of this?" His head swirls around, motioning at the pod. "All of *us*, here? The memories, the photos, are we just supposed to pretend like it doesn't exist? Avoid each other until we get home?"

I'm breaking Logan's heart, but he's doing mine in just as thoroughly.

I'm in love with Silas, viscerally, totally, counting down the minutes until I can get back to him. But like a storm cloud, lightning strikes and thunder follows.

Choosing Silas means leaving bits of my life behind that I didn't expect to have to part with. Stability washed away, guarantees of my future null. The only covenant is him, but that's enough for me.

"When we get back to the Otera we'll figure all of *this*..." I gesture around the space. "...out permanently. For now, we'll just have to give each other space."

Logan holds me there awhile longer, worrying the skin inside his cheek, studying my features and my body like they might dissolve if he lets go. Eventually I tilt my head a bit, giving him a sad smile, and then kick up on my toes to plant a chaste kiss to his cheek.

"That easily?" he says, letting my arms go as I pull away.

"Logan—"

"No—it's fine." He stops me. "I'll give you your space, maybe it's what you do need, actually. We've been stuck in this pod for so long."

I nod, exhaling a bit at the pin prick of progress. "I won't change my mind," I promise him. "I don't want you to hold out for that."

Logan watches me walk back toward the door of the pod and linger. I swipe my journal from the bed on my way and hold it to my chest again, like a shield protecting me from any force resolute to keep me from Silas any longer.

His voice still gives me pause when I pull the slide open before stepping through.

"Just promise me you won't let a few sleepless nights change your entire life."

I give him a sad smile, knowing that it doesn't matter what I say now, because it's all ephemeral anyway. In a few spins Silas and I will be free to be together wholly. Unattached, unshrouded by a past. I've made it my entire life so far loving him in secret, and if I had to, I would love him that way for far more.

When I close the pod latch behind me, alone in the hallway, I remember to breathe for what feels like the first time since

I initially stepped inside. I let a wave of relief wash my body down from my scalp to the tips of my toes. And then another wave prickles my skin all the way back up again, festering with something different. Electric charged with *want*. There's ferocity, an eager begging pulse between my thighs, a flustered, frantic thumping in my chest.

I swallow it all, letting it bundle somewhere low in my belly, and then I go to him.

Silas hasn't moved, not since I left.

His eyes trained on the shadow of me burned into the door like I'll reappear in an apparition.

I promised him I was going to make this right, and maybe that's the truth, or maybe he should have just taken me. Buried himself inside me right there when I told him to and said fuck the rest.

He can feel my hands on his face like they're still there. Can close his eyes and see my lips panting and pursing below the slope of his nose as he mustered the last bit of his resolve to tell me *no, not yet*.

The clock on the wall usually ticks low and slow, but the sound of the arms moving along now is absolutely deafening in the silent space. His eyes flick up and check it, again, as he did ten seconds ago, forty-five seconds ago, three minutes ago.

Silas busies himself stacking the books all around him one by one on the desk again. Thicker bindings on the bottom, shorter, softer ones on the top. In size order so that when he's done he can walk his fingertips down the slope like a staircase—pretending he's this little man without a worry in the world, walking up and down paper flights of stairs.

He taps his fingers on his thigh while he waits, looks up at the clock again—another three minutes, *fuck*. It's been too long.

The door of the pod slides open then, abruptly, without warning or a knock, and Silas leaps up from the bed when I step inside.

We're both trained on each other. I can see the soft heaving of his chest, and the way his mouth parts open a shade, waiting for me to make a move. He's begging me with his eyes, *say something—anything.*

I rush to him. And as quickly as I move to close the gap, he follows. Meeting me hard and desperate in the middle of the room with his arms around my waist, mine tangled around his neck, through his hair, grabbing at anything.

I sigh into his mouth as I crush my lips to his and lick through the seam of them in the same breath. Silas parts for me, willfully, readily, groaning around my tongue, sliding his own into my mouth to grapple with.

His eager hand travels from my hip up my back, pinching the tender flesh at the nape of my neck, making me melt into him. I whine against his lips, biting down on the flesh as he cords his fingers through the hair in the back of my head and holds me to his mouth. Silas kisses me like I've never been kissed before, recklessly, pressing his center into mine with every pass of his tongue, every breathless gape for just a little bit of air to keep us tethered.

Then he lifts me slightly, walking me backward into the wall from which I came, and I feel the hard, cold metal of it against the burning flesh over my spine. I pull away for the first time, long enough to catch his eyes and speak through the breaks in our panting.

"Close the door," I whisper against his lips as our noses spar each other for access. Silas hardly lets the words leave my mouth, humming around them.

And then he does.

13
INSATIABLE

T he thing about myself and Silas, is that we already *know* each other.

The same way the sea will always know the sand. Existing together in waves, rolling, tumbling, sometimes calm and quiet, others like a rip current. The two of us swirl inside one another perpetually, stir and then settle—maybe we could exist apart, but what is more beautiful than the way the surf and sand refuse to stop kissing each other?

It's not the first time, it doesn't look different, the way our body's react isn't unfamiliar. There's no learning to be done, no chasteness, no experimental touches or slow savoring tastes—not at first.

This is a culmination. It's every time Silas and I have ever been one in our dreams, now all at once. Two separate strings existing on the same frequency, bound to travel toward each other for all of time, finally meeting and buzzing voltaic like a live wire in the middle.

✦

He kisses me, hungry. Hiking what he can of my legs around his hips against the hard curve of the wall, fettering me with the heavy weight of his body. We both spar for dominance. My teeth dig into the flesh of his lips, his fingers twist through my blonde locks to angle my mouth where he wants me, where he can reach me deepest.

Silas is intense in the way he fucks. He's task-heady, thorough, brazen when he moves and loves—darker than he cares to admit, but I pull perversion apart with my fangs and feed it back to him.

His mouth dips low and snags at my jaw, my neck. He sucks something fierce into the skin over my beating pulse, and I bray when he lathes the wound with his tongue, like all our urges have been dissolved to primality.

"Tell me to stop now if it be, little bird," he whispers, holding my jaw between his fingers and forcing me to look at him. "I'm afraid you'll soon find me incapable of the word."

I kiss him hard again, grinding my middle into the soft material of his shorts where he holds me straddled against the wall. I *feel* him twitch underneath them.

"Wouldn't dream of it," I breathe.

The pause is short lived before I'm keening again, his lips finding the other side of my neck and pulling a dark oval to the flesh to match the first.

The tank I'm wearing is dainty, Silas hooks his thumbs through the thin straps on both shoulders and lets them drop down my arms. His lips never leave me, it's muscle memory—*down, down, down,* shedding the thin material over my breasts until all that's left of my shirt is hanging off my torso, and the lace of my bra is peeking over the undress.

I twist my arms behind my back, unhooking the clasp between my shoulder blades while Silas's tongue leaves hot trails across my collarbones and the swell of my chest.

As I shrug free of the obstructive layer he exhales shakily, tortured by the sight of my naked chest. "Look at you," Silas mumbles.

He takes his time playing with the taut peaks of my breasts, pinching them, circling the flesh—then takes one with his tongue, flicking the muscle against the throbbing bud until my back arches off the metal and I tug helplessly at the disheveled waves of his hair.

Biting down on the plump round he draws a whimper from me, and *fuck* he loves the sound of it. Diving headfirst then to suck on my other begging nipple before the spit he left behind on the first has time to dry.

Silas leaves me writhing, peppering kisses through the valley of my breasts as he travels my body with his lips like a map.

I feel a twisting ache low in my abdomen, like the slow uncorking of a champagne bottle. Silas isn't taking his time, not letting me breathe. He reacts to the muffled moans escaping the part in my lips, running his nose up my chest to nudge my chin and take my lips against his own again.

"The things I've dreamt about doing to you, Eliza, would make the Gods blush," he confesses breathlessly.

I find the hem at the bottom of his t-shirt, teasing my fingertips underneath the material and feeling the hair that runs along the tight pad of his stomach, disappearing where I want to touch him the most.

Silas flinches, I can hear the catch in his throat when I graze lower, confident as I press my hand against the hard outline of his cock where it's doing no hiding. He sighs into my mouth and closes his eyes for a beat, then licks an aggressive line between my lips to ask permission for more, and I concede. I stroke him *once, twice,* over his shorts before abandoning it to lift his shirt completely over his head.

As if unable to control it, I roll my hips against his again, and he slides a forearm across the small of my back. His other settles vertically along my spine so he can hold me by the neck and press me closer to him while I writhe.

Silas wants to feel that friction, to know my body is begging involuntarily for him like a heated animal.

He knocks several items and loose papers off a countertop to my right, and it's barely a ledge to lean on, but he hoists me the small distance to balance against the edge of the metal, resuming his spot between my legs.

"Impatient." I smile against his cheek, leaving a kiss there and then another at his ear lobe. I bite down on the soft skin and make him growl into the crook of my neck.

"It is high time we stop denying ourselves this pleasure, Eliza," he says, fondling with the drawstring on my shorts and pulling it loose.

I shimmy my hips for him, lifting up on my palms while he drags my bottoms and the barely there cloth of my panties down my legs in one fell swoop. He kneels to help them from around my ankles, discarding them somewhere far and away knowing they won't be necessary any time soon.

Then he kisses the inside of my ankle, my calf, and the warm skin at the bend in my knee as he works himself back up my body.

Silas grunts like he wants to touch every inch of me at once, and is frustrated that it isn't possible. Suddenly in a hurry as my skin tingles for attention, I shed the remaining bunched up material of my top over my head and he lunges forward, kissing the tips of my nipples again and then my mouth.

"Take these off," I mumble as I snake my hands beneath the band of his shorts. I grope his ass, and then help him push the material down his thighs completely.

Silas doesn't wear anything beneath the downy fabric, it catches at his knees and he staggers out of it with an anxious kick. His length bobs heavy and dark between his thighs, drips of himself beading at the tip already, weeping for something to quell the throbbing ache of lust.

We're finally naked for each other, as it has been in every gorgeous dream we've ever had. We both pause to appreciate that.

This is the person I've loved—always, intimately.

I touch his chest with my fingertips over his heart, feeling the frantic thump beneath the skin, and he does the same. We hold each other's true, beating hearts in our palms for the first time. It's no surprise when they attune and pulse the same; they are the same.

Silas slides his hand up to cup my jaw, his thumb prodding softly at the plush pink of my bottom lip for access, and I grant it, swirling my tongue around his finger and kissing it, then kissing him.

We move against each other again, this time completely bare. The hard, velvet head of his cock prods my core, and I grind to meet it as it slides and parts me, spurring my clit so well that I moan into his mouth. Silas does it again, humping through my slit to hear me keen. It stirs heat at his lower back and draws tight at his balls.

Unable to wait any longer, I reach down between our two bodies and take him in my hand.

Silas falters.

Broken, shaking breaths erupt and I swallow them, shushing him with my lips and my tongue, but he can't help the way he jars his hips, slowly fucking himself into the hold of my palm with his eyes closed and head tilted back.

He feels so hard and heavy and *real,* against my fingertips. My pussy aches, fluttering around nothing as every thrust digs the tip of him into my clit over and over again. I'm drowning, warm and ready and slick for him—body humming with need.

Silas comes to and dips his head to suck another mark into the junction of my neck and shoulder. It's frenzied, the way he needs his mouth on me. Constantly, incessantly.

"I want you," he says, pressing his forehead to mine. We both look down at the junction of our bodies, my hand wrapped around him, the glistening round of his dick begging for attention. "I will take my time and taste every inch of your body when I'm through, but for this I cannot be forced to wait another second."

He slides his cock through me one last time, then slots the head where my body opens, waiting for him.

"Don't."

Without another word I usher Silas inside of me, swallowing the tip between my thighs, clenching on the thickness of just the mere beginning of him as my core adjusts.

My body knows that this is *him*. Welcoming an old friend with open arms and tender care. I moan as he inches further, pulling the hair at the nape of his neck and dragging his mouth down to mine. I want to taste the sound of his pleasure as he cracks me open over him.

"Maker, I will never sin again," he swears into the space, slowly filling me to a brim. "I will not tempt you to take this away from me."

Silas's body shudders when I close my ankles around the small of his back and tug him forward, consuming him, wholly, to where he feels his cock brush hard against the catch-all deep inside of me.

"Oh, *fuck*." I pant, tipping my body back just so, opening my throat to him again. I'm unquestionably positive that I've never been so full in my life. He curls himself over me to press his mouth to the skin, spearing his hips steadily while he holds me in place.

The sound of it is messy. He strokes in and out of my cunt, and I revel in the slap of his thighs against the inside of mine.

Silas is always vocal, but now he's just simply mesmerized by the auditory marvel of it all. This could be the one difference, he thinks, *hearing* me. So close to his ear and whimpering, *more, more, more*. The hisses when he bites into my skin, the slick pull of my pussy taking him over and again. It's never been this real, this forthright. He's fuck drunk off the sounds I make alone.

"Sing for me, little bird," he says. "Show me where to find you."

I answer with mumbled praise and half baked pleading. He wants to hear me come apart for him, and I want to make it impossible to forget.

He rocks harder into me, and I curl my fingers into the skin of his back and rake them down his spine.

"Yes—Gods, yes. Please, just like that."

Silas could come right now, in a snap, with the way my insides rub against him—fitting like a perfect glove over his cock. There's been a spark deep in his gut threatening to ignite since I first touched him, and it's growing increasingly hard to ignore.

"Feels so, *fuck*—fucking good," I mumble through bitten lips. The cork is slipping with every thrust of his dick inside me.

"I know, Birdie." He breathes. "I know."

I take to his neck, leaving a trail of my own markings and lashes in the tan skin, then wrap my arms around him—clinging desperately to the last thrumming of resolve we both have.

Silas's hands skate under my ass, pulling me further to the edge of the counter. It's an angle I wasn't expecting so abruptly that I do nothing short of scream. The devastating change of pace and hard ridge of his dick riding over a pleasure point inside of me has my eyes rolling back, my open mouth making rounded shapes as I coo.

"I'm gonna..." I stutter. "Silas—Sy, I'm..."

"Look me in the eyes while I make you come, Eliza." He holds the back of my head in his palm. "I don't want you to forget this moment."

I do as he says, watching the tiny, heaping reflection of myself come undone in the pupils of his beautiful eyes. They swallow me whole, burning around the edges when my core starts to contract around him, choking his cock in short little bursts. He has to hold my hips down with a shaking hand to keep me from arching completely in half as I shatter.

Fuck, it's surreal. It's a spinning room, a black out and come to where Silas is my only focal point. He mimics my face, his own mouth dropping open to gape, eyebrows knitting together when the cord finally snaps.

"Where, Birdie? Where do you want it?"

"Inside—I want you inside me."

He cries out as he loses himself. I feel it happen, ropes of his seed against my walls and the deepest parts of my body. Silas trembles the whole time and crushes himself to me, hugging my rib cage under the weight of his arms, my chest to his chest, his head against my head. We both take time to come down, chests heaving, eyes closed while the sweat from our foreheads mingles and dries where we're connected.

He eventually leans forward and kisses me deeply, lips gliding slowly and gently against one another, neither of us know for how long. When we part, we're both smiling, noses grazing.

"Come to bed with me," Silas says. It's not a question.

The mattress dips as Silas kneels at the foot of the bed and gazes down on my naked body. His dichromatic eyes are lidded and his cock has stirred back to life between his legs, but that's the last thing on his mind with me on display the way I am.

He pinches his arm and I giggle, kicking my foot out to tease him, but he catches it and drags me closer to the edge he's perched on.

"How cruel it would be to wake up from this," he says, kissing my heel, then my ankle, nuzzling his nose into the top of my shin.

I suck in a breath when he bites my calf, then licks it better on instinct and continues his travels, hoisting my knee up to rest on his shoulder.

"I told you I was going to take my time with you," he murmurs, kissing the crease where my thigh meets the back of my knee. "I am many things of a moral dubiety, dream girl, but I am not a liar."

Silas skims his lips down the length of my inner thigh, leaving open mouthed kisses in a trail all the way to my core—then he stops. I sigh and purse my lips, already more than eager to feel him there again, but I know he would never settle for less than near delirium by the time he grants it to me.

He goes back the way he came, this time sucking maroon markings into my skin here and there, possessing me with them, and each time I come a little more undone—my body tells me it needs him more desperately.

Silas mirrors his movements on the other side, this time laying flat on his stomach between my legs while he works. The unruly mess of his hair appears and disappears as his head bobs and he leaves me sweaty and aching.

My legs start to protest, quivering against his assaulting tongue the longer he keeps me bated. I can feel the slick drip of my center when he gets close and then retracts again. The teasing stubble of his chin and cheeks makes me squirm as it brushes over me.

Silas is a vision between my thighs, holding me open with two heavy palms in the hinges of my knees and watching me, waiting for me to tell him what he already knows, that I *crave* him there. He pauses again at the apex, and even the little puffs of breath that leave his lips taunt me.

"I'll beg if you want me to," I mutter, closing my legs around his head. "Just know you're sealing your own fate."

He smiles against my mound, chuckling low and deviously, the vibration of it spurs my clit and catches my breath. Silas pinches his fingers into the back of my thighs to coax me open again.

"Part your legs, little bird. So I can watch you drip honey for me."

It's a divine rediscovery. The push and pull we torture each other with isn't unlike what goes on in my head. He is the man I've always known, how he kisses me, how he worships me, how he makes me come.

I've never experienced a satisfaction like Silas's tongue when it carves me open like this. One pass over the throbbing nerve at my peak and I'm already caving like a half moon, testing the limits that my spine will allow.

He toys with me, licking long, heavy stripes up my core and nuzzling my clit just long enough to feel the muscles in my legs tense and tighten, and then he starts again.

I croon each time, tangling my fingers in his hair, scratching his scalp—he hums when I gush around his tongue and the warm slick walls of my cunt drip for the friction I know will send me over the edge.

"More, Silas," I pant.

I catch his eyes when they flicker up from between my thighs, he runs his nose through my folds, kisses the tangle of nerves and then *sucks*. My limbs turn to putty all around him.

He's devious, but not interested in denying me anything I want from him, so he cards a forearm around my thigh and over the lower half of my belly, holding me down against the sheets as he slips two thick fingers inside of me.

"*Fuck.*"

Silas pumps slowly, curling his knuckles against the heat of my walls, dragging them over that spot again and again. I bite my lip near bleeding and jar my hips into his fingers, ravenous for more attention.

Watching my face distort in satisfaction while he plays with me is like falling in love again. The pleasure isn't all mine though, *Silas gets off on it too.*

He hangs needily between his own legs, grinding himself into the sheets. Every time I whimper and clench around his fingers he feels a devastating tug at his own loins, a pressing reminder of how badly he wants to be inside me again, and then more after that, for as long as I can take him.

He pairs the scissor of his fingers with his tongue, letting his own spit pool at my clit and then licking it off. It's aggressive and insatiable, the way he eats me. Digging his dormant fingertips into the flesh of my thigh when I buck to keep me from stagnating the steady climb.

Silas can feel me, like an extension of himself, start to break. My hands fling helplessly back to his hair, gripping his cheeks—thighs tensing and quaking against the meat of his shoulders. I get *so fucking wet* just as I come undone, and he can feel it around his fingers, hear it in the high pitched cry stuck in my throat.

"Give it to me, Eliza," he beckons my orgasm, curling his fingers inside of my heat. "I want it all over my face."

I clamp down on him instantly, choking out his name.

Silas groans as I come on his tongue, swallowing it all and continuing to drink from me, eyes closed and content, savoring every last taste of me leaking around him.

I thrash when he doesn't let up, licking me over and over until I'm pulsing from overstimulation. I don't need to see it to know I'm swollen and puffy, the pink center of me worn and tired from his lips. But when I look at Silas, face covered in my slick, it's enough to stir something again.

He climbs up my body and kisses me, open mouthed, tongue sliding against my own. It tastes like salt and spit, tangy with my own natural sweetness and Silas's aura tangled in.

"I'm gonna fuck you again," he tells me against my lips.

I open my legs eagerly, nodding consent and holding his face in both my palms so I can kiss him whenever I please.

Silas slips his hand between our bodies and levels himself with me, feeling his cock catch where he needs it, then pushes inside to the hilt in one deep thrust.

I caw—so full of him, so fast. The stretch is searing, even after I just came. He holds still, savoring it again, the feeling of being inside me, his perfect fucking girl. *His* girl.

He groans into my mouth and I return it. I can feel his pulsing shaft inside of me where he's holding himself, and I tease him with a clench of my core to remind him he's still yet to move. It pulls a dark, latent curse from his throat and before I can giggle he pulls back and fills me again, stealing the breath and replacing it with something tortured.

Silas fucks me slow at first, winding his hips in soft circles and short thrusts. He stays as deep inside my pussy as he can, giving me his full length heavy and hard while I'm pinned underneath him.

He hardly ever lets his lips leave my body. If they're not on my mouth, or my neck, sucking dark marks into the meat of my chest—it's because he's leaned back to watch the way his cock slides in and out of me, tugging at the skin there as it comes and goes, glistening thick with my juices, with his.

"You were made for me," Silas praises, thrusting into me harder.

"Maker—*fuck* keep going." I sigh.

He massages a shaking thumb over my clit, the other hand slides up my chest and takes a palmful there, squeezing the flesh until it spills between his fingers.

"I've wanted you like this since I saw you that first day." He gnaws on the words as they slip between clenched teeth. "I should have taken you right there."

"Yeah," I whimper.

It's happening again, I feel it, the same way the sun sneaks up on you; warming your skin, relaxing your body, and then all of a sudden it's burning.

"Should have—should've fucked you in that hallway," he says. "When we realized what we were."

He stabs into me relentlessly, fumbling as he knows there's hardly time left before he loses it too. The fever at his back is breaking.

"I thought about it," I confess hoarsely. Silas's thumb at my peak is withering my resolve, it's fucking killing me.

"In this pod, reading those—*fuck*, those dirty little things you wrote about me in your journal."

I start to squirm underneath him, the far out look in my eyes is a tell, but so is the rush of wetness he feels coat his dick inside me.

"Would you have let me—let me then, little bird?"

He knows the answer, he fucking knows the answer he just wants to hear me scream it.

"YES! Yes—fuck, Silas—*yes*."

I can't believe it, but I'm coming again, the first spasm shutting me up, the second pulling a jagged gasp from my chest. I tremble, finding his forearm because it's all I can reach and stabbing my fingernails into the skin while I *squeeze* him.

Silas is long gone with me.

The way my walls choke his cock steals any rationale from his brain, and all he sees is white—bright and debilitating. He could be alive, he could be dead, all he deciphers is that he's plunging, abysmal.

When I open my eyes it's a cacophony of heavy breathing and panting. The blood rushes out of my ears and back to my chest, Silas is collapsed next to me, skin flushed red, an arm flung over his eyes and forehead cueing exhaustion.

His dick is wet, softening against the damp hair at the base of his pelvis. I know I'm not any better, leaking a mixture of myself and him, feeling it trickling down my ass and thighs.

Several minutes later I lean over and kiss his rib cage, then the peak of his chest. He drags me into his side and I bend my knee over his thigh and rest my head on his shoulder.

"It was never enough to have you in pieces," he murmurs, turning his face into the crown of my hair. "And it never will be again."

My dainty middle finger traces a soft line up the middle of his chest and throat. I look up and he leans down to kiss me, the angle is awkward but it's necessary. He thinks that maybe he can kiss away anyone he's had before me, maybe do the same for me. Erase both of our pasts before this, so all that's left is each other.

"What time is it?"

Silas's eyes flicker to the clock on the table. I'm still burrowed into his side, resting.

Exhaustion is evident, but we can't bring ourselves to sleep just yet. We've both waited lifetimes to feel one another, flesh and bone, and falling asleep feels like a grand disservice when the entirety of our dreams is already here, at this moment.

"Well past mid spin," Silas says. It's been a while since he's spoken and his voice is hard and gravelly, cut up from exertion.

I feel my stomach grumble, like a haggard reminder. *I need to replenish or he'll fuck me dead.*

Silas hears it too, sitting up from the bed, reluctantly unwinding his arm from behind my neck. "I gotta feed you." He smiles.

I chuckle at his choice of words. "I'm not a pet."

"It doesn't change the sentiment," he argues with a wink.

I roll free of the sheets for the first time in hours, stretching my cracking limbs, rubbing the aches in my thighs and knees.

Silas is away from me, sorting through crates, opening and shuffling around in the cooler unit, so I take myself to the weathered mirror tacked to the wall across the room.

It's old, rusted around the edges, and the color bleeds into the glass. The reflection is dirty with smudging and a hairline crack cuts across the middle like a strike of lightning. I imagine Silas lifted it during a dig, stole it from an abandoned camp or snagged it out of the unfortunate remnants of a crash landed pod. Only needing it to shave his overgrown cheeks and take a dull scissor to his hair when it started to tickle his ears.

The mirror matches the rest of him: scarred enough you wonder what happened, transparent enough you can find the answer without asking.

I can still see myself in the muddied reflection anyway, letting a low gasp through my lips as my naked torso waves into focus.

I'm completely branded. Dark red love marks wind up my neck, through the center of my breasts, in little patterns around my nipples, under my ear, tucked against the hinge of my jaw. I touch them tenderly, wincing when I test the press of one along my collarbone and it lightens under the pressure then blooms back to a deep crimson.

I'm disheveled, hair in knots, sweat still dried to the curve of my brow. There's a whole world of *sticky* elsewhere on my body—Silas's spit, his cum, mine. I've never been so *dirty*, I think. But all the while I look at my likeness in the glass and also think: I've never been so *glowing*. Like a fucking beam of light, my complexion is vibrant.

Silas sneaks up behind me and winds his arms around my middle, resting his head on my shoulder and looking at me through the reflection in the mirror.

"I didn't mean to be so rough with you," he whispers, nuzzling his nose and lips into the crook of my neck, kissing a mark he left there. He runs his lips down the slope to my shoulder and kisses one there as well.

I bend my arm to frame his head, brushing my fingers through his tousled hair. He's not unscathed either, I can see the fevered prints I left on him, the visceral instinct written in tongue and teeth across the planes of his body.

"Just marking what's yours," I tell him.

His eyes darken in a snap, and he growls from somewhere deep and hidden, somewhere I recognize, and my body recognizes too. It's instant heat between my thighs again, and suddenly the hunger I felt before has been forgotten and replaced with an appetite for something different.

Silas disappears behind my back, kissing the untouched lines of my shoulder blades, the top of my spine, leaving a trail down the tracks of vertebrae until my skin pebbles in goosebumps.

He puts a heavy palm between the bones at the center of my back and steers me forward. I oblige, happily, catching myself against the wall with hands on either side of the mirror, arching back into the flesh of his hips. He's so hard already that he glides through the skin between my legs easily.

My fingers flex and curl as he takes me by the hips and thrusts in and out of the space between my thighs, the tip of his dick bumping into my clit.

I can see him gaping at me in the mirror, furrowing his brow in concentration. It's so *hot*, this way. Watching him work, watching myself react. This is what it's like when I dream, experiencing the way I make love from somewhere in the second person. I'm telling myself a story in my mind, painting myself a picture in this reflection.

My stomach hums again and Silas feels it under his fingertips.

"I have a protein bar," he mumbles, sliding one hand up my back to hold me by the neck and tug at my hair.

"Fuck the protein bar."

When he fills me this time it's hard and quick, racking his hips in stinging strikes against my ass. A hand on my waist, the other pulling me back by my hair, my throat.

I huff and whine as he takes me by my breasts and pinches the tender flesh—I slide my fingers through my center and touch myself in turn.

We both come in a frenzy, our breath fogging up the mirrored glass, Silas's tongue finding my spine again, muffling his own cries into the sweat-damp skin.

He has to carry me back to the bed, legs still shaking.

We did eat the protein bars. All of them. Hours ago, as Silas held one to my mouth and fed me because I complained, *I'm too tired to eat.*

He chuckled at that, proud of himself for wearing me out as thoroughly as he did. I groaned while I chewed, the bar itself was stale and chalky, but it tasted like a five star meal anyway.

Silas tore the wrapper open with his teeth and traded me bite for bite until the stash withered to null. *You cleaned house, Birdie,* he had said, and I swatted his chest lazily, licking the crumbs of chocolate from the corners of my mouth to savor.

We can't survive on his dried field rations, we'll have to leave this pod at some point, we know that—but it won't be this spin. Him and I are both content to lay in this for awhile, the sweat, the sex, the eroticism of it.

We're infatuated with the feel of one another, our hands never straying too far away. Silas stays touching me, whether it be his fingers wound in mine, his lips on my shoulder, a heavy palm on my thigh. He's trying to keep me tethered, like a kite he's afraid the wind might blow too hard and rip away from him.

Now I'm the one holding him down though, crawling on my knees to perch between his open legs. He flips one eyelid open from where he's resting, one arm tucked under his head, the other tangled in mine.

"What are you up to, Birdie?" He quizzes me curiously.

I haven't even touched him yet, but his dick twitches to life. It's the proximity, the way I look on my knees for him, the insinuation.

"Sealing fate," I tease, knowing for every second Silas kept me bated all those hours ago, I'll give him two more.

Except I don't goad him the same way—I take his soft cock in my mouth without hesitation, making him curse through gritted teeth, because *he was not expecting that,* and the best he can do is hiss and squirm while the blood rushes rapidly downward.

My tongue is warm and wet as I lick eagerly down his shaft until I've reached my limit, then swallow. Silas's head knocks back against the wall, his eyes following on a groan.

I do it again, then again, each time pulling something twisted from his throat. My lips pop off and leave a trail of drool behind, suspended from my mouth to his tip, and he lets out a grated *fuck,* when I use it to pump him messily.

I give him my big blue eyes, my little palm wrapped around him, mouth lapping and sucking at the head. It's almost too much to bear when I dip back down, deep enough to sputter and choke as my throat contracts around him again. He can't take it.

"Ride me," he begs.

So I do.

I hook my legs over his hips and settle down on top of him, eyes fluttering shut as we moan together at the first stretch of my cunt over his cock.

It's like it gets better every fucking time.

Silas tugs me forward, chest to chest so he can kiss me while I move. My lips may be swollen and bruised from the day, but I don't care. I let him bite and suck and lick past them.

As I grind down onto him like I'm in a saddle, Silas meets me halfway. His hips jerking upward in tandem, so eager to please me, to fuck me within an inch of exhaustion.

The way I'm seated, my clit rubs against the coarse hairs at his base and it's fucking debilitating. He's licking the noises I make right out of my mouth and swallowing them whole, hammering into me harder just to force me to cry out to him. One second I'm flying, the next I'm crashing. He's hitting that spot so *perfectly*.

"Silas..." I warn against his lips.

"Me too."

He hugs me to his body, squeezing me so that I can't move as he takes the reins, planting both his heels on the mattress and pumping into me with reckless abandon.

Silas goes first, his thrusts becoming long and erratic, shaking me with the force of it while he buries spurts of himself inside me, and I can't help but follow. He fucks me through my peak, holding me long after the collapse and brushing his fingers through my hair.

When I finally roll off of him, I can't keep my eyes open. I know it's night again, I know we can't keep this up forever, my body can't handle it, the soreness between my thighs is staggering, blatant. I'll feel him inside of me for *spins* after this. Every time I move, wherever I walk.

Silas is weak from exertion too, wanting to drag this out as long as we both physically can, but it's reached its pinnacle. We've wrecked each other in the best ways.

Still he keeps kissing me, rubbing a soft thumb down my cheek as he does. They're slow and chaste, languid and lazy. He only stops when he hears the steady hum of my breathing even out, his own eyes so heavy it's easy to hold me there against him and succumb to it too.

There are still things we need to talk about, obstacles we will need to climb, but that isn't important right now. It all can wait.

The world outside this pod lived a full day untouched by either of us, but inside we lived thousands of days all in one.

We both deserved that. *Being together,* without the utterance of something else. Without the external push and pull reminding us that life isn't always a dream, because today it was. In these sheets, behind these walls, it was.

Maybe that was always the universe's plan, after all. Because we both sleep, and for the first time ever, we don't dream about one another at all.

14
CLANDESTINE

F or as many dreams as I've had about Silas, none of them have
ever felt like this. The steady, thumping beat of his heart
against my spine. The slow, peaceful brush of his breath tickling
the skin of my neck, disturbing wisps of hair around the shell of
my ear.

His arm is slung over my rib cage, holding me to him intimately
with his palm pressed between the soft rise of my breasts, thumb
and pinky finger hooked under the flesh there.

I smell him all around me. In the sheets as I press my nose into
the pillow to inhale the earthen, salty musk of him. On my skin,
despite the sweat that is long dried. The aura of sex is stuck to me
like a pollen. With every shift of my body it tickles my nose and
reminds me of what happened here.

Reminds me *he's* still here.

For the first time ever, a dream that doesn't end. Perhaps we've
switched planes now, crossed over the cosmic wire, entered an
upside down. Reality is now where I go in my sleep, because life
itself is the dream, and it continues on and on and forward and
more, because *he's still fucking here*, and I can feel him in a way
that's all consuming.

Physically Silas is right behind me, chest pressed to the center of my back, one of his legs bent and sandwiched between both of mine, his hips molded against my ass like the slope of a puzzle piece.

But, it's more than that, because I feel him *lingering* too, in places he isn't presently.

A ghost of him inside my body, still filling me, the swollen ache of my sex has a heart beat of its own, it's tender flesh looking for a satiate. I move and my body *feels* it, all at once. My hips are stiff, legs are sore, everything is delicate to the touch. My head throbs a bit from lack of hydration, the room spins, it's like I'm *fuck* hungover.

The cabin of Silas's pod is still dark but it's day now—the eighth spin since he first showed up in my conscious life, and for the first time since then, I think: *Maker, why did it take so long?*

This, is what I've been missing all this time—depriving myself of it for the sake of morality, and Logan, and logic, because that's the type of person I am. I'm a dreamer, not a doer. I've always been perfectly content surviving on the fictional *'what ifs'* of life, living in my head with my daydreams, allowing the happiness of reality in bursts, but still always resorting back to the fairy-tale. The universe though, it always knows.

Silas's other arm is tucked under my neck, cradling my head in his elbow, forearm splayed out across the sheets. I reach over and trail my fingers as light as a feather against the veins of his arm, then the dark roots buried under his wrist that flow into his palm.

When I slip my fingers through the spaces in his, he squeezes them. Encapsulating my palm with his heavy, scar-stricken hand, and running his thumb back and forth slowly, scraping the short nail against my skin. He kisses my neck, digging his nose into the nape where it meets my hair, and soothes my pulse with open mouthed admiration.

"How long have you been awake?" I ask, smiling. I let my head fall back further to present my throat to him like an open canvas.

"Each time you stir, I wake, Birdie," he murmurs into my shoulder. "I'm afraid you might fly away."

Silas's palm between my breasts explores the area, sketching soft circles around my perking nipples, teasing the peaks of them with a brush stroke.

I let out a timid, barely there whimper as he glides his fingertips tauntingly across my chest, the wet trail of his mouth on my neck making my eyes flutter closed again.

"I wouldn't." I sigh, grinding the curve of my ass like a wave against him. "You know I wouldn't."

"But you already have."

I twist my neck to look at him out of the corner of my eye.

"You never came to me in my sleep last night."

"Or you in mine," I confide.

We both ponder it for a second, cradling each other's bodies all the same. Silas moves against me more blatantly, his kisses spread to the hinge of my jaw, down to the corner of my lips as far as he can reach from this angle.

"Does it mean something?"

He hums, tasting the salty sweetness of my skin on his tongue. "It means we don't have to sleep to dream anymore, little bird."

All along, this connection has served as a map. Silas was my destination, my treasure to be found, as I was his. It may have taken us several routes to get here, sometimes a storm would turn us back around and we'd have to go another way, as was life—still every night we'd study each other again, knowing where our travels would eventually take us.

There's a comfortable warmth between my legs the more he moves. I reach back and thread my fingers through the hair at the side of his head, dragging his lips down over my own. It's sloppy, our tongues miss before they find purchase, and the sound is elementary too, the pucker and smooch of it—but it's *sensual*. Hearing ourselves fill each other with this type of love. Silas and

I never had the chance to do this before, we've never savored or explored in a tactile space.

He slides his hand down the plane of my belly, and without hesitation, runs his fingers straight through my slit and I *gasp*.

It's so tender and raw, but still so wet for him. He dips into my center, pulling nectar from within, and slides the finger back out again, outlining hearts against my clit with it.

"Should I be expecting trouble when we finally leave this chimeric haven?" he whispers to me.

My tongue is pinched between my lips as I make breathy little noises with every flick of his fingers. The way I grind back into him is overt now, I can feel the bulbous length of him dotting my ass, smearing precome against my thighs.

"No," I mumble. "I don't—I don't think so."

Silas sweeps heavenly across my throbbing pearl of nerves, just enough pressure, just enough motion, he *knows* me this way. Better than I know myself.

"I wouldn't have pegged Logan as the apathetic type," he says. His voice is drowning behind my soft *oh's* and *ah's* as he baits me. "He truly had no adverse reaction when you told him it was me?"

"He...*fuck*," I bristle. I can feel the tickle of his mustache on my neck again. He bites down and I whimper. "He doesn't know."

My hips keep moving, but Silas's ministrations stop. He holds me still, cupping my sex in his palm, waiting for me to elaborate. When I don't he untangles his fingers from mine, sliding his arm from underneath my head to steady himself on his elbow and look down at my face.

"So you've been dishonest with me?" His eyebrows thread together, expression wounded. "I took you to bed how many times, Eliza—"

"No I didn't—I didn't lie," I turn onto my back to face him, and when he tries to look away I grab his chin with two hands and pull it back. "I told him everything, Silas, I showed him the journal—he *knows* I'm in love with someone else."

"Just not with me." He sits up more.

"He didn't believe me," I croak. "He thought it was bullshit, the whole thing—said I wasn't thinking straight, that we've been traveling for too long and it's gotten to my head."

I reach for him again and he lets me, softening into the hold.

"What good would have come if I told him about you? I was protecting you both." I soften my voice. "It would have been chaos, it would have ruined everything, ruined yesterday."

Silas pinches his eyes shut, because he *understands*. He doesn't want to—he doesn't want to be pragmatic or sensible right now, but he knows this isn't as black and white for me as it is for him.

We've led two completely different lives before this moment—him with nothing precious to let go of if not me, a drifter with a past waning in the current. But for *me*, this was so much more of a change. I have so much more to lose.

"I told him it was over, and that I won't change my mind. That's all that matters, right? That I'm *yours*, Sy. That I will always be yours."

He sighs, deeply tormented, like there's some glaring warning he's choosing to ignore for the sake of me, because he would do anything for me.

"Yesterday was my favorite day, Eliza," he mutters, leaning back down to press his forehead to mine. "I am yours in all the same ways—so if you think this is the best option, then I can oblige."

"Three spins," I whisper, stretching up to kiss his lips, then speaking against them. "We can be discreet for just three more spins."

Silas chuckles, wrapping his arms around my body and rolling me under his weight on the bed. He kisses me back, harder, then nips at my neck playfully as I giggle and thrash around him.

"Let's have discretion begin after this," he suggests, inching down my body and folding his shoulders between my thighs.

"This could be an issue." I blow a raspberry through my lips and look in the mirror.

I've crawled back into my clothes from nearly two spins ago now, but it took Silas a certain *amount* of convincing to even let me get out of the bed to begin with.

Another one, little bird, how many is that? His mouth and fingers had glistened with me as he peeked up at my balmy expression.

I can't...I don't know. I panted in return. *Sy—*

Just one more.

He left me wrung out across the bed, laying on my stomach with my forearm beneath my cheek, knee bent like a right angle. When he tried to run a cool cloth between my legs I hissed at him. *You bastard!* He didn't even try to stifle a laugh, bellowing with his forehead pressed into the small of my back.

No hot water in this pod. Right.

"Remember when you asked me if I really knew it was you all this time?" he'd joked when I turned around, clawing at his chest as he peppered me again in kisses. *"No one else would berate me quite like you do."*

I tried to bite my cheek, but soon we were both in a fit of hysterics, giggling and kissing the smiles onto one another's faces.

"What was it you called me the other day?" I doubled over laughing before he even finished the sentence. *"A fucking magician."*

Now, staring at my reflection again for a second time, I *wished* Silas was a magician.

These dark marks across my chest and neck leave little to assume. If Logan sees me like this, there's nothing I can say or do to revive the dead relationship. It's a *fuck you*, plain and simple.

"What am I supposed to do about this?" I complain, watching Silas slip into his usual attire across the room: fitted green cargos, a black tee pulled over his head. He sees me prodding at my bruising skin, holding my hands over my throat in unnatural poses, trying to hike the flimsy neckline of my tank as far up my sternum as it will go.

"Here," he says, drifting toward me and snatching a piece of clothing off the back of his desk chair. I take it from him and inspect it, just an old, faded field shirt. Maybe it was once black, but it's pilling at the seams and across the stomach a bit, and can't be considered anything more than a heather gray now.

When I slip it on, the collar falls much further up on my neck. With that, and the waves of blonde hair fanning down my shoulders, I cover *most* of the marks, but not all. It's far better than any other option. I pull at the threads and dip my nose into the crew neck, it smells just like him and I hum happily—not even concerned with looking fanatic as I do it.

"This works." I smile, lifting my chin to press a chaste kiss to his lips in thanks.

"You're ethereal, Birdie" he tells me, taking in my body draped in his clothing, feeling a knot of pride and possessiveness tangle in his gut. He holds my hips and pulls me into him. "Perhaps even more so without..." He snaps the band of my shorts against my skin.

"We need food." I shove his hands off my body playfully. "Showers. I need to change my clothes." He nods like he's hearing everything I'm saying but it's going in one ear and out the other.

"I will..." I start to speak, but he cuts me off with a kiss. "Meet you..." *Kiss.* "At concession."

He kisses me again and grumbles, reluctantly slumping away.

"Remember, *discrete*." I point at him as I back up against the hatch door.

Silas leaps toward me a final time, pressing me against the metal, framing my face with his palms and dipping to close his lips over mine. I lick into him first, running my tongue against the soft walls of his mouth and he mimics me. It's quick and deep, the finality of this seemingly infinite moment in time before the slide creaks open and the vortex sucks me out.

"Don't take long," he nudges, pulling the latch behind me.

I finally slip through the doorway, and he watches me until I disappear all the way down the hall.

I stand outside my pod for a little too long, pressing my ear to the wall, trying to hear movement inside. It's not early in the morning anymore, it's past breakfast, but Logan loves to sleep in late if he can, so who knows if this isn't one of those days.

I pull Silas's shirt collar up my neck again and bury my chin in the seam of it. *He's gonna ask where I got this shirt from,* I think. Or maybe he wouldn't. But he would notice it, surely.

I sigh and swallow the lump in my throat, leaning into the door again to knock.

"Logan?"

Nothing. I knock again, louder.

"Hey, are you in there?"

I give it about ten seconds of radio silence from the other side before I try the slide and it jars open.

He's not here.

When I drop inside the space it looks disheveled, like a wind spin swept through and knocked every loose item in the vessel off its balance. The bed is unmade, sheets on the floor, drawers half pulled open, books and paper scattered about. All of my things are still intact, though. I muse the room, bending down to pull a duffel out of a storage hull and then start filling it.

Logan's not here but he'll be back. I got lucky just now, sliding into the fray while he was gone, and I know I can't lollygag and take my time dissecting the mess he left. I have to get my shit and go.

I shove all of what I can of my casual wear into the bag, balling items up in haste and ramming the wrinkled linens into the corners. I smack several toiletries off the counter into it next: shampoo, toothbrush, hairbrush, lotions, makeup bag to cover these Maker forsaken hickeys. Then jog to my night table to grab a comm tablet, my earbuds, the camera.

I catch my reflection in the floor-length mirror as I bustle around and stop to look. My hair is a fucking mess. I'm basically wearing a set of mismatched pajamas. Little bites and bruises are peeking out beneath my shorts on the inside of my thighs that I didn't notice in Silas's mirror. I can't go *anywhere* looking like this in a public space.

"Shit," I whisper to myself.

I look back at the closed hatch door and then at the digital clock perched on the desk.

"*Shit*," I say again, and then start to strip.

Silas's shirt comes off over my head, then my tank. I shimmy the soft cotton shorts I'm wearing down my legs and when they hang on my ankle I kick them across the room impatiently.

I rummage through the remaining pile of clothes that I didn't snag to take with me. There's *one* turtleneck, not usually my go-to item of clothing. It's more of a precautionary piece I pack for cold weather or aggressive atmospheres if it's *necessary*.

Well, *fuck* if it isn't necessary now.

I throw some long forgotten overalls over it, then check the clock again, steadying myself for a final look in the mirror before I sling the duffel bag over my shoulder, and get the hell out of the pod altogether.

Silas is *juggling* in the dining area. Standing in line at several different concessions with his arms already full to the brim.

He doesn't even care how silly he looks; double every item of food available on this transport overflowing in his grasp. Two bagels, two coffees, enough pastries to feed an army. He has a bag of tinfoiled chocolates tucked under his elbow as he balances drinks in one large palm, all so he can pull a few pieces of à la carte fruit off display.

This is something Silas has never had. A *person* to take care of. The delicate soul of another at his fingertips that he has to water, and sun, and tell stories to so that it thrives.

I'm a seedling gifted to him by the cosmos, planted in the muddy cave of his chest under overturned soil. I grow best in his climate, he knows this, we're a perfect match—but it means nothing to be planted without nutrients to survive.

His lips curl into a smirk when he notices the woman at the counter's eyes dip below his jaw and linger there a bit, stuck on the deep ovals of color painted into his skin. She flushes when Silas catches her, her eyes flickering away embarrassed as she hands him two sandwiches wrapped in paper.

He shuffles away from the register, again fumbling several meals worth of food and snacks in his hands when he feels a tap on his shoulder. Silas is smiling before he even turns around, giddy to see my face again, to continue the dream in daylight, to greet me for the first time as *his,* in the world outside his pod.

"Tomorrow we can do breakfast in bed, little—"

He twists around and is immediately cut short by the sobering splash of a face that isn't mine.

"Hey, man." Logan waves, cowering as he scratches the back of his neck nervously.

Putting it lightly, Logan looks like *shit.*

He's folded halfway into his own body, the usual perfect sweep of blonde hair that falls across the crown of his head sticking out in unnatural places. A shirt that was probably once fitted nicely to the grooves of his torso is baggy, wrinkled around the edges and worn. Silas's guess is about two spins worn at this point.

When Logan looks up and Silas meets his eyes for the first time, he can tell they're *tired*. Deep circles that waterfall down his cheeks and add to the dull hue of his skin. Somehow he's both dry and clammy at the same time. Logan looks every bit the scraggly and unkempt man he saw Silas as when he first came off the Pulp. He's a good actor though, keeping up the unbroken facade anyway.

Logan low whistles, chuckling. "Maker, what I wouldn't do to be your woman, what a spread," he jokes as he slaps a palm to Silas's shoulder. It jostles the food a bit, Silas has to sway to keep it cradled in his arms. "Girl from the bar again?" Logan asks him, nudging a second time and nodding his chin toward the markings on his neck with a cheeky smile.

Silas huffs out a humored breath through his nose, squinting slightly at the man in front of him. The best answer he can give Logan is a low hum, treading lightly on the edge of getting immediately caught in a long web of lies he wants no part in.

It's obvious to Silas that Logan is distraught, but maybe it's because he knows the truth of it—that I left him, with a seemingly unbelievable explanation as to why, and he hasn't seen me since. This transport is large in theory, but even the walls whisper. Logan has probably been back and forth down every alley a hundred times, turning over every loose board trying to find me.

What a sight he would have seen if he did.

Silas shifts awkwardly and looks down at all the food in his arms, then back up again. He wants nothing more than to be rid of this interaction completely, but he's quite literally weighed down.

"Listen, man," Logan starts, sensing Silas's utter dissociation from the current topic. "You, um—you haven't happened to see my..." He scratches his jaw. "My girlfriend around, have you?"

Silas's eyebrow shoots up in question. *Your girlfriend?* He knows full well it's Logan's pride refusing to disconnect what they both know is the truth. Still, it makes him hot with *something*. A covetous burn in his throat that he's forced to swallow. What Silas's mouth won't say, his face certainly does, and all of a sudden my voice is in his ear again. *'Remember, discrete'.*

He feels cornered, because, *yes*, of course he's seen me. In every sense of the word, in every position my body would allow, up close, underneath him, most recently sauntering away from the door of his pod wearing *his* clothing.

Silas realizes he actually hasn't said one full word to Logan since the conversation began, and Logan must too, because the longer the silence drags the more accusatory the glances become.

Silas opens his mouth to say something, but just as he does the door to the hall swings open, and out of the corner of his eye, just over Logan's shoulder, he sees me pad inside.

He nods in my direction and Logan turns around.

The expression on my face isn't exactly mortification when I realize what I walked smack into—but it's close. Silas's eyes are pleading for reprieve, while Logan's gleam in relief.

I press two fingers to my temple as I plod toward them, smiling sheepishly, trading glances back and forth between both men as I try to figure out what the fuck their conversation looked like before I came through the doors.

Logan sighs, mitigated for the time being. "Fuck, there you are," he says, reaching toward me awkwardly, and then dropping his arms when I don't embrace him. "What happened yesterday? Where—where did you go?"

He studies my silence for a second, and then looks back at Silas again as he tries to hide the frantic tone of his voice behind a laugh.

This is more than obviously a discussion meant to be between myself and Logan, but Silas still lingers. Unable to allow himself to let us alone together whether it be selfishness, or possessiveness. He feels that *Logan*, if anyone, should be the one to feel on the outskirts of this now.

I look up and down from the copious amounts of food in Silas's arms to his darkening eyes, and I want so badly to devour them both. I hold his gaze for a second too long before I fit it back on Logan.

"Around." I shrug. "Floating, here and there. I slept in the library, it's quiet." Silas catches himself involuntarily nodding along with my story like he's corroborating it, and Logan squints at that.

"The library?" Logan scoffs. "You're being serious? I've been going nuts looking for you, do you know that? All night. You can't just—disappear for a full spin and leave me in the dark." Logan glances at Silas again and then gives me a subtle, confused, *'why is he still here?'* kind of look. It's more than unusual that Silas hasn't yet dismissed himself from this personal conversation, and I sense that, even though I know why.

"That looks heavy, Silas," I say to him, gesturing to the contents in his arms and trying to speak to him through my stare. I know he understands me and he's just being difficult, reluctant to give me and Logan this private space.

"Don't keep her waiting." Logan winks at him, and for the first time Silas shoots him a genuine, appeased smile.

"Wouldn't dare," Silas boasts, finally moving his feet and making his way closer to the door. "I think we're both actually due for a shower."

"Atta boy," Logan hoots at him.

I crush my chin to my chest and stare at the floor as a hot wave of embarrassment douses me. For fuck's sake.

Silas is pleased with himself as he escapes to the exit. I turn to watch him leave and he finds my eyes a final time before he steps out, tilting his neck and shrugging his shoulders suggestively. I can hear him in my ear now too. *"Don't take long."*

When I turn back to Logan his exterior is no longer bright and presumptive, the false mood he laid on Silas is long gone and replaced with something sullen and expectant.

"Hitchhiking?" he bleats, motioning toward the duffel bag hanging from my shoulder.

I sigh and hoist the bag further up my arm. "I thought it would be easier this way," I tell him. "Less taking up each other's space."

"You still don't think this is a little fucking insane?"

"Logan it's been one fucking day, I told you—" I start to raise my voice and then catch myself. "I told you not to wait around."

"We're floating in space, Lize. Look—look at all these people." He points around the room. "They're all traveling just like us, they all know in three spins life resumes. Why don't you know that too?"

I want to shake him. This clueless, naive man that I'm leaving as collateral damage in my wake. I see the sadness buried in his eyes, the flame blown out behind his pupils. He can't quite see yet how this is not in his favor, that there's an impenetrable force that will always send him careening away.

"You gotta let me go," I murmur, because there's nothing else to say. I reach and squeeze his hand once, giving him a sorry smile as I back away. "I'll be around, don't worry about me."

"Eliza."

He tries to get my attention again when I turn to leave, but I ignore my name being called. His voice echoes once more, and this time the sound of it gets cut off when the doors to the hall swing closed behind me.

It's quiet in the communal bathroom. The only sound being the rhythmic pitter-patter of water speckling the floor behind shower curtains and the occasional rubber squeak of my shoes on wet tile.

The glass of the mirrors are fogged to the point that all I can see is my smudged form as I pass, and the collar of my turtleneck sticks to me uncomfortably. Sweat slicks the nape of my neck and plasters my hair to it.

Several curtains are closed, meaning occupied, as I search for a sign of Silas or his belongings—weary not to snoop too close to a random traveler and give them an unwanted shock.

"Silas," I whisper as I walk along. For whatever reason my steps turn to tip toes. "Sy, it's me," I project a little louder.

I walk a few steps further to the end of the row with no sign of him before I stop and start to turn around.

"Silas, where are—"

An arm shoots out from behind the curtain I'm standing in front of and grips my elbow, pulling me into the stall hurriedly. Before I can protest there's a warm, wet hand over my mouth, and he's ushering me backwards against the wall.

My eyes soften when I see Silas's playful smile and the beading drops of water hanging from the dark hair over his forehead.

He replaces his palm with his mouth, licking me open immediately. I taste mint mixed with a tiny tinge of leftover coffee, and it melts me. I slide my fingers through the long, soaked locks behind his ears and tug him closer, opening wider as if he could crawl inside of me, I'd let him. He presses his bare chest against mine, and I can feel the strong, sinewy muscles through the layers I'm still wearing.

"My clothes are soaked." I chuckle as I break free. I thought my outfit was clinging to me in the humidity, but now it's painted to my skin like paper-mache from my collarbones to my ankles. The stream of water from the shower head covers us both, warm and welcoming.

"Not a problem," he mumbles, snapping the clips down off my overalls. He rolls them past my hips, then over my knees and shins until I can step out of the drenched cloth. When he stands, he takes my mouth again and I wrap my arms around his strong shoulders, shuddering as he trails his fingertips up my hips and rib cage to slide the hem of my shirt over my head.

Silas guides me back into the cold tile of the wall when I'm finally naked, then reaches around to feel my ass in both his palms and spreads it eagerly. I smile into his mouth.

"You're gonna fuck me in this shower?" I tease, nipping at his ear, kissing down the thick vein of his neck. "So *discrete.*"

He pulls my hand from around his neck and guides it down onto his cock; urging me to wrap my palm tightly around the heavy length of it. "You see what you do to me?" he asks, grunting against my shoulder when I angle my palm and pump him slowly, up and down.

"Yeah." I gasp. "You get so fucking hard."

Silas sighs and chuckles, it sounds mischievous. I nearly lose my footing when he dips to suck a pebbled nipple into his mouth and bites down on the peak.

"You know nothing about discretion, perfect girl," he assures me. "I saw you that day, right here in these showers." I let go of his dick as he lifts me to straddle his hips. "Cowering like a shy foal behind the curtain when I caught you gawking at me."

He takes my other breast into his mouth and laps at it, tugging the bud with his teeth and curling his tongue tauntingly.

"*Fuck,*" I groan. The water is rushing against Silas's back and falling in hot lines down my chest. It loosens all my muscles and makes me pliant in his arms. "You saw me?"

"Mmmm," he hums, mouth still latched onto my chest. The vibration fucking unravels me. I feel the lash of his tongue pulling at nerves I didn't know possible. In my mouth, in the pit of my stomach, in the dips and folds of my pussy where they haven't already been sparked to life. "I know when there's a hen in a fox den," he mouths, working his way up the center of me, back to my neck, to my lips.

I nestle my hand between our bodies and touch him again, running a thumb over the weeping head where it's waiting patiently at the cusp of my legs. "So what are you waiting for?"

I ask as I notch the thick tip of him between the wet, wanting lips of my cunt, sliding it over my clit. "Devour me."

Silas smiles as he thrusts inside, catching the noises that leave my throat in his mouth. The soft groans reach a higher pitch as he stretches me completely and rocks his hips hard enough to hit the deepest part of my core in one swift stroke.

"Tight little thing," he grits through his teeth, pulling back and then sheathing himself entirely again, opening me around him as my walls pulse and contract to adjust.

"You love it." I moan, crossing my ankles over the tail of his spine. I lean back against the wall in a way that the shower pours down hard on my chest and pools where my body and Silas's connect.

He does love it, watching himself fuck me. The sheer size of his dick looks like it devastates me with every in and out. The gorgeous way my lips frame the thick of it, sucking him in and fluttering like wings when he pulls back. He can't help himself when he fucks me harder, crushing my spine into the wall. He has to wrap a hand around my back when he realizes it, so that his knuckles take the brunt.

"Does that feel good?" He mocks me when I quiet my cries with my teeth sunk into my bottom lip. I only nod to him. "Don't get shy on me, Birdie, go ahead and touch yourself."

He adjusts to let me slip two soft fingers down against my clit, but the water itself is playing with me enough; the tormenting flow of the stream licking at my cunt while Silas spears into me steadily.

I'm floating on it, the perfect fill of him running over the plush edges inside of me, rubbing deliciously over and over again. Then the tandem of my fingers and the shower, and even the cool mix of the tiles as I'm rutted up against the wall. It all makes my eyes roll back.

Silas feels me clench around him, a hot rush of slick coating deep thrust after deep thrust, and he loses it too—squeezing one of my breasts with his free hand to keep himself planted. I bray at the pain but he hushes me—his palm over my mouth again, still hammering his hips up into mine just as rawly.

"If you keep chirping like that, everyone will know you're here, little bird," he whispers. So I bite down into the skin of his hand to quiet the next string of sobs.

I have one forearm slung over his shoulder, bracing behind his neck where my fingertips leave divots in the skin there. The fingers of my other hand spin tight, frantic circles into my clit. I'm so fucking close I can feel the untwisting of the cork begin. The push and pull is paralyzing. My lips are parted in a permanent circle beneath his palm, and Silas gets sloppy—dropping me down a bit and stabbing into me where the ridged head of his cock bumps flawlessly against the soft spot right inside the mouth of my cunt.

"Don't stop—right there, Sy," I cry out. I shirk his hand away and fill the humid stall of the shower with breathless pleading as he fucks me so perfectly.

Silas buries his nose into the valley of my breasts and groans hoarsely, quieting his own desperation as his orgasm sneaks up and overcomes him.

Oh, those sounds I make.

Whining for *him*.

Pleading for *him*.

The supple way his name tumbles off my lips when he's *owning* me in this way.

"Come inside me, Silas. Please, come for me," I beg. There's no keeping him at bay after that.

He unleashes, barreling his hips hard between the spread of my legs as the final string pulls tight on his shaft and snaps forward, jettying his seed in ropes, pumping me *full, full, full* until my body answers back in long tight spasms.

"Fuck—*me*," Silas curses as he feels me go rigid. My legs and pussy flex tight until there's no air left in my lungs, and his own knees feel weak from the passing adrenaline as it filters out of him.

When he finally puts me down, I wobble, steadying myself with two palms against his chest. I can't help but lean forward with my forehead to his neck and giggle. We're both filthier now than when we got in the shower. Exercising the fact that we're nearly *incapable* of discretion so clearly that it's a joke.

He swipes a few wet strands of hair off my forehead where they're stuck and chuckles with me, wrapping his arms around my shoulders and pulling me closer to his chest.

We stand there under the stream of water for a while in silence, just holding onto one another and swaying gently. I realize in this moment that the steady thump of his heart is my favorite sound, my favorite feeling against my skin. It reminds me he's real, he's here—and it reminds me that I am too. A beacon, illuminating from within his body that shows me that no matter the circumstance, I'm where I'm supposed to be. As long as I'm with Silas, I'm home.

He leans down eventually and plants a long kiss to my hair, rubbing his thumb back and forth against my shoulder blade.

"Please tell me you brought some soap," he murmurs. I tuck my head into his shoulder and nod my head, laughing against his skin.

15
MODICUM

It's enigmatic, the way space works. We're always floating. Whether it be on a transport, or on a planet—in circles around a sun. If we're on a moon, we can still float in the skies of that atmosphere. On a pod or in a ship—even then we're floating above a floating rock.

Floating toward something—or not.

Floating forever.

Silas and I stop for a prolonged second in the observatory, pausing the rush back to his vessel, hair still damp from the shower and risking our secrecy just to stare out the window together. The Otera has finally shown up like a distant splotch in the inky black canvas outside, floating too, like a promise to be fulfilled.

This transport *is* going to dock there. I *am* going to begin again with Silas, having become a fuller version of myself since the last time I stepped foot on that soil. He and I, a lock and key together that opens a new door previously sealed to everything worthwhile in life. All of these promises are so near that I squint one eye, reach my fingers out to the glass, and *pinch* them.

My coffee is cold now, but I drink it indulgently, with all the intention of a woman content to never sleep again. We both needed this refuel after running ourselves ragged over taste and touch, until our animalistic energy withered to mere paw prints. Even Silas, who I swore would never weaken, lays full-bellied with a new brightness in his complexion when we finally get the chance to eat together.

"My eyes were bigger than my stomach," he says, huffing a tired, satiated sigh despite the full spread of food still in front of us.

I grunt agreeably, rolling from my stomach to my back on the bed. "I almost mauled you at the concession."

I can't see him where he's sitting up behind me, but he smirks. Silas loves the easy way we both have slipped into the only form of domesticity available. Eating together in his little home, bathing with one another, star gazing over thoughts of the future regardless of the rush and go of it all.

We're *trying* to hold back all of these instinctual emotions, drenching them in a coat of inconspicuousness for the time being—but it's an eclipse; you might have to squint to see it, but no matter how hard the moon may try, it can't completely cloak the sun.

"A bold move that would have been from the preacher of discretion," he teases. "Though I'm inclined to believe Logan still wouldn't have put two and two together."

"He sees you as a friend."

"What a frightening illusion."

I roll my eyes playfully and sit up, scooting closer to him. I don't know if this feeling will ever subside, the spark that accompanies being physically present with Silas, being able to exist in the same setting as him after all this time trapped within the walls of my own subconscious.

Still, I look at him and think: *what a vivid dream.*

I find the need to reach out and touch him, so I trace the whitened flesh of his scarred temple to remind myself he's real.

"An accident when I was a child," Silas confides, and my expression softens.

"Not makoing?"

"Those scars are internal." His guise is unchanged, smiling even over the grimness of it.

It pains me, that despite knowing each other physically—intrinsically—Silas and I are still learning one another comprehensively. All his scars have a story I've not yet heard, the years of his life carry a tone I'm not yet familiar with. I want to know everything about him in this way, too.

His favorite song, his father's name, what he's afraid of, if he's ever been in love. I want to know what made him *mine*—and why.

"Will you show me your treasure?" I ask, leaning down and kissing the half moon mark slanting over his brow. He chases my lips when I sit back, pecking me softly once and nodding his head before standing from the bed.

Across the pod in a storage trunk Silas pulls out a metal case. It's bigger than I expected, but still compact enough to carry with you during travels. He fusses around with it a minute, codes the lock open, and when the cover lifts I can see a glint of golden sheen reflected against the deep greens of his eyes.

"The second most beautiful thing I've ever seen." He winks, motioning his head to the side to cue me over.

"Oh, wow," I mutter as I take it all in.

Shining talismans, jewelry, iridescent green and blue stones, some small, some large. There's things I don't recognize, metals and coins—currency we don't even trade in the main systems.

And then, *gems.*

Gorgeous and demanding, like nothing I've ever seen before. I know as I look that they must be the reason Silas had been on this dig in the first place. Each bulbous oval is translucent to the center, a resplendent core beaming indigo from within it's organic shell. The colors move and glimmer, never resting. Every crystal laid tenderly in foam encasing, each their own shape and size, all more magnificent than the next.

"This is all from your past trip on Dandorma?" I ask.

"Mhm," he hums, stretching his one arm out to the table top to perch on it. He presses his chest softly against my back and looks at the crystalline trove over my shoulder. "The Pulp, however, is much less appealing than the rest of its mother system."

I reach out to touch them, but flinch before I do; unsure the etiquette surrounding it, or if Silas would even want me to in the first place. He sees my hesitation and reaches forward to pick one up for me. It fits perfectly when he drops it in the palm of my hand.

"Heavier than I thought," I admit, smiling back at Silas who seems beyond beguiled, like he's watching his entire world slide together like the teeth of a zipper. I'm curious, and I know Silas won't mind my asking, "I've never seen crystal raw like this, how much is it all worth?"

"You can never be sure. Rates change, supply and demand." He clicks his tongue. "But if things are the same on the buyer's front as they were on my last visit to the Ote, these pearls should be valued at twenty thousand tally."

"Twenty *thousand*?" I enunciate, mouth dropping open like a gaping fish. A twenty thousand tally in any system is striking at riches. Enough for stable comfort and then some if you spent it right.

"Well I have some people I owe a visit to, things I've gotta square away yet," he tells me right off. There's an air of hesitation in that admission. A dimming light in his eyes that passes as quickly as a shooting star.

"And then, *you're gone*," I murmur, remembering what he said that night in the hallway. The first time we were alone together. "I would be gone too with that tally."

"Where would you go?" He watches me put the bulb of crystal back in its cradle, then helps me clasp the case together and puts it back in the chest.

"Everywhere," I marvel. "All the places I've never seen before, but have always read about in books—Prayda system, Corfix system, visit the Ghost Earth in the Solar system." I migrate toward the galactic map Silas has hanging on his wall, running my finger over the clusters of stars, and then pictures he has pinned to the canvas.

"There are still humans there," he jokes, and I sigh out a laugh. "Ancestral roots."

"Everything worth taking from that planet ended up on a ship to the Otera hundreds and hundreds of years ago."

He grunts in agreement.

I stop on a photo of a group of people, recognizing a younger, thinner Silas hanging off the end of the bunch with a sideways smile on his face. They all look to be in good spirits, arms slung around one another, dimpled cheeks. Four men including Silas, and a younger dark haired woman, all dressed in muted greens and grays, red trees blooming sky high behind them.

"Kreda moon," Silas confirms my pondering before I have to ask. "This is Seela." He points at the woman. "Taysh and Lars." The two men standing on either side of her. He stares at the third unnamed man in the photo standing next to him for an extended second. I can see his tongue running back and forth against his bottom teeth between his parted lips. "That's Croy," he finally says.

"Partners?"

"Something like that, Birdie." He smirks. The brief anguish I saw in his gaze is stomped out like a tiny flame. I decide not to press for an explanation. We have all the time in the world to talk about it.

"I envy your travel," I confess. "Have you been to the Glades?"

Silas points a finger at the map where the Glades are tucked into a swirling constellation, and I note there's no pin in place. "I have not. Mako's frequent that land though. There's a native flower called lonokontiko that's worth its weight in petals for many men on the Otera. It's rare. The locals tend to harvest it before anyone else can, though. Their uses are much more... practical."

"What is it used for?"

"It's medicinal." He grins. "Mostly."

My eyes round in surprise. "A drug?" I whisper, as if anyone but Silas may hear me.

He chuckles and pushes a stray strand of hair behind my ear, keeping his palm on my cheek after he does. "A very powerful one, Eliza. When the seeds aren't diluted."

"Maker," I breathe, feeling a certain embarrassment at my naivety. "I feel *connected* to the Glades, somehow. I loved it there. I already want to go back."

"Then we'll do it," he says, matter-of-factly. "We'll go."

"It's not that simple."

"Then we'll stay." He shrugs.

"That's not simple either."

Silas ushers himself against me, wrapping his arms around my waist. "I have yet to find anything worthwhile that can be described as simple, Birdie."

"I assumed you hated the Otera," I mumble into his chest.

"I hate the people," he corrects me.

"Yeah, well, my family is just about as Oterian as it gets—hard to please, incorrigible. They're already less than happy Logan and I flew off without a plan to begin with. My mother called it irresponsible, and immature. Logan could afford to step away from work, but my employment history has been a series of freelancing skills. Photography, tutoring, linguistics. I hate to admit that Logan's been a willing but substantial benefactor."

"And when you return *sans* Logan—"

"Exactly. They won't understand this." I sigh, unwinding my limbs from where they've tangled around Silas's neck. I traipse back toward the bed again and sit. "The same way Logan can't understand this."

This is something I was afraid of, maybe even subliminally from the very first time I saw Silas. That he fits perfectly to me, a jigsaw piece snapping into place—but even so, no one can solve a puzzle on a vertical plane.

Silas sits beside me, putting his hand over mine and rubbing his thumb into the skin. "They're your family though, would they not want to see you happy?"

"It's not about happiness," I concede, lips downcast into a sad smile. "It's the principle. They probably imagine I can be happy with anyone if the price is right."

"They must not know that soulmates exist then," Silas counters, lifting my chin up between his thumb and the knuckle of his forefinger. "Or neither were lucky enough to find theirs." He leans down to press his lips to mine and soothe my up-ticking anxiety, breaking only when he feels me curl into him. "These feelings are not futile, Eliza, they're rooted and watered. We were always meant to grow this way, it's divine nature."

He's right, of course. Before I even knew Silas existed, he was my everything. Tucked away in the lucid musings of my brain, winding like a mercurial vine there. This isn't something my body knows how to reject even if it wanted to, and if anything, this trip has shown me that our pull to one another is magnetic. The closer we are to each other the more tenacious the clash.

The more vivid the dream becomes.

"You're so metaphorical," I murmur, leaning in to bump his nose with mine. "It's sexy."

"Is that right?" He kisses me again, sliding his tongue between my lips as soon as I part them. "I've got more," he promises. "Plenty."

I giggle as he leans me backward and crawls between my legs, laying on top of me. I open my knees to frame his hips and my ankles curl around his thighs, pulling him up all the way until his pelvis meets mine. It's intimate, I feel grounded by the weight of him, less worried about the forthcoming storms we'll have to weather.

"You haven't told me about your family," I say, twirling a strand of his long hair around my pointer finger. "Where are they?"

"I don't know," Silas admits. He's leaning on an elbow so as not to crush me completely underneath him. "I was an orphan. Family has never been defined by blood for me."

"For your entire childhood?" My eyebrow shoots up inquisitively, mouth sloping into a frown.

"The market is small for abandoned, defected children." He points to the mismatched blue and green colors of his eyes. I can't imagine anyone seeing them as anything but extraordinary.

"Oh, Silas." I wallow, combing my fingers through his tousled locks as a comfort.

"As a teenager I was free to do as I pleased though. I found myself more often than not bouncing from system to system with the wrong company—but it was company nonetheless. A togetherness that was unprecedented to me, so despite how toxic or dangerous it became, I was averse to giving it up."

"So how did you become a Mako?"

"It was somewhat dropped in my lap," Silas says. I see hesitation in his features while he thinks of his next words, sucking his bottom lip between his teeth. "I hadn't two tally to show for myself, sleeping on the floor of anyone's pod who would have me, withering away. And then one day that friend just so happened to need a partner for a dig, and I was the willing, willful body that would have done just about anything for a hot meal."

"So you went," I say.

He nods. "I had nothing to lose. I had never makoed before, I didn't even have the gear necessary, and by the end of my first swing to Dandorma my person was so beat up I couldn't recognize my own face in a mirror."

"Well it worked out for you, didn't it?" I gesture to the chest across the room, to the hidden loot with the potential to offer Silas a brand new life if he wanted it.

"I had my feet swept out from under me—my dome rattled several times before I learned to defend myself out there. Crews chewed me up and spit me out, stole everything I ever managed to harvest. I was lucky to be left alive on occasion."

"Why didn't you stop sooner then? If it was so dangerous?" My eyes are blown wide, somehow angry with him for putting himself in those situations, despite knowing he escaped clean. Despite him laying here against me, safe and loved where he's meant to be.

He frowns. "The money was never steady, but it was something—and if I happened to hit it big on a harvest, well, then it was all close to worth it." I nod like I understand, but he stops me with a shake of his head. "Back then, Birdie, I was mindless. Young and cocksure, I'd never had money of my own and I went ahead and squandered every pinch of it time and again. Betting halls, gambling stakes—in my head if I lost everything I could just find it again. Another trip back out to the wild was all."

He seems almost embarrassed about this admission, like he's struggling with spoiling the facade of himself that I've grown in love with.

There's these layers of *darkness* behind him, that he's flowered with fiction and poetry so I can't see the beds they've grown from.

I knew Silas's past wasn't dollied and coddled in the way mine may have been. That there was something that must have pushed him into a life of solitude and zig-zagged meandering, but I wouldn't have surmised he was *forced* into it.

My Silas, always floating, just like the rest of the universe. Not exactly sure where he's going, but believing blindly in a reason behind it. Floating towards me, I realize, and toward the

Otera where this time, he can finally stop—where everything will finally feel grounded.

"That's who you have to pay visits to," I understand now. "All the rest of the people you owe."

"The very last of my debts."

"Who do you work for now?"

I see a muscle twitch in his jaw. He looks down and studies a fraying thread in the sheets underneath my hair, picking at it like it's tedious work.

"Myself." Half truth. "This last trip was for me."

I run a thumb across the bone of his cheek, quelling the fevered skin there as he watches me for a reaction.

Truthfully, Silas could have told me any string of unbecoming things about his past, and I would still recant them. He's never lied to me, remembering now how even before we were together he'd disclosed his pattern of violent misgivings when it came to his trade. It was never a deterrent, more of a welcomed candor, something to remind me that Silas was in fact true and real, not just a figment of my wildest imagination.

"You'll have no part of it," he tells me, eyes dimming a shade darker. "And I wouldn't blame you if the veracity of my past made you question me."

"I trust you," I whisper, hugging him closer to my body. "We're so close to the end of all of this."

Silas reaches out to hold my cheek in his palm, pressing his forehead to mine. "I don't believe our meeting on this transport was coincidental."

I nod against him. "I'm sure now that nothing is."

Silas likes me naked in more ways than the physical. He wants to strip me down to the bare wonderment of my brain and make love to all the dips and curves within my head. It's an alluring chaos when he gets to have both.

It's late.

We slept the afternoon away, but now he kisses desperately into the wells of my collarbones, feeling the points of my puckered breasts against the skin of his chest as he does. My body is damp with sweat and gliding against his, the slick between my thighs coats his pelvis where I grind hard into him, hoping to feel a hint of wanton satisfaction.

"Go on," Silas urges, reaching down to touch himself, pumping his own shaft between my legs as it's aching for me to tell him his next move.

"And then he..." I swallow. "He fucked me with his fingers, slowly, until I begged for the rest of him."

I'm reading to him, my own intimate interactions from dreams written in the pages of my journal. He groans against my breasts, I can feel the twitch of his cock against my hip.

I knew this would happen when he suggested it, wanting to hear more of the dreams I'd kept hidden from him on the Continental. To hear the filth of it.

He presses two thick fingers to my mouth and I open, letting him slide them against my tongue. I suck and lick swirls around the skin, and then he pulls them out and uses them on me, curling those two adept fingers inside of my cunt as I gasp for the air it pulls from my lungs.

"Make those pretty little noises for me, Eliza—*fuck.*" He closes his mouth over the cap of my breast, sucking at it messily while his fingers prod me in and out.

There's something about the twist of them, the way they scissor the soft skin inside of me, stroking and stroking that most sensitive curve. I cry out unabashed, the slip of his knuckles catching all the right nerves, and I *hear* myself get impossibly more soaked. I feel my walls expand as they try to suck him further in.

Silas wants that tightness choking his cock. He's pulled taut, straining against nothing—it's a bundling knot low in his stomach that tightens every time I moan praise through parted lips.

"Maker that feels good, Sy." I gasp. "Fuck you feel *so* good." I squirm my hips up and down to feel that full friction, but it's not enough.

"I know you want more," he instigates me. His thumb connects with my clit and I moan as my spine bends toward the touch. "Let me give you more."

"Yes, I want it." I nod, teeth clamping down shyly into my bottom lip. "I want all of it."

He barely has to rock into me twice before I'm hitting a wall, knees knocking hard against his ribs on both sides to stop the trembling. Silas fucks me through that first orgasm, then pulls me up and onto his lap, kissing my lips raw while he draws a softer, more sensual second out of me.

I'm floating too, just like him. Just like everything. Not sure which way is up or down, only anchored by the gravity that is Silas.

And what a fine way to be.

Where else on this transport is there to go and sulk besides the bar?

At least the world is still moving around him, people chatting and eating. He's not sitting alone in the pod, or walking up and down the hyper-lit hallways looking for me.

It's normal, Logan thinks. For a guy to be having a drink at a bar by himself.

It's alluring, even.

The handsome, anomalous man wiping the sweat of condensation off his cold glass, sitting alone—but is he alone? Or is he waiting for someone? There's a mystery to him. He could still *attract* someone like this, like he did back before he met me.

Logan clears his throat and looks around the room, taking a long swig of the beer in front of him as he does.

How could something as sweet and beautiful as our relationship go so intensely wrong like this? He's calculated it over and over in his head. When my mood started to change, what cues he might have missed. He fucked up that day that he didn't take me to the Continental, this he knows is a fact. There's been something off about me since I came back from that moon. It changed things.

A few stools to his left a woman sits down, fussing with the shawl on her shoulders and folding it over the back of the chair. He recognizes her, tonight she's in a teal blue dress that makes her dark skin look silken. The first time he saw her she was wearing gold. The natural fullness of her hair hides her face a bit, but Logan is sure it's her. He watches anyway until she feels him staring and looks up.

"Do you need something?" Mori asks, annoyed that she's not even been sitting for a full minute and already fending off prying eyes. The men on this ship are pigs, all of them.

"I'm sorry." Logan chuckles. "I recognized you, that's all."

"Well I don't recognize you," she tells him, turning away and smiling at the bartender who slides a wide mouthed martini glass in front of her.

"You know Silas," he says, wiggling his eyebrows. She glances at Logan out of the corner of her eye. "I guess he's probably on his way here to meet you."

"You must have me and the other girl mixed up," she says flatly, her mouth hovering over the lip of her drink before she takes a sip.

"Oh shit." Logan winces, holding his palms out apologetically. "I saw him this morning covered in hickey's and I thought..." He stops. "I didn't know he was getting around."

"All I know is his partner found out about me a few spins ago and she flipped out." Mori rolls her eyes and taps her long fingernails against the outside of the glass. "I guess they must have reconciled."

"I don't think he has a partner," Logan corrects her. "He's traveling alone."

"Whatever she was then." She waves it off. "But, if they can work it out after that, I'm sure anyone can."

Logan's brows thread together, he hums a confused noise and takes another long, gulping drink. Silas is an aberration. He supposes it makes sense that someone so odd and outcast might keep parts of his life private. Maybe even an entire relationship if it was rocky enough to begin with.

"Guess we're both having a hard time at love then," he says to Mori, lifting his glass in toast to them both.

"Sure." She squints, but before she can lift her glass another man greets her, kisses her on both cheeks and takes the seat between her and Logan.

"Cheers," he mumbles to himself. He finishes the last of his drink as he stands, and then takes off, on his way to find me in the library and try his luck again.

16
INTERLUDE

There's waking up next to Silas, and then there's being *woken up* by Silas.

My starving, voracious lover pressing the full swell of his cock into my satiated, slumbrous body. Being stirred awake by the soft pleasure of his lips on my neck, his nose nuzzled into the back of my ear, whispering syrupy staccato, letting it drip off his tongue.

"I couldn't wait to be inside you again."

A tumble of quiet coo's as they fall from his throat onto my skin makes me gasp, and I reach back to hold his head down into the crook of my shoulder. He's fucking me so slowly, deliberately, like he never wants this to end. As if he would give all the hours in his day to me and him in this bed, so perfectly entangled with one another. Just the warmth of my back against his chest, my hips in the palms of his hands, and the cacophonous rhythm of early morning, hushed panting, and the soft steady roll of his heavy length inside of me.

Again, again, again.

My voice is hoarse, unused yet. The meek noises I'm making for him are needy and babbling, they catch and crack, finding a different pitch than Silas is used to hearing; and he loves these new noises. He loves this unsung language I speak to him that only he understands.

"That's a pretty sound, Birdie," he rasps. "You make the—*fuck,* the prettiest sounds."

He holds me open, the bend of my knee in his hand, his fingers digging hard into the flesh there and it stings in the best way. There are bruises still tender and unhealed that he grazes over again, new ones blossoming with every squeeze of restraint that he focuses into his fingertips.

Because he wants to fuck me harder than this.

He always wants to fuck me *more*. Pour all his love into me in every way he knows how—through his words, through his actions, through poetry, through his body. It never had anywhere to go before, and now it does.

I roll my hips back. It's a dance we both sway to—a tango of second nature with the perfect partner. Silas reads my mind, to the left, spin, *dip*.

"S-so...*good*." I shudder, turning to open my wanting mouth to him and he curls over me to catch it with his own. This changes things, pushes him deeper inside me, touches a part of me that was only being teased until now, and Silas feels it too.

The thick rush of slick to my sex that invites him in further tears his breath away and leaves him gasping in return. I consume him, wet and fevered and *saccharine*. It tugs away, licking a heat up his spine, hardening his cock to steel, testing how deep he can give himself to me, and I feel every inch. Feel it in my throat.

"Take it," he whispers. "Take it all." And then, broken: "*Please.*"

Silas controls everything, but still he begs for me in ways that make it feel like I hold all the power. As if I'd ever deny him—ever wish for less than what he's giving me.

I answer in terse nods, threading my fingers into his hair to brace my body, tethering close to him while he drives into me.

He pulls my thigh across his own, hooking my calf over his knee and giving me one hard thrust. We react together;

two harmonious groans of satisfaction when he's completely sheathed inside the tight cup of my cunt.

My breathing shallows while his deepens, as he doesn't dare to move just yet. Afraid the tie will snap too soon. He's too wound up, too inundated, he won't get to feel *this* anymore if he moves, because he'll come, and he can't give that up without pleasing me first.

Silas knows we can't stay here forever, but *Maker*, he will fucking push it. There's another spin ahead of us, a whole day to be lived beyond the heat of these sheets, and he wants to live this day with me—adding it to all the infinite days we will spend together. But if only for a minute, he wants it all to freeze. He wants nothing to exist but him and I, so that he can *give and give and give* me all this love he has inside of him in the most devout way he knows how.

If I recite the scripture, he'll write it on my body with his tongue, burning trails of his faithfulness into me.

He's not moving, and I whine in protest. The throbbing walls inside me weep for friction, contracting in a vice hold around his cock to quell the overwhelming stretch.

Fuck, I just want him to take what's his.

I writhe and he groans in my ear, pressing his heavy palm against the skin between my belly and my core and *holding* me—splaying his fingers out and keeping me from moving underneath them.

"Don't move, Eliza," he grunts. "I can't control myself."

"Silas..." I drop my head back against the damp skin of his shoulder and he peppers feather light kisses to my cheek and the corner of my mouth. "Silas it's...you're...you're too much. I—it's a lot."

His hand on my core snakes up my body, paying small swirls of attention to my nipples with his fingers. I don't regret the way my spine bends in reaction, pressing back against him, pulling him into my body even further, though we both thought it impossible.

I hear him growl through gritted teeth, the hum tickles my jaw, and then he bites down, suppressing that guttural drawl before he gives himself away.

"Fucking—*please*. Just, please move for me Sy. Just—"

I turn my neck and kiss him, slotting my tongue between his teeth and silencing my own cries before they become possessed. The clash is so messy, as everything with Silas is.

Always dripping in honey and hungry.

Even the soft and intimate way he takes me from behind right now, barely out of sleep, malleable, sticky with arousal—has become desperate.

Silas moves, rocking in and out of me. It's barely enough to call it friction, but still I feel it in every nerve ending like a live wire. My stomach goes taut, legs tense, I reach down to touch myself, playing little circles into my own clit, and I *feel him* under the heel of my palm. That's how deep Silas presses inside of me. Just the realization makes me moan, and he's right there with his mouth over mine to steal the sound away.

"Flawless," he murmurs, sliding his hand from my chest to my collarbone, settling it at the base of my neck. "Fucking celestial being, I can't...I can't stop myself with you."

I whimper when his fingers tighten around my pulse. He devours me in every way he can, keeping me close to his body, under the weight of his arms, his palm, toying with air to my Maker damned lungs.

"Fuck me, Silas," I choke out. He thrusts his hips back and forth again at my words and we both hiss. "Take control and *fuck* me."

His teeth drag over my jaw, catching my bottom lip between them. "Is that what you want?" He's teasing despite the way his cock throbs and his hips teeter languidly in and out of me. "Eliza, I will fuck you brainless—is that what you want?" His grip tightens on my throat.

"*Fuck yes.* Yes, I want it," I mumble. Silas hits that deep soft spot inside me on a stroke *once, twice, three times,* but doesn't change his pace and it's debilitating and mocking. I feel my skin prickle and my core suck on him needily. "I want it so much."

He lets go of my neck and pats my hip, gingerly lifting my leg back over his as he nips and kisses a line down my shoulder. "On your stomach," he commands me. "Now."

Silas pulls out abruptly, leaving me clenching around nothing as the loss of him sets my limbs on edge and my spine on fire. My cunt grasps and flutters against itself and I flip without hesitation to my belly while he settles behind me. He straddles my thighs, the thick shaft of his cock laying hard and heavy between the meat of my ass. "Lift these hips for me, Birdie. Show me that perfect pussy."

I whine into the give of his pillows as he kneads me open, swiping his thumbs through my center, parting the lips of my cunt as I drip onto his fingers.

I'm so vulnerable this way. Silas's entire weight holding me down, my legs pressed tight together between his two strong thighs. He leans over, trailing open mouthed kisses across the blades of my shoulders and the wet tickle of his hair sends goosebumps up my body as he moves.

"Inside me, Silas," I demand with my last hanging thread of composure. "Now."

The deep hum of his chuckle on my skin makes me bite my lip. "Querulous woman," he nips. "I own you right now."

I feel the drag of his cock as he taps it against my opening, taunting. The fingers of one hand pulling the tight space between my legs open, the others wrapped mercilessly around himself as he slots into my core.

"Fucking always," I sigh. It breaks into a high pitched whimper when he breaches me again, spearing my wet seam open over his tip. "You own me always."

When he sinks all the way to the hilt he doesn't wait this time, he moves punishingly, hoarse groans attached to the beating sound of him hard against my ass. He pushes my hips down against the bed to keep me exactly where he needs me. Unable to move or writhe or fidget from his hold. I'm completely helpless to the way he jackhammers his hips down into my body.

"*Maker*," he grates through pursed lips. "Oh....*shit*."

Silas can feel the sweat beading on his forehead and as it trickles down the planes of his back. I am a fucking vision, splayed across his sheets like this. Ass bouncing every time he fucks into me, the hardly audible screams of pleasure I'm releasing into the plush of his pillows, my blonde hair matted to my neck. He reaches down and pulls it, pulls me up so he can see my face, even if only from the side.

"This what you wanted, little bird?" Silas mumbles, and it sounds aggressive against the symphony of slaps as he ruts his hips even faster. He's not even sure if he's expecting an answer. He's just speeding toward a rapidly approaching wall with no breaks.

"*Mhm*—oh fuck, there, right *there*." There's a threat of tears spiking at the corners of my eyes as Silas pulls my hair tighter, but the pain is welcome. It shoots down my back and to my core and plucks me there. I feel the pressure like a dam about to break.

"Play with yourself," he tells me. "Fucking play with yourself Birdie, I'm gonna—"

He lets my hair go to grab onto my shoulders with both hands, my back arches to support it, hips lifting up toward him more.

"*Fuck*...oh my *fuck*."

It's a perfect slide, grinding against the deep, soft spot inside me that sends white light to my irises and cancels out all the noise in the background. My head is swimming, floating, I lose track of where I am.

"Come on my cock. That's it, dream girl, I feel it, I feel you—-*fuck*." Silas is just as fucked out as I am, holding on to this with shaking thighs and trembling fingertips because he wants me to milk him dry. He's waiting with his jaw clenched and teeth grinding together for my cunt to grip and choke and suck him empty.

I reach down to rub my clit and it's instantaneous. My mind goes numb, my body goes numb, and all I know is that I'm shaking. Shaking and coming and crying into the hold in Silas's pod as he thrusts me through it, until I can't take it anymore.

"Please...please, please come for me Silas. Fuck, I want it."

He lets it go, stops reaching for the nonexistent breaks and *crashes* full force into that wall—emptying himself into me with short, hard thrusts of his hips that my pussy *pulls and pulls and pulls* out of him. Every overstimulated spasm of my core bleeds him, taking everything he has to give me.

I close my eyes again, trying to breathe in any kind of steady rhythm, but my body denies it. It's all shuddering, short puffs of breath and a harsh gasp when Silas unsheaths himself from me, collapsing down next to my body, cock still half hard against his hip and *covered* in the both of us.

I peek a tired eye open to see him. Chest heaving, the firm gut of his stomach glistening with sweat and sticky dampened hair. He runs a hand down his face and sighs, lolling his head to look at me.

"Good morning." He smiles.

I twist toward him, laying my cheek on my folded forearms. "Good morning," I hum back.

17
MALFEASANCE

Silas walks several steps ahead of me down the transport corridor. He's far enough away that it doesn't look like we're together in stride, and my nose is dipped behind a half opened book as if I'm reading, mildly discouraging any type of passing affiliation.

Just a woman entranced in a book—walking slowly down a hallway. The same hallway, coincidentally, as a man who despite all her dagger-eyed glares, keeps turning back to look at her.

"Silas." My whispered warning sounds like shards of glass hitting the tile. "Turn around." I register his tiny smirk before he faces forward again, throwing his hands up in surrender.

This was his idea. A '*get us out of the pod*' idea.

He had told me that time would move faster if we weren't both staring at a clock from his bed, counting the passing minutes until the ship hits the Ote.

A spin and a half, just a mere meteors throw away.

He still has several books to return to the transport library before departure, most he hasn't even managed through the prologue—too busy tending to his own unfolding story. And there we can both coexist in the same public setting, somewhat concurrently, without raising any eyebrows. There'll be no questioning Silas fingering through the spines of a few hundred novels, and according to me the reading room has doubled as my motel the past two nights anyway. It makes sense if we're both there.

The dull thud of the metal door closing behind me is barely audible, nor is the scrape of my shoes across the carpet and into the aisles. It's quiet, naturally. I see Silas in the corner at the return counter, already steps ahead and remaining aloof as he slides the hardcovers through the slot.

It's so juvenile, the way we both giggle and avert our eyes when we steal a glance. I'm pretending to ogle at the book bindings on the shelf ahead of me, but haven't yet read the title of even one, happily distracted by the man I'm keeping at a distance. Flirting like teenagers.

Instead of dawdling around, I disappear between the cases, out of Silas's sight for the time being while he squares his own affairs away. The library is scarce in new age fiction but bountiful elsewhere. Several genres and languages, the classics of every system obtained in their own neat sections. I scan as I walk, running my finger delicately over the spines. Growing up on the Otera and through schooling I studied various dialects, but some of these publications escape even my realm of knowledge.

Trailing deeper, my eyes wander across the sections of anthologies and nonfiction, stopping to take in all the names of government officials, notable speakers and historical figures that adorn the bibliographies. All these celebrated lives that people wanted to read about and learn from.

I try to imagine having the kind of existence that would garner being immortalized in print. One where even hundreds of years after I've passed, some species, somewhere in the galaxy might be reading about the significance of the life I lived from the small confines of a transport library.

Sneaking a look back through the shelves I can see the outline of Silas standing there, the soft edges of his faded tee tight against the broad span of his back. He's still fiddling around where I first found him, keying things into the machine, probably leaving reviews on the books he returned without reading—he's read them all before anyway.

I smile to myself, then return to dusting the forgotten dissertations with a sly fingertip as I peruse along the cases. I don't really know what I'm looking for, nothing actually. Just a hopeful distraction to take up the slow drawl of time, to keep me out of Silas's pod long enough to stretch my limbs and recover from the raw ache he leaves when he waxes his love into my body.

The books start to fade into informational text: dictionary, encyclopedia, galactic atlases. There's an obvious air of disuse to them. People traveling have every one of these resources at their fingertips in a comm tablet if they need it, it's understandable to see them long forgotten here.

I crouch down and read the titles. There are several alphabetically anthologized series, but one specifically catches my eye.

Intimacy and Intergalactic Definition.

It seems silly for a moment, but soon enough I'm plopping down on the rough, gray patterned carpet with the encyclopedia on my lap, flipping the index open to muse through.

D.

Dalai Lama..

..Dionysus

Divine Love..

And so on through the lettered table of contents. I sigh and curse dejectedly under my breath. There's nothing about dream lovers, or dream connections. As far as I'm concerned, Silas and I are a singular case. I've never met another person who openly found their destined partner through unconscious fantasy—nor has it ever been heard of apparently.

I close the cover, blowing a quiet raspberry through my lips. Maybe I'm naive to think there would ever be any kind of answer to this. It's more than enough to know that somewhere in this universe there's a defining force constantly pulling two incomplete people together, and that Silas and I know as much is true.

The uncanny circumstances of our meeting, the undeniable attraction, the resemblance to the person we've loved and nurtured with our entire souls since adolescence.

There is more to this than even books know to be written about.

I'll never stop thanking the cosmos for giving me Silas, but in the same breath that I've learned of its graciousness, I've also been taught of its blatant discourtesy.

I can have him, surely, but it will be a test. I can love him, wholly, but not without giving up something else. The universe has given me everything I've ever wanted on a silver platter paired with both a fork and a dagger—a fatal ultimatum from the very minute Silas walked through those elevator doors: indulge or it will kill me.

I open the text again, echoes of Silas's voice guiding me across the index this time to the organized 'S' column. I hum in unsurprised approval.

Soulmates.

By literal definition, although never formally recognized as such, the page reads:

"The word soulmate signifies a unique affinity with deep love toward one specific person. It also refers to the mating of two souls, or the mystical notion of one soul shared in two physical bodies."

Below it, a categorical telling of several myths and paths of soulmates as told throughout the universe. Stories from the Hellenistic age on the Ghost Earth, origins of ancient deities, the winding relics of souls crossed through still practiced religions. Maker themself has even left higher powered fingerprints on the idea of romantic twins.

I'm perplexed to read through them all, growing more and more persuaded with the authenticity of my bond to Silas as the lines fold into themselves, article after article. I don't even hear him approach.

"Come here often?"

My eyes flicker up from the page to Silas leaning against the corner of the bookcase. Arms crossed over his chest, ankle over ankle, beaming down at where he found me on the floor.

"Cheesy." I snort, still completely tickled by it nonetheless.

"Some light reading?" he jokes again, pointing at the incredibly thick block of encyclopedia on my lap. The book must weigh as much as my head.

I motion to the floor next to me, and Silas looks around the library once with a skeptical eye before pushing off the bookcase to take a seat at my side.

"There *are* benches here," he chimes. "Couches even. This library is quite the misprized gem on the freighter."

"You carry this thing to a couch." I huff, struggling to pick the book up and show off the weight in my arms.

"Fair enough."

Silas grins as he scans the subject of the open page, charmed by the seemingly never ending ways I find purchase and tug at his heart. The woman he loves is sitting cross-legged in a library, reading of soulmates, recounting it to him. It's incomparable to any dream he could have conjured himself.

"It says in a myth here that soulmates were once one singular being, four arms and four legs, circular bodies that cartwheeled everywhere they went," I point out. "They threatened to take over the heavens, so Zeus had them split in half, and they were so desperate to find each other and reconnect their love, that they became unable to survive without the other."

"And he felt pity for them." Silas continues without even looking down at the page. "So Zeus straightened their bodies, which made it possible for them to, at the very least, breed. Humans now lose themselves in intimacy. Falling in love without realizing that the intense desire to feel completed is inherently normal. We all have an ingrained necessity to seek out the other half of our souls."

"I should have known you'd already read about this," I say, nudging his shoulder with my own.

"Of course I have." He smiles as his thumb traces little circles into my thigh. "I've exhausted the galaxy in search of you—perhaps that's why you're here now. A prize of perseverance."

I hum a satisfied noise, threading my fingers through his on my lap. It's possible, I think, that Silas and I had filtered through all determined pre-destiny. That the universe recognized I was ready for him, and he had more than deserved it.

"Do you believe that story?" I ask.

Silas clicks his tongue. "I have an aversion to the novelty that two individuals must be able to procreate to be soulmates."

"It's impractical," I agree.

"But this one," he points to another subset of the script, "is on the right track." I glance at the text and Silas explains it to me while I read along. "*Twin* souls, predestined by a higher power for one another before birth. Sometimes one soul arrives galaxy-side before the other, which is conceivable in an age difference."

"I'd find it hard to believe that one entity predetermines *every* soul mate."

"That's precisely my own skepticism, Birdie."

I close the book again, huffing out a sigh. Frustrated not at the lack of information, but the reasoning. There's no understanding of this beyond my own imagination, because that's where it lives. And maybe there *are* other people that have experienced this notion of soulmates, but never through a primordial lens.

"I've actually come into a belief myself," Silas says. "Maker approving."

"Oh yeah?"

"At the very least we can contrive that the universe is an omniscient presence," he tells me. I nod. "We are created from nothing, seemingly, but no—that can't be true, can it? We've always been here."

"And where would *here* be, Sy?" I giggle at the twinkle in his stare, the passionate reverie he's presenting.

"The stars."

"The stars?" I wiggle my eyebrows.

"Mhm," he confirms. "There are an imperceivable number of stars in this universe, each made up of two core elements. When one inevitably burns out, the other stagnates to survive—searching for its missing half until it too, perishes. And then the star itself becomes invisible, it just—disappears."

"Stardust," I interject. "It becomes something else."

"Or *someone* else." Silas shrugs. "Two dependent elements separated after millions of years, their dust will always pull in the same direction."

"So you're saying we were born from the same star?"

"That I am." He nods. "Created from the same stardust. As is every person with a star of their own, but you are mine."

This makes sense, for an odd untraceable reason—and suddenly the entirety of the universe makes sense along with it. Every single being created from a timeless repertoire of stars, floating somewhere in the universe—until they're not. Floating until they explode in supernovae and become magnetic, iridescent constellations bred into new life, bound to connect again with their missing particles.

I pull Silas's knuckles to my lips and kiss them each softly, then open up his palm and lean my cheek into the warm, calloused skin.

"Then what about the dreams?" I ask lightly. It's not a matter of being unconvinced, I'm simply just engrossed in Silas's elaboration.

"There lies my greatest supposition, Birdie. But if the universe can conspire, why can't it also leave us clues?"

I grin, biting my lip happily. A whisper of a giggle blends through the breath of my nose. "I think you're right," I say. "Screw this encyclopedia."

I shuck it off my legs and pop back onto my feet. Silas is slower on the limber, but he rises as well, catching my waist in a soft hug and pulling me against his chest.

When I lean in, I kiss the soft hair on his jaw, looking up at him with glossy, mischievous eyes. Then I do it again.

He watches me through his lashes as my lips tease further to his pulse, pinching his lids closed and biting his tongue when my chaste ministrations turn heady. I'm all warm mouth and wet tongue, soothing the rapid flow of blood racing down his neck and elsewhere.

"Careful now, little bird," he warns reluctantly. "You never know what's lurking in the brush."

I pull away and pout, stepping a few paces backward to force the physical distance. Silas is a voice of reason, but that sentiment only goes so far. The undeniable bulge putting pressure on the seam of his pants tells another story. My lips curve into a pleased grin, and he knows exactly why.

"In a library?" I fake a dramatic gasp and hold my outstretched fingers to my mouth.

He rolls his eyes and purses his lips.

"Is this another one of your dream fantasies?" I tease, drawing lines with my fingers against the book spines on the shelf. "Book Guy."

He snorts. "It'd be like fucking you in a church."

I shrug, using my longest finger to hook the top of a novel and pull it from its perch, letting it crash to the floor between us.

"Oops," I squeak.

Silas's tongue darts out on his bottom lip.

I bend at the waist, matching his gaze on the way down and letting the scoop of my collar hang dangerously low across my breasts. I don't miss it when he swallows a low groan as I reach for the book.

"Sacrilegious," he murmurs.

I slide the book back into its place and sigh. He's watching me with incredulous eyes, knowing full well that the siren of a woman in front of him will sing until he's coaxed into dangerous waters.

"An athenaeum of worship," I mumble, turning my back to him. I take a few steps before knocking another novel from the shelf onto the floor. "Who is your goddess?"

I bend again to pick up the strewn paperback, but before I can stand upright my body is being crowded into the book case, chest pressed hard against the cool metal shelving.

"Enough, Eliza," Silas growls in my ear. The warm fan of his breath tickles my cheek as his nose grazes my hairline. He bites down on the soft lobe and I grin playfully, biting the corner of my own lip.

Silas hardly gives me room to move, but I manage a slow writhe of my ass into the cusp of his hips, teasing his length that's stiff and trapped between our two bodies. He answers with slithering hands up the sides of my rib-cage, kneading my breasts hard enough that the meat of them spills between his thick fingers, even through my shirt.

But then he quickly abandons that. Instead, shoving his hands impatiently beneath the thin material of my neckline and bra, splaying his palms over the bare, pointed peaks of my chest.

"*Shit.*" I whine, arching forward and pushing harder against his grip. Those meticulously trained fingers pinch my nipples and roll them tightly between the tips.

"This is my church, Birdie," he whispers to me, dropping his lips into the crook of my neck and lathing an open mouthed kiss to my pulse. "I think I'd like to see you on your knees."

I twist in his hold to face him, so close that our noses brush from the proximity, and Silas leans forward with both arms on either side of my head to cage me in. I'm watching his lips, that plush mouth quirked up in a knowing smirk, parted a bit in the middle and awaiting my next move. Instead of kissing him, I take a handful of his thick swell in my little palm and hum when his breath hitches.

Silas tries to swoop forward and catch my mouth with his own, but sooner than he can, I drop, leaving him staggering to steady himself and looking down into my devious blue eyes as I blink up.

The rest of his body betrays his tongue, because I am Silas's goddess, the eternal shrine he's always worshipped at the feet of in his mind.

My mouth falls open when he reaches down and skates his thumb across my bottom lip. He dips it lower to my chin, and holds the point of my jaw between two fingers. "So pretty like this," he murmurs, then moves his hand to the base of my neck below my ear, stretching his fingers out through the tangle of my hair. "So fucking—"

Silas lets go of me suddenly, turning away on a whim and shuffling across the narrow aisle a fair distance away.

"What are you—" I begin to quiz, but the sound of my name ringing closer than comfort raises the hair on my neck.

I turn to see Logan as he rounds the slim corner of the bookcase and my stomach drops.

"Ah, I thought I heard..." His voice tapers, eyes moving from myself to Silas across the way when he notices I'm not alone. "Something, over here."

"Yeah—hi." I clear my throat as I stand up, putting more distance between Silas and I and taking a few steps closer to Logan. I pinch the bridge of my nose and thank the higher powers of makoing for giving my lover a keen sense of surrounding.

"You weren't, uh—you weren't here last night," Logan says, scratching the back of his neck. He's focusing more on Silas now than he is me. "You said you would be here."

"Right, well I was—are..." I shake my head at him. "Wait, are you *following* me?"

Logan nods a short hello to Silas who's circled back to stand closer. "That's a bit harsh." He huffs. "I'm worried about you. Is that terrible?"

"I told you to stop worrying."

My tone is accusing and fiery, partly because I've been caught off guard, but mostly because I'm mad at *myself*. I could have just fucked this whole thing up by being careless and clouded. Breaking my own rules in a public place for a book-ended quickie.

"You two hanging out or something?" He changes the subject, wagging a finger between Silas and I.

Silas looks at me first for guidance, not because he feels caught, or on the spot, but because this is my line to cast, and he's content to just wade in the water until I need him. But when I do nothing but shake my head and look back at him, he takes the reins.

"I had a few books to return before tomorrow," Silas says, sticking to his guns of sincerity. "Eliza was right here when I found her."

"Binging encyclopedia," Logan digs at me. "And you say I'm not supposed to worry."

"Do you need something from her?" Silas asks, sliding his foot directly across the still wet line of comfort he'd just painted.

"Do you?" Logan squares with him.

"Stop." I step in front of Logan, pressing my hands to his chest.

Silas grinds his teeth together, simmering on the hot coals of Logan's imposition. He sees him as a loud and clumsy animal in the wild, strutting around with a haughty arrogance to match his size, territorial and heavy headed. But even a predator is no match for a stealthy prey, especially one he never sees coming.

"Can I talk to you?" Logan ushers me in the direction he came, toward the front of the library. "Just for a few minutes."

I need to splash cold water onto this, so I agree, nodding my head and following him back around the bookcase. I shoot Silas an apologetic look as he watches me disappear.

"What's up?" I implore once we've pushed into an open sitting area.

Logan seems antsy, tucking his golden hair behind his ears. "I don't really know how to say this to you, Lize," he mumbles, keeping his voice down. "But I don't want you around Silas."

"Excuse me?"

"I got to talking to someone last night," he says. "I know the guy's been nice enough to us, but he's got other shit going on. Do you know he's with someone?"

My eyes narrow. "Who said that?"

"Remember that woman he was with, like—the first night he got here? Really good looking, in the gold dress."

"Yeah, yeah." I stop him.

"She said his *partner* flipped out on him when she found out he fucked around on her." My eyes widen and Logan nods, completely unaware of the reason. "He's just doing his rounds on this transport, making up for seven cycles of jerking himself off in the woods."

"Don't be an asshole," I chastise. "So, what are you saying?"

"All I'm saying is, who knows what he's in here trying to pull with you? He's not a good guy, Lize."

"You don't know anything about him." I shake my head and turn to walk away. "I'm a big girl Logan, I can take care of myself."

I put a considerable distance between us before I breathe again, rushing to the door without giving it a second glance back or even looking around for Silas. I know he'll understand the exit if he hadn't somehow already heard the back and forth.

A spin and a half. I almost fucked this all up with only a spin and a half to go.

"Where are you going now?" Logan raises his voice as I get further away.

"Anywhere that's not here!" I shout back.

18
RECKONING

There's an eerie quiet about his pod now, and Logan fucking hates it.

He's spent next to no time here in the last two spins, because it's just a sick reminder of everything that's been unceremoniously ripped from his life.

All my stuff is still tucked away in crates and bins, sadistically fanning his flames of false hope—and Logan sits at the edge of the tousled bed and stares at it. He wouldn't dare touch it. *Maker forbid I come back to him, see the error in my thought process, realize I miss him just as much as he misses me.*

There's too many things unsaid, too much air underneath it all.

When the freighter hits the mainland it will be different. I'll need to talk to him. To explain this to him, and to everyone undoubtedly waiting for our return on the other end. If he can't reason with me, my family can, our friends can. It's easy now for me to take off into a corner of the ship and avoid him, but this isn't *real*. This is a lull in time, an overzealous hiatus between two places.

Come tomorrow everything will be on it's path back to normal.

Logan looks tiredly around the room and brushes his hands through his thick locks. *The pod has been a mess since I left.*

Things are scattered everywhere, mostly in his own desperate fit of grief that first night I didn't return, and he knows he unfortunately can't leave it this way for arrival at the Otera.

He kicks over an empty bottle at his feet with a sigh before standing from the bed, reluctantly beginning to organize the throws of his displeasure into their original homes.

Piloting manuals back on their podium, communication devices plugged into portals on the wall. He bends down in front of the cooler unit and slides the hatch open. "Fucking leftovers," he grumbles, pulling the untouched trays of food out and tossing each into the small garbage tucked into the corner of the pod.

There's laundry everywhere, collecting in piles on the floor, thrown over the back of the pilot and copilot chairs, sticking out from the covers of the bed. Logan was never the one to keep things tidy, he realizes as he assesses the room. He can't tell what's dirty or isn't, what belongs in what crate. He pulls the hamper over and flips the top open, sorting haphazardly through the garments in front of him. *Dirty, dirty, clean, pretty much clean, dirty.* Then moves to a different spattering of clothes across the way.

He crouches down and picks up some of my abandoned linens: a little white pair of socks, ratty worn sleep shorts, my tank that's tangled with one of his old t-shirts.

Logan nearly tosses it in the hamper but it catches his eye so he pulls it back—because it *isn't* his.

He can tell from the material alone. It's a faded black compression fabric that he's never once owned. He waves the shirt out like a wrinkled sheet to inspect further, pulling the tag out of the back. It's too old and tattered to read.

"What the *fuck*?" he whispers to himself.

This isn't my shirt either, he's sure of it. We both traveled lightly to begin with, but back in the Glades our wardrobes diminished to abysmal, selling any unnecessary clothing in thrift shops to stretch our tally as far as it would go. There's nothing in this pod that doesn't belong.

Except... *this*. This fucking shirt.

Logan rocks back on his heels and huffs a sigh, trying to rationalize this random article of clothing and what would put it here. He shuffles the remaining laundry around on the floor with his hand and finds nothing else, then looks back in the already full hamper at the rest of my discarded clothes and something—- *clicks.*

That night. I was wearing this the night I snuck out and he was up waiting for me to return. The night I came back and broke things off with him, telling him that ridiculous story about the dreams and the journal or whatever the fuck it was. This shirt wasn't here then, and I didn't take anything like it with me when I left.

Logan goes back over to the bed, sitting down with the garment clenched in both his fists. There's an odd familiarity about it, this plain black tee, weathered from excessive wear, dull where it should be dark. He stares at it for a few seconds and then brings the fabric to his face, sniffing the collar, but all he can make out is *me*. Me, and maybe a tinge of something else, like a foreign soap or—a *protein bar,* maybe. The material is a bit heavier than would be worn casually, but maybe for a specific climate, or profession, like a trade worker.

Yeah—*yeah*. He's definitely seen it before, now that he thinks about it, isn't this the same style of shirt that—

Logan's eyes pinch closed as his head tilts back toward the ceiling.

"You've gotta be fucking kidding me."

"It's like you've never seen a camera before." I grin up at Silas from the puff of his comforter I'm laying on top of. He has the thick leather of my camera straps draped around his neck and down the hard planes of his bare chest, fingers fiddling with the buttons and the twist of the lens.

"Not one with all the bells and whistles," he murmurs, lifting the viewfinder to his eye and looking through it.

He's gorgeous standing above me like this, the scars on his tan skin catching against the dim light from the lamp on his desk, showing off all his naturally earned cuts of muscle. Those soft, dark curls that fill in the space above his cock where it hangs heavy and half hard between his legs.

"They all work the same." I roll my eyes playfully as he looks around the room with the camera attached to his face, giving it all his attention.

I'm jealous in a needy way, cursing the contraption for peaking his curiosity in the small duffel bag of things I brought here. Where there's ever a lull between feeding me and fucking me, Silas hasn't yet filled it with leaving me alone.

I pout, stretching my foot out and softly running it up the inside of his naked thigh.

"Sy..." I whine, coaxing him back to the edge of the bed where I lay nude and wanting. He's already had his way with me twice now since returning from the impromptu rendezvous in the library.

"My horny little bird just couldn't wait to be filled," he had teased, pulling my hips to the edge of the bed and sinking inside me in one easy glide. *"Almost got caught on your knees for me."*

"You wanted it." I bit into his shoulder with a groan. *"Wanted to—to see your cock in my mouth in that library."*

"Dirty girl." He grunted before his lips curled into a smug smile. *"How unfortunate, that picture that was never painted."*

He had heard my conversation with Logan, *of course*, tucking himself into the shadowed crooks of the shelves to get within earshot, waiting on standby if he needed to step in.

"*Mori*," I had said, shooting him a telling look as soon as the door to his pod closed behind me.

"*I heard the whispers.*" He smirked. "*He's still none the wiser. I'm tempted to pity the man over sheer lack of cognitive intelligence.*"

"*Yeah, well you're not exactly making it hard to figure out,*" I pushed. "*'Do you need something from her?' Seriously?*"

"*I will not apologize for possessiveness, Eliza.*" He pulled me by my wrists to stand between his legs. "*All my life you have been the only thing I could truly call my own, and that will not be made an exception.*"

Silas drops the camera slowly to rest against the hood of his stomach, it sways there until it settles and I'm satisfied with the change of attention. His smile is warm, the touch of his fingertips to my knee much more of a candle-waxed burn.

"Can I offer you something, sweetheart?" His voice drips in budding innuendo.

I let the same knee he's putting pressure on fall open, welcoming the cool air against the puffy, tender lips of my core. I'm all shiny and swollen, glistening with the remnants of myself and of him where he still drips out of me. Silas hums contentedly, that familiar darkness shining now through his downcast eyes.

"You're a vision, little bird," he says as he runs a thick finger through the valley there, pushing his spend back inside, making me quiver. He picks the camera up again, lifting the viewfinder to his eye and focusing the lens between my legs. "I should take a picture."

The bright flash stuns a girlish yelp out of me, it makes me giggle and fall back against the sheets with a forearm over my eyes.

"I can finally immortalize you," Silas says. "Something that proves you were really here."

I simper again, shy all of a sudden, as if the flash is showing off any piece of myself he hasn't already burned into his memory. The soft stripes of growth inside my thighs, the peppered fuzz of unseen hair.

"Don't get bashful on me," he teases, crooking a finger to gesture for me to sit up in front of him. I concede, folding back up again, and the height is just about perfect where his dick bobs to life, dripping sticky and hopeful in my eye line.

My lashes flicker up at him, lips parting like they want to ask a question—one that Silas answers with less than a nod of his head. I reach for him, tying my fingers in tight little ropes around it first and then open my mouth and let the velvet beginning of his cock sit heavy on my tongue.

Silas sighs through gritted teeth and lifts the camera again. "You look so pretty with my dick in your mouth, Eliza."

The flash doesn't take though, we're both ripped away from the absorption the same way thunder shakes you awake in the night. Stunned to paralysis by a string of loud thumping knocks on the outside of Silas's door.

He sobers immediately, looking from the hatch to me, then back to the hatch again—waiting to see if the noise was a fluke, but then it returns. The pounding of fist against metal.

"Silas!"

Logan's voice booms from the other side and I scramble up and off the mattress, pulling my discarded clothes from the floor in haste to throw them on. "*Shit*," I whisper. "Fucking *shit*."

Silas is doing the same, not anywhere near as frantically. A slip of his shorts back up his legs, not even bothering with a shirt as he walks toward the door. I shoot him a desperate glare, the blood rushing to my ears drowns out Logan's synchronous pounding against the slide. Silas looks too *cool*, I think. My heart is running a marathon while my lover's is taking a stroll through a park.

He flips the locks and takes one steady breath before pulling the door open enough to peek half of his body outside.

"Is she in there?" Logan roars, jumping down Silas's throat immediately. His face is rubbed red, the veins of his neck pulse angrily and slice into his jaw, swelling past the temples on his head.

"Let's slow down," Silas suggests. He glances down and registers that Logan has his old shirt bunched up in a fist.

"Fuck you," Logan spits back. "Is-she-*fucking*-in there?"

Silas bares his teeth, tilting his head in pressing disapproval. "I'm usually a man attuned in ample mediation," he warns Logan, adding something sinister to his cadence. "But I'll have to forgo those pleasantries if you give me but another reason."

Logan can't see me where I stand, trapped in the shadow behind Silas and the door, but he doesn't need to. It's a lost cause to try to maintain whatever shred of this facade is still dangling. Silas has been too good to me, too patient, too understanding and accommodating. I know he would do it for far longer if I asked—pushing his principles to the wayside and stretching the meaning of his own morality, but it's enough. He's taken enough. Before I have a chance to think about it further, I push past Silas to the forefront of the open door.

"Yes, I'm here," I say, slotting my body between the two men. "I'm right here."

19
INDEMNIFY

TWO SPINS LATER

S ilas stands broad-shouldered and shark-eyed in front of the dirt-licked face of an inn room door. It's a sheisty fucking grovel of a place, a real run down scar in the landscape tucked between a flickering neon vacancy sign and a pier that sticks itself out into the Bartanka pool. Floating unknowns wading in the stagnant current. Black water.

The Otera, like any other place, has its beauty and richness, its pristine contemporary foregrounds and city-like brick and mortars. Busy sidewalks and busy people—but not all is glazed in gold.

There are places you don't go here. Dark corners and alleys, oil slicks of metropolis turned criminal after sun down, shadows with eyes. So long as your business is inconspicuous, and the runoff is sorted with a fine toothed comb, no one comes around asking. Like an unspoken partnership between the pier and its patrons.

There's sooty gravel under Silas's boots, sighing softly with every shift of his weight from side to side—a gentle coaxing, or maybe a muttered warning. *Tread lightly.* He's expected here, on this day, at this time. Eight and a half cycles to the exact hour since he was shucked from the den behind this door into the same dirt he's idling in now.

A heavy case is plastered to his side, hanging from a white knuckled grip on the handle just below his hip. Silas can feel that it's shiny with sweat, so he squeezes harder.

The horizon seems to dim a hue as he waits, turned down like a dial from breezy purple to a deep blue. Suddenly the sky is speckled white with constellations waking up with the system's moons. Far away he can hear the hum of the city, but it's quiet at the foot of this entry way, all whistling wind and the sound of his own tepid breathing.

They do this on purpose, he thinks, to keep him on edge as the time dwindles.

Silas hears the sound of a lock unhinging, and he looks up from the scuff on his boot to a man standing in the open door, dark complexion shadowed further by a pair of dark glasses, his body seemingly the height and width of the entrance itself. The man nods wordlessly to him, tilting his head in invitation toward whatever lay inside.

Silas pauses, taking a final look out at the fog spilling into the black water on the edge of the pier before brushing past and through the portal.

It hasn't changed at all since he was last here, though the circumstances are drastically different. The motel-like hole is a front for a games hall, run in part by Oterian elite paired with an underground syndicate, one of many.

A typical money laundering operation. The wealthy filter gambling gains through legitimate sources in return for a cut of the change and a promise of protection. The bosses at Bartanka take care of any *odds and ends,* for their partners. Threat of competition, loose lips, outstanding balances.

The room is littered with several round, felt-upholstered tables. There's groups of players sitting at each, clinking currency together, shuffling decks, croupiers sliding cards across the green where tally is piled and stacked from the ongoing games.

Most hardly look up at Silas as he traipses through. A thick yellow smog of *something* tints the lighting and darkens the wood frame of the venue to deep timber, tickling his nose. He makes his way across the space, avoiding eye lines in a straightaway to the door at the opposite wall. A man stands there too, the same dark complexion and dark glasses hiding his features as the one who greeted Silas, the same emotionless nod to keep him moving in the right direction.

Silas takes it in stride, pacing quickly to his destination and steering clear of the stage that found him in this mess in the first place. His eyes dart onto the tables as he passes, foreign currency lining the playing fields, a hundred sticky fingers *tap, tap, tapping* on the grain as rounds are dealt.

Some men here are regulars, addicted to the come and go of coin, some are likely planted by the Bartanka to level the turf, some have nothing better to do.

Before Silas meets his destination, an arm juts out to stop him in his tracks. It belongs to a dealer at the head of a table donned in a white button up and black tie. He has a pearly pink scar that stretches from forehead to cheek, slashing through the diagonal of his eye with an iris to match it. Silas locks his jaw when he looks up to address him.

"Hey pal, join us for a game."

The dealer's voice is slow and suggestive, he holds his palms face out, a deck of cards in one, the slimy insinuation of non choice in the other.

Silas lifts his eyes to the guard across the room again, feeling out the test, fingers pulsing around the vice grip on his case, to which he gets no expressional answer. Like the option is only his.

He knew that this wouldn't be as cut and dry as it should be. He could never just quietly pay his debts and then disappear. There's a power display to be had, and too many people watching not to make an example out of the lone Mako playing sycophant.

He shakes his head. "I apologize, but I do have business elsewhere tonight."

"I know your business," the dealer implies as his eyes scrape the metal encasement molded to Silas's fingers. "No harm in a round."

Silas sticks his tongue in his cheek, then brings the wet muscle out to dampen his lower lip. The gallery has slowed to all but a stop, games put on hold within earshot to tune into the exchange. His presence is an intrusion—that's blatant. It hangs heavy in the putrefied air all around him, and for a man well versed in violent interaction, Silas is less than reluctant to engage in it here. He knows he's outnumbered.

"I must decline again, friend." He smears on a duplicitous smile to balm the interaction. "My funds are null, I can't provide a fair game to these gentlemen."

Silas waves in the direction of the patrons already seated at the gaming table, several rounds into the night and gussied up in currency they *can* afford to lose. A privilege Silas doesn't have, nor does he wish for any longer in his life. There has been too much *change* these last eleven spins. Perhaps if things had gone differently, perhaps if he hadn't a reason to stay on the Otera now.

"The house will cover you." The dealer pulls out the chair next to him for Silas with a resounding rumble against the floorboards.

"That's a bit counter-intuitive for me," he tries again. There's a thick knot bundling low in his throat like a spool, twisting around the painful realization that this is not an offer to be had, but a demand to be met. "As you said, you know my business here."

The dealer pulls the chair out further, nodding down to the worn wooden bench. "Have a seat, pirate."

✦

Silas doesn't win.

Quazze is a quick game of luck, but it should have been no surprise from where he sat that the luck had run out a long time ago. He was out a thousand tally from the ante-up alone. A beginning bet that set the pace for all three card flips of the game, and by the end of it, Bartanka was adding a mark of three thousand to the bill Silas already owed.

When he's finally ushered through the door of the back room, there's far less burning a hole in his gems case than he anticipated. The harvest that was once abundantly his own dissipating without ever being touched.

Here, there's another table. An empty chair on one side for Silas, the other on the opposite already occupied by a familiar sinister face, hefty and bulbous, greased like the bottom of a sheet pan.

Bazrin Bartanka in all his glory is illuminated by the singular bright spotlight hanging by a chain from the ceiling. Silas sits down and is blinded by it, squinting to the point of impairment. He can only make out the other shadowy figures planted to each corner of the room through the shelter of his eyelashes.

"Silas," Baz booms, a crack of humor to his voice. "I hear you owe me some more money."

Silas shifts the case onto his lap, laying his hands over the width of it. "Reputedly."

"Quazze should have felt like home for you—an easy win to shirk your debts a bit."

Silas chuckles lowly. He knows there was a fix at that table to kick him one more time while he was already down. He could have played a hundred rounds and would have come up short each time.

"I'm not the man I used to be, I suppose."

Baz shifts in his seat and leans forward. Silas can see his eyes now, muddy brown and bloodshot, prickling sweat dotting his upper brows. The room is temperate, but the suit jacket wrapped around and struggling to cinch at his waist looks like it could be cutting dire circulation to the boss's brain.

"How could you be after seven cycles in a fucking pit." Baz spit laughs. Silas sees the precipitation like a dusting across the table under the light. "How'd the pollen treat you this time?"

"As unkindly as it always has, but well worth the trade to be free of any encumbrance put on myself." Silas plays with the dials on the case, cueing in a code that beeps and unlocks. "I have your arrears."

"So quick to get the business underway." Baz shoos him. "Let me enjoy the view. The biggest shit-stain on my reputation coming clean before my eyes."

Silas catches his tongue between his teeth and swallows a thick film at the back of his throat.

"I liked you and your buddy. The funny looking guy, what was his name?"

"Croy." Silas tenses visibly.

"Croy! You two kept it all very entertaining here—had the place figured out, I'll give it to you." He clears his throat. "But all good things must end, you know that."

"I have what I owe," Silas pushes again, opening the case toward the man across the table. "Take your pick."

"Strike a nerve?" Baz asks, his gravelly voice is followed by a yellow grin.

Silas sits silently, holding a stern, unfazed position. He isn't here to relive the recklessness of what feels like several lifetimes ago, nor does his stomach let him regret the events of it any longer.

How could he? That would mean regretting what led him to me.

Baz remains smug as he lifts a hand and flicks two fingers toward the table. One of the men in the room steps forward with a monocle and inspects the contents of the case, moving swiftly from the gold coins and smaller stones to the more demanding and vibrant crystal gems that take up more than half the box. He measures color, clarity and weight, twisting them each around between his fingers and holding them close to the light, then further away. Each piece in the case, one at a time.

When the observation is over, the man leans down to ear level with Baz, whispering something inaudible to the boss who looks to be melting like a candle opposite Silas.

"You continue to impress me, pirate," Bartanka concedes. Silas brushes off the insult for the second time tonight. "Brains and brawn. It's what's kept you valuable—and alive. My guess is in more circumstances than this one."

"Perhaps," Silas agrees, gesturing to the case again. "What'll it be?"

"All of it," Baz tells him without skipping a beat.

Silas releases a humored breath through his nose and shakes his head. "This is worth nearly double what I owe you."

"You owed me ten thousand. You lost your round of Quazze on my coin and now you owe me thirteen."

"It still doesn't add up," Silas interjects, losing more patience than he has.

It was a clear plot of retribution, a robbery far more flagrant. This was all he had, a final comfortable living, a handful of thousands to start anew here or there and put the years of peril behind him. It's what Silas promised himself, what he promised me.

"The rest is interest accrued."

"Interest for what? I'm here, within the decennial rotation as discussed. It would have taken half the time if not—"

"If not for your own recklessness!" Baz raises his voice. "Let me guess, if only you had a partner? Well, lucky you to have been the smooth talker of the two, or you may have found your positions switched and your body adding soil to the black water as your friend's is now."

Silas grinds his teeth and shakes off the wave of rising hairs at the back of his neck.

The last time he was in this room, was also the last time he saw his previous partner alive. Silas struggles now to hide the anguish that accompanies reliving that night. The way the light in Croy's crystal eyes flickered out as he was forced to look on. The tile floor that's currently pristine underneath his feet, then spattered in bright red. Silas's wrists ache in remembrance of the cold shackles that kept him tethered to the very chair he presently sits in.

He should feel ashamed, that for the last cycle and a half the thought of Croy has not but whispered through his mind. Nothing like those previous seven on the Pulp, when the shrill echo of his friend's screaming, bones breaking under pressure, played like a metronome in his mind. When Silas wasn't digging, it was worse. Any moment he allowed himself solace to replenish or tend to his split fingers, he was only reminded that he'd not shed nearly enough blood.

Croy was a hopeful friend, a reliable dig partner and audacious personality that always bit off more than he could chew. He and Silas had formed a bond of sorts over time, running in the same waves of crew, belonging to no one in particular, fighting similar demons. Mako was not a livelihood so much as it was a lifestyle, and when they realized they could make double their earnings through tipping each other off at the gambling tables, the pair made out like bandits. Leaving Bartanka none the wiser.

Silas had warned Croy though—it was too many subtle glances, too many shared tables. They were supposed to be strangers, acquaintances at best. Unfortunately for Silas, circumspection was not his partner's strongest suit.

Later, Croy took a contract on Dandorma from an undisclosed client. A trove had apparently been discovered deep within the Shamzren Root Forest that would take several cycles and steady hands to extract, but the pay-off would be more than worth the work. He and Silas agreed to dig together, to split the wealth and then triple it on the tables. Croy boasted about the prospect, unaware that the very client that hired him was the man he and Silas had taken to conning.

Bazrin Bartanka has eyes and ears everywhere, particularly on the men he's trusting to employ. Before Silas and Croy had even outfitted the pod for departure, they were being dragged into this very office to be made examples of. Silas was the only one to walk out, with the invisible shackle of a solo dig on the Pulp, and an expectation to pay back every tally the two had swindled in exchange for his life.

"And for his demise I will make payment until my dying day," Silas says through gritted teeth. "Thirteen, that is what I can agree on."

"I'll offer you the chance to think otherwise." Baz leans in close to the table again, nodding his head toward Silas. The men around the room to take several steps toward where he's sitting, closing the gaps like predator stalks prey.

Silas allows his eyes to close for a second as a fleeting image of my face passes behind his eyelids.

He would be worth something for me. The only sparkling string of connection tethering him to the ground. Gone are the flightless throes of indirection, the ways in which he has escaped conflict all his life because nothing ever *mattered*. Silas never needed to atone, never needed to be luminary of anything—but now it's the only reverential thing he aspires for. My acceptance, my love, to be able to say I was proud to have shared a sacred attachment.

Silas closes the case in front of him, the lock clicking tightly as he does, and Baz's face falls from expectant to indignant, almost as if he's disappointed it has to go this way. But Silas can't allow it otherwise.

"Unfortunately my pride is no petty thing," he says, bunching his palms into fists on the table as the looming guards close him in.

TWO SPINS EARLIER

Logan paces back and forth a short distance in the empty hallway. One hand pinching the wrinkle on the brow of his nose, the other stuck like glue to his hip.

I fucked someone else, right here on this transport, under his nose, and he should have seen it earlier but it wasn't *like me,* to do that. So why would he?

Silas is leaning against the wall, arms crossed over his muscular chest, his old ratty t-shirt clutched in his hand as he watches the breakdown unfold. He *would* feel bad for Logan. If it wasn't me—if it wasn't him. If this wasn't inevitable, and he didn't have to pretend to play a martyr for my sake.

I'm caught red handed. Bared and vulnerable, trembling through the false front that this isn't tearing through my heart just like it is Logan's. It's like a jagged puncture wound getting caught in all the deepest places. I've tried to pull the spear out through explanation, but it just snags at things that never hurt before I started unsheathing, deepening the gash.

I was drawn to him. I tried to stay away. I will always care about you. He's not who you think he is.

"He's exactly who I think he is." Logan points a finger in Silas's direction, but doesn't give him the respect of eye contact. "He's a stray fucking dog playing lost puppy on this transport. Just looking for someone to scoop him up and take care of him, so that he can feel better about himself."

"You should look a man in the eye when you speak with malevolence." Silas steps away from the wall and in Logan's direction. Letting him know this won't be a one sided conversation where his own character is concerned. That while he's respected my wishes and remained cordial to feign discretion, there's no longer a cause for apprehension.

"Silas," I chide quietly, lightly touching my palm to his chest. He catches my pleading gaze with his own hankered one, and I can see the deep confliction shrouding those ocean eyes.

I know the man that is my lover viscerally. How he thinks, feels, the deep hungered way he loves. The thick, threaded connection rooted in both of our bodies that makes him desperate to provide, to protect, to make proud. Silas cares only for me in the purest, most passionate ways.

I drop my hand when he pushes softly past me. Putting little distance between himself and Logan who rolls his shoulders back dramatically at the close quarters.

"If it's a dispute between you and I that needs to be remedied, let's see it through then. Man to man," Silas offers.

"It's not between the two of you," I point out, exasperatedly. "I did this, Logan. I made my own decision—this is between you and I."

Logan ignores my address, crowding even closer to Silas as a show of size and speaking directly into his face. "And what kind of man are you, to fuck my girl and then shake my hand before your fingers were even dry?"

Silas has a practiced type of patience. Bred from years on the dig, hours spent on his hands and knees extracting from the earth, slow work and gentle forbearance. He weaponizes the tightly pulled string that is Logan's temper, and recognizes that he can win this cock fight without any outward act of brutality. Simply because, *he already has me*. A reality Logan is refusing to live in, acting out against in mocking innuendo and crude misogyny. The woman he thought was his, isn't, and hasn't been, and never will be again.

"You have nothing to offer her and you know that," Logan adds harshly, sticking his finger out to poke Silas's chest and holding it there. "Just some straggler cock and infinite Shakespearean wisdom—don't be fucking selfish."

Silas flicks his tongue out to peruse along his bottom lip, shirked slightly by the fish hook of veracity in Logan's words. He doesn't have as much to offer me as Logan does. That's an unfortunate truth. The simmering guilt of things still undisclosed between Silas and I heats gradually in his gut over it now.

I never asked who or why when it came to his past, so he never told me. It was self-serving in the most dignified definition of the word. Silas never wanted to worry me over things that didn't involve me. Over his own missteps in life, his own qualms to aid. He never wanted me to even hear whispers of the name Bartanka because I was too good, and pure, and beautiful and *safe* for that. That was a dark, dagger-headed piece of his existence I would never be subjected to.

"You don't know what Silas has." I scowl at Logan, the fire of my own possessiveness dipped in petrol and set ablaze. "You don't know what kind of life he's lived."

Logan lets out a condescending huff. "What are you going to do? Take her with you to the wild every time you're strapped for tally? Put her in danger over and over again, digging in some dirt just so you can pay to share a fucking meal?"

Silas drops his eyes toward the floor, briefly, before bringing them back up. A faint, unwelcome sweat flares at the nape of his neck, pins and needles pepper the palms of his hands.

"She *belongs* somewhere, she deserves to feel like she belongs." Logan's assaulting finger against Silas's pulse starts to feel more like the sharp tip of a knife, digging. "*You* don't belong anywhere—don't make that her fate too."

It's more than an empty insult that Silas can contradict, and that knife at his chest feels twisted now. Carving slowly and burning hot into the cavity of his chest, stealing the channel for air to come and go.

He *doesn't* belong anywhere, he never has. The only thing Silas has ever known of belonging is with me, and that's selfish in and of itself; to put so much weight unto someone else, to drag me down that same path. I do belong somewhere, Logan's right—I belong with family, and friends, with stability and hopefulness. Not a castaway in the stars being pulled from one system to the next. Or worse, forced to a place I can't escape because of Silas.

I can see the heft of Logan's words on Silas's shoulders. Pressing him down to a smaller, sodden version of his usual vivacious self.

"You know that's not true." I reach up and pull his chin to me. "Hey—look at me. You belong right here. I belong right here."

Silas nods at my admission with a sad smile. The conflict in his eyes now turned to something more regretful, angst-riddled.

Despite the love seeping from us both, grand and alive and so full to the brim it spills from our every pore just trying to find a place to go—it's not enough. I have roots in him, but I have roots elsewhere too, and he can't dig that up.

The realization burns him, and for the first time, Silas has an anger he doesn't know how to expel taking up all the extra space in his brain. A dangerous fight or flight that's leaning precariously toward the former, and for that I'll have to forgive him in time.

"It must feel like shit Logan," Silas rasps, intent to low blow the man in front of him. To instigate an altercation for his own fucked up reasons. "That she never truly loved you—that it's always been me."

Where Silas is looking for a reaction, he gets one. The already riled up and petulant side of Logan surfaces forthright as he sends Silas stuttering backward with a sharp shove to his chest.

"Shut your fucking mouth," Logan barks.

Silas meets it with an inauspicious grin, like he's happy for the excuse, exulted to participate in the physical back and forth. Not only as a show of his own strength, but as a stress relief. It's like a switch flips and he's the man he was back on the Pulp again. Dangerous, primitive. Unrelenting.

+✦

NOW

"There's no reason to get killed over a box of rocks here, Silas."
Silas turns from his back to his side where he's crumpled over on the floor, holding his rib cage tenderly. He spits a build up of saliva and blood onto the dirty tile and looks up through swollen eyes at Baz sitting in his chair across the table, unbothered. Where Silas thought the single overhead light was blinding while he was upright—this angle, searing into his bruised face from the ground, is damn near debilitating.

He doesn't answer the boss, just lets his head dip down to rest and closes his eyes. He knows there isn't a way out of this room with the treasure he owns. He knew it innately as soon as the words were spoken.

But what kind of man would he be?

A question Silas has been forced to face the past two spins. Ever since the utterance left Logan's mouth—catechizing himself over his own character, what he does and doesn't deserve in life, and now here. What kind of man would rest to let his livelihood be taken undisguised, without a fight, willingly?

Baz tips his head toward Silas again and the lead weighted foot of another guard comes down on a sliver of exposed rib cage. The breath he had just managed to catch gone once more with an agonizing groan. Short puffs of air leave his throat and disturb the dirt below him, he's sticky with sweat and dust cakes to the skin of his cheek on top of it.

"Give me the case code," Baz proposes again as the men back away from Silas. They let him clamber from a fetal position to a lazy vertical, resting most of his weight on a shaking palm.

He squints up at them, passing a quick finger under his nose to snuff the run and clearing his throat. "I'd be misguided to think you won't just kill me anyway."

Baz snivels at that, amused. "I give you my word."

There isn't much of an option between life or death. Silas knows full well from experience that the Bartanka aren't unversed in either.

Croy is a slow leak in his every waking moment, threatening to hit a barbed edge and split the trauma Silas has stitched tightly wide open again.

Then there's other reasons of course to want to be alive, to *need* to be. It's a fucking sour disappointment to swallow. The reality that there's nowhere but down from here unless he makes the only true decision he has.

And just like so many times before, Silas is back to where he was—possessionless, feckless, imagining a life on the Pulp again. After all, gems are replaceable, he can always go back for more.

Bartanka sighs impatiently. He pushes his chair back with an ear splitting scrape across the floor, like metal on metal, as he rises for the first time to get a good look at Silas. He stands above him, gazing down at the misfortuned Mako for a beat, then sucks his teeth and shakes his head as if to show pity.

"Go ahead, boys." He signals to his lackey's around the room with the flick of a finger. They all succeed with overzealous vigor, one pulling Silas's slack body up by an arm, another winding to throw a punch.

"Alright, alright!" Silas calls out, shirking his face away on instinct. "Enough."

TWO SPINS EARLIER

"Alright, enough!" I shout, leaning over the two men rolling around on the tile. I find the hot skin at the back of Silas's neck with a soft palm to pull him out of his devilish reverie. Logan is pinned, flailing underneath him.

Logan had struck first. He should have known. *I* should have known.

There was something swimming in the swell of Silas's eyes unfathomable to us both. Something that only a man who'd been threatened, shafted and forced into avarice could muster within himself.

"You heard her," Silas seethes through gritted teeth. His right knuckles are peach pink, there's a spatter of sweat on his brow, sticking his brown hair to his forehead. "You've had enough."

Logan managed to get in a few hits. There will be sore ribs in the morning, a scratch or two across Silas's already scarred maw; but the shiner on Logan's eye, and split dotted with blood at the bottom of his lip are harsher injuries. One's he'll have to wear with discomfiture and see every time he looks at himself in a mirror.

Stark reminders of Silas. Of everything Silas did to him.

The Mako pushes himself off, unfolding to sit on his heels and catch his breath. There's eavesdropping eyes popping out of nearby pods. Several people wondering what the calamity is, and why there's two grown men wrestling on the ground while I stand owl-eyed over the mess of it.

"This is why I didn't want to fucking tell you, Logan." I'm a step below yelling as I pull Silas up by a bare bicep from the floor to stand beside me, not impressed with him by any means either.

My level-headed lover turned volatile at the snap of a finger over weighted words. It was unlike him. Still, I have to scorn myself over the flare of attraction that stings my core at the way he looked engaging in it. The brutal grip of his hands holding Logan down, his muscle pulling taut over the defined planes of his back. That far out, wild light in his eyes and cathartic sigh as he drew first blood.

Silas had been wanting to do this. Just waiting for a reason.

Logan runs the back of his hand across his bottom lip where it's cut. "You fed me some bullshit story so you could fuck him," he says, standing, albeit slowly. "So you could fuck someone else without feeling like shit about it. I—I was so fucking in love with you. I would have done anything for you."

Silas turns to take a short walk in a circle behind me, staring at the ceiling while Logan speaks, calming himself down. I frown, exhausted by the back and forth of it, the emotional toll of such a poignant climax.

"That's exactly why I couldn't tell you," I say now, softer. "I didn't want to hurt you, I wasn't making it up—it's Silas, okay? It's always been Silas. In my head, my dreams, in that whole fucking journal. And I know it's impossible for you to understand, it's crazy—so I didn't tell you."

Logan rubs at the sides of both of his temples aggravatedly.

"I care about you," I tell him. "I wish it didn't go this way."

"You are an unfortunate casualty, Logan," Silas chimes in, having had his stint of conciliation. "Her and I have been fated far longer than you've even thought of the word love."

Logan snorts, rolling his eyes dramatically and leaving them behind closed lids. "Just...*shut up*." He shakes his head back and forth and a manic chuckle blossoms from between his lips. "Of every fucking person, you had to cheat on me with *Socrates*."

"He never touched me until it was over with you," I admit. "He wouldn't."

"Well I guess some fucking thank you's are in order then," Logan hoots sarcastically. "How ever shall I make it up to him?"

"Logan..." I sigh.

"No fuck that, you know what? I spent the last two days searching high and low for you, worrying over you, *missing* you. And you're down the hall with your legs spread like a fucking whore for this scrag—and now what? The dream is over sleeping beauty. The Otera is where it ends. When you realize he has nothing left to offer you but a book and a warm bed. When that hits you, when you realize that mistake, what then, *Birdie*?"

He spits the nickname at me and it pulls a hot flush to my face. Before I can even process it, Silas is lurching toward Logan again with a strangling grip around his throat and backing him into the wall.

"Silas, stop," I plead. "Let go of him—*let go*."

It's like he's in a trance. Feeling the rapidly declining pulse in Logan's throat against the skin of his palm. Watching his complexion besmear from white to angry red, his eyes agog and searching for reprieve. Silas bares his teeth, grinning sadistically at the choked sound fighting its way up Logan's throat. He adds an extra finger of pressure despite my petition, just to see his face play chameleon from red to a teasing tint of purple.

Silas stops only when Logan throws both his hands up in surrender. My ex's shaking fingertips like a euphoria to him. He doesn't realize until Logan drops to the floor an inch or so, that the race of adrenaline had given him the strength to lift the man—but he can feel it pumping still.

Logan scuffles limply away from the two of us, holding his throat and stumbling backwards down the hall with a bewildered look across his face. "Fucking lunatic," he tries, but it's hoarse and broken. "He's a fu-fucking lunatic."

Silas stands in the center of the hallway as Logan walks away, watching his every move like a threat until he rounds the corner and disappears.

NOW

Silas shifts the slide of his pod open with a weak grunt. The lamp is still flickering on its last leg and illuminating the space enough that the darkness outside doesn't spill in. He's careful when he drops down, gingerly curving his body around any obstacles, tiptoeing through the compartmental area. His hip catches on the sharp angle of his desk and he bites down hard into his bottom lip to quiet a growl, attempting to lessen the pain by introducing it somewhere else.

He drags himself to the makeshift washroom, just a sink beside that jagged mirror, and he doesn't even look up at his own face as he pulls the faucet to run ice cold water. It slaps off the metallic basin and spatters his sweat and blood-slicken tee, wetting the soft hair on his arms.

Silas scrubs his hands raw, scratching his palms with the blunt round of his nails as if he could remove the skin—until the water runs from brown to pink to clear. He pulls his shirt over his head delicately, peeling the material away from his stomach and neck as carefully as possible. But still he feels the hot sprouts of contusion with every shift, the rip of half dried scabs matted into the threading.

He's happy he can't see clearly. The swelling makes the skin around his eyes and cheek tight and abraded. Because if he could, he would be able to see how barren the vessel has become. Not that it's much of a change *physically* from before—but the energy that flowed so seamlessly and freely in the air is gone now, me along with it. There's no soft whispers or hummed conversations. No sighs of satisfaction fluttering through like angelic ambiance.

Ghosts of me, maybe.

The specific way I left a book tilted on the shelf, or the indent of my cheek on that second pillow, the smell of my hair stuck to the sheets—the garbage can across the pod stuffed with food waste Silas is yet to clean.

He bandages himself the best he can, then pulls a stray cold pack from the cooler unit to hold against the lump on his face and takes a seat at the edge of the unmade bed. It's so empty now, and he's afraid to lie down and sleep because he knows what will happen, just as it did the night before.

He'll be met with darkness. With nothing.

When I went, I took those dreams with me too.

Silas shifts slowly, reaching under his disheveled sheets until he finds the lip of his pillow case and tucks a hand inside. He feels around for something for a minute before he finds what he's looking for, closing his eyes and letting his shoulders relax in relief at the small weight in his palm.

One single crystal, smooth and callow, still a fiery, beautiful specimen in Silas's hand as he rubs his thumbs over the width of it. The last piece of anything he truly, knowingly has. A beacon of cerulean fortuity.

He holds it tenderly to his lips and looks down on it like a prayer needs to be said, and perhaps he does say one, in his head, where outward words won't suffice. One lone gem left over from the Pulp, worth not more than a fifth of the entire harvest he had collected, but worth something nonetheless. Worth everything.

Silas inferred what might happen before he took himself to the pier. Knowing full well that Bartanka would, at the very least, want his entire haul. If he only showed up with enough to cover his debts they would know. Baz would have had someone out to scour his pod and destroy his belongings to find the rest as soon as he opened the case. But he couldn't have that, so he brought it all, every last thing worth a tally to his name—minus one perfect little gem hiding under his pillow. A security sheet, small and easy to oversee.

On top of all that, Silas knew if he put up a fight over that case of remaining loot as they took it from him, playing desperate and fragile, willing to die over the harvest like it was his very last shred of existence—well, then they *might* just believe him. So he did.

Silas rolls the stone around in his fingers as he sits silently. It's worth enough for a one way ride and a comfortable place to sleep when he gets wherever he's going. Until he finds a place to make something different of himself, a place where he *belongs*.

He tucks it back beneath the pillow, not his own this time though, mine. He leaves it there under the sheet, and when his hand resurfaces he's holding onto something different. A leather bound journal, tucked and tied with flimsy little straps, the browned pages that he knows so well heavy with love, life and memories that he's content to commit to his own. Living them every night so long as he can, and as long as it keeps me here, in whatever way that may be.

He lays back on the bed, flipping the pages open randomly until the soft swish of paper subsides and lands as an open book would.

"How many can we read tonight, Birdie?" Silas says aloud, holding the script close to his face so as to block out everything else around him.

He can imagine I'm laying next to him, treat this as the dream he knows he won't have. The stories I left him with being the only tangible token that I was ever really there.

20
ARDENCY

"What the fuck was that about, Silas?"
I'm already standing with my arms crossed in the middle of his pod when he returns from the hallway. His bright eyes are still dilated, the crease in his brow more evident than I've ever seen it before.

He brushes past me with his head down and I whip around to force him to confront me, despite the obvious way he wants to avoid it. Avoid talking about this, what he did, who he became in these last few minutes.

Silas still doesn't look up, instead he flips the cooler cover open harshly and shoves his swollen knuckles into the cold compartment, rustling bags of freeze dried foods to rest on his hand. He finally shifts his weight to one leg and sighs.

"Hello?" I goad his silence, shrugging my shoulders in a way that says I'm looking for an explanation.

Part of me knew deep down that Silas was capable of the kind of intensity he showed Logan in that hallway. I could feel it come to fruition now and again when he made love to me, the aching ferocity in his fingertips like a pulse on my skin. Shaking not to squeeze too hard, or touch too hungrily, not to use his hands to hurt me, but to show me he could be good. He could be gentle and careful; he wasn't only his violent life as a Mako. And when I was underneath him, I could see the deep trellis of blackness hiding secrets in the pupils of his eyes. He could rip me to pieces if he wanted to, pluck me apart, crush me. It was frightening, and exhilarating, and—I wanted him to, sometimes. I wanted him to show me everything he could be.

"You could have fucking killed him," I chastise as I close the gap between us, reaching into the cooler to pick up his hand and look at it. I run my thumb over the inflamed bones and he pulls a wince through the skinny spaces of his gritted teeth.

"No, I *would* have." He huffs aggressively. "I would have killed him. I wanted to. That's just the reality of this, isn't it, Eliza?"

I shake my head disapprovingly, lowering his hand back into the cold and then cupping the overgrown stubble on his chin with frozen fingertips. He melts into the touch, the fever of his skin pressing greedily against me like a magnet to metal.

"You don't mean that," I whisper, scraping my thumb over his jaw soothingly. "That isn't you."

Silas sighs through his nose, closing his eyes and squeezing them tightly. He knows I'm doing and saying these things with good intention. I'm leveling with him, pacifying him back to the Silas that I've spent the last three spins with, the one I've been dreaming of since I was a girl. But it's a tedious facade to hold upright where it's waving paper thin in the wind.

Especially now, with the Otera hours away and reality barreling unforgivingly toward the both of us.

"Oh, but it *is* me," he grits out, abandoning the cooler and shirking away from my touch. "You know the dreamy, love-struck, softened version of me, and you're in love with him, but *me?*" Silas shakes his head and grimaces, pouting his lips in a way that presents disgust, but only toward himself.

"Silas—"

"I've kept things from you."

Our voices wrestle with each other but his overpowers. "I have killed men. On the Pulp, on the Helio, all the way from Little Moon to the Breakers—and not always as a means of self-preservation, Eliza. Is that what you want? To look at me every day knowing who I truly am, and still choose me? To know that any place we may go, any planet we may see, there could be a dark shadow of me always walking in our peripheral? I'm not sure I would."

I step toward him again and he puts his hands out to keep me a distance away. He knows he's vulnerable. He knows that if I were to put my hands on him or coo praise in his ear he would buckle and fold; allow me to coddle him and tell him he's not who he says he is—and he can't. Silas needs me to know these things that are inked into his life like a tattoo on skin. Irreversible, permanent, never able to just scrub away.

"I'm living with a false sense of security right now, Birdie. Treating you like the Maker damned Final Oath, because I just..." He waves his hands and shrugs. "I just don't know what's gonna happen when we get off this transport. And that scares the fuck out of me. I should have led with transparency when I laid eyes on you, I should have given you that."

This time when I step closer to him, he lets me. He lets me lift his damaged hand to my lips and kiss the skin. He lets me press his palm into the beating heart at the center of my chest, stretching his fingers to feel the delicate outline of my collarbone.

This glorious man who's on needles over what he feels he deserves, when I know in my blood and my bones, in the stardust that courses through my veins filled with him, that there is nothing in this universe he *doesn't*. That there would never be a timeline in which I would wish or hope him different. That I would regret that he was me and I was him.

If I'm a book, then he is all the lines between every sentence. He's the curve of each letter reaching out to kiss the next, the swooping song of every italic, the pausing breath of well placed punctuation. I am the words, but he is the way in which you read them.

"I don't care what you've done, Silas," I mutter. His brows are still knitted together. I can see the apprehension like a mask across his complexion. His gaze scrapes from his hand on my breast to my lips, then up to my eyes. His lashes look soft, like feathers every time he blinks, and they feel that way too when he lowers his forehead to mine. "I know you, Silas. I know you—and I love you."

He brings both his shaking palms to my face, cradling me delicately, rubbing his thumbs from my cheekbones to the corners of my lips. It feels like he's thanking me silently, teeming dedication into the pores of my skin.

"Had I known you were real—you were out here somewhere," he whispers, the wisp of his breath tickling my mouth as he does. "I would have chosen a different path. I would have been something for you, made something of myself. But I didn't. So Logan is right, I don't belong anywhere and I never have. No one has ever *wanted me,* no one but you."

"You've had other lovers," I protest.

"I don't even remember their faces, Eliza."

I close my eyes and accept it. That Silas has swayed through life on a metaphorical auto-pilot just waiting for the next thing to happen. A drifter.

I knew this, but I didn't truly understand it. It is the farthest thing from the life that I've lived, and I would never be able to fully put myself in those sap-soled shoes.

"You are a divine piece of this universe, and I will not pluck you from your constellation, little bird. Maker will come looking for the missing star."

I smile at him, fractured but unwavering. "We are the same star."

Silas grants himself a softened smile too, running a thumb over my bottom lip once, and then leaning down to press his mouth to mine. It's slow and muted. He doesn't take when I try to give more, instead pulling back and planting a second chaste kiss. He gingerly sets me an arms length away from him with both palms on my shoulders.

"There are things I need to do when we get to the Ote," he tells me. "Dark things that I'm not confident in the outcome of. But I need to *do those things,* before I can let myself have this—have you. I need to be free of the burdens of my prior life."

"Well, let me help you then."

"No." He shakes his head. "And, on top of the inherent danger of it by which I'm plagued—I can't with a clear conscience take you away from something you've always known. Not without giving you at least the chance to truly decide for yourself."

"So what are you suggesting?" I sigh quietly. Obviously displeased, but willing to give Silas what he needs to prove that I won't abandon this. I won't change my mind no matter how much space he thinks is necessary to put between us while he does his bidding.

"We've tasted each other, Birdie, now we need to part to see if that craving returns." He lifts my chin so my sodden gaze is forced to his own. "I have business to attend to in two nights. When we dock tomorrow afternoon I want you to disembark with Logan. See your family, tell them what you need to, give yourself the time to miss me—to *crave* me, if you do. With greater clarity, that's all I ask. "

I bundle the fabric of his waistband in my fists and pull him closer to me. "I promise I'm not going anywhere. I'll do what you need me to do, keep myself out of whatever trouble you're hiding from me." He doesn't miss the disapproving glare I give him. "But leaving isn't going to change my mind, Silas. We *can* find a life with each other. We will."

He runs a gentle hand down my hairline, caressing my skin with his knuckles, holding my gaze like he would the petals of a flower. His beautiful, perfect girl. Finally a tame in his wild. The missing piece in his fragmented miscellany.

"When my pod docks I'll sit in the bay for two spins, until the next transport route," Silas says. "Until it leaves I'll wait for you, Eliza. You come to me and tell me. Tell me what you want to do, and I'll do it. Stay with you, go with you—*leave*. I will do it."

ONE SPIN LATER

My feet touching solid ground for the first time in eight spins feels just as I expected it would. The Oterian concrete is like a new pair of shoes, but the farther I walk down the descent ramp to the waiting bay the more natural it becomes. I don't want to think about the last time I was land side on a system right now. The separation from Silas is torture enough without flashes of the Continental playing on a peripheral projector.

I have an uncomfortable number of bags slung over each shoulder, straps criss-crossing over my chest and undoubtedly leaving red welts there. At the very least they're cutting off some type of circulation to my arms as I feel them steadily go cold and tingly. For barely having any belongings left on the pod after the Glades—I certainly had a fuck ton of belongings left on the pod after the Glades. Not ones I ever suspected would need immediate removal upon docking, that's for sure.

Logan toddles along behind me. He was decent enough to carry one singular box of my random things with him, but the kindness barely makes it past his chest. Bruising has gnarled itself into those first stages of a putrid purple under both his eyes, his nose isn't quite as thin as usual. There's a hairline cut on his bottom lip that has healed better than anything, but it's still unmissable.

When I finally make my way to arrivals, my parents are there, waving their hands excitedly at first sight of us breaching the gate. But the saccharine quickly fades to stagnation as we inch closer and the state of Logan's face is on full display.

I steal a deep breath as my mother's face pales and her bouncy, blonde curls deflate.

"Oh, *honey*, what happened?" She side-steps me, brushing past my shoulder and straight to Logan's side, horrified.

Logan winces a bit too dramatically when she touches his cheek to catalog the damage.

I look at my feet and roll my eyes, shifting the weight of the duffle bags with a curl of my shoulders. My father ignores the coddling of Logan—reaching to me and pulling several bags out of my carry.

"Are you okay, Sunshine?" he asks, quietly bringing my attention to him.

I give him a soft, meaningful smile, because I'm happy to see him again and I'm grateful he asked. I missed his altruistic tendencies.

"Yeah, I'm good, dad."

He assesses me carefully and nods. "You look well," he tells me. "You look different."

My mother drags Logan toward my father and I, looking to me for an explanation with glossed over eyes. As if it were she who had been jumped and beaten in a shadowed alleyway.

"Honey, who *did* this?" she mewls. The falsetto of her voice is like scratching a half healed scab in my ear and forcing it to bleed again. My father squints his eyes, taking in Logan's injuries and undoubtedly making his own assumptions.

"It's a long story." I sigh, finding myself involuntarily looking around the vast arrival gate. I know I won't see him, but still I hope for a shimmering glimpse. An omen or a clue. A little parcel of reassurance that the dream isn't over and Silas is there in the wading water like he promised.

"One your *daughter*," Logan says, shoving the small box of my belongings into my arms, "will have to fill you in on."

He turns on his heel and walks away without another word, leaving my mother's mouth gaping, opening and closing like a fish.

"What is going on?" she manages, hand over heart. "Where is he—why is he..."

"Not here, mom," I dole. "Not in the middle of the port."

She's still slow to move, even when I adjust the weight of all my bags and motion toward the exit.

Fucking Logan, couldn't even give me ten minutes to soften the blow. He had to drop the bomb like a war mongol and taper off to his own safe seclusion, watching me scramble in his wake.

My father takes the box out of my hands and starts toward the door, reading the situation skillfully, never one for obtuse drama or too many lingering eyes. "Let's get you some real food," he offers, giving me an out for the time being. "The muck on that transport probably tasted like shit."

My mother chokes on her beverage, sputtering into the glass and embellishing her poignant displeasure.

"Drita." My father sighs, handing over a linen so she can dab the bright red lipstick from the corner of her mouth.

"A *Mako*." She clutches the napkin in her talons and stares across the table at me. "Eliza, you can't honestly understand the depth of your own actions."

"I knew you'd react this way," I say, abandoning the fork I've been twirling absentmindedly in my plate.

The food in front of me is untouched, unpalatable. There's a very specific type of humiliation that comes with divulging your love life to your parents. One that makes even the most prudish confession pornographic. Despite it, I gave them both the entire in and out. The dreams, the journal, the trip, the transport, the attraction, the defiance, the acceptance, the fight—all the ways in which I can't deny the fate that brought Silas to me. The same way I explained it all to Logan. Transparency is my only grace.

"Is he here, Sunshine? On the Ote?" my dad asks, attempting to subdue the conversation to casual. He reaches across the plates to snag a forgotten piece of bread tucked into a basket.

"Somewhere," I say as my eyes dart through the crowded eatery, as if all this discourse could summon Silas.

"And how does Logan feel about all this, aside from the obvious?" My mother frowns. "Is he willing to reconcile? Is this fixable?"

My father sighs again. "I think what your mother means is, are you positive that Silas is worth this? Are you sure it's what you truly want? It did happen very suddenly, we all know strong emotions can get the best of us." He gestures shortly toward his wife where she's stewing.

"I've known for a long, long time," I say with a blithe smile. "I think I've always known."

Drita waves someone down theatrically for another drink, pulling her shawl tighter to her tiny shoulders as if my admission brought a cool, uncomfortable breeze over her whole body. My father doesn't say anything, instead giving me a compassionate nod.

"You're an adult, Eliza," my mother chimes one last time. "You should think harder about this. You've only known this man for all of a cycle. It's always been a fantasy with you. It's time to wake up."

✦

Downcity is an urban sprawl. Shopping and dining, pristine stone sidewalks that attempt to keep a rustic charm despite the industrialization. Like a gift from the original architects, or a reminder of how new this planet really is.

A glacial current is making a sweep through the system as a new solstice season nears. Meaning unlike my balmy stay in the Glades and temperate ride on the transport, this weather kisses a chill into my skin. It has me holding onto my own upper arms for a tendril of warmth when I step out of the restaurant onto the pavement.

I close my eyes and breathe the bitter air in until it burns my nose. The sun is setting now, leaving a leaky painting of pink and gray careening to the horizon, and there's a tiny shred of brilliance that reaches out and bites the skin of my cheeks. It's going to be night soon, and I'm dreading the inevitable pattern of dreamlessness. Silas is now not only physically gone from me, but subconsciously living a life far away as well.

Still, when I try, I can see him standing there in my head. The soft waves of his unruly brown hair curling defiantly over his ears, tickling the nape of his neck—that shining scar that wrinkles around his eye when his lips curl into a presumptive smirk. The faded t-shirt and dirt scuffed kneecaps on his cargo pants.

I'm afraid that the distance will blur those crisp and detailed lines though. I'll start to forget the way his cheeks dimple when he laughs, or the way his voice sounds when he wakes up in the morning. I might forget the placement of the marks on his skin, or how his eyes drown me in the deepest ocean I've ever seen.

I shake the thought and open my eyes. Only when I do, he *is* there. Across the busy square, tucked into a corner and leaning against a building. He straightens up when I find his stare, seemingly sucking in a fragile breath that does little to hide his vulnerability.

He followed me here. Slinking silently through the groves of pedestrians, keeping a comfortable distance just to get a glimpse at the life I lived before him. To make sure I was okay.

Part of him was curious about my relationship with my parents: how they loved me in ways differently than he did, how he would even begin to compete with all of that affection. Another part of him was simply unable to be fully gone from me just yet.

We smile at each other, with mine escapes a gaspy giggle that he can't hear, but he can see as it bubbles from my lips. Several people cross in front of us both as we stand there, oblivious to everything else, hanging onto the last look at one another before the night truly does fall and the spins begin their slow turn until it's *safe* again. Safe to run across the bustling pavement and into his arms like I so wish I could right now.

My father steps out of the cafe behind me, shrugging on his light jacket. He pauses when he sees me standing on the curb with my eyes trained on a man he's never seen before, planted just as flagrantly on the other side of the road.

I fight back a damp swell in my lashes when Silas nods his head to me. As if to say, *it will all be okay, I will see you soon.* The exchange is wordless and consequential. I don't blame him for coming here, despite the pit that forms when I feel the time I have looking across at him coming to an end.

I mouth a silent *I love you,* in his direction. Then close my eyes to savor the memory when he mouths it back.

TWO SPINS EARLIER

"I can be gentle for you, Birdie." Silas breathes against my neck, nipping at my pulse and then my chin. I'm in his lap, naked and needy. His cock sits hard between my legs, the head of it nicking at the nerves there.

"I know." I shush him, tipping his head back with my fingers knotted through his hair.

I lean down and close my wet mouth over the plush skin of his bottom lip, blistering him with a kiss that turns desperate quickly. Our tongues sweep frantically against one another, testing the depths they can explore. When I release his mouth I take the skin with me, biting the flesh and pulling back until I hear him groan at the pain, then I lick it away.

My breasts are hard against his chest, delighting at the friction as they slide against the damp, warm skin. Silas holds my lower back with a strong forearm, keeping my core mounted against him. His other arm slithers up my spine and takes my neck in the cup of his palm.

"You should have *nev*-never seen me like that." He stutters, reacting to the slow roll of my hips over his shaft. "That's not the kind of man I want to be with you."

"You don't scare me," I say. An echo of so many spins ago when I said those words to him out of primal obligation. They were true then, and somehow even truer now. "Who says I don't want you to be that kind of man with me?"

There's a chaotic glimmer in his eye that shines like lustrous starlight. His pupils dilate and darken, sucking me in like a black hole would in space, like a plaything to the cosmos. He's an open book, but one I can't read right now. There's admiration in his gaze but a host of discernment mars the aura of it, like he doesn't know how to say what he needs to say.

"What is it?" I squint, slowing my hips.

"I love you."

I smile as I hold his face in between palms. I already knew this. Even if he never said it outwardly for the rest of our lives, I would still know it. And I'd know it was the deepest, purest, most saturated, weigh-you-down kind of love there ever was.

"Without you I would know nothing of love, Eliza. You are the definition of it," he says, holding my wrists where they rest underneath his chin. "I am content to be in love with you until the last star falls from the sky."

I don't hesitate to kiss him, deep and smooth. Full of all the layering emotions from the day's past like a dam succumbing to a crack. All the anxiety and anger melts into passion, the rolling current of nervous energy and apprehension flows more like a river of pure adoration.

There has never been a feeling like this for me, nor for Silas. The mask of intimacy I felt with other lovers, with Logan, was a flameless candle in comparison. It was a mocking veil of what the word could really, truly mean.

When we part we stay nose to nose, small shifts of our bodies tease our lips to touch from sheer closeness.

"Love leaped out at us like a murderer in an alley..." I whisper, and Silas grins spectacularly. "Leaping out of nowhere, and struck us both at once."

"As lightning strikes," he recites back to me.

"As a Finnish knife strikes."

He leans in and kisses me again, the damp ends of his eyelashes bat against the tips of my own. Somewhere along the way his eyes have glazed and welled. I realize that I've never seen Silas cry. I've never even dreamt of it.

"She insisted afterwards, that it wasn't so, that we had, of course, loved each other a long...long time," he continues.

"Without knowing each other, never having seen each other."

Silas kisses me again, but this time his hands catch at my hips and roll me beneath him, guiding me so the intention is clear. I wrap my arms around his neck and let him take me this way, one easy push like slipping on a glove, and I am completely at his mercy.

He reacts to my broken syllables as they reach for salvation in the sex-thick air. Fucking me thoroughly, wringing me out for every drop I will allow. He mouths at my chest, my breasts. Swirls his tongue and suckles at them as my hips jar to meet his own.

The soft slip of his cock in and out of me is lewd and intoxicating. I can feel every single ridge of him where it spears into me, hooking onto the soft pleasure center just inside my walls and teasing it with a perfect, debilitating rub of his head. *Back and forth, back and forth.*

I squeeze him inside of me, hooking my ankles together as he hits the deepest part I can allow. Then gasp for air when he pulls all the way back out, using the time to kiss me with an open mouth. We're nothing but teeth and tongue and shattered moans, thriving off of one another like a source of life.

Silas tugs my knees to his ribs, hiking my thighs up higher on his body so he can sink even deeper—until there's no room left inside me to even accommodate a breath of air. He steals the oxygen from my lungs, burying himself again and again until his own thrusting turns jagged and the sound of me coming apart in his ear strikes a match that turns into a wildfire.

He makes love to me like this is the last time, holding my body against his as I shudder.

"That's it, Eliza. *I love you.* I love how you come for me, I love how you feel when I bring you there. I love you...I love you."

He kisses me over and over again. Kisses the salty tears from my cheeks and dries the skin with a press of his own.

I reach down and hold his backside with both my palms, digging my nails in and beckoning him deeper without words, coaxing him to let go, to fill me so I can keep a piece of him inside of me. Even as the new day bares her teeth and the guarantees of this type of fulfillment ever again begins to dwindle.

Silas grants it to me, huffing like a wounded cub when his shaft pulses hot and leaded into my core. I feel every jolt of his spend, every contracting vein on his cock empty itself against my walls. It's euphoric when we cry out together, wailing a siren's song that

will beg to be heard in the empty hallows of our minds for the
forsaken nights to come.

TWO SPINS LATER

I probably should have seen this coming, stuffed into the spare
bedroom of my parents home that was once mine. The paint
is still a sickly mauve that's peeling slightly worse than when I
left it. String lights like my own little constellation hanging, or
half-hanging, now where they used to be stuck to the moldings.

The duvet is even the same. But now it smells like dust, and
the picture frames of me and my university roommates on the
periwinkle dresser across the room are coated in a thick gray film.

Instead of a welcoming space for me to lie down and endure
the remaining days until I can go to Silas again, I find myself
surrounded by boxes. Stacks of brown cardboard filled in
complete disarray with all my belongings that I'd spent the entire
day emptying out of the apartment Logan and I share, or *shared*.

I didn't know if he'd be there when I showed up, but of
course he was. Already piling hangers of my clothes outside the
bedroom, emptying the bedside drawers of knick knacks and
jewelry, stray pens and books I never finished, my vibrator. *That*
he made sure to leave shining at the top of the fray.

It was past reconcile, as I'd suspected from one glimpse into the
condo. Logan, who was implicit to fight for my hand and bury
Silas's confidence into a grave hole, had apparently seen the light
of misdirection. All too eager to rid his life of my infidelity, my
betrayal, all things that made it evident that there was nothing
left between the two of us so long as Silas was breathing galactic
air. And even then, he still wasn't sure.

Logan had told me he had a clearer head now. He was able to speak his own truth and find the clarity that he needed once we got back onto the Ote. He just needed the grounding to do it.

"*So you fucked someone else,*" I'd trivialized him.

He rolled his eyes and threw another item of mine into a box across the living room with less care than he needed to.

"*I went out with the guys last night,*" he admitted. "*They said you're fucked up for this. That you don't deserve me.*"

"*Yeah,*" I agreed.

"*I tried. I tried for no reason. You need to figure yourself out, I can't do it anymore.*"

It stung where it shouldn't have. I agreed with him. He needed to move on from me, but for a tingling reason deep in my chest I was disappointed he gave up so easily. Not because I wanted Logan, but because I wanted him to forgive me. I wanted the fog to lift and for the people looking in my direction with shifty eyes to tell me that *they understood*. A grand realization perhaps, that there was a good and viable reason for what happened on that transport, and I made the right choice. That if someone else were in my shoes they would do the same.

This is what Silas needed me to face. He needed me to understand that loving him meant more than syrupy sex and eternal dreams. That there would be sadness, and hopelessness, and even an outcast shadow nipping at my heels with every step.

He also needed me to understand that he doesn't fit the bill. He doesn't know how to *belong* everywhere that I do.

Staring at the ugly carpet beneath my feet, a soft knock on my bedroom door forces me to blink out of my haze. My dad peeks his bald and shiny head in, the round wired glasses on his face and pajama bottoms let me know he ambled out of bed to come talk to me.

"How are you feeling, Sunshine?" He pulls the door shut behind him with a *snick* and joins me at the edge of my bed.

I give him half a smile, raising my hands pointedly at the boxes of crap loitering in more than half my space.

"Logan wasn't as forgiving as you'd hoped," he observes, looking around and nudging a nearby bag with his socked toe.

"You could say that." My accompanying chuckle teeters off into a sigh.

"Well I was getting pretty sick of being called 'man' anyway."

At this, I genuinely laugh for the first time in days. My smile reaches my eyes, and like a mirror my father's does too. "I know this is a total flip around. I didn't even warn you guys, but sometimes ripping the bandage off is the better way to go."

"You know you're always welcome here, sweetheart. This is your home."

I lick my lips, gulping down the rock of hesitance suddenly lodged in my throat. This isn't my home, it hasn't been for a long time. Even before Silas, my "home" was physically with Logan. Before that among my friends and peers in my years of university. I can count on one hand the number of times I've slept in this bed since my adolescence.

"Or," he corrects himself when I don't rebuttal, "maybe home is something entirely different for you now."

My father reaches over and clasps his hand in mine where it rests on my knee. An act of solidarity, an assurance that I'm not alone like I feel, and the world around me doesn't need to feel so despondent at the moment.

"I've never loved someone so much, dad," I profess, already fighting with my own glistening eyes. Not only at speaking about Silas, but at the closeness I feel to my father over it. "I didn't know it could feel this way."

He rubs his thumb over mine. "I can see it. I see the way you look at him."

I glance over in surprise. "You saw him? Outside the cafe?"

"Hard to miss, the way you were holding up foot traffic."

I laugh again, this time a stray tear finds its way down my cheek and I wipe it away with the back of my sleeve.

"Let me tell you something." My father squeezes my hand tighter. "I've known since you were a little girl, that there was something more to life for you. Something fantastic, and—and *magical*." His dark eyes glisten like a starry night. "Something you would only read about in books."

Silas would love to be a fly on the wall for this. He would probably tell me afterward that everything my father said he could imagine crystal clearly. That the man who raised me was undoubtedly who taught me how to dream.

"You were always a step away from reality, hooked onto it only by the thinnest string, and most times I was on the other end trying desperately to reel you back in," he teases. "If those fantasies are material for you now—you have to pursue them."

Where I thought I had a hold on the teeming emotion, my father's words pull the stopper. I weep freely against his shoulder as he sweeps an arm around my jittering body, holding me close to him. The feeling of acceptance warms my blood and peppers my cheeks with blush.

Even just one person willing to understand this is more than I knew I needed. To know my father would welcome Silas with open arms even if no one else would, exceeds any torn expectations—it breathes air into my empty lungs.

"Thank you." I sniffle and rub my eyes clean with my wrists. "You'll love Silas. He's so smart, the smartest man I've ever met. He travels, and he reads books, and maps and encyclopedias even." I recognize that I'm babbling, but I can't seem to contain it.

"Well, where is he?" My father chuckles. "I want to meet him—officially. Not gawking across the Downcity square."

I look up at the clock and feel an uneasy twist in my stomach. It's nearly a new spin. The skies will stay dark for hours and I know Silas is out there somewhere. Dabbling in a kind of danger he desperately needed to keep me away from.

"Silas had some business to take care of tonight," I disclose. "He had to meet some people. Buyers for his harvest, I'm sure." I'm not sure, but this is the best explanation I can give to my father for the time being. If Silas didn't want me involved in it, I'm positive he wouldn't want my father involved either.

"Tomorrow then," he says, patting me on the shoulder and then leaning over to kiss my temple. "You should get some sleep."

My dad stands and makes his way back to the door, turning the knob carefully because it creaks and the house hears everything. "And don't worry about your mother, Sunshine. She'll come around too." He looks around at the mess of boxes and bags one more time and shakes his head humorously. "Goodnight."

"Goodnight, dad." I grin at him before the door clicks shut.

Then I'm alone again, but slightly less alone than before. I worry about Silas, but I trust him. I know that any danger he's faced on Dandorma and elsewhere in systems all throughout his life can't compete with even the darkest shadows on the Otera. Or I hope that somehow if it does, all the cunning he's pocketed is more than enough to make up for it.

It's still another night without him. Another cold sweat to wake up in, because that beautiful world I went to in my sleep pools in darkness now. Like we both have been plucked out of our story lines and misplaced. The author left an open hole and we slithered through.

His soft hair. The way his eyes crinkle when he laughs. The silvery scar that curves along his temple. The smell of his skin. The sparse hair of his beard.

Don't forget these little details, don't let them fade for lack of attention.

I know I can't sleep, not right away at least. If I felt tired before, the conversation with my dad reignited a sparkless energy. I kick the box closest to me and grumble, uninterested in burning my vigor unpacking any of it at the moment—but I spot a singular duffel from the transport across the room and go to it anyway.

It's the one I had in Silas's pod, still filled with miscellaneous things I'd reluctantly packed away by his request. He didn't want me missing anything, or leaving anything valuable behind. He said it was because it would entice him to bring them to me, making it harder to get through the days. But there was a smidge of vibrato to the words like it hurt him to lie to me like that.

I open the bag and scrounge around inside, the belongings I already knew were in there packed haphazardly into the main compartment, but another item I realize must have been added after the fact is placed upon the rest.

The Master & Margarita, thick and green, makes me smirk when I take it out of the satchel and look at the cover.

When I left the pod I made Silas keep my journal, despite his protest. It was important to me that he had something to remind him that I was coming back. Something that would caress him when I physically couldn't. My dreams to fill the dreamless void we both faced.

I take the novel back to my bed. The springs screech when I lay down and the pillow is too stiff, but I flick on the bedside lamp anyway and thumb through the pages of text. The book snags out of rhythm somewhere and I double back, fanning the worn paper slower the second time until it catches again. I see tucked into one of the nooks is a smaller glossy page, folded over once and tattered on one edge like it was ripped out of its own binding altogether.

Before I open the stray note I look down at the book's page.

The quote, *"Love leaped out in front of us..."* circled in dark black ink, words underlined and marked in pen, Silas's own handwriting in the margins just as I'd seen it the first time I read through: **YOU.**

I run my thumb over his penmanship once before turning my attention back to the piece of paper he'd tucked inside.

I know what it is before it's completely open. The black text on the page indexed into sections gives it away without even having a title. But still, it makes my heart race and my eyes swell again when I smooth the paper where Silas creased it to reveal the contents.

Soulmates.

Followed by all the galactic definitions separated underneath. The tale of Zeus, the twin souls, a couple religious affiliations. And then there's something else. Another entry written below the rest in that sophisticated scrabble of handwriting I've come to know so well.

THE STAR SOULS THEORY

TWO SOULS ARE FORMED FROM THE DUST OF ONE STAR. WHEN THE TIME COMES AND IT CEASES TO EXIST, THE BRILLIANT, SHINING STAR GIVES ITSELF TO THE UNIVERSE—ITS TANDEM ENERGY PARTING WAYS FOR A TIME BEFORE INEVITABLY COMING BACK TOGETHER, DESTINED TO BE BORN INTO THE SOULS OF LIVING BEINGS. THOSE OF WHICH ARE CONNECTED INTRINSICALLY TO ONE ANOTHER ON THIS SHARED PLANE. ONLY THE LUCKIEST ONES WILL FIND THEIR OTHER HALF.

I close my palm over my mouth as I read. Enamored and infatuated, unable to find a voice to squeak out a word into the quiet room if I wanted to.

As if annotating the passage himself, scribbled into the margins next to the *Star Souls Theory,* Silas also added:

I FOUND YOU. THE OTHER HALF OF MY STAR.

21
DRUTHERS

The singular gem in Silas's hand might as well be burning a hole through it. He stares at it too long and the color starts to bleed from the indigo center to a druzy haze.

There's a hideous kind of quiet in the land-docked pod that, while supposed to quell the ache in his head, does the exact opposite. It just lets every thought he has about me and this situation run unattended like an adolescent through the halls—knocking over knick knacks, bumping into bookcases, screaming at the top of its lungs.

He doesn't have to look at himself in the mirror to know that on top of his bloodshot eyes, there are brash circles of discoloration masking his high cheekbones. Scabbing lacerations that make him wince in discomfort when he runs his hands absentmindedly over his now-crooked nose.

Silas paces back and forth, rubbing a thumb against the hard shell of the little crystal and stopping in front of the slide, *once, twice*—back toward the disheveled bed and then to the door again—*three times.*

"Fuck it," he mumbles to himself, shoving the rock into the back pocket of his pants and stepping outside.

Immediately the sun is too bright, thick, and demanding. Even if his injured face wasn't already crying for shelter, the waves of light would burn right through the thin layer of his eyelids and wrestle with his retinas. He pulls a dark shade of eye-wear from his front pocket and fits them to his face, hiding the bruising about as well as a bandage might hide a disembowelment.

The terminal is as busy as it usually is, travelers galloping from place to place as the transport floats high above. Restock pods fly toward it on a seemingly never-ending conveyor belt, getting the ship ready for its next route out.

Silas chances a look up at the massive vessel and immediately regrets it as a stab of pain nips at the base of his skull, igniting like candles down every vertebrae in his back. He swallows the grunt that tries to escape before it has the chance.

Silas sees this moment as he sees many things: a sign, superstitiously. It's the universe reminding him that he doesn't want to go up there. He doesn't want to get on that transport alone.

The gem grows heavy where it's slotted in his pocket and he looks around again, trying his hardest not to let his posture slump or too much of his face to show. Somehow the black shirt he wears that's usually like a second skin sags awkwardly and hangs longer at the wrists than usual. A physical representation of the shrinking man he feels laying claim inside his body.

This is risky, and Silas knows it is, but there's no getting on that transport unless the rock in his cargo pants is traded currency. Physical, palpable tally that will not only fund the ride he's about to take, but stake him somewhere far away from all this. Maybe in the mountains on the Tlo, or a farm off the Lagrom system.

A place where he can build something. *Begin* something.

He spots the closest exit, scuffling in that direction at a pace he shouldn't be. His rib cage pulses angry under his skin and his lungs protest with every reach for breath through broken bone. He keeps his head down, eyes navigating inconspicuously through shins and shoes as they pass around him, never looking up to chance giving away his identity—as if the obvious limp wouldn't do it anyway.

A quick slip out of the street-bound outlet, and a brisk walk through the congestion of Downcity would bring Silas to the hoarding-hovel of a trading outpost he needs to get to. It's a gimcrack shop. The walls are lined with shelves and novelties, pawned forget-ables and glass cases where all valuable trades are kept under careful eye.

It's a place where you could offer a precious rare crystal for thousands and the person next to you could be bartering a stuffed animal at the same time. There, the owners know Silas by name. Whether that's on good or bad terms fluctuates with his visits, but this time around it could lean either way.

He's nearly to the exit, travelers dissipating somewhere behind him the closer he gets, but just as the crowd splits Silas notices he's being watched.

Two men uniformed in black the same as they were in that dark room last night, arms crossed over their hard chests, sunglasses that give away nothing but a shadow of a face. Suddenly it's as if the terminal is empty save for Silas and his aggressors.

"Maker," he murmurs under his breath, scratching a nervous hand down the back of his neck.

They're looking straight at him. Daring him with a deadpan expression to leave the docks so they have an excuse to finish the job that Silas talked himself out of not even half a spin ago.

If he tries to leave, they'll follow him. If he goes to the trading outpost, they'll know he kept part of his harvest to himself. If he tries to *run*...

Silas nods at both men, communicating his understanding with them silently. He has to swallow the bile rising in his throat as he turns back the way he came, forced to reconvene a plan in the cage of his own pod.

Inside, the clock on his desk mocks him with dwindling time and he angrily swipes it off the surface. He ignores the sting of limbs and the broken appliance as he steps over it and sits down on the edge of the bed.

Silas is out of hours and options, and worse than that, he knows I'll come to him soon. Full of expectations—love and hope for the future that he's going to pull out from underneath me.

It's a punishment worse than death, he thinks, because death would be peaceful and I might still love him in the end. I might still love him anyway, resentfully. Forever at tempestuous odds with the universe for giving me everything and then taking it all away.

I take a shuttle to the transport station. The distance is walkable on a temperate day, my parents living right on the line between Downcity and Up, but the air outside is frigid. As soon as I breach their entryway I have to double back inside and pull a forgotten sweater out of a packed away crate.

It makes me miss the Glades almost immediately. That weather I yearn for and thrive in. The breeze that doesn't bite like this one, but caresses like a lover instead.

If Silas is anything like me, he's likely been awake for hours. If he even found it in himself to sleep at all. I had to convince my father to stay home for now despite his protests, wanting so innocently to come along and meet my other half as a show of good faith.

Maybe it's selfish, but I need my lover all to myself after three spins alone. I surmise the reconciliation will be as explicit as it is implicit—speaking first in tongues and teeth before words.

This is the day I've been incandescently waiting for. The first *real* day of thousands still yet to be lived on the other side of the subconscious wall I've broken through with Silas.

It's as if every dream I've ever had was just a preview. Little glimpses at what the rest of my existence has in store, black and white memories meant not to be remembered but instead, re-lived. In vibrant unforgettable color.

For now though, with nothing left to hurdle, we can just enjoy one another without fear of the future.

Silas's pod is easy to find, the beaten panels of well-used metal are dented in some places, patched in mismatched colors in others. It sticks out in rows of manicured alloy the same way his cool stare does, always causing people to look twice. I suppose after years on this pod the man and the metal might become tangible representations of each other, the same way an animal grows to resemble its owner.

He doesn't answer the door when I first knock. There's a long pause and I shift on my heels and look around the terminal for a sign of him before trying again. "It's me," I say when I do.

I realize I'm nervous for some reason, enervated by emotions that wrap around my insides like the coil of a snake and squeeze until I forget how to breathe.

I hear him sigh from inside, the sound too faint to properly identify, but it's a noise nonetheless. Suddenly I'm pulling the latch without an invitation until the slide creaks open and the sun pours into the dim, airtight pod. It leaves my shadow on the floor in front of me like a foreboding vignette.

"Sy?" I search as I step through the threshold.

I see him there, head hanging into his own lap, back against the wall behind his bed. He's rigid as a board, like he hasn't moved from that spot in three whole spins, and maybe I'd suspected correctly, that the man did in fact become one with his pod.

I know something is wrong before he has the chance to tell me himself. The longer it takes him to lift his head, the larger the pit grows in my stomach, until I'm sure that all my intestines have been entirely swallowed and replaced with a gaping hole. When he does finally decide to look up, I feel my knees buckle underneath my weight.

"Eliza."

"Who?" I gasp. It's strangled somewhere in my throat and muffled by the trembling palm I instinctually bring to my mouth. "Who did this, Silas?"

My brain immediately screams Logan, the only tangible explanation. Him and his fucking friends. It must have been.

"Did Logan do this to you?" I ask, crossing the small distance to Silas and crawling up onto the bed on my knees. I reach out and hold my fingers to his face, touching the curve of his chin gingerly but his jaw still flexes in pain.

Dark purple welts cradle his tired eyes like half moons. The usual dewy olive tone of his skin is muted and pale, stretched taut by swelling that hides the sharp features of his face. He's burning against my graze, feverish and sticky to the touch. His eyes swim in and out of focus, dehydration visibly attested.

"Not Logan," he finally grits out.

I lift his shirt and we both wince together this time. The skin peels away from the fabric it's stuck to with a layer of sweat. Dark abrasions puddle around his ribs and disappear with the bow of his back.

"Broken," he manages lazily.

I leap from the bed and fling the cooler unit open. The search is scarce, one cold pack the size of my palm is the only thing worth aiding him with. I bring it back to the mattress and have him hold it to the side of his face against one blackened eye.

"Where is your med kit?" I ask while I'm already shuffling things around on his shelves, stepping on broken shards of a clock and discarded clothing piled on the floor. I see it before he says anything, half open on the desk with ointments and pill bottles spilled into the previously organized box. At least he had tried to help himself.

"Birdie, stop."

"Can you walk?"

"Little bird."

"You're low on everything in here, we have to go to the hospital."

"I'm not going to the hospital."

"At least to my parent's then, you'll need an antibody boost." I shake an empty bottle of liquid at him. "There's none left."

"You need to stop and listen to me."

"I'll listen to you when you walk out of here." I grab his hand and yank to help him stand from the bed but he doesn't budge.

"I'm not walking out of here, Eliza." His voice is deeper now. He squeezes my elbow and pulls me down closer to his face so I'm forced to look at him. "I can't."

I stare deep into the pits of his eyes, they're tired and pleading. I know he's exuding energy he doesn't need to in an attempt to keep me here, but still he tugs my arm down until I reluctantly sit in front of him on the bed. I can feel the frantic skitter of his breathing brush across my lips and without hesitation I kiss him softly, it's so chaste I can barely sense the touch against my skin.

"What happened?"

"I got lucky," Silas answers honestly. He lets a short pitiful laugh escape as he exhales. "I made a deal with the devil, little bird, but now I must vindicate."

"Is this over the harvest?" I implore him. "What do you mean, deal?"

"The harvest is gone," he tells me. "It turns out they wanted a lot more than previously discussed. Now my hand has been forced, and I can't stay here anymore on the Otera. That was the deal." The admittance tastes sour on his tongue.

I stare at him blankly, as if I can't fully register it, like the words were said in a language I don't speak and my ears are full of sand.

He doesn't say it again, instead searches my eyes back and forth and frowns. That's how I know it's the truth.

"Before we met, I was on Dandorma, yes," he explains. "But what I failed to disclose to you is that, that dig was done in exchange for my life, Birdie. I was there to repay a stolen debt that got my last partner killed right in front of me."

"That man from the photo," I connect. "Croy."

Silas nods solemnly. "They wanted my life last night despite my restitution. My only other choice was to leave this place." He makes sure I'm fully aware of the words before he says them. "I need to leave."

"That's bullshit." I scoff. "You're not going anywhere, you're safe here. With my family, with me."

"I'm not, and neither are you the longer you stay in this pod."

"Who?" I raise my voice. "Who could possibly have that kind of leverage, Silas?"

"The Otera isn't all framed flowers and Downcity stucco, Eliza. There's people I've found myself affixed with on this planet even your night terrors would recoil to. I told you there were things I'd kept to myself, because I was selfish, and I wanted you—this is undoubtedly my repentance for that."

I turn away from him and squeeze my eyes shut. I can feel the creeping twinge of tears stinging to the surface. It could never be easy. I was naive to assume that the last three days were strictly Silas protecting my autonomy, when I know now the distance was just a way for him to keep me safe. Safe from the things that haunted him when I wasn't there, from the people that left him bloody and broken and willing to leave the Otera behind without protest.

"So tell me, then," I insist. "Make me understand."

LAST NIGHT

"I'll give you the case," Silas relents. His throat is dry and he can taste blood on his teeth as he lets his tongue pass over them.

"That's better." Bartanka grins. He waves off the men surrounding Silas and they drop him back to the floor where he lands in a heap on his knees.

Baz takes his time bringing the gems around, leaving Silas in a limbo of suspense. No doubt conjuring the ways in which they'll dispose of the Mako once they've gotten what they want out of him.

The hanging lights have become dimmer, or maybe it's the swell around his eyes that causes the hue. Silas feels like he's in a fish tank. He knows he's encircled, but nothing comes into focus if not directly in his view. Baz doesn't kneel to his level, instead he whistles Silas to his feet on wobbling legs, tisking at the time it takes him to clamber up and look at the boss where he stands.

"Open it." Baz pushes the case into Silas's arms. The force of it knocks him back a step but he regains his balance, turning the locking side of the silver box toward himself.

"I'll open it," Silas mumbles, "on the condition that you'll let me walk free from this venture debtless—and alive."

Baz barks a laugh. His lip curls into a snarl and he gives Silas another shove that disorients him more violently this time. "You open the case and I'll do what I please with it, and you."

"Just end my life then, because I have nothing left to give. I'll be Maker damned and burning eternally before I let the snake that bites me take everything I'm worth with it."

Baz snivels, but Silas doesn't waver. He puts the unopened case on the floor between himself and Bartanka and lowers himself onto his knees, as if surrendering to his fate.

He's only half bluffing. If this goes the way he wants it to, Baz will spare his life even if just for greed. Silas knows the boss isn't partial to reprieve, but Baz cares more about the riches in the box than he does about a nameless harvester that no one will ever miss.

No one will ever even remember.

If Bazrin Bartanka wants to fertilize his pool with another body, he'll do so without the money he was owed, without the crystals he truly values.

"Smart boy. Such a smart boy you are, Silas."

Silas looks up and Baz is grinning, touching the sole of his now-bloody shoe to the top of the case. He pushes it back in Silas's direction where it skids and kicks up a cloud of dust.

"Here's what we'll do," Baz barters. "You'll open the case, and I'll let you live. But the condition is this: tomorrow when the transport leaves again on its scheduled circle-out, *you* will leave with it. And there will be no circle-back. Do you understand? If for some reason you decide to stay, I will find you. If for some reason you decide to return, I will find you. And if there is a soul in this system that cares about Silas the pirating thief, I'll be elated to introduce them to your old friend Croy, and make certain you're there to witness it."

The ultimatum is clear. Either die now without a chance to say goodbye to me, without a trace, forcing me then to always wonder where he went, how he could leave me, why he didn't have the gall to tell me himself.

Or at the very least, the ability to offer me an explanation. To make sure I know that everything he did was to keep me safe, and that he will love me with every beat of his heart from wherever he ends up on this sordid plane.

It's a simple choice.

NOW

I'm silent for a while after it all comes out. The pills that I fed to Silas from the bestrewed medical kit have given him a renewed poise, and where I should be the caretaker, it's him holding me now.

"You have to forget about me, Birdie. You have to live your life, promise me that."

"Silas, I'm not letting go just like that."

"You have to." He jostles me a bit, holding me firmly by the arms.

"I'll come with you."

"No," he scolds. "If you leave here with me, there's no coming back. You'll never see your family, you'll never be able to come home to the Otera. I love you too much to do that to you, Eliza. I *won't* do that to you. I know that now it doesn't seem like acquiescence, but in time you would grow to resent me. Maybe that's my predilection for selfishness again, but I'll take a chance with your brooding on the mainland over indignation in a distant system. These men are *bad* men, little bird, and they are watching my every move. My every breath. You're safe now, but if you get on that transport with me, you'll never be safe here again."

I suck my bottom lip into my mouth and feel a fresh rush of emotion gather in the wells of my eyes. He's not making this easy. He's not giving me a chance to argue with him either. I know Silas believes he's doing the right thing, because only twelve spins ago he was all but a pipe dream to me. Now I'm attempting to mediate a permanent relocation from everything I've ever known before him.

"There has to be another way."

He holds my face and swipes the unshed tears from my eyes with his thumbs. He doesn't have to say anything for me to know what he's thinking. It's always been this way with Silas. A glance that speaks everything we can't. From the very first time we saw each other on the transport to the quiet, seldom lulls of inactivity between his sheets. But those glances usually whispered things like, *I know you—I want you— I love you.* This one just screams, *I need you to be okay.*

"I'll thank the cosmos endlessly for granting us Elysium, even if just for the few spins we had together," he whispers. "For showing me I wasn't wasting my life in waiting for a fantasy."

"This isn't how this was supposed to go," I croak, tears flow freely down my cheeks as he kisses them away. I lean my forehead gently into his.

"I know," he says, pressing a hard kiss to my hairline. I don't need to see his face to know he's fighting back his own flood of emotion. "One thing we failed to remember is that not every story has a happy ending, Birdie, or even a fair one. And sometimes the best ones leave you gutless and aggrieved, wishing you could tell the people between the pages what to do to make it right before everything goes wrong."

"What would you have told us?"

Silas looks up from my head and across the room to his marred reflection in the hanging mirror. He knows what he would have told himself: to stop gambling his life, to stop running with the wrong crews, to learn a trade that warranted a title or a nuance of respect when he threw it around. Then he could have had me, he could have had everything.

That's not the poetic silhouette he would leave me with, though. That's not the Silas I wanted to remember.

"I would have told myself to kiss you earlier," he says. "Read to you longer, never to fall asleep." My breath catches on a sob as I lean against the shoulder of his shirt and he shushes me tenderly. "To forgo the formalities and tell you I loved you beneath the shade of that yellow flowered tree on the Continental. Because I knew it then, and long before that moment."

I smile at that. A sad, pathetic smile, but the image of it all makes me grateful. I finally look up at Silas and kiss his bruised cheeks one at a time, and then his lips.

The clock is gone, but Silas knows that time between now and his ascent to the freighter is diminishing with every passing second. He can't keep me here much longer, and he can't let me leave without asking one last favor of me either.

"I need you to do something for me, Eliza." He reaches behind himself and sifts through the pocket at the seat of his pants, pulling the last rock of crystal out and holding it in the space between us.

"I thought you said they were gone," I mumble, taking the tiny gem from his fingers and rolling it between my own.

"I stowed this one. Then prayed to Maker that it wouldn't be missed, because I had a rightful inclination that I might be needing it."

"To leave," I understand.

"In case."

It's just as pretty as when I first held it, I know it's that same gem, I'd never forget. The shape, the edges, the color against my skin, the weight of it in my palm. I wonder if Silas chose to keep this one for that reason. Because it was touched by me, a part of me and him, something he didn't want to part with for menial, but meaningful reasons.

"What do you need me to do?"

"This gem is no good to me in it's current embodiment. I also can't roam freely Downcity without eyes on my tail. There's a gimcrack shop not far outside the terminal entry that will offer you a tally for that rock. You tell them my name. Take whatever they give you, don't barter, don't worry. I just need you to be careful and to keep your head down."

"You want me to fund your departure?" I force a laugh, attempting to joke but it doesn't quite come out like one. Silas doesn't try to fake a grin either.

"Tuck it into your bag, and go."

"Go?"

"We're running out of spin, Birdie. The freighter won't wait, and I need ample time to..." He pauses. "To really say goodbye."

I hesitate, my eyes flutter closed and tears roll down my cheeks defiantly.

How could he expect me to do this? I'd been willing to sacrifice every piece of my life to keep Silas close to me. Throw away years of a committed relationship, lose friends, disappoint my family if necessary. I'd spent the last three spins wide awake and committing the likeness of his face to memory lest I forget it in that short span of time. Now I'm battling the reality of truly forgetting it forever.

"I'm sorry," he says, finding the strength to stand from the bed and pull me up with him.

"Sy, I don't know if I can do this."

He kisses my mouth hard and abruptly. I can feel the fever breaking through the skin of his lips as he does. My arms wrap delicately around his neck as he walks me backwards toward the slide, thinking that if I hold on tighter he might not let me go.

"You can," he mumbles against my lips, smoothing my hair back on my head and holding me close to him.

I shake free of his hands and bury my face in the dip of his collarbone, inhaling the sweetness of skin that is uniquely his. Salt-tinged copper, earthy and herbal—another thing I will fight not to forget. The warm scent that soothed my sleeping body, wrapped around my flesh in the dead of night, stayed stuck in my clothes and my hair, on my skin, even hours after we'd parted.

I feel the press of the slide against my back and Silas reaches for the hatch behind it, still hugging my body to his, not yet keen to let me go.

"Will you ever forgive me?" he asks.

I finally slide the gem into the pocket of my bag as I look up at him. The time has passed to remain in denial, and I know that his entire life now sits in my flimsy linen satchel like a powder keg. If I don't do this he's in danger, there's people here who will hurt him. And even if it's the hardest thing I've ever had to do, there's no other way.

"Forgive you for what, Sy?"

"For waiting for you."

I reach up and run my thumb over his cheek, wiping his watering eyes away.

Even if I'd read the last chapter first, if I'd seen the ending before the start, I would have done it all again. Maybe each line would sting a little harder, every word would read a little sweeter, every miscommunication would hurt so much deeper. But so would all the love.

"Don't ever apologize for giving me the fullest life I could find," I tell him, and then kiss him a final time.

I don't make it ten steps outside the terminal before my heart falls like a block into the pit of my stomach. There is nothing that could have prepared me for this bottomless feeling. It's more than losing a friend, or even family, those wounds take time but they heal—*this*, this is like tearing off a limb. Before Silas, my soul was incomplete. We didn't stitch together, we *grew* together. Two pieces into one, no longer recognizable apart. I can't just exist wholly on my own anymore. There will forever be an open gash.

22
PIKE

The shop is exactly where he said it would be. I stand on the sidewalk across from the dirty business windows and stare blankly inside for way too long.

Everything is a tacky yellow, too bright to be appealing. The awnings outside, the shelves on the interior. There's shit in there I know will metaphorically die stuck to those ledges. Costume jewelry, outdated lamps, hats and scarves and vintage art. There's a spindle of stray keys: skeleton, Abloy, dimple, double-sided. This is all surface level frontage.

Despite nothing of terrific value on display, I know that if Silas sent me here with a crystal worth somewhere near three thousand tally that there's little to assume from the staged facade.

I reach into the bag hanging at my hip and feel the loose gem inside, wrapping my fingers around it until it's enclosed in the palm of my shaking hand. The wind is colder now than it was before, and I feel it skitter like a spider down my back in spite of my layers.

I want to move, but my shoes seem stuck to the pavement. My legs disobey my brain, like the cord has been snapped sending function from my frontal lobe to my feet. *You can do this*, I hear Silas's voice in my head coaxing me on. Except the voice is wrong. I can't.

I couldn't even muster the courage to tell Logan I wasn't in love with him anymore. I couldn't handle the feeling of disappointing someone important to me. I couldn't get out of my own way time and time again when the love of my life begged me to. I spent eight spins on that freighter sleepless, inebriated and playing a game of avoidance just so that I didn't have to face the literal powers of the universe, fearing that they might fucking overcome me. And then they did.

I couldn't handle all of that emotion, so how did Silas expect me to be able to handle this?

Saying goodbye to him is one thing I will never be able to do. One thing I will never do. He has to understand that.

I let the gem go loose again in my bag and then sling it behind my back, leaving the shop behind and dashing toward the shuttle line back in the direction of my family's home. I struggle to hide my anguished complexion from prying passengers, pulling my knees up to my chest and burying my face into them.

The time on my watch blinks aggressively. That freighter will dock before mid-spin is up, and I know Silas is waiting for me. Pacing, hand on his hip, fingers smoothing out the fine lines over the bridge of his nose.

When I went, he watched the entire way. Until my body disappeared through the crowded terminal and past the exit, extending his physical time with me, enduring the sight of my leaving. If not to punish himself further, to prepare himself for when the time comes that I don't turn back around.

.✦.

My father is in the main room when I return, bounding up expectantly to meet me at the door. His excitement tinkers softly to worry when I traipse in alone. He can see the heartbreak like it's wearing itself outside my skin. The puffy saddles under my eyes, the crease folding over itself between my brows.

He pulls me into an embrace that makes me feel like a little girl again. Coddled in my father's arms after bloodying my knee while learning to ride a bike. When my childhood pet ran away and I searched for days but he never turned up. The first rejection letter from university—and then the second before I ended up By The Sea. All of those things seem so inconsequential compared to this.

"What's happened?" he murmurs into my hair.

"It's too long a story, and we don't have the time right now, dad," I say as he peels away from me with a raised eyebrow.

I could be okay, I think. The goodbye didn't need to be accompanied by a bold stamped '*The End*' as a book would have it.

I had said what I needed to say to Silas. I had loved him, fully, until the time ran out, and left him with a vision of me that said not farewell, but see you soon. He didn't have to live with that final goodbye, and neither did I.

"I'll give you the full explanation later," I tell my father. "Right now I really need you to do something for me."

23
TREPIDATION

Silas doesn't have the blinking cursor of a desk clock anymore, but the trill announcements over intercom from the freighter above are mildly worse. Reminding him every mid-hour to get ready for transit, and that the on-board docking will begin soon in all garage bays.

He doesn't dare step outside for fear of drawing attention the closer it comes to departure. All he can do is pace, and prepare—waiting blindly for a knock at his door he both yearns for and also hopes will never come.

There are ascension protocols in place. Silas leans down and messes with the switches of the control board so they'll lift the vessel into orbit on autopilot regardless of whether he's in the pod or not. This way he doesn't have a choice but to leave. He can't hesitate, or run, or think twice about closing me into this pod and taking me with him.

I would hate him. He has to keep telling himself this. I would miss this place and my family. I would crave the routine, and simplicity, and accommodation that he may never be able to guarantee.

The crystal should be worth three thousand. It *should*. But that's it. Not enough to travel like he promised me when half that harvest was still his and the future was endless. Not enough to live luxuriously or worry free. It's only enough for a cycle or so on the freighter until he finds the right moon to disembark, a modest place to live, and a thin cushion of currency to stretch thin while growing new roots.

The comm buzzes to life and chokes out a staticky dispatch. *All pods intent to travel must ascend to transport by the new hour.* Recur. *All pods intent to travel must ascend to transport by the new hour.*

Silas sucks his teeth and stares at the hatch as the comm clicks off. "C'mon, little bird," he murmurs to himself.

He's nervous now, thinking that something must have happened. I must be in trouble with Bartanka and he was heedless to ask me to do that type of bidding for him, no matter how unsuspecting. I should be back here.

Without a second guess he bounds toward the door, thoughtless to the people who may notice once he crosses that threshold, more than willing to die over it if that's what may be.

But then as if it was only a test, there's a knock. It stops him cold and tampers the boil in his veins on contact.

"Maker's men." He exhales, pulling the latch and sliding the door open. "You don't know how worried—"

If the knock was a cold bucket of water, this feels like a frigid, howling wind. He's frozen in place.

"Hello, Silas."

Silas recognizes the man, my father. Even though he'd only seen him once, across a busy intersection days ago. Silas doesn't say anything, he just swallows and nods his head a bit, daring a look behind my dad as if expecting me to follow. My father frowns.

"She's not here," he tells him.

Silas's pulse starts to race, his mouth suddenly bone dry. He licks his lips and clears his throat, then regards the thick green book in my father's hands that he hadn't yet noticed. His insides feel like a melting candle. Slowly dripping wax that sears as it moves and puddles in his stomach.

"She—she isn't?" Silas rasps. "Did something—"

My dad, Kian, shakes his head at Silas and frowns again. He must be a sight to see. I had warned my father, of course, not to be taken aback by Silas's state. That something had happened and it wasn't important right now; what was important was getting the traded currency from the outpost Downcity and bringing it to him. Just to take the gem and mention Silas's name and the brokers would take care of the rest.

"Do you mind if I sit down with you?"

Silas still isn't fully accepting this turn of events. He's spent hours thinking he would have another moment with me, another chance to hold me and touch me, brand my body one last time with his love.

He doesn't know this emotion well. It isn't anger, or sadness. It's not resentment, nor does it scratch the surface of betrayal. Maybe he's felt it before, but only in traces. When I was holding Logan's hand the first time he saw me on the freighter. A pinch of it again when I was in Logan's arms the night I told him about my journal. Then as I walked away from him in that observatory when things came to light with Mori. It's not envy or hopelessness either, it's something stronger, it's all of these things.

It's heartbreak.

"Come in." Silas ushers aside to let my father pass. He pulls a chair out from where it's tucked into his desk and offers it, then takes a seat at the edge of the bed across from him.

"I think this is yours." Kian fishes into his front pocket and hands Silas a fold of cash. "Three thousand tally, that's a pretty penny for a rock." He grins a bit.

"Thank you," is all Silas says back.

My father leans back in the chair and studies Silas's face. Through the unflattery, he can still see his grief. The tired maw of confusion and sadness like a desolating elixir.

"She wanted me to tell you that she couldn't do it," Kian says, spurring Silas to pinch his eyes closed in a futile attempt to keep himself from breaking. "That's why she didn't come. She didn't want to have to say goodbye to you. I've never seen her torn like this over something, Silas. That's my little girl, I feel all the pain she does. Maybe in a different way, but, nonetheless."

"I understand." Silas nods. "She's doing the right thing for herself, and that is my only salvation in this, I promise you that."

"I take it by your face that not everyone on the Otera is your best friend. That's why you're in a bit of a rush to leave again."

It's not a question, but it's open ended, and Silas feels he owes it to my father to attempt an explanation. If he doesn't, I'll probably have to. And if I didn't even want to see him again, then talking about the reason we were forced apart may not be something I'm happy to do either.

"I just want you to know that I love your daughter more than this universe must know what to do with. That's why it's taking her away. It's too bright for anyone, too blistering. You can only burn so hot for so long before it all gets stomped out.

"Before I knew her, I dreamt about her. I searched for her in strangers and waited all the years of my life for a catalyst to show its hand, because I *knew* what I wanted. Nothing else mattered. And *that* there, is the impetus of this entire untimely predicament.

"A Mako only makes money one way, and I never made a ton of it. What I did, I was acute to squandering, especially when I was young and green and had nothing but time to fill my cup. But with that kind of mindset also comes greed, and credence. I was a prized mare one day and a shit kicking stable boy the next.

"I crossed the wrong people." Silas pauses. "Without a second thought at how that may affect me ten cycles down the float, but now here I am, atoning, and this conclusion feels like one long lesson I've spent my entire life learning.

"I can't take her with me, because I can't come back. And if she detests me forever, I'll wear the blame like a scar, but at least I'll do so knowing there's a family here that loves her, and an opportunity for a life that still serves her well."

My dad sits up in his chair and rests his elbows on his knees, clasping his hands together under his chin and baking in the kiln of Silas's monologue.

"I can see why she chose you, Silas," he finally says. "And I understand. Loving someone is one thing, feeling incomplete without them is another."

Silas's expression is grateful, then inquisitive.

"She told us—about her dreams, the journal. Everything that happened on the transport route back here."

"*Everything?*"

Kian chuckles a bit. "Everything."

Silas hums and readjusts himself on the mattress, glancing down at the sheets we rolled around in, trying and failing to remain astute.

"I don't know what really connected you two, but if she believes in it, then I have to," my father says. "And now that I've met you, Silas, I know that there must be truth to the madness. I'm sorry that it couldn't have gone differently."

Silas feels a lump in his throat again. He manages a tight smile and a nod of his head. "Me too."

The intercom whirs to life on the control dash and interrupts, a filtered female voice chiming through.

All pods please ascend to transport at this time. This is the final docking call, all pods please ascend to transport at this time. Thank you.

Silas releases a choppy breath when Kian stands first. He thinks it must be his attempt at making things easier—aiding him to leap into the breach. There's still the book, sitting now on Silas's desk ledge and my father gestures to it softly.

"She said it'd be easier, if you took it back."

"She's probably right."

Kian starts walking toward the door and Silas stops him. "And this then," he says, pulling my journal from underneath the pillow and bringing it over to my father.

When the pod opens this time, Silas does step outside. Even with the lackey's still there waiting. This is the last time he can touch ground on the mainland without repercussions.

"I'm glad to have met you," Silas says sincerely. Their interaction was another piece of me that he gets to take with him. A person to remember him on the same plane of my existence. Someone to remind him that it was all real. He extends his palm out to my father for a handshake. His knuckles are bruised and his normally stable fingers tremble, but he offers it anyway.

"Likewise, Silas." Instead of shake, my father tugs him gently into an embrace. Silas is slow to react, half unsure of the etiquette, half completely resigned from any kind of paternal affection. It's new to him.

The crowd around the terminal has nearly dispersed. Everyone traveling is on their ascent to the freighter, the bustle of commuters has reduced to just hands waving up at the sky, final goodbyes.

Kian pats Silas's back and takes a step away, intent to leave, but just as he tries Silas's focus is elsewhere, over my father's shoulder. It's glossy and gazing, lips parted in a trance as if he's discovering a new constellation right before his eyes.

And maybe he is, because it's me. Like a North Star in a fog. Hugging my arms close to my chest with an oversized duffle slung over my shoulder, weighing me down.

Silas doesn't know what it means, but when my father finally turns around to garner a look, I start to cry.

I couldn't say goodbye to him, so I didn't. I wouldn't.

I knew my father would do anything I asked, and I wanted him to meet the man that changed my life, but it couldn't all exist at once. Not in a simple or organic way, and not with the threat of waning time biting at my heels.

The truth is, I knew standing in front of that gimcrack shop this morning that if there was anywhere in the universe I needed to be, it was with Silas. That he wasn't the only one who had to concede to make this work. He had done that, time and again on the transport for me, and now it was my turn. There was never a sign so poignant as the way the two of us found one another. Without him I'd spend the rest of my life half a human, in limbo between tolerating what I have and craving what I need— knowing he was out there somewhere craving me as well.

You can't pull roots this deep from the ground and expect them to grow back the same.

My father gives Silas a last meaningful nod. There's a lifetime of love in the gesture, an expectation to withhold that kind of endearment with his daughter, and a trust that he knows he will.

I smile, meeting my dad halfway in a tender embrace that leaves a dark line of tears staining the light fabric of his shirt. He smooths my hair from my face, wiping the tears from my cheeks with his thumbs.

"Dad..."

"No, Sunshine. No explanation necessary." I tilt my head into the palm of his hand. "Now go," he tells me, pressing my journal back into my arms. "Go dream."

I stifle a new rush of tears and press up on my toes to kiss his cheek. There's less and less going on around me, the pods are flying quietly into orbit, Silas's being one of the last still on the dock. There's no more time for goodbyes and my father senses it, stepping aside so there's nothing now between me and my other half.

Silas is stone-still outside his pod, hoping that if he doesn't look away I won't disappear. The sound of motors whirring to life inside the vessel gives me move though, and I find myself floating toward him, fast and desperately, wanting nothing more than to be in his arms and closed into the pod where it's real. Where it's me and Silas against all.

He's at the hatch when I reach him, holding the slide open as the pod kicks up sparks and dirt around us both, threatening to launch itself without passenger's if we don't move quickly.

It's a frantic dash, we fall into the pod the moment that it's lifting, our clumsy bodies hit the floor and the latch is slammed and sealed shut at what seems like the very last second before the ground is left far beneath us.

Silas finds my face with his hands and pulls me to his mouth like he needs it to breathe. A hard, slow press of lips and then tongue, soft sighing as we become weightless on the floor.

"You shouldn't be here," he whispers, holding me close to his body. "I told you not to come with me, you belong down there."

Even as he says the words they sound lamenting. An echo of all the things I've already decided against and have brought me to exactly where I'm meant to be right now.

"I belong with you." I hush him again with my lips. He should be distraught with pain holding onto me the way he is, but it's as if he can't feel anything that isn't me. "I could never say goodbye to you, I couldn't even sleep without you. I was *afraid* to," I tell him, tracing the scar over his eye with my fingertips then running them softly through his dark hair.

"I was terrified that if I closed my eyes for too long I would start to *forget*—with all that darkness where I used to dream. I would forget the little things. The way you smell, the way that light reflects your eyes, the way you feel when you hold me like this, when you kiss me, when you make love to me. I couldn't let myself. I couldn't just forget you."

He presses his forehead to mine. Before this, Silas thought the only feeling greater than knowing I existed, was knowing that I loved him back. But now, knowing that he was the choice I made against all else, and that every day he spent wishing his life was like his dreams was now reality, was better than all the rest.

"Oh, Eliza," he says against my lips, "you will forget me not."

24
ELYSIUM

Silas didn't blink an eye when I suggested the Glades. In fact, he didn't even really need me to say it. *Of course, Birdie,* he'd murmured, tracing my lips with his fingertips.

We didn't get out of bed much those first few spins back on the freighter, making up for the lost time in the prior three—but to be honest it felt less like reconciliation, and more like setting the precedent for forever. I woke in the morning to Silas curled around me, nibbling softly at the flesh of my ear, running his lips down the length of my spine, notched, head or hips, between my legs. Then in the night he loved me to sleep.

It was all a long, fantastic dream.

When we finally disembarked over the cerulean moon and watched ourselves and the pod descend, it was like a revival. There was no plan further than that, no where to start first or dig in. It was learning how to walk again, but this time, unafraid to fall. Silas was just happy to go where he knew *I* wanted to. To the place that had grown to mean so much over such a short period of time. The islands I couldn't wait to get back to, introduce him to, fall impossibly more in love with him on.

The currency from that little gem found us a home right next to the sea, surrounded by tumbled dunes and thick grassy brush that gave way to soft, black sands and the open ocean.

The windows were always swung wide, and the breeze was always warm. We had a big bed, and a little kitchen, rolled and faded wooden beams that Silas hung salt white gossamer from like angelic drapery. In one corner there was a nook for me, styled with hand-picked shells and home made candles from the markets. I stacked Silas's books and my journal in shelves cut from the wall, and pressed snug pillows into the window seat he made sure was mine. There, I could sit and watch the waves in the day, and at night when the sky bled purple and the sun kissed the horizon, I could listen under bright hanging constellations as they faded into the bay.

Silas learned new trades with his hands. Fishing, weaving, thread melding. He helped build dwellings, and shared stories; reading his books to the children on the islands as if they were his own. He spoke to anyone who would peruse past his foreign accent and listen.

He knew so much about so many things—a beautiful emanation of his non-traditional upbringing. He was strong and smart, naturally gifted with the ability to adapt in any way he was needed. More than anything he was trustworthy, veritably charming and intensely understanding.

The Glades were home to abundant raw resources. Timber, straw, fruit, sand—there were plants on the moon that shed seasonally, unwinding like snagged fibril, and those coats were thinned and strung again into things like clothing, fabric, canvas and paper.

When the locals came upon a deposit of natural crystal sleeping deep in the banks of overturned jetty, Silas was the only one they trusted for extraction. Those stones were sacred and respected, a rare material mostly rumored, but when uncovered, able to harness and scale tidal energy into solar electricity, amongst other things. It felt again as though the universe had willed him to be there.

As the cycles passed, the need for routine became all but obsolete. There was no impending danger or lingering deadlines. No expectations to withhold outside the things that already felt important enough to maintain. Silas's handiwork amongst the villagers, his makoing skill-set on the jetties when called upon, his ingenuity, eclectic knowledge and occasionally his personal library—were all of good use.

It was the first time Silas was ever able to do something meaningful outside the chains of necessity. That, or at the benefit of somebody else in order to survive. Here he could choose. He was never underappreciated or underestimated. In the safety of the Glades, he never had to give himself away. All the little pieces he lended, he knew he would be getting back.

I, like a dovetail to my lover, tended animals on the moon. Aquatic species as they prematurely sluiced in with changing tide, endangered amphibians that needed preservation where floods had washed away ecosystems, domesticated creatures missing from their owners. More than once Silas had come home to chittering beasties soaping away at my hand in the stone basin, a feeling like pride and love and *want*, swirling deep in his gut at the image of it.

Then he would press me against the sink just as I stood. Hands first heavy at my hips, trailing up my ribs, skating over my breasts in faint, teasing circles. He would nip and lick at the nape of my neck, the soft hairs above his lip tickling me until my skin heated and my breath hitched. And with his nose nuzzled into my salt swept hair, he would ask me if I wanted him—and it was always *yes*.

Yes, in front of the marble trough sink. Yes, after a long day under the cold stream of an outdoor shower. Yes, when the breeze kicked through the circular windows of our bedroom every night. And yes, always yes, tucked between the brush and the tides, sand in my hair and shells pinching into the meat of my sweltering skin when he got me underneath him on the beach.

"Fuck, Birdie."

Silas dragged his tongue down the valley of my stomach, lathing open mouthed kisses to my belly, my hips, the dip of skin just beneath the line of my swimsuit. The strings were a tease, a bullshit barrier he snapped into my side with a flick of his finger.

My top was long thrown across the sand, peppered in twinkling black grain. When I looked down, I saw that same shimmering dust in patches across my body. Silas's fingers were rough with it, it scratched and bristled, but it looked like a fucking work of art, and I loved when he took me like this. So impatient, so unable to just carry me ten steps to the house. Instead laying me down in the malleable seaside and tearing my ocean-soaked suit off with his teeth.

The land was private where we were hidden away, nothing but the birds and the leaves, the swell rushing out and back to wet the sand. Foam kissed our toes, and the waves rushed over our bodies, naked and gorgeous, sunkissed in the wake. And this way, Silas could fuck me frantically. Racing the climbing tide to my climax, rolling my body in deep, thick thrusts against his. Everything was salt and grain, my lips on his lips, his chest, his neck. I swallowed the groans he didn't bother to hush when my nails tore his skin and the briny water stung like new scars into flesh.

When I came he licked into my mouth, tangling his tongue with mine. Fucking me breathless, wrung out, teetering on another crest until I felt him ridge and spill inside of me.

We would often lay like that, stuck in the sand with each other until the sky turned color and the water went cold with the night. Later we would stir and make love again in darkness under the stars.

✦

Then one day, there was a letter. A message over comm. We had gotten few before, from my parents after we settled, promising to find a way to visit soon. Another on my birthday, then again on Silas's. This one was different, unexpected.

Silas and I opened it over breakfast in the morning, just a photo in a hologram came to life. It was Logan and a curly haired woman, his arm draped over her shoulders, her cheek pressed into the side of his chest. She had a sterling smile, just like his, and a dimple in one cheek. Pretty, I thought. Beautiful even. They looked like perfect halves clasped together like that. In floating text the caption read:

I believe you now. I'm sorry it took so long.

Even after everything that had happened, Silas grinned, squeezing my fingers tight within his own.

He finished his coffee and stepped out through the open deck doors, looking out at the ocean longer than usual, more thoughtfully. When I finally joined him, flanked by the yawning stray-turned-homely orange cat Silas called Gem, he told me there was still one thing yet he wanted to do.

And so, the ram-shack bungalow of a book exchange Silas built and maintained in the village all by himself was born. We call it The Nest.

A library of second-hand reads. All the novels he had stowed away once upon a time sit in perfect disarray around the cozy, quiet room. It retains its authenticity with dark wooden shelves and billowing curtains that let in only natural light. There's thrift chairs and mosaic artwork, his own old maps and found photographs lining the walls.

It's Silas's silent metaphor for all things in life being derivative. Everything you touch, the universe has touched first.

People who come and go through the Glades as travelers read while they're on land. Some leave behind new books they have no use for anymore and thicken the already off-kilter stacks. Over time it's become somewhat of a haven for history as well as fiction. The people that visit The Nest remember Silas long after they've gone, sending letters and sometimes gifts to add to his ever growing collection.

At first, I wondered why he was so willing to part with all of his books. Why he was able to let them go so easily knowing what was written like poetry between the pages, hooked in his handwriting next to all his favorite lines.

"I don't need to read a different story anymore, Birdie, because *ours* is my favorite one."

He told me that he'd found who he needed those pages for, and that maybe, just maybe, all that chicken scratch would offer the same prosperity to someone else. I, on the other hand, was disposed to let all but one of those storied books find a new home.

There's a little bell above the entry that jingles now as someone new walks into the shop. Silas greets them from behind the shoddy counter, and I look up from where I'm lounging across the room on the chaise with a pen between my teeth.

Silas's weathered copy of *The Master and Margarita* sits open in my lap, the pages are freshly marked and tagged in my own pen. New annotations and underlines, my scribbled love letters next to his between the margins anywhere they'll fit.

I feel like this little moment of my life has already happened—in a thought, maybe in a dream. When Silas turns his focus and smiles at me, the grin reaching his eyes and warming my cheeks, I know that it has. I know that the universe always speaks to me in subtle revelations, and that *this* is exactly where Silas and I are meant to be.

25
EPILOGUE

The sea air soothes in the mornings. I feel the ocean all around me before I even open my eyes. It sings to me in crashing waves and fly-over birds, in the sway of palm leaves brushing against one another in every gentle breeze. Some days it lulls me back to sleep and tucks the sheets tighter to my body, the dawn coolness nipping at my naked toes. Other mornings, like this one, I feel warm sunshine dancing in shapes on my skin, tiptoeing up my back and neck, kissing my hair and leaning in.

As if trying to whisper in my ear, *wake up, wake up, wake up.*

"Lize?"

A soft shake.

"Babe?"

Another.

My head feels ten pounds heavier as I try to lift it. My eyelids are stuck together with sleep, I can feel the furrowed wrinkle in my brow as I blink away the sedation and my vision adjusts to the room. The brightness hits me first. A beam of light through the open window that triggers the sensitivity in my blue eyes and illuminates the sand colored walls of the bungalow.

"Maker, you knocked the fuck out."

I hear a jingle of something. A rattle of a bottle as I groan and stretch the muscles in my legs. Finally I'm able to roll over from my side to my back and take in the entire space.

Logan.

No.

I close my eyes again. Attempting to catapult myself back into the unconscious world I was just living in.

"Herbals here are no joke, Lize." He shakes the little bottle again and the glass dropper clinks against the inside of it. I must have left it half unscrewed on the bedside table in the middle of the night. "Where did you get this, anyway?"

The fresh market a few spins ago. An older woman behind an artisan table had suggested her own homemade, holistic remedy for insomnia. The way I explained my inability to sleep soundly had her thinking it was nightmares keeping me awake, when that couldn't have been further from the truth.

I wanted to forget.

The time I had spent with Logan on the Glades had made me want to finally, unequivocally forget about the man stealing my every dream at night. I wanted to move on from the delirium of false hope. So I bought a tincture from her, and took her photo too, hoping at the very least to sleep deeply enough to muddle the dreams into something relatively unsatisfying.

Logan twists the bottle in his palm and reads the handwritten warning label out loud. "Lonokontiko seed has been known to cause side effects such as snoring, rash, fatigue, cold-flashes, increased appetite, and in extreme circumstances—moderate hallucination and astral projection. What the fuck is this, Eliza?" He laughs, but I'm entirely numb to it.

All of a sudden I feel reality slam into my conscience like a freighter.

Silas? *Silas.*

He was here. Or—I was there. Where was I?

His pod. The transport. The *Glades.*

Silas.

I gave him a name this time.

"How much of this did you take?" Logan asks.

Double the recommended dose. In my attempt to black out completely, I'd seemingly done the opposite. Having had the most vivid and unforgettable dream of my entire life.

"Maker, fuck." I sit up and look around abruptly, as if the entire plot just came full circle. This bed, this shack, the dull sound of waves crashing in the surf in the distance. I search the sheets and the fluffy, white down comforter with my hands frantically, lifting the blanket and finding what I need to.

My journal. I toss it open to the last page I'd written on.

Are you ever going to tell him about me?

Logan sits at the end of the bed with a dubious look on his face. His perfect, strawberry blonde hair pushed back off his forehead and curling behind his ears. He's dressed for departure.

Departure.

I feel twelve spins of motion sickness swirling in my gut.

"I thought I'd let you sleep. I tried once already to wake you up and you basically growled at me."

I hold a palm to my clammy forehead. "I don't think I've ever slept so deeply."

Even so, I'm not the least bit relaxed. I feel like my body has lived an entire cycle without me and I'm now just struggling to catch up.

I dream about Silas every night, but this was different. Like the teeth of every previously mismatched key in a lock finally sliding into place. A door opening to a different world of connection.

I can still *taste* him. I press a fingertip to my bottom lip as if it should be plump and swollen, and I'm disappointed when it's not. There are days worth of dreams swimming in my head. Fragmented pieces floating deeper and deeper, threatening to be forgotten with every passing second of consciousness. It's all too much to remember.

A book.

Books.

A foreign moon.

A *woman*. Who was that woman?

Gems.

A fight.

Sex... *a lot* of sex. My cheeks heat and my core tightens.

"I packed up your little library already." Logan puts his palm on my bare knee and it makes me flinch. He raises an eyebrow.

The bungalow is empty, save for a few last minute items. Our sheets need to be stripped from the bed, and my toothbrush and a comb sit out on the basin counter across the room. There's a folded pile of clothes Logan put out on a chair for me to slip into, and a backpack I had filled last night with all the things I wanted to take from this treasured island back to the Otera. Maps, photographs, some of the moon's natural indigo crystal.

I kick myself clear of the comforter and stand on wobbly legs. Despite already being on land, the movement feels like grounding after having floated for a long period of time.

"You okay?" Logan stands and walks to the wide opening of the front door with his arms crossed over his chest. He looks so tanned in his white linen shirt, a few of the buttons are popped open at the top.

I stare at my feet and clear my throat. "Yeah, it must just be the sleeping aid. Remind me never to take it in the middle of the night again."

He chuckles a little and blows a chaste kiss across the room toward me. "I'm gonna head down to the pod to fire her up, take a walk when you're ready? Transpo is floating in..." His watch beeps. "Twenty."

"Yeah." I force a smile to my lips. "Okay."

Logan raps his knuckles on the door frame and turns to walk out just as a green warbler flaps its way through the threshold and purchases on the windowsill nearest to me. It fluffs its feathers and whistles.

"Stupid little bird." Logan shoos a lazy hand in its direction, but the bird doesn't budge. "Get outta here."

"Leave it." I traipse to the sink and usher away the uncomfortable twist I feel in my gut. "It's not bothering me. It's making sure I'm not late."

"Heavy task."

I stick my tongue out at him and hear his laugh fade away with his steps as he takes off down the black sand beach.

When I turn I catch my reflection in the circular mirror. Wispy blonde hairs curtaining across my forehead, freckles spattered over the natural bronze on the bridge of my nose and cheeks. My under eyes are puffy and I rub them with the pads of my fingers and groan. With only twenty minutes until ascent I barely have the time to dress and pack away our remaining belongings, never mind sitting down to try and recollect last night's fever dream in the pages of my journal. I wouldn't even know where to start.

All I know, is that was the realest my life has ever felt on an unconscious plane. Much less like a dream, more like a premonition.

"Silas."

I say his name out loud for the first time. Let it flick off the tip of my tongue and into the quiet bungalow, as if speaking him into the universe itself. The little green bird tilts its head toward me from its perch on the bay window, and I decide that if I can't write it, I should at least tell someone about the dream. So I do.

I tell this tiny bird every detail I can remember as it watches me dance around the sandy shack house, stripping the bed sheets and brushing a comb through my hair. I tell it how Silas and I fell in love. How hard I fought, and how *easy* it was once I finally let go. I tell it about the bartender, and the other woman, and the static remnants of the day we spent on the Continental moon. About these giant mammals fucking in a meadow just as I was drunk enough to let Silas kiss me.

"Do you think I'm crazy?" I ask it. "Is there something deeply wrong with me?"

There is obviously no answer.

I spin away and scan the emptiness of the shack one more time, doing a last sweep to make sure that nothing is left behind or under. I lift the bed frame, open the small cabinets twice. I shove the clothes I'd worn overnight into my canvas backpack, slinging it over my shoulder, and when I turn back around to head to the door, the little bird is gone.

"Are you gonna eat that?"

I blink out of my daze and stare directly at Logan where he sits across from me in the metal booth. The sounds of chatter and utensils clinking together in the cafeteria consort tune back to full volume from a previously muffled haze.

"What?"

"Are you going to..." He points at the sloppy tray of food in front of me. "Eat that?"

I haven't been hungry yet today. I can't even focus on a conversation, let alone eating a meal while engaging in one. My stomach pangs in a way that tells me if I were to try to digest something, it would just come right back up.

"The food's not that bad, Lize." Logan reaches over and stabs a fork into the brown meat on my plate. "Nothing like the Glades, but—"

I look around the communal dining area. The space is like a shopping center food court, several ticky-tacky shacks with different cuisines lined up next to one another. Every-which gender and species scattered about at their own little tables. Maybe families traveling to visit more of their own, maybe friends headed to a vacation spot. Possibly a lone straggler starting a new life on whatever system the ship happens to pass.

Some of the faces I see are ones that I strangely remember.

I look back at Logan who's shoveling the food from my tray onto his own with a spoon. My eyebrows furrow as I start to sense an eerie familiarity about the interaction. Like this exact moment has already happened, and I'm now reliving it.

I turn my focus to the giant screen hitched on the wall. It shows that the freighter is currently floating over a cluster of moons in the Dandorma system. A red blinking light indicates that there's a pod on-load docking currently in the garage bay.

I squint, my lips parting slightly as I stare at that little blinking cursor on the wall under the universal clock.

Time passes so differently in space. In some systems a spin can be as long as a cycle is in others. What is a day, or an hour or a minute even? It's been several long, slow hours since we touched down on the freighter, but back home an entire day has passed. I think of how many spins came and went in my dreams last night. Now, the seconds tick like an internal metronome.

My eyes shift back to Logan, who's wiping at the corners of his mouth with a napkin.

"You've been all spaced out today. What's up?"

"Nothing," I lie to him, but then I shake my head and backtrack. There's no reason to lie. It was all just a *very* vivid dream, one that I can't seem to let go of. I'm convincing myself that this day is a serious case of déjà vu, when the reality is that I'm just not all here right now. "I think that herbal really—"

The sound of the steel elevator across the area dinging draws my attention away.

"Ah look, new travelers just pulled in," Logan says.

My breath catches in my throat as I watch the doors slide open.

THE END.

ACKNOWLEDGEMENTS

There are no words in this world to properly acknowledge every single person that made this book a possibility. When I started writing Forget Me Not in March 2021, it wasn't even meant to be a novel. It was a fun delve into scifi fan-fiction that quickly took on a life, universe, and characters of it's own. Five months later I had written a hundred thousand word novel, and so many readers online had been there, cheering me on and reaching out in messages every single week to tell me how much they loved it. Without that, I wouldn't have even thought this book was worth anything. So thank you.

My husband Joe, the most fierce and loving support system in this universe. He beta read every single chapter of this story after I finished it. He believed in it every step of the way, and I don't even know what I could have done in life to deserve him. Babe, I know I made you want to rip your hair out some days when I was so lost in this process of writing and revising. But, this story is for you. You're in every line. I love you.

Kelli Mazanec, the greatest human being I think I've ever met in my life. One of the greatest *writers,* I've ever met in my life. The hours of communication, text chains, messages, Discord chats, sending inspiration and discussing this book. You organized my thoughts, my schedules, my breakdowns, beta-read. I don't even know what to say. You are a light in my life, Kelli, I will forever be indebted to you.

Charnie, apart from the obvious dedication to you in this book ;), thank you for listening, bouncing ideas off of me, and always being a soundboard over text and Zoom where I needed it. You are so immensely talented and well-written, I'm in awe of how lucky I got to have you in my corner and, I cannot wait for your career to absolutely take off when the world gets to read the masterpieces of Charlotte House for the first time.

Alex Thomson, for designing the most kick-ass cover I could have ever imagined and being such a great friend to me over the last two years. You were there from the very beginning and I love you always for it!

My parents, who will never know about this book, because I've hidden it behind a pen name. Thank you for giving me this gift of love for writing. I don't know where it came from, but you still have that first children's book I ever wrote when I was six years old. So I think our best bets are there.

My in-laws, who are too smart for their own good and figured this pen name out anyway. I hope none of you ever read this, truly, but if you do—it wasn't me.

Rachel, CiCi, Ren, and Rachael.

Every single person on Tumblr that read this story in its original glory. I love you.

And I'd be remiss if I didn't also thank Pedro Pascal, Zeek Earl and Christopher Caldwell for inspiring this world and its characters.

ABOUT THE AUTHOR

Karissa Kinword is a zillenial mother taking her passion for writing, romance, and the things that stick with you long after they're gone, to paper. She lives in the Hudson Valley of New York with her husband and toddlers.
You can follow her on social media:

Instagram: **@karissakinwordwrites**
TikTok: **@karissakinwordwrites**
Twitter: **@kjkinwordwrites**
You can find book aesthetics and character inspiration on her
Pinterest
Join Karissa's mailing list to receive updates on all her books.

Made in the USA
Columbia, SC
18 November 2022

71553021R00209